FUSION NIGHT

FUSION NIGHT TRILOGY #1

For Bill and Diane,

ELLIE A. GRAY

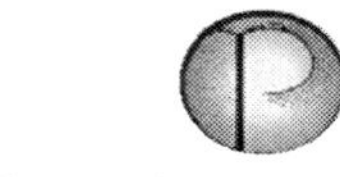

Outskirts Press, Inc.
Denver, Colorado

This is a work of f ction. The events and characters described herein are imaginary and are not intended to refer to specif c places or living persons. The opinions expressed in this manuscript are solely the opinions of the author and do not represent the opinions or thoughts of the publisher. The author has represented and warranted full ownership and/or legal right to publish all the materials in this book.

Fusion Night
Fusion Night Trilogy #1

v2.0

Outskirts Press, Inc.
http://www.outskirtspress.com

ISBN: 978-1-4327-7852-1

PRINTED IN THE UNITED STATES OF AMERICA

*For my dad and Mallory, for your support,
and to Emily Schoon, for believing I could do it.*

Prologue

Seven-hundred years ago, Werewolves and Vampires lived in peace. Humans had a surplus population, and life was good for them all. That is, until two of them fell in love. One was a Vampire named Lucas, the other a Werewolf named Victoria. They secretly married, against all laws, and had a son, which they named Rafe.

Victoria sent their son to be raised by Lucas, since the child had fangs and drank blood. Lucas lied to his Coven by saying he'd fallen in love with a Vampire named Juliet, who was the King's daughter, in which he purposely killed. He told the King she'd been murdered by a Werewolf by the name of Michael, whose existence he thought he'd made up. But Lucas did not know that Michael was actually a real wolf. To add to that fact, Michael was also Victoria's brother, and the uncle of his son. The King sent his best Warriors to kill Michael, but there was an ignorant young Vampire Guard in the Coven.

His name was Joshua, and he either did not understand the mission, or just despised the Werewolves so much his demons possessed him. For, when the Warriors left to kill Michael, he joined them against order, and killed the Werewolves' Alpha Female instead. This started a war between the Minuit Coven and the Glace Pack.

Rafe, meanwhile, soon became a high honor. He lived in the middle of the battle, considering that after the Werewolves' revenge got Juliet's father killed, it made Lucas King. That meant that Rafe had become the Prince of his Coven. But just before he turned eighteen, the other Vampires in his Coven started becoming suspicious of him. He was faster and stronger than the rest of them, and the greatest and swiftest fighter. And when the day came of his eighteenth birthday, he got the ability to transform into a wolf.

His father was terrified when Rafe showed him what he could do. He banished his son from the Coven to Chiroux, France, and gave him his own race name. Fusion. He told all in the Minuit Coven that their Prince had been killed in battle. And so, Rafe lived alone for four hundred years, until another Fusion came to live with him. Her name was Amaury.

Rafe fell in love with her, and after living with her for almost twenty years, both of them frozen at age eighteen, he discovered she loved him back. They were both happy living in secret, and Rafe was finally glad of what he was. So much so, that he didn't know of any threats towards Amaury and himself.

Nonetheless, one day a young Vampire by the name of Baron had become curious of his past. Lucas had stepped down from the throne by this point, and was no longer the

King, but ordered Baron to keep away from the records nonetheless. However, the youthful Vampire disobeyed, and snuck into his ex-ruler's chamber, despite his warning. Amongst the bookshelves all over the darkened chamber, he found two books: *Ancient Battles of the Minuit Coven and Glace Pack* and one that said only on the cover, *Victoria's Diary*. Baron read each, cover to cover, and learned of the whereabouts and existence of Rafe Gautier.

He rounded up many of his fellow Vampires, and teamed against Lucas. They killed him, and then paid a visit to the Werewolves. When they found out what Victoria had done, they murdered the Warrior carelessly. The Coven and Pack teamed up then for the first time and went after Rafe.

When the Werewolves and Vampires came to kill him, Rafe hid Amaury. They didn't know she existed, so he made her hide until they were gone. Fusions can only be killed by other Fusions, unless they bleed to death (or if the proper weapon is used). So, Rafe died, and both races resumed with their war. And only one knew of the last Fusion. A Vampire named Magdelene. And if she reveals the secret that the Fusion race isn't dead, all hope of peace will be gone forever.

Chapter 1
Fusion by Blood

Amaury:

I began to write to my sister, frustrated. Nothing was going right whatsoever. As a Fusion, a combination of Vampires and Werewolves, I must remain hidden. The only person, I mean, *being*, that knows I exist is Magdelene. My half-sister has always been there for me. She is a full-blooded Vampire, and I deeply envy her.

We shared the same mother, Annabel de Pompadour, who married her father, David de Pompadour, and she was born soon after. Magdelene told me that our mother had cheated on him with a Werewolf named Daniel Pale. The result: Me. Being a Fusion is hard. I am socially disconnected, except for my letters to and from Magdelene.

I had to kill my parents long ago. Magdelene killed her father as well. We did it to protect me. If we wouldn't have, they would've exposed my secret to the entire Vampire and Werewolf races. The Minuit Coven and Glace Pack would be in peace for a short time, only to destroy me. Then their war would resume, and all hope of peace would be devoured by nightfall.

Magdelene feared it would happen to me, just like it happened to Rafe Gautier. He was the greatest man I'd ever met, so sweet and caring. And he'd died to protect me. When the Vampires and Werewolves came for him, he hid me, since I was unknown of, and made sure I'd be safe. I still remember his black hair falling over his worried, smoky eyes as he told me, "Stay hidden and don't move. I'll be back soon."

But he never came back. They killed him, exactly three hundred years ago today, in 1574. Today is January 18, 1874. I'm writing Magdelene, in hopes she finally got through to King Benjamin. Ever since my older sister was born (four years before me to be exact), she'd loved King Benjamin, even when he was a prince. A few days ago she wrote me, saying to be careful, because the Humans were growing more suspicious of everyone. She also advised me that my future predicting would be coming in good use right about now, as with her mind reading.

Vampires are given three gifts. They have extraordinary strength, impossible speed, and can read minds or predict the future, one or the other. Werewolves have two, the ability to shift into wolves, and their venom kills Vampires instantly. Fusions have the same Vampire and Werewolf qualities, except their venom destroys both Vampires and Werewolves. And as legend goes, if a Vampire bites a Human they become one, same with the Werewolves.

If I were to bite a Human, they'd become a Werewolf with incredible speed. If my genealogy was switched, however, they would be a Vampire that can read minds and predict the future. A lot of ignorant people get confused with this process. But, as I write to Magdelene, I have failed to mention what I'm thinking. So, I continue to write:

Dear Magdelene,

Each day seems to drag on even longer. I am so desperately lonely. If you weren't around to talk to, I probably would've exposed my secret by this point in time. Now if Rafe were still here, then it'd be a different story. He lived alone for four hundred years, and I'm afraid I'm going to end up in following his footsteps. But Magdelene, I greatly don't want that to happen. I need to find some friends outside my little solitude fortress, or I think I'm going to go crazy.

Speaking of friends and boys though, have you gotten to Benjamin yet? I know you've chased him for as long as I've lived, so I hope he finally comes to his senses. You are a Vampire Lady, an heir to the throne if something were to happen to him. I think I might just go over there and knock some sense into him if he doesn't open his eyes soon. You're very lucky, Magdelene, to live in high respect amongst people who love you. I wish that someday, that'll be me.

Yours truly,
Amaury

I folded the letter neatly and stuck it in an envelope, and sealed it with a wax sigil. I blew out the candle on my desk and picked up the encased note, walking out the door. I set the letter on the ground and went into my wolf form. I was so glad I could transform with my clothes on, unlike the Werewolves in all the books. I picked up the envelope with my teeth and trotted into the forest, heading all the way to the Fanges Castle in Maufanges, France, only about two miles away.

I walked through the dense woods for a while, until I finally came upon a looming Gothic castle. It only took me a moment to squeeze through the iron bar fence and pad along the castle walls, until I found a tiny window. I faced the familiar old oak tree that was behind me, and ran towards it. I ran up the side of the tree and jumped in the air, spinning, and clung onto the wooden window sill for a few moments, sliding the letter securely under the crack in the window. Then, I let myself fall a story, landing unharmed.

Still in wolf form, I sat, threw back my head, and howled loud enough to wake Magdelene. A few moments later, I saw her come to the window. She smiled, her black hair in a mess, black eyes tired looking. She took the note and nodded to me, and as I stood and turned, I looked back and returned one to her. Then I padded away at a steady trot, turning down the path home. But something inside me forced me to stop.

I looked to my right. If I turned now, I could reach the town Guéret, France in just less than two hours, probably less since I had amazing speed. I was unsure, but in the end, I began to head toward the Human invested town. I had no intentions of killing any, since I don't *need* blood (I can eat Human food too), but it felt like I was being drawn there. I had no idea what was in store.

I was running full speed, and about to Guéret by that point. I began slow down and stopped, sitting to take a rest. I was panting heavily, so to help calm myself, I looked up at the sky. The moonlight bathed the treetops, the stars twinkling all around it like a million eyes. As my breath began to even out, I stood, muscles sore, and began to walk down the cool dirt pathway.

The only thing I saw for a long time was the light from the moon. But as the forest became less dense, I saw a field to the right of me just outside of the trees, and a fairly unnatural light glow. I looked around the field, slowly making way towards the tree line and instantly saw a small white house, with a light emanating from one of the windows. I'd never noticed the small house before, and as I stopped for a moment to study it, the light was suddenly was gone. Whoever was in the room had obviously blown out the candle.

The house's door opened then, creaking in a haunted manor, and a man stepped out. He wore jeans and a light yellow jacket, so light it was nearly white, that reached his waist. But I really couldn't distinguish him until he turned around. He wore a midnight black shirt and had matching hair, which was long, about chin length. His eyes were a pale, icy blue, and his skin was very tan, like all he did was work in the sun. He also wore a scornful expression, as though he was bitter towards the world. And there was another thing. He was a Vampire.

I wasn't controlling my legs, but I felt myself walk forward, ever so cautiously. I noticed him tense, just barely, before he turned to face me. He drew back his lip a bit in a sneer, but I quickened my pace toward him anyways. I drew to a stop and transformed into my "Human" form, smiling.

"Hello," I said politely.

"Who are you?" he asked, his expression still derisive.

"Well, Vampire, I'm not a Werewolf if that's what you think," I said, hoping to confuse him.

"Well, that was obvious. I smell your Vampire blood, Fusion."

"How do you know what I am?" I asked, blue eyes wide with shock. "No one's heard of us for over three hundred years!"

He laughed at that. "How old do you take me for, a hundred?"

I shrugged. "Who are you?" It was my turn to ask.

He gave a sly smile. "My name's Radder."

I was again stunned. "You mean, Radder Thor, King Benjamin's brother?"

He rolled his eyes. "Unfortunately, yes."

Then I remembered something. Benjamin had taken over Radder's rightful place as King of the Vampires when his brother challenged him to a duel. He somehow lost and was banished from the Coven. I guess that's why he lived here. So I asked him.

"You live here since the fight with your brother, right?"

He nodded. "Yes. But it's none of your concern."

I shrugged again. "It could be."

"And why do you say that?"

"I like to help people. It might make you feel better if you opened up to someone."

He suddenly grabbed my wrist, squeezing it harshly. "I tried that once, and let's just say it didn't work out."

"So now you distance yourself from the world?" I snapped.

"So do you. You have for three-hundred years."

I yanked his hand off my wrist and pushed him against the house. "Don't… ever… touch me like that again."

He smiled again. "What if I do?"

"I'll bite you and end your life now. You know my venom will kill you, right?"

"Obviously. But on the contrary, I don't think that would be wise." He drew his fangs out, intimidating me. "You don't scare me," he added.

"Oh, but I should."

"I'll never be scared by a girl."

"Oh, so now you're not only a complete jerk, but you're sexist, too. Real nice, Radder."

"Thank you," he said, "your offenses mean nothing."

"What is it with you?" I asked.

"With me?" he said. "You're the one who came randomly to my house in the middle of the freaking night looking for conversation."

OK, so he had a point there, but still. "Do you know what it's like to live alone for *three-hundred years?* No socialness at all, no friends, family. Try that."

"I do." His eyes clouded with an unknown sadness. "Just not in the same way you have to."

I let him go then. "What do you mean?" I asked.

He looked angry now. "What do you care?" he asked. "It's not like my life should mean anything to you."

I slowly backed away from him. "I'm sorry. I was just trying to..."

He put his hand up to stop my words from slipping out. "I think you should just go, before you cause any more trouble."

"But..."

"I don't want to hear it," he said. Then Radder turned and began to walk away.

If he thought I'd give up so easily, the poor boy is sadly mistaken.

"Why won't you talk to me?" I asked, falling into stride with him.

"Uh, because you're annoying as hell."

"Well, you're just so kind, now aren't you?" I said sarcastically, a smile on my face.

He stopped, turning to face me. His eyes were pinned down into a vicious glare.

"God, what is with you? I have never met anyone as frustrating as you in my entire life."

"Well, after you live in nearly complete solitude for over three-hundred years, you can get to be a little stalker-like."

"I'll say," he said.

"Well, other than for me being annoying, I know for a fact there's more reasons you won't talk to me. So, spill it."

He closed his eyes, drawing in a sharp breath, taking too long to exhale. His hand ran through his hair briefly, before he spoke. His icy eyes opened suddenly, too, making him seem malevolent in every which way.

"You really want to know why I don't talk to anybody?" he asked. As I nodded, I noticed his fangs were still drawn out.

He gave an evil smile. "Let's just say that if I ever let anyone into my life again, not only will it kill me, but they'll never take another breath for all eternity. How's that explanation for ya'?"

I smiled. "Much better, thank you."

He continued smirking for a minute before he said, "You best be getting home, Fusion. Chiroux is a good hour from here."

I nodded. "I guess I'll see you around, then," I said, "so, goodbye."

His smile grew a bit. "Au revoir," he said, "à bientôt." Then he turned and walked away again. This time, though, I didn't stop him. I felt myself shift into my wolf form, and as I sprinted back to Chiroux, those words kept running through my mind.

Au revoir, à bientôt.

Bye-bye, see you soon.

The thought sent a chill through me as I ran down the familiar path home. I wasn't entirely sure why, but there was a haunting hint to his words. I shook my head as I continued my mad dash back to my home. *Get a hold of yourself Amaury, it means nothing, he's just psycho and he scared you...* However, my thoughts couldn't convince me otherwise from the truth. Those words meant something hidden, like a heavy burden you can't shake off.

Au revoir, à bientôt.

Bye-bye, see you soon.

And I knew from there, everything would be different.

Chapter 2
The Intruder

Amaury:

Mars 19, 1874; Minuit
(March 19, 1874; Midnight)

Dear Diary,

I decided yesterday (as in a few minutes ago, since it is midnight) to leave Chiroux and take a walk to Guéret as a Werewolf, after giving my most recent letter to my sister. I decided to go as a wolf so I wouldn't scare any ignorant Humans I came across... as much. As I walked along the forest I met a Vampire, one you may've heard of. His name is Radder Thor, King Benjamin's brother. He was banished from the Coven because he was a bad leader. His past is very... dark. He told me if he let anyone in, it would kill him. I wonder what he means by that. I wish I could learn more about him, but he's like a huge book that cannot be opened, no matter how hard you try. I guess I'll just have to get it out of him. Somehow.

-Amaury de Pompadour

As I shut my diary, I thought about Radder's words again. I told my diary everything, considering it was the only entertainment source I had, other than writing letters to Magdelene. This is why I was surprised when I chose not to tell the old, leather covered book about his words, and how they haunted me so. Any time I felt scared, or lonely, the diary had brought me solace. But not today.

Since it was midnight by this point, I decided I better get to bed. I went upstairs to the powder room, changed into a white nightgown, and brushed my hair. I went down the empty hallway of the castle, taking a turn on the left and opening the door there.

As I walked into my bedroom, I noticed one of two things right away. My window was wide open, causing the wind to blow my light purple curtains fiercely. I ran quickly to shut it, securely locking it after. I then turned and surveyed the damage. A few random papers were strewn all over the place, but that was no big deal.

I didn't detect the second thing until I noticed the spot where the papers had come from. My dresser mirror reflected the moonlight fairly well, and shone a soft glow over the wooden surface of the actual dresser. That's when I saw that the box was gone.

There had been a small box sitting on the dresser. It was trimmed with gold and decorated in rubies and diamonds and sapphires. In fact, it was probably worth thousands of dollars just by itself. But it wasn't the box that mattered to me. It was what was inside.

It had held the most beautiful necklace. The necklace was a striking little replica of the full moon on a leather cord.

And at night, if you caught it just right in the moonlight, it shone brighter than a star. The most disheartening thing about its disappearance, though, was that it had been a birthday present. From Rafe.

I silently went around my room, picking up the scattered papers. Some were unimportant, but a few were some poems Rafe had written me for another birthday present, and seeing them made my throat feel tight. After they were all back in a neat stack on my dresser, I sat on the side of my bed. I grabbed a small red pillow with gold-colored fringes on it. I twisted some with my finger for quite some time, before I realized it was yet another gift from Rafe. That's when I began to cry.

My first thought here was that I was in the middle of a field. It was wet, covered in dew. The night sky was bright, thanks to the full moon, which also made the dew sparkle. My back was against a tree, but my head was on someone's chest, their arms around me. Yes, I knew exactly where I was.

I lifted my head and looked into Rafe's smoky gray eyes. He smiled at me and ran his fingers through my hair. I placed my head between his neck and shoulder, while he continued to stroke my hair. He lifted my chin up then so I was looking into his eyes again.

"I got something for you," he said, smiling broadly.

"You know you didn't have to," I said, feeling rather guilty.

His smile widened. "But I wanted to," he said. He reached

into his pocket, pulling out a small box, placing it delicately in my hand. It was the most beautiful thing I'd ever seen, engraved with golden designs and covered in various jewels.

"Open it," he said, now twirling a strand of my hair with his finger.

I did as he asked, and when I saw what it held, I gasped. I felt my eyes twinkle as I took the item out of its wooden encasement. It was a stunning replica of the full moon, so much like it, it was like I held the whole moon in the palm of my hand.

"Oh my God," I said, gasping once more, "it's beautiful."

He smiled. "Watch this," he said. He picked it up by its brown leather cord ever so gently. Holding it up towards the moon, and a little to the right, it suddenly shone brightly. It was a gallant white light, like a star itself. Then he brought it back to us, snapping me out of its striking spell. He returned it to the box, closed it, and set it on the ground. Then he turned to me.

"Happy birthday, cherie." he whispered. Then he kissed me. He drew me nearer to him, but eventually pulled away. He still smiled though as he looked into my eyes.

"Je t'aime," he said, kissing me once more.

When I awoke from my dream, or I guess memory, there were tears running down my face. Every time that recollection haunted my dreams, I would put on the necklace. It seemed to lull me to sleep, keeping the bad dreams away. But tonight, I didn't have the precious memento from my time with Rafe.

I clutched the small pillow he gave me tightly. I continued to cry softly, my face buried deep into a bigger pillow. That is, until I suddenly heard a loud crash come from downstairs. I bolted upright, and quietly slipped out of my bed as another crash sounded, a little softer than the first one. I smoothed down my tangled hair, beginning to silently walk across the wooden floorboards. I was suddenly thankful I knew my way around the castle, since I knew exactly which boards creaked and which didn't.

I silently slipped down the stairs. The moon shone in through the windows, and only strengthened my senses. Even for the near darkness, I could make out the features of the intruder. It was a Vampire, with black hair and bright green eyes. He wore a hood over his head, probably to hide his identity. A thought crossed my mind then at that moment as I studied him, though.

He's a Vampire. He could be able to read minds.

Careful to keep my mind blank, I continued down the last of the stairs. The Vampire was holding something in his hands, and smiling thoughtfully. Finally reaching my destination, I made my move. Under the cover of darkness I changed into a wolf, stepped a few feet, my claws making a *click click* noise on the floor. Then, I growled deeply at the invader of my home, baring my teeth in a wicked manor.

He silently set down what he'd been holding, an item that looked like a picture frame that I'd never seen before, and turned his green eyes on me.

"Well, what do we have here? An outcast Werewolf?" he

smirked at me, but his eyes hinted evilness. "Oh, but wait," he continued, "none of the female Werewolves have black fur, and you're obviously not a boy, so, who are you?"

I glared at him with my sharp blue eyes. "A better question would be who are *you* and what the hell are you doing in my home?" I said, bitterly, releasing another throaty growl.

He chuckled a bit. "So, this is your castle? Man, you are one lucky puppy."

"Answer the damn question."

"Well," he said, "I can tell you what I'm not doing here."

I felt my anger rising, and my muscles began to tense. "You better spit it out right now or I swear I'll kill you."

"Now, see here wolfie, you don't want to do that." He then drew a dagger out from his sleeve. He put the tip against his finger, twisting it slowly back and forth with his opposite hand. Each time the surface faced me, it glinted a bright silver in the moonlight.

Silver.

My mind raced. Silver was supposed to kill Werewolves, but not Fusions. As soon as he sliced me with it, he'd expect it to kill me almost instantly. But it wouldn't; in fact, it'd heal faster than the blink of an eye. I gulped, glared my eyes, and growled again.

"You don't scare me," I said nastily, "not with that pathetic little thing."

"Really?" he asked. Before I knew it, the dagger was flying across the room. Straight towards me. Suddenly the sharp little blade was piercing the flesh of my left shoulder. The dagger fell to the floor, and I could feel the blood running through my fur, warm and sticky. I suddenly realized that if I was a Werewolf, I'd be dead by now. So, I rolled my eyes into the back of my head and fell on my right side. I breathed slowly, so it would seem as though I wasn't at all.

I heard his footsteps as he came closer. He picked up the dagger then. Then there was a rather lengthy pause, and I felt his eyes watching me. I knew what he was thinking just before he spoke.

"Wait," he said, stroking my fur where the wound had been. "What the-?"

I shot my head up then, biting his leg fiercely. He plunged the dagger at me again, this time hitting me square in the chest. It hurt, only for a second, but I winced anyway. The Vampire took the small advantage to grab my throat and rip me off of him. He began walking backwards with his hands and feet, watching me in utter fear.

I stood then, staring at the wounded Vampire, both of us panting. His blood ran down my muzzle, staining my teeth and adding a revolting copper-like taste to my mouth. Thinking this, I suddenly realized the extent of what I'd just done.

He was a Vampire.

I was a Fusion.

My venom is supposed to kill his kind.

The Vampire had slipped into unconsciousness exactly two minutes after I bit him. I morphed back into my "Human" form, hurriedly going upstairs to change into decent clothing. When I came back downstairs, I gently picked him up. I slung his arm over my shoulder, and began to drag him like that. As I got outside, I noticed the stars were fading. I needed to move, and *fast*. I contemplated changing into a wolf and dragging him with his cloak back to the Fanges Castle, but decided against it. The only way to get him there before dawn was to give him a piggyback ride and run as fast as I could.

I knew how stupid I'd look, but I figured that if I didn't want my head ripped off by pissed off Vampires, I'd have to make the sacrifice to my self-esteem. So, I flipped him around and threw him onto my back. His breathing was growing shallower by the minute, and his skin grew even paler than the deathly white it already was. I knew I was nearly out of time. So, instead of running him back to his Castle, I set him on the ground.

I sighed as I drew my fangs out. But if I didn't get the venom out of him now, he'd be dead before I reached Maufanges. So, I knelt beside him on the ground, set his head in my lap, and pierced my fangs into his flesh. Since they were still coated in venom, though, I wasn't sure it'd help. But it seemed to.

After about a minute, his blood got its normal taste restored to it. Even though I'd already been alive over three-hundred years, I would never understand how things worked. After all, by all logic and common sense in favor, a second bite to the throat should have killed him. But, alas, it didn't.

I picked him up with me as I stood. Again, I swung him onto my back, piggyback style. Only this time, I was able to run without the threat of him dying. Then again, there was still the threat of an angry Vampire community revolting against me if they discovered that I had harmed one of their own. Remembering this, I grabbed the Vampire's legs tightly so he wouldn't fall. I began to run then, challenging the wind with my speed.

It seemed to take forever, but I finally recognized a few of the trees on the winding dirt road. I thought I saw something in front of me, but I was going so fast that I didn't realize what it was until it was too late. I felt myself crash into it, hard, as I fell to the ground. The Vampire on my back rolled off of me at some point in the collision, but I hardly even noticed. I was staring at who I'd run into.

Clad in his yellow jacket and a pair of jeans, Radder Thor was kneeling on one knee a few feet away from me. His hand was on his forehead, his eyes were closed tightly, and his teeth were firmly gritted. Suddenly his eyes opened, looking at me with a blazing fury.

"You!" he said bitterly. "What the fuck is your problem?"

I stood, brushing off my black skirt. "Radder, I'm sorry, but I was trying to-"

He put his hand up to stop me. "Forget it. Just, just forget it."

I walked towards him, reaching my hand out. "Do you need help?"

"I don't want and I don't need your fucking help you stupid Fusion!"

"I hope you know that I do happen to have a name!" I snapped. "You have no right to treat me like I don't!"

He was suddenly standing then. He grabbed my wrists tightly, his eyes filled with rage.

"For the record, I wasn't. So, what is your name then, Fusion?"

"Amaury. Amaury de Pompadour." I said, staring into his eyes with pure frustration.

"Amaury," he repeated. "I like that name. It suits you." His angered expression turned into a wicked smile.

"How so?" I asked.

"What, you're not a mind reader like myself?" he asked, smirking. He loosened his grip on my wrists a bit, letting some circulation back into my hands.

"No, I'm not," I said. "Anyways, you should know that if you're one."

He chuckled. "Very true," he said, finally dropping his hold on my wrists. "So, any particular reason you chose to "run" into me today?" He chuckled again. "Pun intended," he said.

"Well," I said, indicating to the Vampire who now lay face down in the dirt, "I was trying to get him back to the Coven before dawn, but-" I trailed, staring at the pink sky. The day had officially begun.

"Maybe I can be of assistance," he said, "let me just see who this is."

He walked over to the injured Vampire and kneeled down, turning him so he lay on his back. His expression looked stunned, and with a shaky hand, he lifted the Vampire's eyelid to see his eye color.

"Oh shit," he said, "Amaury, what the hell were you thinking?"

I walked over to him at a brisk pace. "Why? What's wrong?"

He sat up on his feet, wrapping his arms around his knees. He stared to the trees on his right, as though something in the forest had captured his interest. Sighing, he turned to face me.

"You have absolutely no idea who he is, do you?"

I shook my head. "No, I don't."

He drew in a sharp breath, exhaling slowly. "Amaury," he said, "this is Benjamin Thor. The King of the Vampires."

I felt my eyes widen. "Oh shit," I said.

He shook his head. "How'd you get to him anyway? Don't you know how much danger you're in now?"

"Hey," I said, putting my hands up as if to block his words. "He broke into my house! What was I supposed to do, sit at the bottom of the stairwell and watch as he stole my possessions and learned my secrets by reading my diary?"

He smirked again. "You have a diary, huh?"

"Oh, shut your damn mouth," I said.

"Sorry," he said, though the smile was still on his face. He looked at his brother. "Now, what were you doing snooping around her house, bro?" he asked the comatose Benjamin. "I always knew you were a stalker, but, I mean, really?" He shook his head in disgust.

I giggled. "OK Radder, I'm sorry to ruin your little chat, but we kind of need to get him back before the rest of the Coven murders us. Is that alright with you?" I asked the last question sarcastically, smiling.

He smiled back at me. "It is perfectly fine with me, Madame," he said. Radder picked up his brother, holding him up carefully. "Who's faster?" he asked.

"Me," I said, grabbing Benjamin. "What do I do with him when I get there?"

He shrugged. "Just dump him outside the door, I guess. They'll find him sooner or later."

I smiled, but apparently he wasn't kidding. "I'll meet you there," I said. I threw Benjamin onto my back, secured his arms around my neck and held onto his legs, and took off running. Soon enough I saw the Gothic castle. And by the looks of it, no one was stirring about its rooms.

I set the Vampire down as I slid through the towering iron bar fence. After I'd made it successfully through, I reached across the other side and grabbed Benjamin by the hood of his cloak. I dragged him like that until his shoulders were in grabbing distance. When that moment came, I hauled his unconscious self through the gap in the fence.

When both of us were on the Minuit Coven's side of the fence, I set his arm over my shoulder, beginning to drag him like I had at the start. It was about twenty feet to the large oak doors, but we got there surprisingly fast. I dropped him on the cobblestone path leading to the doors, leaving him there, as I dashed quickly back to the fence. I was back in the blink of an eye, sliding through the fence a second time, and ending up right in front of Radder.

"Nicely done," he praised with a smile, "I especially enjoyed the part when you dumped my brother face first onto the stones." At first I thought he was joking, but soon saw that he was dead serious (no pun intended).

"Well," he said, "we better get out of here before-" He stopped at the sound of a creaking door.

"Run!" he said, and before I knew it, he was gone. I dashed into the bushes behind me. I sat behind one, carefully moving branches and leaves out of my way, nearly soundlessly, so I could see.

There was an unfamiliar Vampire standing in the doorway. She had long, flowing blonde hair, and from what I could see, brown eyes. Her face was drawn in a mix of horror, disgust, and anger as she stared at the King of her Coven laying unconscious outside the castle. She went inside for a moment, then returned, bringing with her another unfamiliar Vampire. This one had bright red hair, and her eyes were a cool ocean blue. She flipped her hair, seemingly unconcerned about Benjamin.

Soon, the two had him picked up and were carrying him inside the Fanges Castle. As soon as they were gone, Radder was beside me.

"The redhead is Maryanne Bosquet," he said. "The other, the blonde, is Razza Lacoste. I think my brother is in love with her."

I looked stunned, and I knew it. "No," I disagreed, "he isn't. I think he likes Magdelene."

"Magdelene de Pompadour? No, they're just-" he trailed, thinking for a moment. "Wait, what's your last name again?" he questioned, giving me a rather funny look.

"de Pompadour."

"So, you two are half-sisters, then?"

"Yeah," I said, "we have the same mom."

"Huh," he said. "You learn something new every day."

I nodded. "I guess so."

"Well," he said, standing. "We best be getting to our rightful places. I don't know about you, but I have things to do."

"Oh," I said. "Right. I have… things, to do too." I suddenly felt extremely disappointed.

"I'll see you around though, right?" Radder asked me.

"Maybe," I said. "I don't go out much though, because I don't want to be noticed."

He paused for a minute, thinking about what I'd just said. "Right," he said then. "I guess I'll just see you when I see you, huh?"

I nodded. "Sure," I said. *As if*, I thought unwillingly, suddenly remembering his ability to read minds.

He looked at me with somewhat shocked eyes. His expression looked hurtful, and then he walked slowly away.

"Goodbye," I whispered. I had the strangest feeling that I wouldn't be seeing him around any time soon.

As he walked, I watched him go. *Did he hear me?* I thought.

He stopped suddenly, turning around to face me.

"Of course I heard you," he said, his eyes pinned down, "Why?"

"I just didn't want you to leave on a bad note, that's all."

He raised his eyebrows. "Oh, well, sure then. That makes sense."

"Radder, listen, I'm being really rude to you and…"

"Amaury, it's fine."

"Je suis désolé. I'm sorry. Really."

"Amaury," he said, walking back over, "I said it's fine. You don't have to apologize."

"But I wanted too. I'm being a total jerk to you."

"Yes, you are. I forgive you though, 'cause I'm being a jerk to you, too." He smiled down at me from where I still sat on the ground.

"Hmm. Still, anything I can do for you?" I said, still feeling guilty.

He looked at me. "No. Why would you have to?"

"To prove that I really am sorry."

He chuckled. "You don't have to do anything for me," he said, "except…"

"Except what?" I asked, faking irritation.

"You have to do me a few favors."

"Which would be?"

He paused for a moment, thinking. "Five favors. First of which, starts now."

Oh no, I thought. "OK," I said, "what do you have in mind, Radder?"

"Just follow me," he said.

I looked up and stared at him. He reached his arm outwards for me to grab. His black hair fell over his blue eyes, and I had a painful flash of the last time I saw Rafe. I gulped, and looked straight ahead of me, hoping the comfort of the trees would help brighten up my now sad memories.

"Hey, are you OK, Amaury?" Radder asked.

I snapped out of my trance, looking up at him, nodding.

"Ready?" he asked, arm still extended so I could take his hand. I just stared up at him.

"Come on, you can trust me," he said. "There's nothing to be afraid of, I promise."

Although he was talking to me like I was a dog, I placed my hand in his. He helped me stand, and then began to walk. When he noticed I wasn't following, he stopped and looked at me over his shoulder.

"Come on," he said, "follow me."

I sighed, and then walked fast to catch up with him.

"It's almost a two hour walk to Guéret from here," he said.

"I am quite aware of that."

He smiled at me. "I was hinting something there."

I thought for a second before finally getting what he was hinting at. "So, we're going to Guéret, then?"

"Precisely," he said.

"Why do you live in Guéret?" I asked.

"Well, I'm not allowed in Maufanges. I was banished."

"Then how come you were here when I ran into you?"

He looked straight ahead of him. "I was taking care of some business."

"Oh," I said, knowing not to push it on that subject. "Well, why'd you choose Guéret? I mean, there's a ton of towns all around here."

"I chose Guéret because it had the most Humans." His smile was gone.

I nodded, thinking it'd be stupid to just say, "Oh," again.

He sighed. After a few moments he said, "You know, I hate being what I am."

Again I nodded, since I had somewhat of an understanding of why he'd say such a thing.

"I just… I hate killing people. I mean, occasionally I'll drink an animal's blood, but I can't survive on it totally. I mean, I'm a murderer. A killer." He shook his head in disgust.

"You can't blame yourself," I said. "It's not your fault you were born a Vampire. Blame your parents."

"I do. I curse them every day of my life. Especially Brock though. I hate him most of all."

I wasn't aware why he particularly hated his father, Brock Thor. He had been King before Radder, and gave the throne to him over Benjamin. This wasn't supposed to happen though. Since Benjamin was the eldest child, he was supposed to inherit the rightful place as King of the Minuit Coven.

"Why? He gave you the throne, he-"

"Listen! It's none of your concern as to why I hate him. Just, just stop asking personal questions. I feel like you're stalking me."

I was quiet as we continued down the dirt pathway. Guéret was still a little over an hour away at the pace we were going. I studied the trees on the side of the pathway, watching as the occasional squirrel ran up the side of one, and listening to the birds sing marvelous little songs as the day progressed. I was lost in a trance of nature, and just barely heard Radder as he broke the peaceful silence.

"Listen," he said, "I'm sorry, OK? I just don't want you to learn my past. I don't want you to get hurt."

I wasn't sure how he'd meant the last comment to go through to me, but I took it as simply the fact that he didn't want *anybody* to get hurt, not just me in particular.

We continued walking. "Tell you what, since I'm being an asshole, I'll cut one of the favors. You only have to do four now."

I still didn't speak, just kept walking forward.

He turned towards me. "Amaury, please say something."

"Merci," I said. "For cutting a favor."

He gave me a tiny smile. "Votre accueil." he said. Then he sighed. "I'm sick of walking." he stated.

"Tired?" I asked, giving him a sarcastic smile.

"Ha ha, very funny," he said. He turned right and walked into the woods a little bit. I followed him into the thick forest, and found him sitting on a rotten log. He smiled as I approached, motioning for me to take a seat beside him on the fallen tree. I did, watching him pick up a few smooth gray rocks that were at his feet. He stuffed them into his pocket while I gave him a strange look.

"Um… what are those for?" I asked, a little creeped out.

He smiled, looking straight ahead. "You'll see."

I shrugged, looking onwards. "Does it have to do with one of the favors?"

"Perhaps," he said. "But that's for me to know and for you to find out."

"Whatever," I said.

He chuckled, scooping up more rocks with his palm. He also spooned up a handful of dirt this time, and pulled the rocks out. The earth in his hands fell back into the place it'd come from, while the rocks remained in his palm, as well as a few chunks of dirt that didn't make it with the rest. Slowly he took the rocks and wiped them off on his yellow jacket. It stained it brown a bit with the earth, but he didn't seem to mind.

Radder looked at each stone carefully before placing them in his pocket with the others he'd taken from the ground. One though, he picked up delicately with his fingers. He twirled it around with his fingers, studying it intently. It was a smooth, pure white stone, clearly in the shape of a heart. It seemed to have a glass coating over it, and it shone in the still-rising sun that just barely came in through the dense treetops.

He smiled at it before placing it in his pocket with the others. "That stone reminds me of you," he said.

"How so?" I asked. But he just shook his head and smiled, slightly laughing at his own private joke. He bent down again to pick up a few more stones, and I decided not to ask again. Radder surprised me though. Instead of picking up some rocks out of the many at his feet, he picked up a tiny little flower.

It was a deep purple wood violet with four petals. The throat was a mix of a deep yellow and black, and even the whole flower wasn't as tall as my pinky. In fact, it looked almost dead. He began spinning it with his fingers by the stem, and we both watched as it twisted this way and that. Then Radder unexpectedly picked up my right hand.

He turned it so my palm was facing up towards the light blue sky. He placed it in my hand, closing my fingers around it tightly, but not as much as to crush the delicate flower in my palm.

"Keep it," Radder told me, "for as long as you possibly can." His expression was serious. He kept his hands over mine, and for a moment, I thought he'd kiss me. And, somewhat to my horror, I wanted him to. But too soon he took his hands away. He stared at the ground, and knowing he'd been reading my thoughts, I felt my face flush.

He sighed again, picking up three more stones. After cleaning them off, he studied each individually. The first was too sharp for his liking, and he threw it violently into the dense, dark forest. The second he stuffed into his pocket. But the third, a small, smooth, and also heart-shaped gray stone with little black flecks, he put back on the ground. Leaning down, he covered it over with more dirt while I just looked at him.

"Let somebody else have it," he said, aware of the look I was giving him.

He sat back up, folding his hands together and placing them between his knees. I put my hands on the log to keep my balance as I stretched my legs out in front of me. I kicked the dirt a bit with my shoe, watching it move. Out of the corner of my eye, I saw Radder run a hand through his hair. He leaned down again, picking up yet another rock, cleaning it off, and sticking it in his pocket.

Suddenly he stood, brushing off his dirt-covered hands on his jeans. "Let's go," he said, and started to walk back towards the path. I quickly stood and followed him. For a Vampire, Radder was awfully fast compared to most others. It took me a moment to find him, and I nearly had to start running to catch up to him. But, finally, I did. It was apparent he was frustrated with me, mostly because his eyes were turned down in a glare. So, I just put my head down, stared at the ground, and kept an even pace with him.

We continued walking in silence. That is, until Radder finally spoke.

"We're almost there. It's about a twenty minute walk from here."

"Great," I said, "can't wait."

He smiled then. "We could make the journey there a little more interesting if you like."

I looked at him. "And what would that involve?"

His smile widened. "Amaury, I, Radder Thor, challenge you to a race."

I gave him a wicked smile. "You are *so* on."

He pointed ahead a few feet to a towering oak on the side of the path. "We'll start there. The finish line will be the edge of the forest in Guéret, where it comes out onto the road. I mean, I'd make it the gate, but we don't want to risk revealing our existence, you know?"

I nodded. "Then it's set."

He smiled at me as we neared the oak. He walked a little ahead of me, grabbed a stick off the ground, and drew a perfectly straight line with it across the road.

He looked at me as I approached, his blue eyes shining bright with anticipation of the challenge.

"You ready to run?" he asked as I got closer still.

"You know it," I said, "prepare to be beaten."

"As if. You're gonna get your ass kicked, girl."

I pouted. "You mean, you're not gonna let me win?"

"No, I'm not. Sorry, but you must win this on your own."

"I was gonna anyway. I've seen snails run faster than you."

"Snails don't run."

"Oh, whatever," I said, "are we gonna do this, or not?"

He smiled. "OK. Ready?"

I nodded, getting into a running position.

"Alright then," he said, following my example. "On your marks, get set, go!"

We both took of at lightning speed. Around me, the trees blurred past in a flash of brown and green. Everything was so hazy; I couldn't even make out the smallest details of the forest I'd been so careful to study earlier. In fact, I couldn't even see Radder. Which meant, he was either extremely far behind me, or way in front.

I turned a few times on the indistinct pathway, and, spotting a town in the distance, I willed myself to go even faster. Before I knew it I was at the edge of the woods. As I looked around me, I saw Radder hadn't shown up yet. But as soon as I thought that, he came up behind me.

"Damn," he said. "I lost."

I turned around and smiled at him. He was smiling back. "I so let you win," he said to me.

"You so did not," I said.

He got a little closer. "How are you so sure? As far as I'm concerned, you can't read minds, so really there is no logical way you can prove that I'm lying."

I stared at him. "Maybe," I said, "I just know that you wouldn't lie to me."

He chuckled. "Smart girl. Come on, let's go."

We moved through the bushes that were all around, but finally came into a marvelous field. There was long, flowing green grass all around us.

"Are you sure this is Guéret?" I asked, "because this doesn't exactly look like a town."

"We have about a two minute walk through the field to reach the gate. If you look out a bit, you can see the main road to get there."

I shielded my eyes with my hand, looking farther away. Sure enough, there was a dirt road, crowded with people and carriages and horses.

"What's going on?" I asked.

"There's a bazaar in the town square today. There's probably a lot of good stuff, too."

"So, what's the favor I have to do, exactly?"

He smiled, looking forward, and walked on. "You'll see."

We soon reached the stone arch that held the iron bar gates. This was the only way to get into the city, and the only way out. No wonder it was so crowded. Guéret was completely surrounded by dark stone walls to ensure the city's protection. Radder and I joined the huge mass of people wanting in and out of the city's encased walls.

It was so crowded, in fact, I could hardly breathe. Radder took my hand in his so I wouldn't loose him, and I felt myself flush a bright pink. He smiled at me as we walked under the stone arch. The gates had been swung out of the way as far as they could go, as not to disturb the visitors and locals. After we'd crossed over into the city, Radder led me down the cobblestone road until we reached the town square.

It was actually a giant circle over a square, and in the very center was a giant fountain. Water spewed out from the top, glistening in the afternoon sun. Around the rim were people resting, and many children eating treats. All around, in front of all sorts of buildings, were tiny wooden booths. All sorts of things were being sold, from elegant vases to creatively designed blankets.

Radder let go of my hand, although it was even more crowded here then on the pathway, and walked off. I soon lost sight of him in the cluster of people, and sighed, knowing it'd be impossible to find him here. So, I went around looking at booths. I went to one where an old man sat, carving little wooden figures. I looked at some on display. There was a bear, an eagle, and even a tree.

I studied the works, very impressed. But then I saw three,

in the very back, that sent a chill down my spine. I picked the first up, looking down at it with a look of horror.

It was a Vampire. Actually, it looked just like a normal person, except, it had fangs. It didn't look like any Vampire I knew, but still, it was scary.

The second was of a wolf. Its fur was bristled, ears back, teeth bared viciously. It looked like an ordinary wolf, though, so I placed it back by the Vampire. When I picked up the third, though, I almost fainted. It was another Vampire, the same one as before, only this time its mouth was open, fangs showing, and he was lunging in an attack-mode sort of way. It was reaching for a wolf that looked similar to the other figure I'd picked up.

I stood there holding and studying it for an unknown amount of time. Eventually, the old man put down his knife and the newly-carved figure and stood. He stretched, briefly, and picked up the figure again. It was a butterfly, sitting on a leaf. He set it on the stand with the others. Then he looked at me holding the Vampire and Werewolf carving.

"The Vampire is named Brock," he said, "and the Werewolf, well, he's actually a mix of the two. His name is Rafe."

I nearly dropped the figure on the ground. I set it on the table with shaky hands as the man watched me.

"You know of them, do you?" he said.

I nodded. "Yeah, I do."

He picked up the figure. "Brock and Rafe are real, you know."

Stay hidden and don't move. I'll be back soon.

"Yeah. I knew that," I said.

"Well, they're not anymore. Rafe got destroyed, and Brock got killed by one of his sons."

My eyes widened. "Which one?"

"Well, I don't know either of their names, but it's the kid with blue eyes. That's all I know."

Radder.

I nodded. "So, was Brock the only one who killed Rafe, then?" I felt this was my chance to learn who had killed him, and possibly, get revenge once and for all.

"No," he said. "One of his boys helped. Don't know which though. Sorry. In fact, maybe they both did. Again though, I'm not sure. I mean, I wasn't alive three-hundred years ago, you know?"

But I *was.* "Yeah, I know exactly what you mean."

"You know, you seem awful young. I mean, I only know because one of my ancestors was killed by a Vampire, but, how do you know so much about the Vampires and Werewolves and, oh, what are those things called? The hybrids?"

"Fusions." I dragged the word out slowly.

"Yeah," he said, "those."

"My parents were hunters, until they got killed," I lied.

"Oh, well, I'm sorry to hear that. Who killed 'em?"

"Um…" I thought quickly. "Maryanne Bosquet, I believe."

"Never heard of her."

"She's a newer Vampire. Hasn't been alive a century."

He nodded. "Right. I'm not too aware of them as I used to be, but you listen here girl, you need to watch your back. I know there are still a whole lot of them out there. Now, the Werewolves, they'll protect you. If you're in danger, find a Guard. I'm sure those Fusion things are all dead since Rafe.

And, if you see a boy, tan, black hair, blue eyes, run. It could be a person, or it could be one of Brock's boys. Anyways, he's probably the most dangerous Vampire there is. He's completely psycho, too. I've heard rumors that he can be extremely nice, but you say one wrong thing to him, and your head will be off your neck."

I nodded. I knew Radder's mood could change fairly quickly, like it had this morning. One moment, angrier than hell, the next, a total gentleman. The thing I couldn't believe though, was that he could've been an accomplice to Rafe's murder.

"I'll be careful," I said, "no way one of those Vampires is gonna get me."

"Smart girl," he said. I remembered Radder saying those exact words to me earlier.

"Well, I guess I'm just gonna go-"

"Amaury, there you are! I've been looking all over for you!"

Radder came up behind me. He placed his hands on the stand, looking at the figures. His eyes fell on the one, then, of Brock and Rafe.

"This is amazing," he said, picking it up to study the detail. "You do these by hand?"

The old man nodded, keeping his eyes trained on Radder's movements. I could see the suspicion in his eyes, and could almost hear his thoughts.

Tan boy. Black hair. Blue eyes. VAMPIRE!

"Yeah," he said slowly, "I do."

Radder set it down. "Brock and Rafe, am I correct?"

The old man's blue eyes widened in shock. He nodded quickly, and again I knew what he was thinking.

VAMPIRE VAMPIRE VAMPIRE!

Radder saw it too, only he actually *could* read the man's mind. He chuckled. "I must say, it is *very* impressive woodworking of my father."

That did it. He backed up as far as he could in the tent over his stand. He put his hands up in surrender. Then he pointed towards Radder. "You- you're a Vampire!" he said, so quietly you could barely hear him.

Radder's fangs drew out. "Got that right, old man."

"Radder, stop!" I said. "Leave the poor guy alone! He hasn't done anything!"

The man turned to me. "And you, what are you? You're not Human! But-"

Radder frowned. "She's a Fusion."

I saw him turn to look at me. I hung my head down so I wouldn't see the horror in his eyes. "Radder," I whispered, "let's go."

He smiled at the man. "Au revoir," he said, grabbing my hand and practically dragging me away. We weaved through the crowd of people. I couldn't believe that nobody had just seen that ordeal. Radder led me to the giant fountain, let go of my hand, and sat on the edge. He patted the open section of stone beside him, motioning for me to sit down next to him.

I did, but I didn't look at or speak to him. Well, until I noticed his fangs were still drawn out.

"What do you think you're doing?" I asked.

"Relax. Everyone's so busy shopping they won't notice."

"Well, fangs are a hard thing to miss, considering no Human has them."

He sighed. "Would you please just calm down? It's really not that big of a deal."

"It is to me."

"What is your problem?"

"Hmm. I don't know. Maybe I'm just a little angry because you scared that poor old guy. You said you hated hurting people. So, how come I just witnessed you harm someone? On *purpose*, even?"

He put his hands on his temples. "Would you just let it go? Jeez."

"No, I won't." Then I stood up and walked away.

"Hey! Amaury, get back here!" I could here him call after me, but I ignored him.

I weaved through people, trying to find the way out. But, I didn't know which way we'd come in, and I couldn't see the stone arch anywhere. Frustrated, I went with the sea of people. I was practically the only one who remained, since everybody else was either going out of the crowd to shop, or joining it. I didn't see Radder anywhere. I figured that he thought I went off to look at more of the booths, so I just tried to blend in with the crowd. He could've left the city, too, and gone back home.

Lost in thought, I barely stopped myself before running into a lady. She wore a brown dress, a peasant's dress, with a hood over her head. Conveniently, the hood was attached to her dress. She was carrying a whicker basket with a white and blue checkered cloth covering its contents. I couldn't make out her hair color beneath her hood, but her eyes were as brown as her dress, and they looked wide with shock.

"Bonjour, Madame." I said. She just stared.

"Um…Enchanter de te connaitre." I added.

She looked at me. "Um… Je ne parle pas très bien le Français, pouvez-vous me parler en Anglais?" *I don't speak very good French, can you speak to me in English?*

"Certainly," I said.

She sighed in relief. "Thank you. No one else here seems to be able to."

"Do you need help?" I said.

"Yes, yes. I'm looking for someone."

"Who?"

"A friend of mine. Kind of tall, tan, black hair, and blue eyes. He's probably wearing a light yellow coat. Have you seen him?"

I gasped. I knew she was talking about Radder. "What's his name? He sounds familiar."

"Radder." My suspicions were correct. "You know him?"

"Yeah," I said, "I know him. I don't think he's here though. I haven't seen him."

"Hmm. Oh well."

"What's your name?" I asked.

She paused for a moment. "Raven," she said, "Raven Navre."

It was evident she was lying, so when she asked for my name I said, "Ava Davis."

She nodded, her lips pursed. "Well, it was nice meeting you."

"You as well," I said.

She nodded again, and then began to walk away. As she began to disappear, I saw something on the ground. I picked it up, seeing it was a crumpled up piece of paper.

"Hey, you dropped this!" I called after her. But when I looked up, she was gone.

I opened up the ball of paper out of pure curiosity. Surely if she dropped it and didn't return for it, it was unimportant. I smoothed out the paper, making out a small poem written in a terrible scrawl. It read:

You can run Fusion,
But you can't hide.
Find who you're looking for,
And they'll serve as your guide.

I stared at the small piece of paper in my hand, feeling myself shake. For the record, I had no idea I'd been searching for anybody. Plus, how could anyone be my guide? Only three people were even aware of my existence, and even then, only one of them was actually a person. *Who are you Raven?* I thought.

I jumped when a cold hand touched my shoulder. I turned around to see Radder standing behind me, frowning.

"It's about time I found you," he said. "I thought you'd left."

I shook my head. "I couldn't have left without you."

"Why?" he asked, "are you so excited to do your favor for me that you couldn't bear to leave?"

"Actually, I just couldn't find my way out. But if you want to put it the other way, then sure."

He didn't look amused. "Well, are you ready to do your favor?"

"Sure," I said, "why not?"

"Alright then," he said, "follow me."

We weaved through the crowd, but this time, I was careful to keep him in sight. We made it out of the crowd fairly quickly, and started walking down a road that went out of the square. There weren't many people here, but there were a few random booths.

"What am I supposed to do, exactly?" I asked as he started to make way towards a booth.

"You," he said, "are supposed to stand here and be quiet while I buy you something."

I felt my eyes dilate. "Wait, *what*?"

By then, though, we were at the booth. There was a woman sitting behind it, placing a few beads in a careful pattern on a new leather cord. The booth was full of all sorts of little trinkets: wind chimes, necklaces, bracelets, rings, and even little bells.

Radder leaned over and whispered in my ear. "Pick anything you want." I felt my face flush.

I saw the neatest little thing right in front of me. It was tiny little blue bell, attached to a black leather cord. I picked it up and it rang, making the most beautiful sound.

"I like this," I told him. He took it for a second, considered it, and grinned.

He asked the woman making the necklace how much it was, paid her, and then turned back to me. He brought his hands around my neck and clasped the necklace, then backed up a bit.

He slid his hands around my waist then, smiling. "Beautiful," he said, and then he kissed me.

My head felt light the moment his lips pressed against

mine. I felt it when he pulled me a little closer, bringing his hand away from my waist, and instead tangling it in my black hair. But suddenly, without any given warning, he pulled away, though kept his arm around my waist, bringing the other back down to join it. We were both smiling broadly at each other. I felt myself blushing as he held me there, feeling the lady at the booth's gaze and knowing she was smiling in amusement. The kiss had only lasted a few seconds, but I felt as though I was on top of the world.

His hand grasped mine for the third time that day, and we began to walk a little farther down the road. My mind was buzzing. I couldn't believe he'd actually *kissed* me. And right now, I didn't care that he could read my mind. It was all I could think about. He appeared to be smiling, though, as we continued down the road. We stopped in front of a dark alleyway then, and he turned to me, letting go of my hand.

"Wait right here," he said, "I'll be right back."

He started walking towards the alley then. Out of the darkness, I could make out the shape of what appeared to be a person in a cloak. Radder approached them, talking in a low voice for a few moments. I saw him hand the person something, and watched them give him something in return. Radder's item shone for a moment before he placed it in his pocket.

Then, he nodded to the person. They said a few more things before Radder came out of the alleyway and strode over to me. The figure still stood, though, watching us in utter silence.

"Hello," he said, wrapping his arms around my waist again. "Are you ready to go, or would you like to shop a little more? I'll buy you whatever you want."

"I'm not really sure," I said. "I mean, I don't want you to waste your money on me or anything."

He stifled a laugh. "I'm not wasting my money, trust me."

I shrugged. "Still."

"Tell you what," he said. "How about we go look at the booths, and if you see something else you want, then I'll get it. If not, at least you got that pretty little bell around your neck."

I felt myself blush for the umpteenth time today as Radder smiled at me. He bent his head a bit to kiss me lightly on the lips, and then we started walking away. His arm was still around my waist as we walked along the cobblestone road. I turned my head then while he wasn't paying attention, hoping to get a glimpse of the hooded figure. But, he was gone.

Radder and I had visited many booths throughout the day. The first we visited was another trinket booth, where there was a beautiful silver necklace with a black onyx pendant hanging from it. I stopped for only a moment to look at it before Radder purchased it. Since I had nowhere else to put it, he placed it in one of many of his pockets.

Radder eventually left me alone for a few moments. When I asked why, he only said that there was a particular booth he wanted to visit. I shrugged as he walked off, walking over to another booth. A rather plump woman sat behind it, a fake smile plastered on her face. Hundreds of vases sat all around her, colored with remarkable colors and decorated with beautiful hand-painted designs. I had a hard time believing that this individual lady had made all of these.

"Can I help you?" the woman asked in a snooty voice, her smile gone.

"I'm just looking," I said. She rolled her eyes.

"If you aren't going to buy anything, I say you should just leave."

"Excuse me?" I asked.

"No one here likes annoying people coming to their booths to just "look." It's either come and buy or keep on moving."

"Well," I said, "how the hell are people supposed to buy things without looking at them and deciding if they want them first?"

"Obviously, you don't. You just pick something and buy it. We don't care if you want it or need it or not. We just want money. And if you aren't willing to give us that, then we don't want you near our booths. How stupid are you?"

"Excuse me?" a voice said behind me. "What did you just say to her?"

I somewhat moved away as Radder appeared next to me. And, to be honest, he looked rather pissed. I put my hands on the stand and looked down, preparing for his rage.

"Is that how you treat the people who give you your profits? The people who give you money to pay for food for you and your family?"

"Yes, it is. But as long as I do get paid, I don't care about being hospitable to my customers."

Radder shook his head, though a smile remained on his

face. I knew that this was about to get ugly. Without saying a word, Radder picked up a rather pretty vase, examining it. Then, without warning, he threw it on the ground, smashing it to pieces.

"Hey!" the woman said, her eyes wide, "you're gonna have to pay for that!"

Radder picked up a few more of them then, throwing them on the ground to join the other broken vase. The woman looked at him in horror. By now, people were gathering around to see what all the commotion was about. I stared up at Radder, feeling my heart skip a beat. His fangs were drawn out, and in plain sight of all the people around us.

Everyone was staring at him and his fang-revealing smile by now. One little boy, holding his mother's hand, pointed at him and said, "Mommy, what's wrong with his teeth?" Radder heard this, or perhaps another comment, and laughed menacingly. He placed something on the booth then, some type of very expensive coin I'd never seen before, and said to the woman, "Keep the change."

Then, he backed up a bit, ran a few steps, and jumped high into the air. He landed on top of a roof, while the crowd gasped. I gave him an And-What-The-Hell-Am-I-Supposed-To-Do-Look, watching as he looked at me with a smile on his face. He waved to the citizens of Guéret, and said loudly, "Au revoir." Then, he turned around and ran, jumping from building to building until he was out of sight.

Figuring that I had nothing to loose, I followed his example. Except, when I was on the roof of the building, I didn't turn or wave or speak. Instead, as the people again gasped, I followed Radder's scent among the building tops. I jumped over tons until

I reached the stone wall. Gliding over it and landing softly in the grass, I stood, brushing off my skirt. I didn't see Radder anywhere.

I jumped though when someone's arms slid around my waist, until I realized it was him. He kissed my neck and whispered in my ear, "Bonjour cherie." Again, my face flushed, especially when he turned my head to kiss me on the lips. Too soon though, he pulled away and started walking. I was a little angry that he'd only kiss me for about three seconds. But, regardless, I hurried to catch up with him. He placed his hands in his pockets, not speaking, as we cut through the field to the forest.

After we'd reached the woods and found the path, Radder took my hand in his. We walked along it until Radder suddenly stopped.

"We have to run," he said, "they're looking for us. And they're close."

"Won't they be able to see our footprints on the dirt? And hear my bell?"

"We'll run beside the path. Take your necklace off and hold it tight, so it doesn't make noise."

I did, nodding, only then remembering I was holding the flower, too. I swear that somewhere along the lines I'd let go of it, but no. It was still encased firmly in my palm. I placed the bell in my opposite hand, following Radder to the side of the path.

"Let's go," he said, and then he took off.

I ran until our paces were even. "Wait," I said, "won't they be able to follow our footprints from earlier?"

He slowed a bit, forcing me to as well. "Good point," he said. "Tell you what, you run on to your house, and I'll meet you there."

"Oh, alright." I said. I felt extremely worried for him.

He stopped, and I did too. "Amaury, I'll be fine. I promise." Then, again, he kissed me. He pulled me nearer, holding me close for as long as he possibly could. When he pulled away, I felt like I was flying, my head in the clouds. At least it had been longer than three seconds this time.

"Don't worry," he said, "I'll take care of this."

I nodded. "I'll see you soon," I said, and as I ran away, I felt terrible. I already missed his presence. Perhaps though, even worse than that, was the fact that I felt like a traitor. Rafe had been just as sweet as Radder, maybe even more so. And yet, I was starting to forget him. It used to be that he was always on my mind. But since I'd met Radder, I was slowly letting his memory slip away.

I began to run faster then, hoping to keep the sad thoughts of Rafe and me out of my head. I felt a tear run down my cheek, but it was quickly gone, considering how fast I was running. Before I knew it, I had reached my castle in Chiroux. As I walked in, I felt its emptiness sweep over me. I felt so alone here.

I lay down on my couch, placing my head on a pillow. I longed for Rafe to be here, by my side. But as much as I wished and hoped, I knew in my heart that he was gone forever, and he would never be coming back. I shed another tear, just as I heard a knock on the door. I wiped the small trail of water off my cheek and smiled, knowing it'd be Radder.

When I opened the door, he stepped in, pulling me into an icy embrace.

"I told you I'd be alright," he said. Then he kissed me. He pulled me closer to him, and after a few minutes, he pulled away, but rested his forehead on mine.

"I need to be getting home," he said, "but I don't want to leave your side."

I was glowing inside. "Will I see you tomorrow?" I asked.

"Of course," he said. "As if I could stay away from you for an entire day. I'll be here at dusk."

"Alright," I said. He kissed me one more time, lightly, before he walked out the door. I shut it softly behind him, keeping my hand on the knob as I smiled broadly. Then, I remembered he had my black onyx necklace. I opened the door, hoping to call to him and tell him, but he was gone.

I went upstairs to my bedroom, the bell necklace and the small purple flower still in my hand. When I opened the door I walked over to my dresser, setting the bell necklace in front of my small stack of papers. Then, I noticed that my black onyx necklace was on top of the papers, next to a blood red rose. I looked around, but I was alone in the room. There was no trace that Radder had been here; even his scent was gone. And yet, I knew he had been.

I picked up the rose and made my way downstairs to my kitchen. When I walked in, I found a tall turquoise-colored vase. I filled it up with water and placed the rose in it. The violet, though, would need a smaller one. So, I searched rapidly through my cabinets for something I could put it in. I had to place it in the smallest thing I could find, which happened to be a wineglass. I filled it with water too, just as I had for the vase, and set it next to the rose's vase. I put my elbows on the counter, resting my head in my hands as I stared at the two beautiful flowers. Then I smiled. This had been the perfect end to a perfect day.

Chapter 3
Benjamin

Magdelene:

I heard myself mumble when Razza and Maryanne entered my room. Razza came over to my bed, shaking me. "Magdelene!" she said. "Get up!"

Slowly I lifted my head. My darkened room was invaded by the light coming in through my door. I threw my black quilt over my head, listening as Maryanne walked around my room, opening the curtains. Razza threw the quilt off my head, forcing me to see the light.

"Come on," Maryanne said, "rise and shine."

"There's something wrong with you if you shine after you wake up." I said, getting out of my bed and rubbing my eyes. I made my way over to my dresser mirror, picking up a hairbrush and brushing my somewhat tangled hair. Then, I turned to face the other Vampires in my room. I noticed Razza had on a long, flowing black dress. Maryanne wore the same thing, only her dress was red. *Typical Mary,* I thought, *always wanting to be who she's not.* I was suddenly very thankful I was the only one in here who could read minds. On that subject, I found that Maryanne's mind was completely content, while Razza's had a worried vibe to it.

I looked at her. "What's wrong?" I asked.

"It's Benjamin."

I felt my heart skip a beat. "What about him?"

"Get dressed and we'll tell you," she said, walking out the door with Maryanne behind her. "We'll be downstairs."

As she shut the door, I looked at myself in the mirror. Had Benjamin been destroyed? I doubted it, but still, it was a possibility. I hurriedly changed out of my black nightgown and into a white t-shirt. Over it I put on a small black vest. I also put on a black skirt that went down to my knees, and black high heels. Checking my hair once more, I walked out of my bedroom.

I made my way down the long flight of stairs in the Fanges Castle, then headed into the parlor. I found Razza and Maryanne sitting in chairs, which were scattered all around the room. Adam Carpentier joined them as well. As I entered the parlor, they all turned to look at me, and then at the only couch in the room. *Benjamin.* Again my heart skipped a beat, and now my throat felt tight.

I walked around the green couch, looking at him. Benjamin was sprawled out on it, looking as though to be asleep. I would've thought he was dead, had his chest not been continuously rising and falling.

"What's wrong with him exactly?" I asked.

Adam answered. "He's unconscious. Razza found him laying on the pathway this morning."

I looked at Razza, glaring. "What were you doing outside?"

She put her hands up in self-defense. "I was going to check on the plants to see if they needed watering. What'd you think, I was going to go and murder a Werewolf?"

"Knowing you, you probably were."

She rolled her eyes. I continued speaking. "Does anybody have any idea what happened to him?"

Adam walked over, kneeling on his knees by Benjamin's head. "No," he said, "but we did notice this."

He scooted along the floor on his knees down by Benjamin's feet. Adam drew his black cloak up over his left leg. There was a giant gash in Benjamin's leg, which looked similar to a Werewolf bite. His leg was soaked with his own blood, and the wound, while deep, should've healed by this point.

While it was indeed strange, I ran my finger over his blood and smelled it. "The scent in his blood is normal," I said matter-of-factly, "no trace of venom."

Adam followed my example. "She's right," he declared. I glared at him, angry that he had been trying to prove me wrong. But that was just Adam, he always had to be the right one. I looked again at the wound.

"Looks like one of the damn Werewolves got him." Adam said as he noticed my observation of the wound.

No, I thought, *for once Adam, you're wrong.*

I swiped up more blood with my finger. Still no venom. "Damn," I cursed. I looked up. At some point, Razza and Maryanne had left the room. Rolling my eyes again, I suddenly noticed a dark spot on the left arm sleeve of his cloak. To inspect it, I'd have to find a way to get Adam to leave the room, or at least distract him somehow.

"Where'd Maryanne and Razza go?"

He looked up too, surveying the room. "I dunno," he said, "I'll go find them."

I watched as he left the room and into the kitchen (we had a kitchen as to not be suspicious. It's not like we use it). I took my opportunity alone to investigate the dark spot. Sure enough, it was sticky and smelled of blood. But it wasn't Benjamin's. I lifted the sleeve up a bit to smell. It wouldn't completely reveal the identity of the one who bit him, but it would at least verify if it was indeed a Werewolf. So, I smelled the sticky dark spot.

It had a Werewolf's scent.

But also a Vampire's.

"Amaury. You bitch." I whispered, sucking in a breath. I couldn't believe that my own sister had tried to kill my soul mate. Well, my soul mate who doesn't acknowledge the fact that we truly are soul mates. But still, it counts. Suddenly Benjamin turned, making me jump. He mumbled in his sleep, saying unintelligible words. He moved his injured leg, causing his face to have a pained expression appear on it.

I ran my hand swiftly through his dark ebony hair. I longed to do this every day, while he kissed me sweetly and held me tightly to him…

"Magdelene? Is that you?" a drowsy voice asked.

Oh no, I thought.

Benjamin can read minds.

"Yeah," I said, "it's me alright."

He smiled. "Of course. I'd recognize you anywhere."

I felt myself blush, though I wasn't sure if it was intended as a compliment or not.

"How's your leg?" I asked, hoping to keep him from reading my mind. I felt my own dive deep into his, seeing that so far, he hadn't read a single thing I'd thought all day. Phew.

He winced as he turned again. "Pillow…please," he begged, his voice revealing his pain.

My eyes scanned the room quickly, my only focus finding one for him and helping to ease his pain. Spotting one on the chair where Adam had been sitting, I walked over and picked it up. I felt a gaze burning into my back, and turned, still clutching the pillow, to see Benjamin looking at me. I made my way back toward him with the pillow in my hands, watching as he smiled widely; so much so that it reached his eyes.

I lifted his leg up and set in on the silky white pillow as carefully as possible. He winced, clenching his teeth together as I set his wounded leg on it. Moving my hands away from his leg and standing, I asked, "Do you need anything?"

"A cup of Type A blood would be nice." He smiled weakly at me, then leaned his head back against his pillow. His eyes squeezed shut then, and he brought his arms behind his head.

"That fuckin' hurts you know," he said.

"Well I'd imagine so," I said, "it's, like, three inches deep and makes up half of your lower leg."

He chuckled. "I guess so."

"Do you want me to bandage it up or something?" I asked.

He nodded. "I'd like that."

I nodded back, though his eyes were closed and he couldn't see me do that. I bolted up the stairs, silently, and ran to the nearest powder room. Opening a cupboard over the sink, I found some bandages fairly quickly. Unfortunately, we didn't have anything to clean the wound with. I shrugged at nobody, running back down stairs with the bandages. I turned into the parlor, only to see Razza leaning over Benjamin's leg, wrapping it for him. While I felt my insides bubble with anger, I kept my thoughts as silent as possible, so Benjamin wouldn't hear them and know I was there, listening.

"There you are," Razza said, finishing up.

"Thank you very much," he said sweetly, a smile showing in his voice.

I felt my hands ball up into fists. "Oh, it's no problem," she said kindly. "Anything else I can get you?"

"Well, I want some Type A blood. Very badly."

"Of course," she said. She walked swiftly into the kitchen, where I silently followed her. I watched as she opened the fridge, searching for a container holding the blood Benjamin so desperately wanted. I leaned against the counter, hidden in shadows, and asked, "What do you think you're doing?"

Razza jumped, startled, while I smiled evilly. She turned to face me, a puzzled look plainly displayed on her face. "What's it look like?" she asked, "I'm getting a drink for Benjamin."

"Which is my job, in case you haven't noticed," I said. I set the bandages on the counter.

"Your job? He asked me to do it."

"Yeah. *After* he asked me."

She rolled her eyes. "What is your deal anyway? I mean, it's just a drink."

I rolled my eyes back at her. "As if it wasn't obvious enough."

"Mags, I really don't know what you're talking about."

My anger rose even more. I felt it take over. "Don't talk to a higher Vampire that way!"

"What 'way'?" she said. She was ticked off now, too.

"Don't call me "Mags." That is *not* my name." *And anyways, only Amaury calls me that.*

Razza looked as though she'd break something. "Oh yeah?" she asked. "Well soon enough, you'll be thankful that I acknowledge you, once you lose your high position."

"Lose my position? What the hell are you-"

"Ladies, ladies, please! Stop!" Maryanne bustled in, the skirt of her red dress swirling as she walked. "Let's not kill each other now."

Razza said the most immature line in the book. "Well, she started it."

Maryanne rolled her eyes at Razza. "Guess what? I don't care who started it, I just want it to stop so I don't end up having to clean blood off the kitchen floor! Now, somebody get Benjamin the blood he's begging for, and one of you can go and fluff his pillows or something."

I smirked as I walked by Razza. "I got the blood," I sassed, watching in amusement as she stormed off. Maryanne shook her head while I searched for the right container of blood.

"What is it with you and picking fights?"

I continued to smile. "I don't like people interfering in my little game."

"And what is your little 'game,' exactly?"

I giggled. "You'll see."

She stepped back. "You are *really* starting to creep me out."

"Oh well," I said, shrugging. After digging through the fridge, I finally found what I was looking for. I grabbed the container out of it, shut the door, and set it on the counter. Searching trough the cabinets for a glass, I was aware of Maryanne staring at me.

"Can I help you?" I asked her, turning around.

She just shook her head. "I just don't see what you have against Razza. I mean, she's really nice."

"Uh-huh. Whatever you say. She's just trying to steal the very thing that's mine."

"What are you talking about, Magdelene?" Her blue eyes revealed her confusion.

"I already told you, you'll see. Someday." I continued to rummage through the cabinets until I located a wineglass. Grabbing it, I set it on the counter next to the container. Slowly, I poured the blood into it, which started to make me thirsty. So, I got another wineglass from the cabinet, and turned back to Maryanne, who was still just standing there.

"Want some?" I asked.

She nodded, so I grabbed another for her. I quickly poured blood into the wineglasses and handed one to Maryanne. The other, I guzzled down. I felt some of the blood flow down my chin, which I quickly swiped away. Maryanne watched me, sipping from her glass every so often. Something was bugging her.

"What's wrong, Mary?" I asked.

She looked at me, wide eyed, and said, "Nothing."

I glared, trying to dig through her mind. Nothing was out of the ordinary, until I felt my mind slam into a wall of some sort. She was blocking some of her thoughts!

"Why the shield?" I asked her pointedly.

She glared at me. "There are just some things that you don't need to know." And then, she walked off.

I shook my head in disgust, putting my empty wineglass in the sink and picking up Benjamin's full one. I began walking towards the parlor, glass in my hand, when I saw Razza searching in a closet, looking for something. Doing my best to ignore her, I walked into the parlor and stood next to Benjamin. He looked up at me, and then snatched the glass out of my hand furiously.

"Took you long enough," he said gruffly. I hadn't noticed it until now, but his eyes were a bright red, a sure sign that he needed blood. He gulped down the contents of the glass quickly, and soon his eyes returned to their normal green color. I took the empty glass from him, and asked, "Do you want any more?"

He shook his head. "No, I'm fine. Thanks."

I stood there a moment longer before I said, "Well, I'm just gonna go and-"

"Please don't," he said. "Stay here."

I felt my face flush, though I wasn't sure he saw. I set the empty glass on the coffee table in the center of the room, and then returned to the couch. I sat on the edge by his legs, and placed my hands between my knees. Benjamin closed his eyes, and soon he was fast asleep. Slowly, I rose from the couch, and grabbed the empty glass on my way out.

I made my way back to the kitchen to put the glass in the sink. That's when I ran straight into Razza, who was headed for the door. She wore the same outfit as before, only she looked, *different*. Also, she was carrying a whicker basket, its contents covered with a blue and white checkered cloth. She looked at me, then down at the basket, then at the door. Biting down on her lip, she turned back to me, knowing what was coming.

"Where do you think you're going?" I asked, crossing my arms over my chest.

"Why is it any of your business where I go and don't go?" she retorted.

"Because I do what's best for the Coven, and I don't want any Vampires sneaking around and getting into trouble. *That's* why."

"If you must know," she said, "there's a bazaar in Guéret that I want to go to. Ya' know, to do a little shopping." She shifted the basket with her arm and raised her head high, trying to intimidate me.

Glad to be able to rid of her, I said, "Have fun."

She looked at me, somewhat surprised, but was out the door before I could change my mind. Quickly, I took the glass into the kitchen and washed it, as well as the other dirty wineglasses. I put them away in a neat row, then went upstairs. Walking down the long hallway, I finally came to my familiar white door. Opening it, then shutting it just as quickly, I stepped into my sunlit room. I was careful to stay away from the sun's rays shining through my two large windows, and my smaller one.

It wasn't like they'd do anything to me. I mean, the whole myth that Vampires burn in sunlight is a bunch of bull crap. We just don't especially like the light, which is why we usually prowl around and hunt at night. Unfortunately, Werewolves get strength from the moon, so that's when they hunt, too. Only, not for food. But for us.

Making my way to my closet, I opened the two large doors that led inside. Moving aside my many dresses and other various outfits, I walked into the closet. I saw fairly well in the dark, so it was easy to locate the candle I had in there, along with my box of matches. Slowly I took one of the matches out of its encasement and swiped it on the box, igniting it on the first try. Lighting the candle with the match, the room suddenly became much brighter.

I threw the match in a bowl of water that was next to the candle, as to prevent it from becoming aflame once more. I picked up the candle and slowly stood, walking over to the wooden crate at the end of the room and sitting down on the pillow in front of it. On top of the crate was the thing I'd spent the past three-hundred years trying to retrieve. The bejeweled box, and inside, the rarest necklace known to mankind.

I'd spent so long trying to find it, only to find out that Rafe Gautier had bought it for God knows how much money, and ended up giving it to, of all people, Amaury. She didn't know it, but this necklace held a few powers. It also had a special name, which was coincidently, the Fusion Night Necklace. In short, it was a necklace that looked like a miniature moon. As legend has it, the necklace was created by Lucas Gautier to protect his son from evils. However, when he gave it to Victoria so she could distribute it to their son, she was killed, and the necklace was stolen and unfound until centuries later, when its owner was destroyed.

So, Rafe had found it at a secret booth in a Guéret bazaar three years before he died. He bought it, and knowing its powers, gave it to my half sister in order to protect her. What he didn't know was that after he died, she rarely even glanced at its box anymore, let alone wear it. And so, under the cover of night, I stole it as she wrote in her diary about her encounter with Radder. It made me laugh to think that only hours earlier, she'd delivered me a letter, completely trusting me.

Amaury hadn't known anything about her necklace, other than the fact that it shone in the moonlight. And, to be honest, I was glad that she didn't. Because, the necklace also had a dark side. Lucas had been so frantic to construct a protective necklace for Rafe, that he hadn't taken the time to remove any defective flaws. If you used the right amount of black magic and said the right spells, the white full moon necklace would become completely black, but only on the inside.

When that happened, anything but Fusions could sense its dark energy. Then, if a Fusion wore it, it would suck out their energy and eventually kill them. After the Fusion was dead, though, the spell would reverse, and the necklace would be good instead of evil again. I'd have to choose the exact time to return it to the Sleet Castle, otherwise known as Amaury's home, so she wouldn't be suspicious of where the necklace had been. Then, maybe, she wouldn't be able to part with it, and my plan would work perfectly.

Greedily, I ran my fingers over the bumpy surface of the small golden box after I'd set the candle down beside it on the crate. The jewels were all real, and the box alone was probably worth thousands of dollars. Maybe even millions. I began to run my fingers between a few rubies, until I found what I was looking for. The box had a secret latch, camouflaged within the field of jewels, so it couldn't be opened easily. However, the latch was extremely easy to locate. So, slowly, I unlatched the box. When I opened it, I felt my eyes widen as I gasped.

The inside of the box was completely empty.

I blew out the candle and threw it on the ground in a rage. I stormed out of the closet, not even bothering to hide my secret little space or to even shut the doors. Walking straight in the sunlit parts of my room, I made my way out into the long hallway.

Razza. Maryanne. Adam. Even Benjamin. There were so many suspects, I didn't even know where to begin. But I decided to start with Maryanne. I mean, she had managed to block her thoughts from me earlier. What else would she be hiding? Then again, I didn't know what Razza had been hiding in the basket she was taking to the bazaar. One thing was clear though, I was going to watch those two like a hawk.

I loudly made my way downstairs, not even trying to mask my anger. I passed Adam on the stairwell, and he gave me an odd look, asking, "Jeez, what is your problem?"

"Oh, shut up," I said. He shook his head in disgust, but continued on his way upstairs.

What a jerk, I thought.

I finally hit the bottom of the stairs and angrily started towards the door. *OK, Razza, prepare to be-*

"Jeez, what is up with all the stomping and yelling?" a voice said. *Benjamin.*

I changed my path away from the door and hurried into the parlor instead. Benjamin sat on the couch, rubbing his eyes. Removing his hands from his face, he blinked, and looked around.

"Magdelene?" He suddenly sat up, frantically trying to locate me.

"Are you alright?" I said, hurriedly walking over to the couch.

He smiled, but quickly wiped the look off his face. "What the fuck? I thought you were going to stay here with me."

"Well, I was, but you fell asleep, so I went to go do some dishes."

"Is that it?" his eyes challenged me. I considered lying, but, what good would that do?

"No. It's not," I looked down. *Oh man, this is gonna get ugly…*

"What else were you doing?" he asked, his bright green eyes holding mine, intimidating me.

"I… I was in my room," I stammered. He was making me uncomfortable.

"Go on," he coaxed. He was enjoying my struggling.

"I… I was just checking on the necklace. Going to perform a spell or two."

"The necklace?" he thought for a moment. "Oh. Right. The Fusion Night one or whatever the hell that stupid ass Lucas named it."

"Yeah. That one."

"So. What'd you do to it? Is it almost ready to be used to kill that stupid sister of yours?"

"Well, uh…no."

His eyes pinned down into a glare. "Magdelene, what did you do?"

"I didn't do anything!"

"Then what happened? Spit it out already!"

"I opened the box and it was, well, sorta…gone."

"Gone? What do you mean it was 'sorta gone'?"

"It was just, gone. It's not in the closet or anything."

He didn't say anything; just looked ahead. I noticed his hands balling up into fists, his knuckles a pure white.

"Benjamin?" I said, my voice quivering.

"How the *hell* did you manage to lose it?!?" he shouted. That's when I noticed that his fangs were drawn out, and I began to shake.

"I… it was in the box…"

"Uh-huh. Sure. Because it's just so easy for me to believe that your stupid self didn't manage to misplace it."

"Benjamin, I set it in the box the last time I had it…"

"Then what the hell hap-," he turned to face me, only to see that I was shaking.

"Magdelene?" he said. His voice was quieter, softer. It wasn't until then that I noticed there were tears running down my face.

"Hey," he said. He reached for my hand, but I stepped back.

We were both silent for a moment before he said, "Listen, I'm sorry, OK? It's just, I'm angry about the wound, and-" he stopped, realizing that his words had no effect on me whatsoever.

"Will you please talk to me?" he asked.

I sighed. "Only if you promise not to blame me for losing that stupid necklace."

"Well, who else could've lost it?"

"Razza or Mary probably stole it." I said quietly.

"Now why blame them?" he asked, somewhat agitated again.

"Because, today, Mary was blocking her thoughts from me, and Razza left the castle carrying a basket to take to a bazaar."

"Now, with what Mary did, that's suspicious. But Razza, she was probably just carrying an empty basket to carry stuff back in."

I felt a prick of jealousy that he was defending her, but tried not to let the thought go through my mind very long. He leaned his head back against his pillow, which looked recently fluffed, and looked as though to be deep in thought.

"Well," he said, "I don't know who did it, but I do know that we need to find out."

"Impossible."

"Impossible?"

"There was no scent in the closet other than my own and yours."

"I don't believe it." He started to stand, which only caused him to sink back onto the couch, and make his face go whiter than it was.

"Be careful!" I said, kneeling by his head. He was obviously in a lot of pain, and I didn't know what to do.

"Is there anything I can do to help? Get you more blood maybe?"

"Just…stay. Don't leave my side." I didn't know how he'd meant for that to go through, but I felt my face flush for a second time that day.

"Are you gonna be alright?" I felt so concerned for him, and I wished there was some way to ease his pain.

"I'll be fine. I've been through worse." He smiled.

"What could be worse than *that*?" I asked, motioning toward his injured leg.

"A lot of things that I've been through."

"Like…?"

"Well, let's just say a lot of it had to do with Radder."

"Oh."

"Yeah."

"So, I'm gonna take it as you two hate each other as much as I hate Amaury?"

"Precisely. But, you already knew that, didn't you?"

I nodded quickly in understanding, then said, "Speaking of her, you should read the stupid letter she wrote me." Then I remembered that she'd mentioned how much I like Benjamin.

"Well," he said, "bring it here. I'll read it."

"Later," I said. "You're exhausted. I can tell."

He sighed. "I guess so. But I don't feel much like sleeping at this particular moment."

Again, silence pierced through the room.

"What happened last night? I mean, what'd she do to you?"

"Well," he said, "it all started when I broke into her house." I smiled and thought, *been there done that.* We both laughed before he continued.

"I was snooping around, and I found her diary. Not that I was going to read it, but I figured I'd skim through it a bit, to see if there was anything about me in there."

I felt the color drain from my face.

"Well, I picked up the stupid book, and, what do you know, a vase falls over and breaks. So, I scooted the shards underneath the desk with my foot, and my hand is on the stupid old desk, and another vase falls off and breaks! So, by this point, she's heard me, of course, and starts coming down the stairs as silent as possible. Well, I know when I've been caught, so I brought out the tiny little frame from my coat. You know, the one with the note in it?

Anyways, I set it down by her diary, and all of a sudden I hear this really low growl coming from the shadows. I mean, at first I didn't believe you, about how she was a mixture of a Vampire and a Werewolf, but as soon as this huge black wolf comes out of the darkness, well, let's just say I nearly had a heart attack. So, we started talking, and then I-"

"Wait," I said, "what did you two say?"

"I don't remember the exact words," he said, "but, it was pretty much 'Who are you?' and 'Who are you and what are you doing here?' That's about it. So, as I was saying, I drew the silver dagger out of my sleeve and start intimidating her with it. And she's all like, 'You don't scare me with that.' And so, I threw the dagger and cut her shoulder. She fell over, and I thought she was dead, that I was right and silver would kill her.

So, I walk over there and pick up the dagger, and she's just kinda layin' there. And I'm thinking, 'What the hell?' because, I mean, she's not bleeding or anything. So, I kinda brush back her fur, and the scar is completely healed! Then, all of a sudden, she gets up and bites my leg, so I stab her with the dagger, but she barely even blinked! Somehow, though, I managed to throw her off of me."

He paused, taking a breath.

"Well?" I asked, "then what happened?"

"I remember I fell over, and was just kinda laying there, and then I see her morph back into a freaking person. She went out of my range of vision for a minute, but then she comes back. I didn't know what she did, but I couldn't even think. Because then, everything just went black."

"So, that's it?" I asked, disappointed. I was hoping for a bit more than that.

"Well, yeah. After everything went black, all I remember was waking up to see you leaning over the couch staring at me."

I blushed, again, and saw him smiling at me.

"I was just checking on you," I promised.

"Well," he said, "I'm glad that you were, or else I couldn't have nagged you to get me a drink."

The smile on my face widened, but quickly vanished as Maryanne and Adam entered the room.

"Hello Benjamin," Adam said, "glad to see that you're finally awake."

"I'm glad to be awake," Benjamin said, drawing his attention away from me.

"Sleep well?" Maryanne asked.

I saw the suspicious look he gave her. "Yeah, I did as a matter-of-fact. At least I couldn't feel the pain of my wound."

She nodded, but seemed unconcerned that he was in pain. Adam had the same attitude, but at least showed a little bit of concern.

"That's good," she said. "I wish there was something we could do to help."

"If you wanna help, stay here and keep me company." He smiled. So, it wasn't that he wanted just me in there, he'd take anybody. I felt my heart sink.

"Well, I have things I need to do," she said, "but I'm sure Adam would *love* to keep you company." She gave Adam a sharp, meaningful look that said *play along*. I narrowed my eyes. Something was up. I tried to read both of their minds, only to see that they were severely blocked. Benjamin noticed this too; I could sense his mind trying to read theirs.

About to ask what was up, Maryanne bustled out of the room, almost as if she knew what I was about to ask. I felt her anxiety as my suspicious gaze followed her out of the room. Adam sat down in the green chair he'd sat in earlier, placing his arms behind his head and leaning back, his eyes closed. To just anyone, he'd seem normal, relaxed, but I knew better; the vibe from his mind showed that he was scared about something. *If I just found a hole or weak spot in the wall blocking his thoughts, I might just be able to-*

Don't. The command was heard simply in my head. Benjamin was looking at me, his expression unreadable. *We'll find out sooner or later*, he thought. I nodded to him, and he returned one to me. Adam's eyes opened, and he flew forward in his seat. Suddenly he stood, and said, "Excuse me, but I, um… I gotta go." In a flash, he was gone, and I was alone with Benjamin once more.

"Well that was odd," I said. I sat up a little, readying to stand so I could follow Adam. But, Benjamin grabbed my hand. "Stay here," he whispered. He opened his mouth to say more, but quickly shut it. I tried to delve into his thoughts, to see what he was going to say, but was met by a mental wall. Why was everybody blocking their thoughts today? Jeez. Benjamin's eyes began to flutter, though he tried to hide it. He gripped my hand tighter and looked at me, his eyes pleading for an unknown reason.

"You're tired," I said, "you should sleep."

He just looked at me for a moment, but finally, his weariness overwhelmed him. Slowly his eyes closed, and soon his breathing slowed. Silently, I left the room and started up the stairs. I was in no hurry. Taking the steps one at a time until I reached the top, I made my way to Adam's door, which was wide open. Maryanne's door, which was just down the hall, was shut, as was Razza's. I stood outside of Adam's door, trying to remain undetected.

Slowly his thoughts began to pour out. He didn't notice my presence, and probably assumed I was still downstairs with Benjamin. Unimportant words were streaming around his mind. I was about to leave, thinking all of his important thoughts were hidden. That is, until I noticed a blackness he was trying hard not to think about. *Come on Adam*, I thought, willing him to replay vision he'd had, *show me what you saw*. Then, without warning, my mind was swelled in darkness.

I found myself standing in the shadows of a very dark room. A few candles suddenly lit up the small space, and I saw Maryanne hurry into the dimly lit area. The room was totally empty, except for countless candles scattered randomly around the room. That and, in one corner, a wooden cradle. Maryanne hurried to it, and slowly lifted a small bundle from the tiny bed. A loud wail sounded as she picked up the wad of blankets, and I heard myself gasp. A *baby*?!?

"Hush, hush," she said, slowly rocking the infant. Eventually, the child's sobs died down.

About the time it stopped crying, someone else entered the room from a different entrance. I couldn't see who it was at the angle he was at, but one thing was clear: he had black hair. *Is it Adam?* I thought. It wasn't Benjamin, and he was much to pale to be Radder. It must be.

"Hey," he said to Mary. It didn't sound like Adam's voice, or anybody's I knew for that matter. But, still, it couldn't be anybody else.

"Hey," Mary whispered. Just as soon as she'd said it, she began to cry. The man held her as close as he could with the child still in her arms, trying to comfort her.

"Mary," he said, "sh, it's alright, OK? We're gonna be fine. All of us. Ya' hear?"

Slowly, Maryanne nodded and wiped the tears from her face. She looked at the infant in her arms, holding it tightly. Looking up at the man, she said, solemnly, "I'm scared. Especially for him."

"Well," the man said, "I'm not gonna let anybody hurt either of you. OK? I promise."

Another tear ran down her face, which he wiped away. Gradually, she removed herself from his embrace and walked back to the cradle. Ever so gently, she set the baby in it, watching him for a few moments. The man blew out a few candles, then walked out of the room, without so much as a goodbye. Mary just stood by the cradle, her hands on its side, staring at the sleeping baby.

"Oh, Jay," she whispered, "what are we going to do with you?"

Then, everything blackened once more.

I opened my eyes and found myself sitting on the floor, leaning against the wall outside Adam's room. I didn't sense anything on his mind, so, I stuck my head in the doorway. He lay sleeping on his bed in an awkward position. I shook my head, unable to fathom how both of us had managed to fall asleep. Then a sudden realization hit me. I *hadn't* been sleeping.

The memory of Adam's vision flooded into my mind. It didn't make sense, though. First off, Adam and Maryanne had lived in the Fanges Castle with Benjamin and I for over three-hundred years, and had never shown any interest in each other. That's why it didn't add up that a child would be involved, let alone that it was in fact Maryanne's. Is that why Adam had looked so shocked when he had the vision? I was scared and shocked, and I had just watched it. But if Adam lived it, I could only imagine his fear.

Slowly I stood and stretched my arms, stifling a yawn. As quietly as possible, I managed to slip past Adam's dark room without waking him. All of his curtains were drawn, so I couldn't look outside and guess the time. I made my way down the long hallway until I came to my bedroom door, which I opened and shut in the blink of an eye. Safe from everyone else's thoughts in my comfortingly tranquil room, I let out a content sigh.

Walking over to the window closest to my bed, which was the small window that Amaury had been outside of last night, I studied the sky. Judging by where the sun was in the sky, it was nearing three o'clock in the afternoon. I sighed. Then I remembered something. Razza had left at about midday, and she should be back by now.

I turned away from my window and made way for the door. Opening it and stepping into the hallway, I started for the stairs, not even bothering to close the door to my room. I walked along the hallway at a fast pace, but was careful to slow and quiet down as I walked past Adam's open door. As soon as I reached the stairwell, though, I found myself nearly flying down them. When I reached the bottom, I saw that Razza hadn't come back yet. Her scent was stale.

Shaking my head in disgust, I made my way into the parlor, where Benjamin slept on. I went around the couch and sat near his legs. Benjamin looked so peaceful in his sleep, and it made me smile to know that, for the meantime, he wasn't in any pain. His mind was completely blank from the looks of it, so it didn't seem as though he was dreaming. I found that fact hard to believe, so I tried to dive deeper into his head. Suddenly, I found myself lost in the depths of his mind.

I still felt myself sitting on the couch, but my mind was inside Benjamin's head. I was confused and lost there, and I began to wander around. His mind was filled with darkness, but finally I saw a bit of light. I began to will myself toward it, and, when I passed through, I found myself in the castle. I could see Benjamin frantically moving about the rooms, until he opened a closet. He stood there, just staring in, and I tried to see what he saw. Then, he moved just out of the way, and I saw myself in there.

Slowly, I watched as he reached his hand out, watched as I took it. He helped me stand, and then he whispered, "Hurry. We've got to hide. They're here."

He led us down the hallway and I said, "Where are we going to go? That was about the only place to hide, which is why I was there."

"They'll find you too easily. I can't let them get you."

"Oh, well, that makes sense. I guess."

"Come on," he said, leading the way. "Hurry!"

Suddenly, I heard footsteps behind us. We took a turn and ran into my bedroom, shutting the door as quickly as possible. Benjamin held the door so whoever was chasing us couldn't get in. I grabbed a chair and placed it under the doorknob, so that he could leave his station. I walked over to my desk and grabbed a box of matches and a candle, since my curtains were drawn and the room was pitch black.

I grabbed a match out of the box and struck it, then brought it to the candle's wick and ignited it. I threw the match in a bowl of water that was on my desk, and took the candle over to the bed, which Benjamin sat on the edge of. I sat down right next to him, and looked over to see him staring at me. Watching all this from the other side of the room, I felt extremely happy that we were trapped in the same room together.

"Benjamin," I watched myself say, "I'm scared."

"It's OK," he said, "everything's going to be fine. It's just a few crazy Humans. With stakes."

I looked at him, wide-eyed and hoping he was kidding, but his face was serious.

"Magdelene, I promise you, we are going to be fi-"

Before he could finish speaking, the door burst open. Someone undistinguishable stood in the doorway, holding a stake in each hand. A girl walked into the room, and I could clearly see that she had brown hair and sharp blue eyes. She walked closer to Benjamin and I, the stakes still in her hands and said, "So Vampires, are you ready to pay?"

Then Benjamin woke up.

He sat up, gasping rapidly, and I felt my mind snap away from his. "Benjamin!" I said, sliding along the couch until I was by his head. "Are you aright?"

He nodded, slowing his panting. "I'm fine," he said, "it was just a nightmare."

He sat back, leaning his head back on his pillow. "You were in it, you know."

"I know," I said. I felt his gaze burning into me. "I could see it."

"And you were looking in my head, why?" His anger was shooting off of him.

"I didn't mean too. I saw blackness, and I was just trying to figure that out, and all of a sudden my mind was swept into yours, and I couldn't get out. It wouldn't let me go until you woke up."

"I see," he said. "Still, you shouldn't have been snooping around in my head in the first place."

"I'm sorry," I said. "I only saw your dream, if you were concerned about what else I might've seen."

"I have nothing to hide, so don't worry about that. I'm just saying, it doesn't please me to know that my Coven's top Vampire was peering into my head."

"Again, I'm really sorry Benjamin."

"Again, I don't really care. As long as it doesn't happen anymore."

"It won't. I swear."

He sat up as much as his leg would let him, which brought him awfully close to me. "Good," he said. "Come to think of it, there is *one* thing I didn't want you to see."

I almost asked *And what would that be?*, but figured it'd make me look stupid, considering he had said he didn't want me to see it. So, I just shrugged.

He came a little closer to me. "Come to think of it still," he said, "I could just show you."

I gave him a puzzled look, not having any idea about what was on his mind (especially since his thoughts were severely blocked).

He brought his face closer to mine. "There's something I've wanted to do for a *very* long time," he whispered. Then he brought his lips to mine. I brought my arms around his neck while his snaked around my waist, only bringing us even closer. My head felt light, in the clouds. This was the one thing I'd wanted forever, and now, it was finally mine. I smiled in spite of myself. Benjamin pulled me closer still, never drawing away, until we both heard the door open at the exact same time.

We both pulled back from each other as Razza walked into the room. She smiled at Benjamin who quickly said, "Razza, glad you're back."

"Glad you're still up," she said, turning and making her way upstairs, leaving me and Benjamin alone.

Your face is red, he thought, a smile wide on his face. *Oh, you're* real *funny*, I thought back, though I knew he wasn't kidding. I wasn't surprised I was blushing after he'd just kissed me. I turned away, looking out the parlor window. Still feeling his gaze on my back. I turned back to see him smiling widely at me. I smiled back, weakly, and heard various footsteps coming down the stairwell.

Razza, Maryanne, and a very drowsy Adam all entered the room. Maryanne held a few things in her hand and said, "OK, Benjamin, I'm going to stitch up your wound to help it heal."

"Like hell you are," he said, though his thoughts clearly displayed that there was no way to resist what was coming.

So, Maryanne walked over and sat next to me, only closer to his legs. She lifted up the cloak and got to work. Benjamin grabbed my hand and squeezed it, while I knew he would only feel the pain for a second before it was gone, he just wanted some comfort. Adam strode over to his chair, and Razza just stood behind the couch, engrossed in Mary's sewing.

"So, Ben," Adam said, "what exactly happened to you?"

"I'm not sure," Benjamin lied, trying not to reveal Amaury's existence. "I remember walking through the woods, and a wolf attacked me, but that was it. Then I woke up in here. I can't even remember why I was outside."

"But if a Werewolf bit you," Razza pointed out, "you'd be dead."

He shrugged. "Maybe somebody sucked the venom out."

We were all silenced then. I turned my attention to Mary, who was stitching his wound so fast her hands were blurs. Finally, she stopped and announced that she was done. I helped her to rewrap Ben's leg. When we finished, she stood.

"I'm going," she proclaimed, then walked briskly out of the room. Bored, Adam and Razza soon followed her. Once they were all gone, Benjamin sat back up, and brought his lips to mine once more.

Chapter 4
The Mysterious Radder

Amaury:

I drew out a sharp, angered breath as I surveyed the damage in my parlor. All around my desk were the shattered remains of priceless vases. Not to mention, there was a tiny frame on my desk. Inside of it, there had been a note, similar to the one Raven had given me. Only, this note read:

You can run Fusion,
But you can't hide.
Learn to trust no one,
Because everyone lies.

This note terrified even more than the one I'd received yesterday, especially since I knew who the person was who had left it. In fact, someday, he may be related to me by being my half brother-in-law. Although, the way things were moving along, I wasn't sure if that would happen. Sweeping up the rest of the shards, I quickly went outside and dumped them by a dead tree. Sighing, I made my way back into the castle.

I was trying to make my home look as nice as possible, considering Radder was coming over at dusk. It was about five o'clock in the afternoon. After my long day yesterday, I'd accidentally slept in this morning until about noon. I was glad drowsiness hadn't taken over me, or else I didn't know how I'd be able to keep up with Radder.

He's probably the most dangerous Vampire there is.

The old man's words swam through my mind, and I shuddered. I didn't believe Radder to be evil though. Sure, he was a little confused, and to be honest, very unpredictable, but still, he could also be nice. *Very* nice. I felt myself blush at the thought. Making my way over to my desk, I sat and opened up my diary to a fresh page, and began to write.

Mars 20, 1874; L 'apres midi
(March 20, 1874; The Afternoon)

Dear Diary,

I am so excited about going out with Radder tonight. I have no idea what he has in mind for what we are going to do, but I am absolutely bubbling with excitement. Honestly, I've no idea why he likes me so much, and vice versa. I mean, yesterday was the only real time we've had together, and already he's kissing me. While it feels awful, it also feels… right. I mean, it's almost as if we're meant to be together.

If that's true though, there's just one thing I don't get. If we are supposed to be together, then why was I tortured by loving and losing Rafe? What's the point in loving someone that you're just going to lose? I don't get this game called life. But I guess I have to be like everybody else and just play along.

-Amaury de Pompadour

The last paragraph I wrote brought tears to my eyes, but I did everything in my power to not cry. Slowly shutting the leather-bound book and placing my feather pen beside it, I stood up. Making my way into the kitchen, I decided to grab something to eat.

Opening my refrigerator door, I saw I had one thing left to eat, which was a few segments off a wheel of cheese. I grabbed one and started to eat it slowly, leaning against my counter.

I studied the two flowers on the other side of the counter. The impeccably beautiful blood red rose, and the small, imperfect wood violet. Both appeared to be thriving in their vastly diverse vases, though the rose was at least ten times healthier. I knew neither of them would live for very long without their roots, but I could at least try to help them. So, finishing the last of my slice of cheese, I took both of the flowers out of their water-sources and picked up the vase and wineglass.

Finding my garden tools in my mudroom, I picked up my spade and made my way back outside. Going to an alive tree in my yard, I sank to my knees. After dumping the water out of the vase and wineglass, I dug the spade into the earth. Filling it with soil, I poured the dirt into the vase. Then, I did the same thing as before, only I poured the soil into the wineglass.

Picking up what I'd carried outside, I hurried back into the castle. Returning to the kitchen, I set down the vase and wineglass, and carried the spade back to the mudroom with the rest of my gardening tools. I made my way back to the kitchen then, and picked up the long-stemmed rose. I placed it in its turquoise vase, trying hard to get the bottom of the stem into the soil. Then, I filled the vase with more water.

After returning the vase to its spot on the counter, I repeated the action with the violet and the wineglass. With both vases back where they belonged, I stared at them for a moment longer, smiling. I couldn't wait to see Radder. I felt a pang of sorrow and betrayal, but it quickly faded. Rafe was dead. I knew that. There was no getting him back, no matter how much I wanted him to still be here.

Taking a deep breath, I moved away from the counter and headed into the parlor. Going up the stairs, I quickly took a turn into my room. I shut the door softly behind me and walked to my closet. Opening the large doors, I began to sort through different outfits. *What should I wear?* I thought. Nervously, I pulled out a plain white blouse. It seemed decent enough, so I placed it on my bed. I shut the large doors then, and walked over to my dresser.

I opened the second drawer from the top, where I kept a few skirts. I pulled out a black one that went down just past my knees, and also matched the blouse perfectly. I shut the drawer, and then changed into the new outfit. After I'd changed, I stood in front of my dresser mirror and studied my appearance. My hair was a complete mess, which angered me. I ran a brush through it countless times until it looked decent, but it refused to be tamed.

Angry, I threw my brush back down on the dresser where it belonged, and considered putting my hair up. I decided against it though, considering it'd make me seem like I was trying to hard. Making my way to the powder room, I decided to run a bit of water on my hair, which would hopefully flatten it out some. I also applied a bit of makeup, but not too much, and looked in the mirror.

I thought I looked good enough, though I wished my hair would lie flat. Sighing, I wondered when Radder would be arriving. I made my way downstairs to wait for him on the couch. I relaxed on the couch, laying down and staring at the ceiling. My hand slowly slid up to my neck, where the little blue bell necklace was. I twisted it slowly back and forth, smiling all the while. I couldn't wait for Radder to come and wrap his arms around me and kiss my lips…

Stay hidden and don't move. I'll be back soon.

I gulped, and blinked back my tears. *Rafe's gone. Deal with it.* Taking a breath, I tried to focus on Radder's arrival. Slightly, I sat up, just enough to turn around and glance out the window. The sun was sinking lower in the sky, and the light was beginning to fade. *Radder, where are you?* I really couldn't get mad though, I mean, it *was* still dusk. But, something wasn't right.

I sat up, folding my hands together and placing them between my knees. *He'll knock on the door any second now,* I thought, glancing out the window once more. However, the only light left against the blackness was a thin ribbon of orange. I sat there for a long time, watching the color fade, until there was finally none left to see. I felt a tear run down my cheek. I'd been stood up.

You stupid girl. You knew this'd happen. I brought my hands up to cover my eyes, and I cried as silently as possible. I couldn't believe I'd let myself come to like someone else, just knowing that everything I've ever loved has been taken from me. I wiped the tears away with my hand, and just sat there, looking out the window, and watched as stars began to dot the sky.

I was so overcome with my sadness, that I almost didn't see the vision. But, when I closed my eyes, I could see Radder. He was at his house, and while I didn't know why, he was crying. I didn't even consider that he might be in too much pain to come here. But, why?

Slowly, I stood up. Something was wrong with him. As I hurried out my door and into the dark night, I felt myself transform into a wolf. Guéret was over an hour away. Sighing, I took off running through the woods until I found a dirt pathway that led to the Human infested town. I ran at full speed, even faster than I had yesterday when I'd raced Radder, and watched as everything around me blurred.

Before I knew it, I'd arrived at the town's gray walls. The giant iron-bar gates were shut and locked, and while the town should've looked peaceful with everyone in their homes, it seemed more like a prison. I stopped to study it, standing beside the gates. A man walked in front of the gates, and came to an abrupt stop. I guessed that he was patrolling the city's barriers to make sure there weren't any intruders. I looked up at him, studying his face. He looked a little bit like Benjamin, considering he also had black hair and green eyes.

"Hey, Sam!" he called, startling me. He motioned for another man to come over. I watched though as not one but two silhouettes made their way toward me and the man.

One of the silhouettes stepped out of the shadows, the one I guessed was Sam, with a woman beside him. Sam had golden blonde hair and light blue eyes, and the girl beside him shared his eye color, but was a brunette. Had his arm not been around her waist, I would've considered them to be siblings.

"What is it, Jared?" Sam asked, obviously annoyed.

"Well, if you would look behind the gates, you would notice that there's a wolf there."

"A wolf?" The girl asked, sounding more suspicious than surprised. Slowly she came forward, and kneeled down right by the gates. She stuck her hand through the bars, gesturing to me in a friendly manner. I shied away, trying to seem as normal as possible so they would leave and I could be on my way. *Can't you people understand that I only stopped for a second and that I'm in a hurry?!?* I pinned my ears back, growling in annoyance at the girl.

"Ruby, be careful," Sam said cautiously. "The last thing we need is for you to loose a hand."

"Oh, stop worrying about me," she said, although she did stand up and move away from me. "I can take care of myself."

I felt my fur bristle as I scented more Humans approaching. How many of them haven't seen a wolf before? Another couple came out of the shadows then. The boy had blonde hair like Sam, only he had hazel eyes. The girl had brown eyes and matching hair.

Ruby turned to the other girl. "Hey Hazel," she said, smiling.

Sam and Jared turned to the man. "Hi Hugo," they said politely, though I got the vibe that he was the last person they wanted to see.

"Oh my gosh, a wolf!" Hazel exclaimed staring at me.

"Careful," Sam said, "he's mean."

I growled. *You mean* she *you idiot.*

"Here's what I don't get," Ruby said. "How come there's a wolf here, and yet, no wolves live around here?"

"I dunno," Jared said. "But it's pretty cool."

"What's around its neck?" Hazel asked.

Uh-oh. I shied away more, my ears laying flat on my head.

Jared kneeled down and peered at my neck. "It looks like a bell."

That's when I took off running. I didn't care if I was a blur to them; all I knew was that I had to get away from that town. They lived there. They must've been at the bazaar yesterday. And, who knows? Maybe they saw the booth with the little bell necklaces. Heck, they might've even seen Radder buy it for me.

Nervous, I ran at an impossibly fast pace. I cut through the meadow, went through the woods a way, and finally came to a small white house. Slowing, I could see light coming from the windows. He was home. I went into my "Human" form, and slowly went up to the door. I knocked, thrice, and waited for a few minutes. Nobody answered.

OK Radder, if you want to play this game, then you better welcome another player.

I opened the door and walked inside, so shocked I was nearly unable to close the door. There were lit candles everywhere, and I mean *everywhere.* On his kitchen counter, on the cabinets, even on the floor. I turned left, leaving the kitchen, and entering a living room. Radder was sitting on a worn brown couch, his face in his hands as he cried. Just as my vision showed me.

"Radder?" I asked, making my way toward him.

His sobs were cut off then by the sound of my voice. "Amaury?" he asked quietly.

"Yeah," I said. "It's me."

"Go away," he said. "Now."

"But, Radder, I-"

He stood as quick as a flash and glared at me, tears streaking down his face.

"Get. Out. NOW!" he said.

I stood and stared at him, willing him to change his mind. "Well," he asked, "what are you waiting for? Go!"

I backed away, not saying another word. *I was just trying to help*, I thought, walking away. I was back in the kitchen when I heard him sigh.

"You know what?" he said. "Get back in here."

I slowly turned around to face him, since he was in the kitchen doorway now. "Make up your mind, will you?" I said angrily. I was fed up with his changing attitude.

He looked at me, eyes wide. "Please?" he asked, cocking his head to the side.

I let out an angry sigh, but came toward him anyway. As I walked by him, he grabbed my arm with his hand and spun me around so that I landed in his arms. He wrapped his arms around my waist, and before I could get out of his grasp, he kissed me. Angered, I pushed him away from me and slapped him across the face, watching in amusement as he rubbed the red spot on his face, even though it vanished quickly.

His gaze darkened. "What the hell was that for?!?" he asked furiously.

"Uh- for standing me up. *That's* why."

"Standing you up?" he asked, "what are you talking about?"

"Don't you remember? 'As if I could stay away from you for an entire day. I'll be here at dusk.' How could you forget?"

Slowly, realization crept into his eyes. "Oh my God, Amaury, I'm so sorry, I-"

"Just drop it," I snapped. "There is no excuse for why you should lie."

"I didn't lie. It's just, I remembered something else, and I forgot-"

"You just don't get it, do you?" I was on the verge of tears.

"What is so bad about me forgetting?"

"You didn't forget. You lied."

He sighed. "Do we have to go through this again? I didn't lie, I-"

"Do you know what happened the last time a guy promised me he was coming back?

"Coming back? I-" he paused, thinking for a moment. "Oh my God. You mean-"

"Rafe. Yeah, I mean him." I felt a tear run down my cheek, which he wiped away. He pulled me to him again, my head on his chest as he whispered, "Please don't cry. I'm sorry."

"It's just, I had a vision, and I thought something had happened to you."

He tilted my chin up so I could look into his eyes. "Something did. But it was a really long time ago."

I rolled my eyes. "You're talking to me like I'm a little kid. What's the story?"

He flinched. "It's kinda boring. I don't think you want to hear it."

"Yes, I do, especially if it explains all these candles." I motioned around us. "Besides, I'm kind of curious about who you are."

He smirked. "I'm Radder Thor. Pleased to meet you."

Again, I rolled my eyes. *Smartass.* "You know what I mean."

He sighed. "Maybe you should've just left."

I glared. "Fine," I stated, trying to get out of his grasp.

"On the second thought, I kinda want you to stay and keep me company. I'm feeling kind of lonely."

"OK, seriously, you changing your mind every two seconds is starting to get annoying."

He chuckled again. "Why don't we go and sit on the couch? If you want to know about my past, you might want to get comfortable, because, let me tell ya', it's a long story."

I shrugged. "I don't care. Let's hear it."

He let go of me then and walked back into his living room, while I trailed behind him. He sat in the same spot he was when I got here, so I decided to sit next to him. He wrapped his arm around my waist, pulling me to him so that I was leaning against him.

"Are you sure you want to know?" he asked.

"For God's sake, yes," I said, still rather annoyed.

He looked at me jokingly. "OK, I'll tell you, but then I'll have to kill you."

I just looked at him. "Well, the first time I met you, you did say that if you told anyone about your past, it would kill not only you, but them too. So…?"

"I'll make an exception with you," he said, kissing me lightly on the cheek. "I'll warn you though, my story is kind of sad."

I shrugged, looking up at him. "That's OK," I said quietly.

He nodded. Then began to speak. "Well, it all started about three-hundred-thirty-nine years ago."

"Wait," I interrupted, "is that number also your age?"

He nodded while I said, "Jeez, you're only a year older than me!"

Radder opened his mouth to comment, but quickly shut it. Finally, he just said, "Anyways, I'm gonna continue, if that's alright with you?" I nodded quickly.

"Alright then," he said. "Well, I was a baby then, so I can't really remember everything. But this was how Benjamin described it to me. He was three years old, and was with Brock. They were out hunting, since Brock was teaching him the ropes of how to get a Human as prey. Brock's wife, Veronica, was with them too. So, they brought Ben to a house they'd been targeting, which was a small log cabin. Inside, there was a man named Jackson, his wife, Heidi, and their son." He stopped, taking a deep breath.

"Who was the son?" I asked, intrigued with the story.

He looked at me, very seriously, and said, "Me."

I heard myself gasp. While it had been pretty obvious, I hadn't been expecting that.

"So, Brock isn't really your father then?"

"Right."

"And you were Human?"

He nodded. "Yes, but I'll get into detail on that later."

I nodded in response, so he continued. "Well, Brock and Veronica kept tormenting my parents. They'd open and close the door, knock on the windows, anything to scare them. And they did it so fast. Ben said that my parents were absolutely terrified; they didn't know what was happening. Then he told me that all of a sudden, the house burst into flames. His parents had set it on fire, and he could see his mother inside. She was trying to kill my parents, and Ben told me that Heidi was screaming, "Save Radder!" to my father. And then…"

I noticed that he'd started to cry. I leaned closer to him and wiped the tears off his cheeks. "Radder," I said, "I'm so sorry."

He took a deep breath, then spoke sharply, "It's fine. I shouldn't be crying over people I never even knew in the first place."

"But, Radder, they're your parents!" I exclaimed.

"I know that!" he snapped. His blue eyes were on me, his gaze as cold as ice. "But I never even spoke to them. They don't matter anymore."

"But, think, you wouldn't even be here if it weren't for them."

"Yeah. And I'd be better off not being here. I'm so sick of living."

I looked at him, utterly shocked. "How can you say that? Being what you are is a gift-"

"A gift?!?" he snapped. "How is living forever a *gift*? A curse is more like it!"

"Well, I don't think so," I said. "I love the fact that while for everyone else life goes on, and the whole while I stay the same. I mean, it really sucks that I don't really have any friends or anything, but still. Think about it, Radder. It's amazing!"

"I do think about it," he growled. "I think about how I

have to kill to survive. About how, while everyone else gets the relief of death after under a century, I've already lived over three lifetimes and counting. About how much pain I've caused this place by killing others loved ones. I mean, I killed a man last week. Who knows? Maybe he had a wife and children and tons of friends, and I ended his life in order to extend mine for a week or two. I think that it's anything *but* amazing."

I sighed. "I guess I don't really get your situation. I mean, I don't need to drink blood."

"Exactly. You can't argue with me if you don't know my pain."

We both sat in silence for a moment, before I finally mustered up the courage to ask, "So, what happened next?"

He sighed angrily, but continued with the story anyways. "And then," he began, "She, Veronica, she killed my mother. She began to drink, not bothering with me or my father. But then, a pillar fell from the ceiling and trapped her in the building. Brock ran in and tried to get to her, but, he couldn't. Ben said that just after Brock left the spot where she was trapped, another pillar fell and crushed my father, who was trying to get my mother. Brock had told me that it'd startled him, and then he saw me, just laying in a little wooden cradle. The cradle ignited, and- he saved me. He picked me up and took me out of the burning house just before it collapsed."

"But, that doesn't make sense," I said. "Why would he have saved you if he was trying to kill your family?"

"Veronica was pregnant, and was supposed to have another son. He told me that even though the house was on fire, I wasn't crying. He figured I'd make a good Vampire, because I was "tough," and would be a good replacement for the son he never got to meet."

"That's awful," I said.

"I know it is," he replied. "Anyways, Brock took Ben and I home. Ben told me that he'd asked his dad where his mother was, and, plain and simply to his three-year-old son, he said, "She's dead." No wonder he's so traumatized. I mean, watching your mother die right before your eyes? That's insane."

I nodded, urging him to go on.

"So," he said, "My earliest memories are from when I was about five, when Benjamin and I would play games outside. The first thing I'd noticed was that he was extremely fast. We tried to play hide and seek, and he'd find me in about five seconds. Then, when it was his turn to hide, he'd leap into trees so that I could never find him. I couldn't understand. Then we played tag, and he'd run, tag me, and then be gone so fast that it was like he was never there at all.

Then, when I was ten, Benjamin got fed up with those games. So, instead, he'd challenge me to races, and we'd bet on who'd win. And, of course, he always did. I didn't understand. I mean, I grew up amongst all these people who drink blood, and I ate Human food. I lived with the Vampires in that stupid castle. It didn't make sense as to why I was so different.

So, one day, I decided to ask Brock about it. That's when he told me that I was in fact a Human. I asked about who my real parents were, but he wouldn't speak. So, I asked Ben instead. It took him awhile to remember everything, but eventually, he did. When he told me, I didn't speak to anyone for months. Everyone was so worried about me, and tried to get me to talk, but I just couldn't deal with the fact that they had raised me as their own, had lied to me, and had killed my family nonetheless.

I began to secretly plot how to run away. I knew that there were hundreds of people in Guéret, and since we traveled there to go to bazaars often, I knew that it'd take about two hours to get there on foot. So, I began to steal some food in the kitchen that was there just for me, and packed it away. One Vampire, an elderly lady who begged someone in the Coven to bite her so she wouldn't die, found out was I was doing. She was kind of the Coven's maid and was like a grandmother to Benjamin and I. Her name was Dina. I was sure she'd tell Brock what I was up to, but, to my surprise, she actually helped me. She said that if I didn't want to become a Vampire, then I should be able to choose if I was turned or not." He paused to take a breath, and then continued.

"So, we both found out that there was a bazaar in Guéret happening a week after I'd planned my escape. When that day came, Dina woke me up before the crack of dawn; made sure I had plenty of food, and showed me the hidden dirt path. She told me to stay on the side, so I wouldn't leave footprints. I made it to the city at dawn, right when the gates were opening. People were starting to enter, so not many paid attention to me. I was swept into in a crowd of people, and I tried to get out so that I could talk to a police officer that was nearby. I knew I couldn't tell him that Vampires did exist, but I could at least say that I'd come all the way from Maufanges in order to get some help, since I'd seen a man get murdered, and that his killer had drunk his blood from his neck.

I was nearly out of the crowd when somebody grabbed

me, clamped a hand over my mouth, and spun me around. It was Brock, and I remember being extremely terrified. The cop saw this though, and said, 'Hey, you! What do you think you're doing?' which made Brock turn his head. Then he looked back at me, drew out his fangs, and said, "Play along, Radder, or else." So, Brock practically dragged me to the cop, since my legs were weak, and introduced himself. He told the cop that I was his son, and I'd just gotten lost in the crowd, and he'd been trying to find me. The stupid cop trusted him, since he thought we looked like each other, which we didn't, and let Brock take me back home. We walked back to Maufanges, and he was quiet, so I figured he'd gotten over it. I was wrong."

He took another breath and swallowed hard. "Radder?" I asked. "Are you alright?"

"Yeah, I'm fine. This is just where it starts to get ugly."

I felt my eyes widen. "Ugly?"

"You'll see."

"Well, go on," I urged him. "I'm intrigued."

He chuckled. "OK. But don't say I didn't warn you."

"I won't," I promised.

"Good," he said. He leaned down to kiss me, briefly, and then rested his forehead on mine. He opened his mouth to say something, but decided against it, and drew away from me, though his arm was still around my waist. I leaned against him, since I'd drawn away, and waited for him to continue the story.

"He- he took my back to the castle. He let me go in first, and when he was inside, he just walked around silently. I followed him and kept saying; 'Dad?' I was hoping it'd make him a little more pleased that I was respecting the fact that he was my dad now. We went into the kitchen, and he turned around, and he- he hit me."

"He *hit* you?"

"Yeah," he said. "He punched me in the nose, and broke it. Then he pushed me into the table, which made me fall onto the floor. I remember I was crying, because it really hurt. Benjamin walked in and just stared at me. Then I remember Brock saying, "See? You're not one of us, or else you'd be healed by now. Why don't you remember that the next time you decide to run away?" It didn't really all fit together, but, I got the message. He left the castle then to do God knows what, and Ben helped me up and took me to Dina. She helped fix it up and stop bleeding. She had to reset the bone while I was conscious…"

Radder closed his eyes and grabbed my hand, squeezing it tightly. "I've never heard anything so awful in my whole life," I said.

"Oh, don't worry, it gets worse," he promised. I gulped.

"After that, I was very wary around Brock. I tried not to provoke him, but if I ever showed a sign of weakness because I was Human, he'd beat me. Like, badly. I'd often have bruises all up my arms and legs, and more than a few times I'd have a black eye or a bloody nose or lip. Benjamin tried to protect me, but there wasn't very much he could do. One day Brock got mad at me for eating some bread and came after me, and Dina got in the way. Then- he killed her. I watched him kill her. I'd never seen anything so horrifying, and it made me want to be a Vampire even less, if I had to kill others like that to live. I'm still horrified by it in fact, but, that's besides the point. So, things went on like that until I was seventeen-"

"He beat you for *seven years*?"

He nodded. "Yeah. Every single day."

"Oh my God," I whispered.

"Hey, it's OK. That was a long time ago."

"I know, but still, that's terrible."

He nodded, and then decided to continue. "Well, when I was seventeen, he let up so he could train Benjamin. Ben had gotten his fangs two years before I turned seventeen, since, as you know, Vampires, Werewolves, and Fusions all stop aging at eighteen, and had gotten a lot stronger and faster. Benjamin was training to be a Warrior and Guard, since he was a Prince of the Coven, so Brock was pretty busy training him. And then, before I knew it, the day of my eighteenth birthday arrived.

I woke up on my birthday to find myself in a chamber, with a steel anklet around my left ankle, which was attached to a chain and nailed into the wall. I stood up and I could only move about three feet. There wasn't any food, or water, and it was pitch black. I couldn't see anything, and I was scared half to death."

"Well, that's a lovely birthday present now, isn't it?"

He chuckled. "Seriously, it was the worst birthday *ever*. Anyways, the chamber door opened, and I saw Brock. He came over to me, grabbed my shoulders, and said, "Welcome to the Coven." Then he bit me, and I just sank to the floor. Right after that, he left, and I was alone in the darkness. I'd heard stories from Dina about how much being transformed hurt, but I mean, I had no idea it'd be so bad."

"What was it like?" I asked.

"It was as though my entire soul was on fire. I was screaming, and shaking. I rather would've broken my nose and had the bone reset a thousand times than feel the pain of being turned. It just went on and on, for about three hours, and right before I thought it'd kill me, it ended. Just like that. I'd been squeezing my eyes shut for the last hour or so of it, and when my eyes opened, I could see everything in the dark cell. The rats, the stone pattern, even a few puddles of water that came from God knows where.

I could hear the rats gnawing on food and other things, drips of water on the other end of the cell, footsteps three stories above me on the top story of the Fanges castle. But, other than my heightened senses, the thing I felt was the worst. I felt sick, like I'd throw up. And I wanted blood. I needed it so bad, I could feel the redness of my eyes. While I'm sure it was just a few minutes that seemed like forever, Brock finally came back into the chamber. I scented him before I saw him. I was laying on the floor still, and as he approached me, I jumped up and punched him in the face. I was just so angry, after all the beatings, and after he turned me.

So, I broke the chain that I was on, and I totally attacked him, just took all my rage out on him from the past seven years. He tried to fight back, but he couldn't dodge me. When my rage ceased, he had so many bruises and broken bones that it took him a long time to heal. He crippled up on the floor, and, when all his injuries did heal, he got up, and he laughed. He just laughed and laughed, and I got so mad that I made my fangs draw out for the first time. I wasn't expecting it, so I fell to the ground with my hand over my mouth.

My gums were bleeding really badly, I mean, my fangs

had like, pierced through them. In fact, they were bleeding so much that the wounds wouldn't heal. Brock helped me stand up, and told me that I shouldn't have let them draw out because of anger the first time. Once they finally did heal, he taught me how to draw them back in, and then out again, without breaking my gums. Then, he took me up the stairs of the chamber and back into the castle. When he opened the door, the entire Coven was there. Mariah, Sandra, Abel, Vladimir, Gabriel, Rebecca, Amy, Russell, Lucas, David, Annabel..."

"And who are these people?" I asked, somewhat confused, because I only knew Annabel and David.

"Vampires who have been dead for centuries. Then, of course, there was Maryanne, Adam, Razza, Benjamin, and Magdelene. Everyone was just staring at me, completely silent. Brock told them all to leave, except for Benjamin. That's when I started to hear voices. Everyone was talking so loudly, but their lips were shut. That's when I realized that I could read minds. I mean, it made sense, because Brock could too, and he was the one who bit me. After everybody left, things went silent. But that was because Ben and Brock knew how to shield their thoughts. I didn't think that they'd bothered to read mine though.

So, I just blurted out, "I can read their minds." They both looked at me, and then led me outside. They began to teach me how to hunt people, how to scent and listen and watch, how to strike at just the right moment and drink every ounce of their blood. They taught me how to fight. Brock watched every training session I had, and I was so scared that he'd find a way to hurt me if I failed, that I tried to succeed in everything. And I did. I was an overachiever, and I'd beat any Vampire in a fight, no matter how experienced they were.

Finally, Brock chose a day to step down from the throne. Everyone had gathered in the parlor, all of them expecting him to make Benjamin the new leader of the Minuit Coven. At the ceremony, he said, and I quote, "I have chosen the strongest and greatest Vampire in this Coven to take over from now on." Still, they all expected it to be Ben. I could hear it in their minds, they were all ready to cheer, *especially* Magdelene. But then, he chose me. And everything went quiet, even their thoughts. That's when I knew that everything would change.

Everyone's eyes fell on me, Ben's came last. Half of the coven had a happiness shining in their eyes, despite the circumstances, and the other half were glaring at me like they all wanted to drive a stake through my heart. Brock was motioning me forward, so ever so slowly, I went to the front. I had to do this thing where I kneeled before the current King and swore loyalty to the Coven and all this bullshit, and then I guess I just became the King.

It was scary after that. I mean, nearly everybody wanted me dead so that Benjamin could lead the Coven. I mean, I didn't blame them either. He was technically the first-born, and, I mean, I wasn't even Brock's kid. Plus, it's not like I wanted him to choose me. But, I guess that Brock was a little more bronze than brain, so he thought it'd be wise to put the strongest Vampire in charge. Since I hadn't trained to be leader though, and Benjamin had, I kept him as my second in command, just so he could help me learn the ropes. I made it clear to him, though, that if I were to die, I'd want

Benjamin to take over. So, the days went on, and-" he cut himself off, thinking for a moment before he continued.

"And, one day, I decided to visit Guéret, to run a few errands. There, I saw this girl. She was beautiful. She had curly black hair and pretty brown eyes, and, I guess I kinda had a "love at first sight" kind of moment."

"What was her name?" I asked, feeling extremely jealous.

"Her name was Audrey Williamson, as I later found out. After the first time I saw her, and I will admit, I kind of followed her around, trying to get her attention and find out a little bit about her, nothing more. I found out her name of course, and that she was eighteen, and that her father, Roger Williamson, was the richest man in Guéret. I could ask anybody about her; everyone either knew her or was in love with her too.

One day, I mustered up the courage to go and talk to her while she was in the town square. She thought I was cute, and she was curious as to why she'd never seen me before. When she asked for my name, I realized that her dad, or someone else in her family could be a Vampire Hunter, so I decided to stick with a fake name."

"Which was...?" I asked.

"Richard Thompson," he said, smiling in amusement.

"Wow," I said, "that even sounds fake."

"I know. But, hey, she bought it. She introduced herself, although I already knew who she was, and said she had to go, but hoped to see me again soon."

"Sounds like she was trying to get rid of you."

"That's what I thought at the time, but a quick glance into her thoughts told me that she wasn't lying. So, I waved her off as she walked away. I wasn't aware at the time, but I later find out that someone had been watching me."

"Who was it?" I asked, anxious to hear the answer.

"I'm getting to that," he promised. "Anyways, I ran into her "randomly" over the next few weeks, and each time she grew happier to see me. After knowing me for about a year, she invited me to attend a ball that her father was hosting at Guéret's concert hall. She said that her father wanted to meet me, being as we'd never met before, nor had he ever heard of me. So, I decided I'd go, just to humor her. I didn't want anyone at the castle to become suspicious of my whereabouts, so I just told her that I had some errands to run and would probably be late."

"Random question," I said, "what year was this?"

He looked very seriously at me before finally saying, "1573."

"That's a year before Rafe died," I whispered. My heart ached.

Radder took my hand. "I know. I'm sorry."

I shook my head. "It's fine. Just, continue, if you will."

He looked at me for a moment before agreeing to my request. "Well, I managed to fool everybody so I could leave, though I don't remember exactly how, and went off to Guéret to attend the ball. I had to hide a tuxedo in the bushes earlier in the day so I could change into that once I'd left the castle. So, after I did change into my tuxedo, that's when I went along the dirt pathway.

I arrived at the concert hall an hour late from when it had started. I spotted Audrey right away. She was wearing an elegant red dress, and some boys were literally drooling over her. I made my way toward her, and she greeted me excitedly, and told me to follow her. She took me over to a rather fat man and said, "Daddy, this is Richard. Richard, this is my father." So, I shook the guy's hand, trying not to laugh at the fact that she was calling me Richard.

So, after a brief introduction to Roger, we made our way to the dance floor, and started to, well, dance. We were having a lot of fun, and everyone thought I was normal, and I was just having the absolute best day of my life. But, a thought struck me then. It was Audrey's, and she was thinking, *'I love him so much.'* That's when I knew that I had to tell her the truth. I mean, if she did want to be with me, she deserved to know the truth about me, ya' know?

After one of the slow dance songs, I asked her to join me in the garden behind the concert hall. She agreed, so we made our way outside. My plan went along in my head: She loved me, and when I told her what I was, she'd let me bite her, and I'd actually get to kiss her…"

"Wait," I said, "you never even kissed her?"

"No," he snapped, then continued a little softer, "I never did. Anyways, she asked why I wanted her out there, so, I drew out my fangs, and told her, 'Audrey, I'm a Vampire'."

"What did she say?" I asked.

"She just backed away from me and pointed at me. Her voice was shaky, but threatening, and she said, "I'm going to tell them all. I don't care if I love you or not Richard, I want you dead. I'd rather it be you than me." So, I grabbed her wrists and said, "First of all, my name isn't Richard, it's Radder. Secondly, if you do tell anyone, I'm not afraid to end your life and the life of anyone you speak to." So, she screamed for help, and I- I did what I had to." He swallowed hard, tears forming in his eyes.

"You killed her?" I asked, though I silently thought, *Yes!*, trying to shield it from his mind.

"Yes," he whispered, "three-hundred-one years ago to this day."

"So, I guess that explains the candles then, huh?" I asked.

"Yeah," he answered, "every year on this day I make a little "memorial" type thing out of candles for her. Yesterday, when I told you I'd come at dusk today, I didn't even think about it. In fact, I was getting ready to go and get you, when I remembered. So, I did stand you up. But, you of all people should understand. I mean, the person you loved died too."

"Yeah, he did," I said, "but not the same way yours did."

"Good point. I had to leave quickly because some people heard her scream and came running. They figured out pretty quickly that it was a Vampire that had killed her, though only one person figured out who it was."

"Who?" I asked, puzzled.

"That old man at the bazaar yesterday. His name was Anthony Smith. Apparently, Audrey had a sister named Allison, and he's a descendant from that side of the family."

"Really? That is very ironic."

"Tell me about it," he said. "I really thought that Audrey and I were meant to be together. I mean, this will sound stupid, but I actually went to a psychic once, and she told me that my soul mate's name started with an "A." So, I guess you can see why none of it made sense."

I nodded, trying not to think about how I'd seen that my

own soul mate's name was supposed to start with an "R." I gulped. *Rafe...*

"So, what happened after Audrey died?" I asked, trying to get my mind off of Rafe.

"There was a bounty set for me. Anybody who had any information on who had killed her was supposed to come to the police right away. But nobody knew it was me. That is, until Benjamin found out."

"But, how?" I asked.

"He was following me, watching my every move. He felt my pain at losing her, and his lust for power became too great. So, he decided to challenge me to a duel over my position as King. The whole time though, I couldn't stop thinking about Audrey, and, so, he beat me. I got banished, and was only allowed to pass through Maufanges. If the Coven caught me living in the city, they would kill me. So, I moved to Guéret.

Not soon after though, I got a letter from Brock, telling me what a disgrace I was. That's when I snapped. I was so angry at myself for taking all that shit from him for all my life, and losing what I'd always worked for, and just plain sick of him always criticizing my actions. So, I ran to Maufanges, snuck in the castle, and went up to his room. Brock was writing something, and when he saw me he laughed and said, "Why, if it isn't the failure himself..."

He was going to say more, but before he could I grabbed him by the throat. I punched his nose until it broke, then reset the bone myself so he could feel some of the pain that he caused me. I wanted him to feel the pain of being transformed, of being beaten so many times for so long. Unfortunately, there was no way I could've done that. So, I just hurt him as much as I possibly could, and then I drove a stake through his heart.

After that, I just went home. It felt good to have him dead, though I knew the Coven would want to kill me even more than they already did. But I didn't care. The bastard deserved to rot in hell for what he did to me. I mean, I wouldn't have to have gone through all that pain if Veronica had just lived, or if he'd just let me die with my family. Then Audrey could have lived, and Brock would still be alive, and Ben would've been King right from the start. This world would be so much better without me."

"Now, you know that's not true," I countered. "Think about it. If I hadn't met you the other day, I probably wouldn't even be alive right now. It's nice to have someone who knows somewhat of what you've been through."

He looked at me and smiled, pulling me closer to him. I asked quietly then, "So, what happened after you killed Brock?"

"Nothing," he said. "That's practically my whole life right there."

"I see," I said. Then, curiosity sparked in my mind. "What was the favor I was supposed to do today?" I asked him.

He shrugged. "I can't even remember," he confessed, "but right now, there is something you can do." His voice was choked, and he brought his other arm around my waist, resting his forehead on mine again.

"And what's that?" I asked, feeling the water from his tears on my cheek as he began to cry.

"Just stay here with me," he whispered, "don't leave my side."

Chapter 5
Bitten

Amaury:

I woke up the next morning in Radder's arms. It took me a moment to realize where I was, but I soon remembered how Radder had cried himself to sleep, and how he begged me to stay. So, I'd decided to just stay the night. Slowly, I sat up, being as he was still sleeping soundly. As I looked around Radder's small living room, I was thankful I'd managed to blow out all the candles the night before, or else there definitely would've been a fire. That brought back the memories of the story he'd told me, and I shuddered. I couldn't believe that he'd had to live through all the pain and suffering that he did. Nobody deserved that.

I slowly drew myself away from his embrace, deciding I'd better head home. It didn't seem as though Radder would be waking up anytime soon, so I figured I'd better write him a note, just so he'd know where I was going. I made my way into the kitchen, where I opened a few random drawers (most of which were completely empty) until I found a piece of paper. On his table there was a conveniently placed ink-well and feather pen, which I used to write with. I kept the note short and simple:

Radder,

Just so you don't worry about me, I went home. I'm so sorry about what happened to you, though I know I don't and never will fully understand. Still, I'm sorry.

-Amaury

I shrugged to myself after I'd written it. I had no idea what I was supposed to say. *Oh, I'm sorry your adoptive dad practically tried to kill you and then made you a Vampire, and that you killed the love of your life. I hope you feel better about it later today.* Yeah, I don't think so. I figured what I'd written was good enough, considering there wasn't much else I could say.

So, I stood, and quietly made my way out the door, as not to disturb Radder. I decided I would travel faster in wolf form, so I quickly transformed and made my way through the field surrounding his house and into the woods. Quickly finding the dirt pathway that would lead me home, I remembered the last words he'd said to me last night.

Just stay here with me. Don't leave my side.

Even though I'd just left his side, I felt my heart ache for him. It was the weirdest feeling in the world. Here was Radder, a practical stranger that I'd only known for three days, and I was already falling in love with him. It just didn't make any sense, especially since our first encounter didn't leave either of us with the best first impression. And two days ago, only the second time we'd ever spoken, he'd kissed me. Multiple times, even.

It had taken Rafe six years to even make a move on me, let alone kiss me. I didn't know it was possible to fall in love so quickly. It was crazy. Stupid, especially. And I don't want to love him. The only person I'd ever wanted to love was Rafe. The only person I couldn't have. I felt tears pricking in my eyes, but blinked them back.

Don't cry. You're stronger than that.

I decided to go from a steady trot to a full out sprint so I could get home quicker. To keep my mind off of Rafe and Radder, I tried to remember everything I had to do today since I'd fallen a bit behind on my chores. Right as I began to make a mental list, though, I heard a crack right above my head. I skidded to a halt, distorting the prints I was leaving in the dirt, and whipped myself around.

There was a Human standing before me, a young boy with golden blonde hair and sharp hazel eyes. He looked to be only about fifteen or so, and he was staring at me curiously. I wasn't sure if he knew I was a wolf or thought I was a dog, or if he had seen me running so fast that I was blur. He had a strange atmosphere around him, but the oddest thing was that while he was in fact a Human, he had appeared literally out of nowhere. There was no scent, no trace of him ever being there before. It didn't make any sense.

Slowly, he knelt down, holding out his hand in a friendly gesture. "Here girl," he said quietly. So he thought I was a wolf. Nothing more.

He reached into the brown jacket he was wearing and pulled out a bit of meat (why he had meat hidden in his jacket I will never know). He placed it in his outstretched palm, gesturing for me to take it. Cautiously, I padded forward. A normal animal might have leapt at the chance to get free food, but I was smarter than that, even if the giver was a harmless Human. As I got closer to his hand, I could smell the meat. It was tainted, probably with a drug or some type of poison.

I growled, but before I could turn and begin to run back home, I felt someone grab me by the neck. I yelped in surprise, recognizing the scent of my attacker. It was Magdelene. I snapped my jaws at her, but her arms were just out of reach. And, the Human boy was gone, with Benjamin standing in his place.

"Well, well, well," he said, "if it isn't our dear Amaury. So Fusion, how are you?"

He knows what I am?!? I thought frantically. *How could Magdelene have told him about me?*

"I told him about you because I couldn't keep it a secret forever," Magdelene hissed, answering my unasked question. "Anyways, if he'd found out I had kept it a secret, he'd have my head."

"Exactly," Benjamin cut in, "anyways, she would've thought about it at one point or another."

"OK, I really don't care anymore," I said. "Who was that boy here a minute ago? The Human?"

"His identity is a secret," Benjamin said, "but don't worry, you'll find out eventually. That wasn't the last time you'll see him."

"Or, maybe it is," Magdelene said, smirking. "Considering we're about to end your life."

I felt as my eyes widened, felt as I struggled to release myself from her grasp. I raked my claws down her arm, hoping that it'd make her loosen her grip, but she wouldn't let down. I was trapped. I was going to die, unless I made a move to escape. So, I did the only thing I could do. I shifted.

Magdelene had her arms bent to hold a wolf, but the space was too large for me in my "Human" form, so I was able to slide away from her. However, she saw this coming. As soon as I got out of her grasp, she lunged on me, with her fangs drawn out. She bit my arm, which caused blood to instantly drip onto the forest floor, but the wound healed fast.

I drew my fangs out, threatening them both.

"I hope she told you that my venom kills you," I said nastily to Benjamin. "I hope you know that the wound on your leg was from me, and that it could've killed you."

"Ah, but it didn't," he pointed out matter-of-factly.

"And why do you think that is?" I asked him. He didn't have an answer. "I saved your life, Ben," I told him. "So, don't you think you should be thanking me instead of attempting to kill me?"

"Fine," he said. "Thanks. Now, if you don't mind, we're going to end a life that never should've existed."

Magdelene had a tight grip on my arm, but I found it easy to get away. I took a split second to shift, then I bolted. I was three times faster than either of them, plus on all fours I was even faster. However, Benjamin and Magdelene both knew where I lived, considering Magdelene had delivered letters to me before, and Benjamin broke into my house two days ago. So, even if I did beat them to my house, there was still a chance that they'd break in and try to kill me. I wasn't safe anywhere.

Still, it wasn't like I had much of a choice to go anywhere else but home. So, taking a deep breath and picking up speed, I decided I'd accept my fate, whatever it may be. Before I knew it, the path took a hidden turn left, out of the woods and into a field where a small castle sat. I was home.

I morphed back into my "Human" form, slowly approaching the door to my home. I went inside, quickly shutting the door and locking it. Making my way over to my desk, I opened my journal, sat in my chair, and began to write.

Mars 21, 1874; Le matin
(March 21, 1874; The Morning)

Dear Diary,

Well, I went to go and see Radder last night after he stood me up. He told me his entire past. About how he was born a Human, but Brock adopted him after killing his parents, and how Brock beat him for seven years. Then, he turned Radder into a Vampire on his eighteenth birthday against his will. He made Radder the King of the Coven, which started a somewhat verbal war between him and Benjamin.

Then, one day, he met a Human girl by the name of Audrey. He fell in love with her, and one day at a ball, he took her into the garden behind the concert hall and told her what he was (and showed her). She threatened to tell his secret to everyone, so, he had to kill her. Benjamin found out about it, and challenged him for his position as King. They had a fight over it, which Ben won, because Radder could only think of Audrey. So, Radder got banished from the Coven.

After he was defeated, Brock sent him a letter telling him what a failure he was. He snapped, and snuck into the castle and killed him. He said that was basically his whole life. He didn't want me to leave though, so I stayed the night at his house. On my way home this morning, though, I got attacked by Ben, Magdelene, and some random Human boy. I thought I could trust my half sister, but apparently, she exposed my secret. I did manage to make it home safely, though I have a fear that Benjamin and Magdelene are going to come here. We'll just have to wait and see.

-Amaury de Pompadour

Shutting my worn, leather-bound book, I slowly stood. I walked over to one of the windows in my parlor, peeking outside. Nobody seemed to be outside, but you could never be too careful. So, I locked the windows, too. Then, I made my way into the kitchen to check on the flowers on the counter.

The rose was starting to get a little black, but the little purple flower was thriving. It didn't make any sense that the healthier flower was dying before the sickly one. But, it was true nonetheless. After monitoring them for a few moments, I made my way into my mudroom to get my watering can, so I could water my garden outside.

When I had the watering can, I cautiously made my way out the door. There were no suspicious scents anywhere, no eeriness amongst the trees. I felt safe, for the moment at least. Slowly moving around my small castle, I dipped the watering can to water the thirsty plants. The soil drank up the moisture quickly, assuring that the plants would continue to grow. I noticed a few more flowers, a couple pansies and some tulips, had literally grown over night. I knew though, that soon enough the flowers would be dead, no matter how hard I tried to keep them alive. That was the fate of everything, even immortal beings like myself. Death was inevitable, even if you were promised forever.

I made my way around the flowerbeds fairly quickly. A few times I had to go back inside and get more water, but I still watered each plant faster than I ever had before. When I finished, I glanced up at the sky. It was probably nearing noon, considering I'd left Radder's house around ten o'clock this morning. Making my way back inside, I wondered where Radder was. I replaced the empty watering can to its rightful place in the mudroom, and began to go upstairs. Before I set foot on the first stair, though, my door burst open.

"Amaury!" a voice called. It was Radder.

I made my way towards him and said, "What's wrong?" His eyes were wide, and his hands were shaking, though he was trying to hide it.

As soon as I was close enough, he slid his arms around my waist and pulled me to him. "Are you OK?" he asked me, his voice as shaky as his hands.

"I'm fine. Why?"

He took a deep breath. "I scented Ben and Magdelene in the woods, as well as your blood. I thought something awful had happened to you."

"Magdelene just bit me. It was no big deal."

"What were they going to do though?"

"Huh?"

"They obviously attacked you for a reason, and, knowing my brother, he told you why you were being ambushed. So…?"

"They said they were going to kill me."

He withdrew away from me, backing closer to the door. "That's it," he said. "The bastard's crossed the line this time." He turned and stormed toward the door.

"Radder!" I called after him. He stopped, but didn't turn around. "Radder," I said again, "they said they were going to kill me. But they didn't. Just calm down, OK? I'm fine."

"This isn't just about you," he said, slowly turning to face me. As he said the words, his eyes turned from an icy blue to a bright red.

"Radder," I said for a fourth time, "calm down. You're just thirsty and it's making you mad. Maybe you should just..."

"Don't tell me what to do!" he snapped. "They could've killed you, don't you see? Don't you understand that it's all Benjamin's fault that I lost everything I'd worked for?"

"But, I thought you didn't want to be king?" I said.

"I didn't. But I worked to be respected. When I became king, I got what I always wanted, and what I wanted the least. And he took it from me. The sick bastard. And then he almost took you." The redness in his eyes lessened a bit, now having a reddish-blue hue.

"Hey, it's fine, OK? Nobody got hurt. It was just a failed attempt on their part. I'm OK, you're OK, they're OK."

"They won't be for long," his eyes lost their bluish tint, and were now fully red.

"What do you mean?" I questioned, worry growing inside me.

"I am going to end this. Now." He turned around again, but this time, he walked out the door.

"Radder," I said, following him out the door and catching up to him, "what do you think you're doing?"

"I'm going to kill them." He said it lightly, but his expression was serious. "You're free to join me if you like."

"Will you just listen to me? Why don't you hunt and see if it calms you down?"

"I'm not thirsty," he said, though his eyes showed proof that he was lying.

"Yes you are. Your eyes are red."

He sighed, long, and said, "Fine. Just if it makes you shut up about it."

"Well, aren't you kind," I said sarcastically.

But he didn't hear me; he was already running into the forest. So, I wandered around the field until I spotted a familiar little patch, where four logs lay, creating an imperfect square shape. In the center of the square was a fire pit. Back when Rafe was still alive, he'd bring me here for a little campfire, in which we'd just sit on the log farthest from the fire, where we'd tell stories or jokes or just make out the whole time. The memories made me smile, until I remembered that this time, Rafe wasn't with me.

I swallowed hard and sat on the log opposite to the one I'd always sat on before. My stomach growled loudly, reminding me that it was lunchtime. I didn't understand why Radder had to get so mad about something that wasn't even that big of a deal, especially at this time of day. Right as I began to think of him, he appeared right in front of me, smiling as I jumped. He sat down beside me and laughed.

"That was *not* funny," I said.

Still, he smiled. I was glad to see that his eyes had returned to their normal blue color.

"I brought you a rabbit," he said.

My eyes widened. "You did what?"

"Well, there aren't many people around these parts, so I drank a rabbit's blood to sustain myself. And, I know you can drink blood, and I figured you were hungry, or, I guess thirsty, so I brought you a rabbit." With saying that, he suddenly presented a very dead bunny, which he was holding by the ears. It made my stomach turn over.

"I hate drinking blood," I said. "Why do you think I stick to Human food?"

"Well, you don't really have much of a choice, now, do you?" he said.

My stomach growled, as if on cue, and I knew he was right. Reluctantly, I grabbed the poor bunny and drew out my fangs. I hated this. I pierced my fangs into the rabbit's neck and began to drink, resisting the urge to get sick (though it's not like I could anyways). After all the blood was gone, I felt better, and yet worse.

My teeth were stained with blood, and I was embarrassed to the fullest. If I ever drank blood, I usually did it in private. But, Radder had been sitting beside me, watching me the entire time. I wanted to crawl into a cave and never come out. I dropped the dead corpse of the bunny and stared at the white ashes in the fire pit. The ones that had been there for centuries, and had never let the wind carry them away. It made me remember Rafe, and I had to fight back tears. But, this time, I couldn't fight them off. I felt the tears run down my face, and Radder slid his arms around me.

"Hey," he said. "Don't cry. It's just a bunny. Nobody's gonna miss it."

"This isn't about the damn rabbit," I said.

"Then what's wrong?" he asked.

"You're the mind reader," I said. "You tell me."

"This is about Rafe, isn't it?" he asked.

"Wow, took you long enough to figure that one out," I said.

"Listen, he's dead. OK? Time to move on."

"I could say the same thing to you. Your girl died, remember? She's the reason you stood me up last night." That shut him up.

Then he spoke again. "It's different when you kill them, though," he whispered. He pulled me closer and kissed my cheek.

"Maybe," I said. "But either way, they're both still dead."

"Good point," he said. "So, with all due respect, let's go take our anger at their deaths out on two certain Vampires."

"Why? Can't we just get revenge on them later?"

"Perhaps we could, but I have the urge to kill a certain somebody right now."

I slid away and put my hands up in a defensive mode. "OK, just as long as it's not me," I said seriously, though I smiled to let him know I was joking with him.

He chuckled and stood, brushing off his jeans, though there wasn't any dirt on them.

"Well," he said, "what do ya' say? Ready to go kill some Vampires?"

I took a deep breath. There was no talking him out of this. "Why not?" I said. "I couldn't stop you if I tried."

"No, you couldn't," he agreed. "Walk or run?"

"I prefer to walk, if you don't mind," I said.

"Fine by me," he said.

"Good." I stood then too, blushing as he took my hand and began to walk in stride with me toward Maufanges. It would take about forty-five minutes or so to get there by foot, though Radder would probably challenge me to a race again. I smiled at the thought of how I'd beat him, and glanced over to see him smiling, too. He squeezed my hand and looked at me.

"I wish you would've woken me up before you left," he said. "I gladly would've walked you home."

I shrugged. "You looked happy. I didn't want to wake you up."

"I was having a good dream," he said. "Nothing more."

"What was it about?" I asked, rather curious.

He shrugged. "Stuff," he said.

"Great description," I said sarcastically.

"Why, thank you," he said. "I'll make note of your compliment."

I rolled my eyes. "Seriously, what was it about?" I asked.

"I told you. Stuff."

"You are absolutely hopeless," I said, shaking my head. "What's so secret? It was a dream."

He sighed. "Let's just forget about it, OK? Move onto another topic."

"OK," I said, "What do you want to talk about?"

"How about," he said, "what our battle plan is."

"I don't even really want to do this, let alone talk about it."

He sighed, but didn't say anything. So, we just walked along in silence, his hand gripping mine tightly. It brought back a flash of my time with Rafe, which I tried hard to keep out of mind. Like Radder said, it was time to move on. So, I took a deep breath, and just kept walking forward.

It seemed like forever of just us walking in silence, but finally we reached the Fanges castle. Radder slid through the fence first, waiting for me to follow. The castle had an obscure feel to it, as though something important was going on inside its dark stone walls. Silently, I slunk behind Radder. He obviously knew what he was doing, considering he'd broken in here before.

We made our way past the front doors, then had to duck to avoid the windows that seemed to cover every square inch of the castle. Eventually though, we made it to the castle's back, where there were no windows, except for a small one near the ground. While tiny, both Radder and I could easily fit through it.

"How'd you know about this?" I asked.

"It leads to the dungeons. I noticed it when Brock was leading me upstairs, after I got turned." His gaze seemed to wander far away for a moment, before he shook his head, bringing himself back to reality.

"OK," he said, "let's do this." He put his hands on the sides of the window and swung it open easily. He propped it up on our side of the wall so that we could both go through without difficulty.

"I'll go first," he said, "you jump down and I'll catch you."

"I'll have you know that I'm wearing a skirt," I said.

He smiled. "Oh well," he said.

Before I could respond, he had jumped into the darkness, his back to me. I decided to go in the same way. I peered down into the blackness of the dungeon area. Though I knew he was right below me, I couldn't see Radder anywhere.

Trusting my instincts, I slid through the window, instantly swallowed by the darkness. I didn't know how far I'd fallen, but I soon felt arms around me. Radder was holding me, and yet it was so dark I still couldn't see him.

He set me down on my own two feet, which made me stumble a bit. He helped steady me, then wrapped his arms around my waist. He was about to kiss me; I could even feel the closeness of his face to mine. But suddenly a huge, bright beam lit up the dark room. I saw a silhouette against the bright light, but before I could catch the person's scent, Radder grabbed me and pulled me behind one of the cell walls, where we sat, crouched as low to the ground as possible. He held me as close to him as he could, his tenseness telling me to stay as quiet as I could.

I heard footsteps, saw the shadows in the light. *Oh God, they know we're here!* I thought, too frantic to obey Radder's quiet command to calm down. Suddenly, I heard two distinct voices. Neither belonged to Benjamin, though, or Magdelene, or anybody else in the Coven. And yet, they were oddly familiar.

"Do you see anybody?" a male voice asked.

"No," a female voice responded. "Nobody's in here."

"Listen, maybe he's not even here. Maybe the wolves took him. But, if we don't get out of here soon, the Vampires are going to find us and rip us to pieces."

"Oh, no they won't," the girl promised him. I heard as she shuffled around in what I assumed was a bag. She drew something out rather loudly, and by the way Radder's muscles tensed, I could tell that the item she was holding was a stake.

"Sam," the girl said. "These damn creatures took my little brother. And I am going to find him and bring him home, no matter what it takes."

Sam spoke then. "This is crazy. You're going to get yourself killed, Ruby."

Wait. Sam and Ruby? Those were the Humans I'd seen in Guéret yesterday on my way to Radder's house.

"I don't care," Ruby suddenly snapped, bringing my attention back to them. "They took Rocco, Sam. I have to find him."

"How do you know? Maybe he just ran away."

"Please. My parents taught me all the ropes to Vampire hunting. They showed me how to tell if it was a Vampire who broke into your house or just a normal person. But now that my mom and dad are dead, I have to look after my little brother. And you think I'm just gonna sit back and watch as some stupid Vampires kill him? Or recruit him, even?"

"Ruby, calm down." I watched as one shadow moved closer to the other. "Rocco's going to be fine. He's fifteen. He can take care of himself."

"No, he can't. He's stupid, and I promised my parents that if something happened to them I'd protect him. Now look at what's happened!"

"Well, if you want to find him so bad, don't you think we should get out of here and go look for him?"

I heard Ruby sniff. I hadn't even realized until now that she'd been crying. "OK," she whispered. I listened as she silently followed Sam out the door. As soon as the door shut, Radder and I were again swelled in darkness.

"Well, that was close," Radder said.

I let a breath that I didn't even know I'd been holding. "So, now what? There are a couple Humans running around trying to kill the Coven."

"A little more than a couple."

"What do you mean?"

"I mean there are five, not two."

Of course. Jared, Hazel, and Hugo had to be with them.

"So, how is this plan going to unfold?"

"Well, we'll just let the Humans distract them so we can kill them. Seems easy enough."

"When are we going upstairs?"

Suddenly he stood, and while it was dark I could tell he was offering me his hand. "Right now," he said.

Reluctantly, I placed my palm in his. He pulled me up easily and started to make way for the door. I somewhat trailed behind Radder as he pushed open the door, letting the light flood in the darkened dungeon. I exited with Radder, and waiting for him to close the door, I stared around the beautiful inside of the castle.

The dungeon entrance was on the back wall on the left of a long staircase. The floors were a luminescent white linoleum, and before the staircase was a red carpet, with golden designs interlaced within it. Everything about the place was elegant. To the right of where I stood was a beautiful parlor, and to my left was a kitchen. I knew that the only reason it existed was for show, but there was also the fact that it had been used at one time. I shuddered at the memory of what Radder had told me. Before I could totally let it get to me though, Radder slid his arm around my waist.

"The bedrooms are almost all upstairs," he said truthfully.

"Almost all?" I questioned.

"There's a hallway just off the parlor, he noted, "and the kitchen, too. They meet together in the middle. Mostly higher class stays there, since there's only four rooms, but since I killed Brock only Ben lives down here."

"What about Magdelene?" I asked. "And, wouldn't it make more sense if the higher class stayed on the second floor? Or the third, even?"

"There are not enough Vampires to inhabit all three floors. The Coven's population is dropping rapidly. And, if you were an attacker, where would you think to look for the leader?"

"The second floor."

"Exactly," he said. "It's reversed, so you'll actually get the entire Coven, mostly Warriors and Guards, instead of who you're looking for. Then, you'll most likely die."

"I see," I said, "smart strategy."

"Isn't it? Now, let's go find who we're looking for."

We began to walk away from the door to the dungeon. This place looked so much different from my own castle, with its wooden floorboards and unexciting furniture. Though, I'm sure one of the Coven's Vampires would be just as shocked at the appearance of my home as I was theirs. Radder turned in the parlor, and I could see his nostrils flare as he scented the air.

"Ruby's been through here. So has Ben." He began to head towards the staircase then, as I followed closely behind him. When we reached the stairs, he began to fly up them, and was at the top before I could blink. Following his example I reached the top very quickly, but Radder was out of sight. I'd have to follow his scent.

I noticed that on the path he took were the mingled scents of Ben, Magdelene, and Ruby. There was one door at the end of the hallway, on its right side, where Magdelene's scent overwhelmed the others. I figured this had to be her room. The door was swung wide open, and I saw a small light. A candle had fallen, starting a small fire. Radder was in the room, holding a girl's wrists and telling her to calm down while she struggled and fought against him. But, she was Human, and it was no use.

Her brown hair was partially covering her piercing blue eyes, but you could easily see the anger in them. She was trying hardest to release her right hand, I noticed. Then, my heart skipped a beat. She was holding two stakes, and one was covered in blood.

The fire was beginning to spread over the dark brown carpet, lighting the room a bit. I couldn't see any dead bodies, which was relieving, but I could plainly see the fear in Radder's eyes, and could tell he was scared at the thought of losing someone else to a fire. *Me?* I wondered. I didn't know if there was anyone else in the castle he cared about.

The girl, who I assumed was Ruby by the way she looked, started to scream for help. She must've thought Radder was going to bite her.

"Shut up!" Radder yelled at her. The flames continued to grow. "Where did they go?" he asked, loud enough for her to hear over the sudden roar of flames.

"They-they jumped out the window!" she shrieked. "Now let me go!"

He threw her backwards so she couldn't plunge one of the stakes into his heart when he walked away. He came towards me then, standing in the doorway, and said, simply, "We need to get out of here."

"I couldn't agree more," I said.

"You didn't let me finish," he stated. "We need to get out of here, but only after we get Ben and Magdelene."

"Oh my God. This place is on fire, and your only concern is getting those two?"

"Yes," he said. "In fact…" he didn't have time to finish, because, before I knew it, he was crumpled on the ground in pain. As soon as he fell, I heard myself gasp, because behind him stood Ruby. In her left hand she held the bloody stake. Her right hand was empty. Ruby began to laugh at Radder's pain. I wasn't sure if she'd stabbed his heart or not, but I wasn't about to take the time to find out.

I lunged toward her, pushing her back beside Magdelene's bed, where the flames made an almost ring. I picked up the dropped candle which was near the bed, and quickly dipped the wick into one of the nearby flames. Ruby stood, watching in shock, as I took the candle in a half-circle, igniting the carpet and surrounding her in flames. The flames rose, taller than me, and it came to a point where I couldn't see Ruby anymore. There wasn't anyway she could get out now. So, with that being done, I made my way over to Radder. He was doubled over in severe pain, his eyes tightly closed.

"Radder!" I said. The roar of the flames was getting louder still, and nearly the whole room was on fire. "Radder, come on," I said nervously, fearing for his life. "Get up. Let me help you."

He seemed to be frozen in pain, as though he couldn't move. I would've thought he was dead if I hadn't felt his pulse and confirmed that his heart was still beating. He had curled himself into a ball, and I had to move his legs and arms away from his chest. Ruby had been pretty off on her aim, and instead of plunging the stake through his heart, she'd pierced it through his back, about three inches above his bellybutton. The stake had gone through his back and came out the other end of his torso, soaked in blood. It made me feel sick.

The scariest thing, though, was having to pull the stake out of his back. I got it out as quickly as possible, and Radder never made a sound. I threw the bloodstained stake into the fire, which was growing so close I could feel the heat from it. Radder was still just laying there, bleeding, and I had no idea what to do.

"Do you need some help?" a voice suddenly asked.

My head snapped up, only to see another Human standing beside me. I'd been in such panic I hadn't even scented or heard her.

"Yeah," I said. "I do."

"I'm Hazel," she said. *Of course.* "Who are you?"

"I'm Amaury," I said. Then I motioned downward with my head. "This is Radder. He won't talk to me and I- I don't know what to do."

"Is he your boyfriend?" she asked, smiling, although this wasn't the best time to have such a happy expression.

"Yeah," I said.

"So, what happened?"

"Ruby drove a stake through his chest."

"Ruby?" she asked. "Do you know where she is?"

Caught in a ring of fire. "No. She ran as soon as she stabbed him."

"Of course. I was trying to tell her not to come, mostly because I don't believe in Vampire hunting, but, she's too stubborn to listen. Does what she wants, even if it is a bad idea."

I knew someone like that too. Now that the stake was out of his chest, I turned Radder onto his back and propped his head up in my lap. The flames were starting to get dangerously close.

"OK," I said, "I don't mean to be rude, but we kind of need to come up with a plan. Like, now."

"I concur," she said. "He's probably in shock. Try talking to him. Maybe he'll snap out of it or something."

I highly doubted it would work, but I tried anyway. I shook him lightly and said his name, told him to wake up. So far, Hazel's theory was proving to be inaccurate. So, I tried one more thing. I kissed him, lightly, on the lips, and whispered, "Come on, Radder. Get up. Please?"

Slowly, I saw his eyelids flutter. I couldn't believe he'd woken from my kiss. In fact, I shouldn't have believed it. Because, as soon as his eyes opened fully, he jumped up and stomped his foot repeatedly. He'd woken up because his shoe had caught on fire. Once the small flame was out, he looked into Magdelene's room.

"Oh shit," he said. "Time to go."

"Finally," I breathed to myself, unsure if he'd heard it or not, but I didn't care.

Hazel had already left, probably to search for Ruby, so I followed only Radder down the stairs. But, halfway down the stairwell, we ran into none other than Benjamin and Magdelene.

"Going so soon?" Ben asked in a menacing voice.

"Yes, in fact, we were," Radder replied. "Thanks for having us over. We'd love to visit again."

Ben frowned at Radder's sarcasm. "Well, then if you like the place so much, why don't you just stay for a little longer?"

Radder had a barely-there smile on his lips. "We really need to get going. We're having dinner with the Werewolves. I'm so sorry we couldn't stay longer."

Benjamin grabbed Radder by the shirt collar, obviously extremely angry.

"You think this is all fun and games, Radder?" he asked in a threatening voice. "Well, here's some news for ya'; it's not. Give me one good reason as to why I shouldn't end your life right now."

"Because you're my brother," Radder said.

Benjamin's green eyes flamed with anger. "I am not your goddamn brother!" he screamed. I could just barely see Radder's smile behind his upturned coat collar. *He's enjoying this.*

The hand Ben was holding Radder with started to shake violently. He suddenly released his hold on Radder's shirt, causing Radder to stumble a bit. He quickly reached for the railing in order to keep his balance. But before it was within his grasp, Benjamin grabbed his unstable arm and threw him down. Radder winced, because of the wound in his chest, but didn't try to fight back.

Then, to my dismay, Ben kicked Radder down the stairs and lunged towards me, as did Magdelene. But, I was too fast, and was at the bottom of the stairs before they even noticed I had disappeared. Radder lay at the bottom, his arms wrapped tightly around his chest. He groaned in pain, and I noticed that his left arm had been cut somehow, his jacket was ripped too, and was bleeding all over the red rug, making it an even darker shade of red.

Suddenly, Benjamin and Magdelene were at my side. Ben grabbed me, while Magdelene knelt beside Radder. Slowly, she drew his arms away from his stomach. I had a dreadful feeling she was about to do something awful. But I wasn't about to sit back and watch her. So, I drew my fangs out in an intimidating manner, but only for a brief moment.

"Don't touch him," I said in a low voice. "Or you're going to be sorry."

"Really?" she said. "And what are you going to do, exactly?"

I didn't tell her, though. I showed her. Somehow, I was able to slide away from Benjamin's hold on me, and I dived at my sister, grabbing her arm before she could react. I sank my teeth into her, poisoning her blood. She was going to die, I knew. As soon as I was sure she had the poison running through her veins, I withdrew my teeth from her arm. Magdelene's arm dropped from my grasp. She was staring at the ground, not saying a word, but she began to shake. Benjamin was staring at us both in utter horror.

"What have you done?" he whispered, barely audible. Slowly, he walked towards Magdelene, catching her just before she fell over. She let out a pathetic little whimper of pain, and then did I realize the extent of what I'd just done.

"Magdelene?" I said, suddenly worried.

She talked, just above a whisper. "You worthless bitch," she said. "I told Annabel you were good for nothing."

"Well, excuse me that your mom cheated on your dad. That's not my fault."

"You just don't get it, do you?" she tried to make her voice harsher, but she was starting to loose conscious.

"What don't I get?" I asked.

"You just can't understand what I've tried to tell you for so long. Annabel isn't your mother."

I was so shocked by her words that I almost couldn't speak. Though, I did manage to say one thing. "What?!?"

"Annabel wasn't your mother. Your mom was some girl named Adra. She and Annabel were best friends, and your mom told mine about you when you were about three. There was a battle then, and your mom died, so mine took you in. And you killed her. You-"

She stopped talking then; her mind had slipped into unconsciousness. Benjamin stared down at her. If I hadn't known any better, I would've thought he was on the verge of tears.

Radder's eyes began to flutter, although I hadn't even noticed that they'd closed. He tried to sit up on his own, but I had to help him. Soon enough though, he was on his feet. Benjamin didn't say a word to either of us; he just stared at Magdelene, not taking his eyes off her for one second. I watched him for a moment, before I felt Radder grasp my hand and lead me out the doors. But right before the door closed, I swore I heard sobs.

Radder began to lead us toward Guéret, but I protested. "My house is closer," I said.

"I don't care. I wanna go home."

"Well, I think it's too far of a walk, especially considering your condition."

"I'll be fine," he said, though he changed directions and began to head towards my house. "So," he said, "what happened while I was out?"

"Well, Magdelene told me that we're not really half sisters. In fact, we're not even related."

"Do tell."

"What more is there to say? Just that Annabel and my mother were best friends, and that my mom died, so Annabel took me in and made up the story that she'd just cheated on David and that I was her daughter. She convinced Daniel to stick with that story, and that's about it."

"What was your mother's name?" he asked.

"Adra," I said.

"Adra?" he repeated, surprise evident in his voice. "Adra Lacoste?"

"I'm not sure what her last name is, but probably. You knew her?"

He nodded. "Razza is her little sister. She died when I was about four in one of the battles."

"I know. Magdelene told me that. I have a question."

"What is it?"

"What was she like?"

"Well, she and Razza were both a lot alike, personality wise. Both of them were smart, but they didn't look anything alike. Razza has blonde hair and brown eyes, right? Well, your mom looked just like you; she even had the same shade of black hair, only she had hazel eyes, not blue."

That made sense. I knew my dad had brown hair, and that my eye color had come from him.

When I didn't answer, Radder said, "Your mom was pretty, you know. You look just like her."

I blushed, pretty sure that was meant to go through as a compliment. I decided to throw the topic off a bit just then, to go along with what I was thinking. "It's strange, you know," I said.

"What is?"

"The fact that my last name should be Lacoste, or Pale, instead of de Pompadour."

"I know what you mean."

"What would your last name be, if you hadn't been turned and all that?"

"Thompson," he said, smiling broadly.

"Isn't that what you told Audrey your last name was?" I asked.

"Yup," he said. "I thought I should be somewhat truthful with her, even if it was only partially."

"Well, at least you were being thoughtful." Again, there was an awkward silence between us.

"Amaury Lacoste," he said suddenly. "Doesn't have much of a ring to it, does it?"

"Neither does Radder Thompson."

"Maybe your mom thought it would sound better if you added your middle name?" he suggested, the smile on his face growing.

"Amaury Roslyn Lacoste? No, I think she just picked a couple random names."

"Really?" he said. "I actually think that sounds pretty."

"Hmm. Well, I think it sounds odd. What's your middle name?"

"Andrew."

"Radder Andrew Thompson. Now that sounds better."

"I'll agree with you on that. Although, I think my current last name sounds better with it."

"Sounds good with both," I stated. I hadn't noticed it before, but I suddenly realized that the trees were beginning to thin out. We were nearing the castle. Radder must've seen this, too, because he suddenly picked up his pace. Before I knew it, my home was just barely visible behind the trees.

"Come on," I said, willing him to go faster. I wanted to make sure his cuts were healing.

He was a little reluctant at first, but he soon matched his slow pace with my faster one. We reached the castle fairly quickly, and when we went inside, I ordered Radder to take off his jacket and his shirt.

"Why?" he asked.

"Are you stupid? Ruby drove a stake through your chest. That's too large of a wound to heal on its own. Same with the one on your arm. Plus, your jacket's going to need stitching."

"I'll be fine Amaury, I promise."

I rolled my eyes. "Come on, Radder. You know I'm right." Without another word, I went upstairs into my powder room. In the medicine cabinet, I had everything I'd need to stitch his wound and clean it out. Grabbing what I needed, I made my way back downstairs. Radder was sitting on the couch, head in his hands, with his jacket and shirt laying beside him. I sat down on his left side, placing a hand on his shoulder. Slowly, he lifted up his head to look at me.

"It really hurts," he whispered.

"Well, then move your arms so I can help."

When his arms were out of the way, I began to clean the dried blood off of his chest and back. Then, I proceeded to stitching the wounds. It didn't take long, and before I knew it the stitches began to vanish, a sure sign that his injuries were healing. So, I moved onto his arm, which was still bleeding, so it took a little longer to stitch. When I finished, Radder wrapped his arms around me and kissed me lightly on the lips.

"Thank you," he whispered.

"You're very welcome," I said.

He smiled at me, then drew away, turning himself around to pick up his shirt.

"I think that's ruined," I said truthfully. There was a giant hole going all the way through the center, and blood stains made it blacker than it already was.

"Oh well," he said, shrugging and putting it on anyway. "I'll throw it out later. Are you going to fix my jacket, then?"

"Yes," I said, standing up. I picked up all the utensils I'd used to stitch his wounds, and headed back upstairs. Once everything was back in its rightful place in the medicine cabinet, I went back downstairs.

Radder was still sitting where I'd left him, so I went and sat down next to him. I bent down and reached under the couch; that's where I kept my sewing kit. Once I'd retrieved the wooden box, I found my needle and a thread closely colored to match his jacket. Then I got to work on sewing the frayed sleeve. Like with his wounds, it didn't take very long to stitch up the jacket, and I was done in a matter of minutes.

While I had been sewing the jacket, Radder had gone into the kitchen, though I had no idea why he would. I figured he was just exploring my house, trying to map it all out. When I finished sewing though, it was as though he sensed it, for he appeared back next to me. I noticed that the stitches on his chest, back, and arm had both disappeared, which I was relieved to see. Radder picked up his jacket, inspecting the now-fixed sleeve.

"Nice work," he said. You could barely even see the stitching. "Thanks."

"It was no big deal," I assured him as I packed up my sewing kit.

He looked down at the ground, but didn't say anything.

"Are you staying?" I asked him curiously.

"Well, actually, um… I need to get going."

"Oh," I said. I was actually hoping that he would stay a little longer.

"I'll see you soon though, OK? I promise."

That's practically what you said yesterday. "Yeah. OK."

He sat down next to me then, pulling me closer to him so he could kiss me. He rested his forehead against mine and just barely whispered, "I…" but didn't say anything else.

"You… what?" I said as he pulled away from me.

"Uh- nothing," he said. Something about the way he said it gave me the hint that I wasn't supposed to have heard him.

"Whatever," I said as he stood.

He lingered for a moment before whispering, "Goodbye." And then he was gone.

I stood and walked to the window, hoping to catch one last glimpse of him walking away. But it was as though he'd vanished into thin air. Sighing, I made way into the kitchen, hoping to find a snack. What I found instead was a small note, sitting beside the wineglass that held the small violet. It said, simply:

Glad you decided to keep this.
-Radder

Right above his name, there was a blot of ink, as though he was going to write more, but decided against it. I stuck a corner of the note underneath the wineglass, so nothing would happen to it. Then, I made my way back into the living room, just to glance out the window one more time. I wasn't exactly sure what was going to happen, but I had a dreadful feeling that nothing good would come out of this day.

Chapter 6
An Unexpected Visitor

Amaury:

Mars 22, 1874; Le matin
(March 22, 1874; The Morning)

Dear Diary,

Yesterday was, in one word, hectic. Soon after I got home, Radder burst in the door. He'd scented Ben and Magdelene in the woods on the way to my house, and, of course, my blood from when Magdelene bit me. He was scared to death about me, and honestly, while I know it's awful, the thought makes me smile. Nobody's cared about me this much in a long time.

After I assured him that everything was OK and that I was very much alive, I offered he go hunting, since his eyes were red and betraying his thirst. So, I thought that would calm him down, but I guess it just made him angrier. He brought back a dead bunny (poor bunny) so I could drink, since it was lunchtime. Then, we went to Ben's castle and snuck in the dungeon to lead a surprise attack on the Coven. While we were in there though, two Humans I've seen once before named Ruby and Sam came in searching for someone and talking about killing the Vampires. When they left, so did we.

We went upstairs to Magdelene's room to find a distressed Ruby. Radder tried to find out where Ben and Magdelene had gone by asking her, but all she said was that they'd jumped out the window. So, Radder came over and started talking to me, when all of a sudden Ruby came up behind him and drove a stake through his back. I pushed her into Magdelene's room and trapped her in a circle of fire. I think she's dead.

Another Human, named Hazel, helped me with Radder. I got the stake out of his back, and he got woken up by having his shoe catch on fire. Hazel left, and I started to lead Radder down the stairs, when Ben and Magdelene met us before we could take a step downward. Benjamin took hold of Radder's shirt collar, and after an exchange of harsh words, Benjamin threw him on the ground and kicked him down the stairs. He and Magdelene tried to grab me, but I ran down the stairs to help Radder, who had cut his arm in the fall, and was temporarily unconscious.

Before I could get him out of the castle, Ben and Magdelene were at my side. Ben grabbed me, and when Magdelene attempted to hurt Radder even more, I released myself from his grasp and went towards her, and, I bit her arm. Basically, she collapsed and Ben went into this trance, and Radder woke up. But before she passed out, Magdelene told me that Annabel isn't really my mother. My real mother was named Adra Lacoste, Razza Lactose's older sister. Apparently, she and Annabel had been best friends, and my mother died in a battle when I was three, so Annabel took me in.

After Radder woke up, we began to walk back home, and he

told me that Adra and I looked exactly alike, except she had hazel eyes, not blue. Moving on, though, when we got back to my house, I stitched up his wounds and fixed his jacket for him. Then, he basically just said thank you and left. Although, he did leave me a note by the little purple violet, saying he was glad that I'd decided to keep it. To be honest, yesterday was a drag. I'm scared that something bad is about to happen. And soon.

-Amaury de Pompadour

Iclosed my diary with a loud *Thwack!* and stood up. It was a beautiful spring morning, and the day seemed promising. It was rather warm out for being so early in the morning, so I decided to go outside and water my flowers. Retrieving my watering can, I stepped out the door to be greeted by the warm sunshine. As I walked in the grass along my flowerbeds, I could feel the dew seeping into my shoes.

Each flower had dewdrops on its petals, which shone brightly in the still-rising sun. With my watering, though, they only got wetter. Some more flowers had again sprung up overnight, this time it was mostly snapdragons and marigolds, and a few morning glories.

I smiled at the population of flowers in my garden. I worked hard to keep the flowers growing, mostly because it was something to do, but also because it was fun and took my mind off things.

Finishing up watering the plants, I made my way back inside and returned the watering can to the mudroom. I didn't know what else there was for me to do. It was just like every other day, before I met Radder. I figured I should probably go to Guéret and get some food, being as all I had to eat was cheese, but I decided to go later on today, or perhaps tomorrow. Today, I felt like staying at home, or at least close to it.

So, I decided I should go upstairs and try to find some entertainment there. I entered my room, looking amongst my possessions. Nothing was out of the ordinary; everything was in its place. Except for one thing.

Under my closet door, a piece of paper was sticking out. I didn't think much of it, but thought it to be odd, so I walked over and opened the door. Instantly, a whole stack of papers slid on the floor. Sighing, I began to sort through them. None sparked any particular interest to me; most should even be thrown away. So, I just sorted through them briefly into two piles, one to be tossed and one to be kept.

Then, I saw a paper that caught my attention. There were three different scrawls covering the paper, and some looked oddly familiar. When I started to read, though, my heart nearly came to a stop:

Rafe,
Just so you know, we've alerted the Werewolves of your existence.
We're all plotting on when we're going to come for you.
If you have anything to hide, we suggest you do it NOW.
We're coming for you, Rafe. There's no escaping us.

The note didn't have a signature on it, so I had no idea who the trio was that had wrote it. The paper was yellow from being over three-hundred years old, and had a haunting atmosphere to it. I quickly placed it in the Throw Away Pile, piling more papers on top of it. I never wanted to look at it again.

After I'd sorted out the papers, I threw some back in the closet were I'd found them. The rest, I picked up and carried outside. Slowly, I walked towards the fire pit and the four logs where Radder and I had gone yesterday. I placed the stack of useless papers in the white ashes and went off to find a branch to place on top of them so they wouldn't blow away until I started a fire. After that was done, I walked back to my house. I decided to start the fire later tonight, when it'd go more with the nighttime surroundings.

As I walked through the door to my castle, I again felt its emptiness sweep over me. I sighed as I wandered around, not knowing what to do. As sick and awful as it made me feel, if I hadn't met Radder the other day, I probably would've found a way to end my life. The rest of forever spent in solitude? No thank you. Radder was right then, about living forever being a curse over a gift. I mean, once you've seen and done everything, what else is there to live for?

I trudged slowly up the stairs and returned to my room. Perhaps I could read a book, or maybe paint. I needed to do something. Just then, though, as I began my ascent up the stairs, I heard a creaking noise. It sounded like an opening door. So, I stopped where I was and turned toward the door. And, sure enough, it was open, with a figure standing in the doorway. A figure that could only be Radder.

I instantly felt myself smile at his being here. In fact, I was so glad, that I found myself standing by him within seconds. As soon as I was close he pulled me into an embrace and kissed my forehead.

"Hello, cherie," he said. "How are you today?"

"I'm fine, thanks for asking." I said. He smiled at me sweetly, and I felt myself blush.

"I want you to do a favor for me," he said. I felt my smile slip away. He laughed.

"Trust me, it's not too bad."

"Then what is it?" I said.

"Are you aware of Ruisseau de Chiroux?" he asked.

"You mean the lake?" I asked. It wasn't too far from my castle.

"Precisely."

"Well, of course I know about it. It's a five minute walk from here!"

"Exactly," he said. "So, why don't we head up there?"

I was a little cautious. "And, what for?" I asked.

"To swim, of course! One of the many things water can be used for."

I blushed. "I'm not so sure."

"Well, it's not too hard. All you gotta wear is a sundress or something and jump in. Not too hard, now is it?"

"Um… I'll have you know that I am aware of what to wear when I swim and how to get in the water."

"Are you now?" he said. "I'll only believe you if you agree to come swimming with me."

I rolled my eyes at him. "You always have to have it your way, don't you?"

"Yes, I do. Now, let's go."

"If you've forgotten, I'm not wearing any swimwear yet."

"Then go and change!" he said. "I'll wait here."

And so, I found myself climbing the stairs and entering my room to change. I sorted through my closet to find a plain white sundress and quickly changed into it. I sighed, wondering why nobody could just invent a certain outfit made specifically for swimming. Shrugging, I made my way back downstairs to where Radder was waiting.

"Hello," he said as I approached him. It was at that moment that I saw he was wearing jeans and a white t-shirt.

"You're swimming in *that*?" I asked him.

He shrugged. "Why not?"

"Um... *hello*. Your jeans will stay sopping wet for, like, the rest of the day."

"I'll change. It's simple."

"Whatever," I said. "Anyways, lead the way."

We walked out the door then, which I didn't bother to lock since I had no key with me, and I followed Radder through the field. After just a few steps away from the castle, he grabbed my hand and intertwined our fingers. It didn't take long to cross the field, and then we had to maneuver through a small stretch of trees. Finally, when we reached the tree line, we were met by a small segment of field. About five yards away was a huge, sparkling lake. Ruisseau de Chiroux. Radder drew his hand away from mine and took his shirt off, throwing it randomly onto the grass, and started to head towards the water. That made me blush as I slowly began to follow him to the sparkling blue lake.

There was a dock that went out a couple yards into the lake, because occasionally people were riding in their boats here, most likely fishing. But today, it was just Radder and I, with no one else to bother us. While that made me happy, it also made me a little wary. So, I slowed my pace, watching as Radder took off and did a cannonball into the lake, which made me laugh.

When I stepped a few feet onto the dock, Radder's head came out off the water. As I neared the end of the dock he smiled at me and somewhat shook his sopping wet hair.

"Come on, get in," he said. "The water's fine."

"I'll get in in a minute."

"Why not now?"

"I don't know, I just..."

I didn't even have time to think before he grabbed my arm and pulled me into the water. I felt the water surround me, and felt as my head went under, the water seeping into my eyes and making them burn. Radder had let go of me, and so I shot my head up out of the water, rubbed my eyes, and turned to glare at him. He smiled at me and laughed at my anger.

"That wasn't funny," I said crossly.

"Really?" he said. "'Cause I thought it was."

"Well, you thought wrong," I said. Then I grabbed my mass of hair and began to wring it out.

"Now, tell me, what's the point in that?" he asked me.

"The point is to get my hair a little dryer."

"Why? You do realize that we're swimming in a lake, right?"

"Yes."

"So, why would you be trying to dry your hair? There's no point if it's just going to get wet again."

"I know that, but, oh well."

"You're crazy," he said. He swam a little closer to me and wrapped his arms around me. Then, he brought his lips to mine, kissing me briefly. "But, oh well."

I smiled up at him, hoping he'd kiss me again, and trying

as hard as possible to hide that one little thought from him. However, he did hear my thought about the kiss, so he bent down to kiss me once more. As he did, I brought my hand back in the water and splashed him in the face. He drew away from me, his fangs drawn in defense, and rubbed his eyes. When the water was gone from them, he looked at me, smiled evilly, and said, "It is so on."

So, from that point on, we had a splash fight. Then, after getting drenched in the face a few times, I dove deep underwater to the point where I knew he couldn't see me. But, I could see him. I swam around until I was behind him, then came up to the surface and dunked his head underwater. When I let go of his head, he shot up and turned to face me.

"Now *that* wasn't nice," he said.

"Let's consider it payback for dragging me into the lake."

"But that was different. You had to get in sooner or later."

I just shrugged, watching as he inched closer to me and again wrapped his arms around me. Then, of course, he kissed me. I was expecting that, of course. But what I wasn't expecting was that the now blowing wind would carry the scent of Werewolves. The second I smelled them, I drew away from Radder.

At first he didn't know what was wrong, and was a little creeped out by my sudden fear. Then, I guess he scented the air, because he looked at me, and that was all it took.

"Come with me," he whispered.

He grabbed my arm and together we swam a few feet, ending up underneath the dock. Radder pulled me close to him, and we had to tread water for a long while. Suddenly he tensed, and I smelled the wolves, even stronger now. Then, there was a noise above us, an ominous little *click click* kind of noise, like nails scraping wood. Or claws. From the dock above, I heard the sound of sniffing, followed by voices.

"Someone's here," a female voice spoke in a threatening tone. I recognized the voice as Angel Rousseau's, who was the Alpha of Glace Pack. I felt my heart stop. Then, a quiet male voice took over.

"I think you mean someone *was* here," he corrected Angel. I let a soundless breath escape. The water would have to be confusing them.

"No!" Angel suddenly snapped at the other wolf. "Someone *is* here. A Vampire. But I also smell wolf."

"Maybe it's dog-"

"NO. It's wolf. Don't deny it. I know you smell it too."

Again, there was that *click click* noise from above, and I could tell the male wolf was backing down.

"I want a search ran through the woods around here," Angel ordered sharply to her pack members. "Every single inch from here to within a ten mile radius."

"Shit," I cursed softly under my breath. They'd surely find my castle if they were searching that short of a distance.

Suddenly, everything seemed to stop. The wolves stopped scenting the air, the clicking noises receded; even the water was still.

"Did you hear that?" a new voice suddenly piped up.

"Of course I heard it," Angel said.

Another different voice spoke. "It came from under us."

Radder and I exchanged an anxious glance. Thanks to my carelessness, they would find us. And, of course, they'd destroy me, and Radder too for harboring me.

Radder leaned in as close as he could to me and brought his lips close to my ear, whispering an almost inaudible sentence.

"I'm not going to let them hurt you."

Then, before I knew it, I was again swept underwater by him. I barely had any air in my lungs, and the second I realized it might be a bit before I could surface, I thought I'd die. Especially because, in the hurry to submerge us, Radder hadn't taken into consideration that I might've swallowed water. He still held me close to him though, and that made the pain a little more bearable. Together, we both looked up to find the wolves looking over the sides of the dock, into the dancing blue water. And then, as if they were ghosts, they vanished. Completely.

Radder noticed this right as I did, and swam back to the surface with me in his arms. The second my head was out of the water, I was coughing and trying hard to breathe. Radder let go of me so I could get some air, but still left his hand on my shoulder.

"Amaury, you alright?" he asked me in a worried voice.

I nodded, though I was still gasping for air. I wasn't really all that sure as to why I was about to die from lack of oxygen, and yet it hadn't even seemed to faze Radder. As my breath just barely started to come back, Radder held me again and kissed my neck.

"I don't need to give you CPR, do I?" he asked jokingly.

"I highly doubt that's necessary," I said. "Especially since that's only used when your heart stops beating. Which, mine hasn't."

"Smartass."

"Well, you're just so kind, now, aren't you?"

"As a matter of fact, I am," he said. "Now, do you mind if we get out from under the dock? I'm starting to get claustrophobic."

"*You* are? You aren't the one being held in a death grip."

He laughed at that, and moved away. Then, he swam out from under the dock, and very cautiously I followed him.

"It's fine," he promised me. "They're gone."

So, I made my way back out into the light of the day, glancing quickly around the vicinity of the woods to be sure no wolves were on the prowl. It felt good to be back out in the hot sun of the afternoon instead of under the dock hiding for my life. In fact, it made me so happy that I didn't have to hide anymore. So I started to laugh. Well, I guess it was more of a giggle, but still.

Radder gave me a weird look, though he was still smiling, and said, "You really are crazy."

That comment, of course, only made me laugh more, and the only thing that made me stop was a quick movement along the trees. I barely saw it out of the corner of my eye, but it was there. A little black blur. Radder must've heard me think about it, because he stopped smiling and surveyed the woods around us.

"Babe, nothing's there," he assured me. But I knew better.

"C'mon," he said. "I promise you, nothing is out there. The wolves are far away."

"How are you so sure?"

"Well, for one I can read their minds for about as far as five miles. And, since I hear nothing but your thoughts and my own, then they're obviously not anywhere near us."

I shrugged, still a little wary. "OK, but-"

Then, a familiar voice pierced through my words.

"Who the hell are you?" it asked.

Busted.

Radder and I both turned our heads simultaneously towards the source of the words. By the shore of the lake, only three feet away from us, was a black male wolf. His teeth were bared, and his brown eyes looked fierce and angered. Radder instinctively pulled me closer to him, and I just barely noticed the glint of his fangs as he drew them out. It didn't take me long to realize that this was the same wolf who had back talked Angel on the dock.

"You could answer the same question," Radder said in a rough voice.

"My name is James," the wolf replied. "Now, again I'll ask, *who are you*?"

"My name is Radder," he said. "And this is Amaury."

James squinted, studying us. "Are you both Vampires?" he asked.

I drew my fangs out too. "Of course," I said, hoping I'd persuaded him to believe my words.

He stepped a foot closer to us, and I saw his nostrils flare, scenting the air around us. "You smell like wolf."

"Well, your Pack was just here," I said. I figured he'd believe my reasoning, but the look on his face told me he wasn't convinced.

I could almost read his thoughts on his face, considering how plain it was. He was debating over turning us in or not. Right as he was about to speak though, Radder interrupted.

"I'm curious," Radder said. "How were you able to block your thoughts from me?"

James's eyes grew wide, then he stuttered, "I…I can't tell you."

"Sure you can," Radder said.

"Let's just say a friend of mine taught me how to."

"But, Vampires are the only ones who know how to do that. Does your friend happen to be a Vampire?"

"Maybe so," he said. His eyes were still wide, and I could evidently tell by the tone of his voice that he'd decided not to turn us in after all.

"Isn't that practically betraying your pack, though, by being friends with the enemy?"

"Well…I…" Radder had put him at loss of words. Suddenly though, his expression became furious. "Aren't you betraying the Coven by sneaking off during the day?" he asked.

"We don't live with the Coven," Radder said.

"Well, then where do you live?"

"Wherever we want. We're, I guess to say, Rogue Vampires."

James shied back from us the little bit, and opened his mouth to speak, before a long howl pierced through the sky. Everything went silent for the second time that day, the birds, the insects, and again even the water.

"I've gotta go…" James said in an awkward voice.

I nodded at him. "We understand," I said.

"Have fun James," Radder said in a sarcastic tone.

Slowly, without so much as a goodbye, he began to pad away softly through the field. I watched him until he had completely gone from sight. When he had, I didn't speak until the insects began to chirp and the birds began to sing once more. Once they had, I turned to Radder.

"I thought nobody was here?" I said, smiling sweetly at him.

"That damn wolf blocked his thoughts. It's not my fault I didn't know he was here."

"Didn't you scent him or anything? Or hear him creep up on us?"

"No, and, judging by your thoughts, you didn't either."

"I told you I saw something."

"Whatever. It doesn't really matter anymore anyways."

"Just don't doubt my amazing instincts next time."

"Your instincts aren't amazing," he said insultingly, then dared to kiss me briefly on the cheek. "But *you* are."

"That was probably the cheesiest pick-up line I've ever heard. It was also inaccurate."

"How so?"

"Well, you said I was amazing but my instincts aren't, but in all technicality, my instincts are a part of me, aren't they?"

"Again I say smartass."

"I'm not being a smartass, I'm just correcting your error."

"So, you're being a smartass."

I rolled my eyes. "Whatever."

After that, an awkward silence passed between us. It seemed like forever until he asked me, "Are you hungry?"

I hadn't even noticed until now that I was starving. It was afternoon, after all. So, I just nodded my head, and Radder let go of me, and began to move towards the dock. He grabbed the side and swung himself up, and when he was standing he said, "C'mon, let's go find you something to eat."

So, I waded over to the dock, and Radder reached down

in the water to grab my arm and help pull me up. Once we were both on the dock(soaking wet, I might add), he leaned in once more and kissed me, only this time, it was on the lips. After a minute or two, he took my hand and led me through the field. When we came to where his shirt lay upon the ground, he made me stop for a moment and let go of his hand while he put it back on. Afterwards, we continued on our way.

"Where are we going exactly?" I asked him once we had reached the forest.

"My house," he said.

"You have food there?"

"I do now."

"That's a little odd."

"Well, it makes it seem less suspicious if I have food there. I mean, if someone were to search my house, they wouldn't believe a Vampire lived there."

"Unless you sleep in a coffin."

"Ha ha, very funny."

"Do you?"

"Now you know as well as I do that I, as well as every other Vampire on this planet, sleep on a bed."

"Jeez, I'm just joking with you. Chill."

He just shook his head at me and continued to lead me through the trees. I was afraid that I'd angered him, since his expression looked annoyed, so I kept quiet for a long while. The silence seemed to drag out the time span, and since it took over an hour and a half to get to his house, it seemed like forever. Finally though, after what seemed like an eternity, a little white house was just barely visible through the trees.

I turned to Radder, smiling cautiously. "What do you say we make the rest of the journey to your house a little more interesting?" I asked, somewhat quoting what he'd said only three days earlier. I couldn't believe that we'd only met each other four days ago. It seemed like we'd known each other forever.

Radder turned to me and smiled. "It is so on. Oh, and before I forget, I need to remind you of something *very* important."

"And what would that be?"

"Snails don't run."

"You're mean."

"Don't forget it," he said, the smile on his face growing wider by the second. Then, out of nowhere, he took off in a full sprint.

Cheater! I thought as I started to run. I didn't think I'd be able to catch up to him. And I was right. By the time I reached the house, he was already there. He was leaning against the doorway, arms crossed, a smug look on his face.

"Took you long enough to get here. I figured I'd die of old age before you even got halfway here."

"You can't die of old age you idiot. And if you've forgotten, last time I totally beat you."

"I let you win."

"Uh-huh. You keep telling yourself that."

"Well, I won this time."

"That's because you took off before you even said go!"

"Well you should know me well enough to know that I'd do something like that."

Again, I quoted him. "Well, I do now."

"Good," he said. Once more, there was an awkward silence between us. So, I did the only thing I could do to break it, and that was to go inside his house.

When I walked in, he followed me and began to head for his bedroom.

"I'm going to change," he said. "Help yourself to whatever you find."

Once he left, I began to open cupboards and such in search of food. Apparently, he hadn't had as much food as he thought. In fact, there was practically nothing. *Where'd all of it go?* I wondered. Crumbs were scattered all over the shelves, but other than that there wasn't any proof that food had ever existed in these cupboards.

My stomach began to growl loudly, verifying my hunger. There had to be food somewhere. I began to wander around his kitchen, until something caught my eye. There was a window over his sink, and from that window you could easily see the forest. But in the small stretch of field surrounding his house, an apple tree stood, completely isolated in the vast field.

As quickly as I could walk, I went outside and made my way toward the tree. It was a lot taller up close, and the best apples were way over my head. So, I climbed fairly high up the tree and grabbed a couple of them, then hurriedly slid my way back down and headed back to the house. When I got inside, Radder was still in his room, so I began to eat one of my apples. It didn't take too long to finish, and I'd just taken a bite from the other when he entered the kitchen.

"Apples were the only thing in here?" he asked curiously.

"Are you kidding? Your cupboards are completely empty."

"What?" he said. His face had a mixture of emotions. "That's impossible. I just bought food this morning." He began to go around the kitchen then, opening the cupboards to find them empty, slamming each one in turn.

"I don't believe this," he said.

"Well, what do you think happened?"

"I'm not sure, but I'm going to find out."

"Not right now I hope?"

"Of course not. You're here, so you have my full attention." He gave me a weak smile, and I gave him one in return.

"I want to see your room," I said out of the blue.

He just looked at me, his smile gone. "Why?"

"I don't know, I just want to."

"It's nothing special."

"Oh well," I said. I walked past him and began to head toward his bedroom.

"Amaury," he said, starting to follow me. When he was within reach of me, he grabbed my wrist and spun me around to face him.

"Why don't we just go hang by the lake for a while?"

"What is so bad about your room?"

"Nothing, I just-" he was at a loss for words. He loosened his grip on me, making it easy for me to free myself, then continued towards his bedroom door.

The door was open a crack, so I just pushed the door to reveal Radder's room. I instantly saw why he didn't want me in here. I mean, it wasn't like it was disturbing or anything; it was just a little shabby. For instance, his clothes were strewn along the floor, with an unkempt brown carpet just barely visible beneath them, not to mention his dressers were full of clutter. His bed was awfully tiny, strictly a one person only kind of bed, and it was unmade and extremely tattered.

My eyes must've scanned the room for some time, since Radder said, "I know, it's awful, but I haven't had much time to clean or anything lately."

"Why not?" I asked.

"I've been...busy."

It was apparent he wasn't willing to say more about the subject. So, I turned my focus to something on his nightstand and headed for it.

"What is this?" I asked him. In my hands I now held a large, blue suede bag. It was fairly heavy, and as I was about to open it Radder snatched it from my hands.

"You'll learn in good time," he said. "I promise."

"Well I better," I said sarcastically, "or I will hold a grudge against you forever."

He smiled at my comment, while I walked over to his bed and sat on its edge. Radder stood by his nightstand for a moment before sitting beside me and pulling me into an embrace.

"I promise I'll clean it up as soon as I can," he said.

"It's alright," I said. "I don't mind."

"Well, I'm not doing it just for you. It needs to be cleaned."

"True, but still. It's not your fault."

"How is it *not* my fault?"

"Because," I said. "You've been spending most of your time with me."

"Well there's nothing wrong with that," he said, his smile growing.

We sat there like that for some time, just me in his arms, ignoring the rest of the world, when he offered to go back to the lake. Not exactly to swim (unless I wanted to), but moreover to sit and enjoy the rest of the day by the water's side.

"I'd like that," I said.

He kissed me tenderly on the cheek, then stood up, all the while still holding me. In fact, he kept his arm around me as we made way to the door. I did make him pause briefly though, on our way out of his room, so I could pick up a comb that was laying on his dresser and run it through my damp hair. Then, with smiles plastered on both our faces, we made our way out of the room, out of the house, and into the warm spring sunshine.

I hadn't realized how much time had passed. The sky was beginning to turn pink as the sun sunk lower into the sky. Plus, it'd take a long while to get back to the lake from here. It didn't really matter to me though. Because as long as Radder was by my side, every minute was worth its while.

Radder continued to smile, mostly at my thoughts I was guessing, and pulled me as close to him as I could get. I tried as hard as I could to shield the rest of my thoughts from him though. I didn't want him to hear me unless he didn't feel completely the same way. The truth was, I loved him. I really, truly did. Even if this was just a game for him, or he didn't really care about me, I was in love with Radder Thor.

I was absolutely sure he hadn't heard me, since I'd tried so hard to block my thoughts that it gave me a headache. But, in case he did, I tried to keep my mind focused on my surroundings, hoping it'd eventually slip out of his mind. He didn't say anything to me about it though, so for now I assumed I'd gotten away with it. So, I gave out a relieved sigh.

"You seem happy," he said.

"I am."

"I'm glad. Especially since we're almost there."

"We are?" I said. I was actually rather surprised. In fact, I couldn't even fathom how we'd walked so far so fast. Radder gave me a sly smile, then began to pick up the pace a bit.

As we walked, I began to actually notice my surroundings and not just pretend. The sky had become a deep mix of pink and a light violet, splashed with a radiant glow of amber against the setting sun. The birds were still singing beautiful songs as a solute to the fading light of day, and, as we exited the forest, I saw that the lake still sparkled like a jewel. The whole of it was absolutely breathtaking.

"I used to love coming here as a kid," Radder said. "Brock would bring me and Benjamin and everyone else here for a little "picnic" sort of thing, although I was the only one who actually ate. But still, it was fun. All of us kids would go swim while the adults did whatever, and at the end of the day we'd sit and watch the sun set behind the treetops. I always loved those days. Well, until I was ten..." his voice trailed, and I caught a hint of sadness in his eyes that was gone about as soon as it arrived. But it had been there.

"I'm sorry," I said.

"It's fine," he said. "It's over now, so don't worry about me."

"You didn't deserve any of it," I said. "You were just a kid looking for a taste of freedom. That's all."

"I wish he would've seen it like that."

"I do too," I said.

"He's the reason I'm so screwed up," he said.

"Don't say that. You're not screwed up."

"If you're saying that, you don't know me."

"Well, you do still have some secrets to tell me."

"I'm not telling you. At least not for a long while."

"Why not?"

"Because you don't wanna know. Trust me."

"If you love me you'll tell me," I said, only half joking.

He took a deep breath. "I promise I will. Just not today."

He took a long pause before he spoke again. "What do you say we go sit down somewhere?" he offered.

"Sure," I said. "Better than standing."

"I hear that," he said, a smile returning to his face.

He began to walk away then, letting go of my waist and grasping my hand instead. We headed straight for the lake, and stood on the dock. Out of nowhere, Radder suddenly withdrew a small pile of rocks. I recognized them as the ones he'd collected in the forest days earlier.

"What are you doing with those?" I asked.

He didn't answer me; instead, he threw the rocks, one at a time, into the lake. They skipped along its surface, covering half the lake, before they finally sunk. At least I somewhat knew why he'd been collecting them now.

"I used to always love doing this as a kid," he said.

"I see."

"The other kids and I would have a contest to see who could make them skip the farthest."

"Let me guess," I said. "Your Humanness caused you to always lose."

"Actually, I always won."

"Really?"

"Yeah. None of the Vampires could get it quite right."

"You should teach me how to. Every time I attempt it the rocks just sink."

He chuckled. "I will. Someday."

"Promise?"

"I promise."

We smiled at each other, and then he asked, "So, would you like to go and sit for a while?"

I nodded, and so we walked about halfway up the small slope, so we weren't too close to either the forest or the lake itself. We sat down at the same time, and the second we were on the ground Radder pulled me to him. The trees behind it began to cover the lake in darkness as the sun lowered in the sky, making its lustrous appearance fade. Everything about this place was so just so beautiful. And it made me think about how, while sometimes life is hard, if you take the time to admire it, it is absolutely perfect in every way. I felt happier now than I ever had before, and it seemed as though nothing could ruin this moment. Well, that is, until I glanced over to see a red-eyed Radder.

He noticed I'd caught him, and he became angry, though I think mostly at himself. "I'm sorry, OK?" he said. "I just... I can't help it."

"Go and get a drink," I said. "I know it won't take very long, so just go."

"No," he said. "I wanted today to be perfect, and I'm not ruining it now."

"It's been perfect enough for me," I said. "And you'd be in a better mood if you quenched your thirst instead of trying to ignore it."

He sighed deeply, but finally gave in. He kissed my forehead, then stood and said, "Don't worry, I won't be gone long."

And then, he vanished.

So, I sat there in the grass, waiting for him to return. I watched the sun sink lower in the sky, saw as the first sign of stars began to dot the sky, and watched as the lake lost its sparkle. When the color in the sky began to fade, I began to panic. Radder hadn't returned. And I worried even more when the darkness overcame the amber sky, and the stars invaded its surface. I wouldn't believe that he'd stood me up again. I couldn't. But, when the darkness came, so did my realization that he really had.

I was so angry that I wanted to scream. But at the same time, all I wanted to do was curl up in a ball and cry. I'd trusted him. Gave him a second chance to show me that he wasn't this type of person. In my mind, I figured that I should wait for him, just in case something had happened and he was just really late. But in my heart, I knew that he wasn't coming back anytime soon.

So, with tears filling my eyes and staining my cheeks, I stood and slowly made my way home. With the moon as my only light, and the resting woodland animals as my only company, I felt so alone. I hugged my arms to my chest as I wove my way throughout the trees. The scent of wolf was incredibly strong here, and that's when I realized how close they were to my castle. So, in an utter panic, I broke into a run, afraid of what I might find.

Chapter 7
Captured

Radder:

I was having the best time of my life. I don't think that life could be more perfect. I'd never had so much fun at the lake before in my entire life, and even though Amaury saw my disastrous room, it all still turned out pretty good. Especially since, on our way back to the lake, she declared how much she loved me. Well, it was in her head. And she was trying hard for me not to hear it, that much I could tell. So, I went along with it, pretending I hadn't, while on the inside I was happier than I ever thought possible.

The whole day was completely flawless. Until I became thirsty. The feeling came on suddenly; I hadn't even expected it to come. But, the Thirst was undeniably there, and I was about to tell Amaury when I saw how happy she was. So, I decided not to, so I wouldn't spoil her happiness. But, being as attentive as she is, it didn't take very long for her to notice.

She told me to go and hunt. Insisted I do so. But I fought with everything in me to let her let me stay and just ignore it the best I could. I mean, everything was going just right for once in my life, and I didn't want the monster inside me to snatch it away. But the Thirst always wins. I had no choice but to give in.

So, I stood, kissed her on the forehead, and said, "Don't worry. I won't be gone long."

Then, as hard as it was, I ran away from her and into the cover of the darkening forest. I tried to scent something I could find quickly and drink from quickly, just enough to quench my thirst, so I could get back to my girl. Unfortunately, all the rabbits around here had disappeared for the night. I'd have to go deeper into the forest to search. In fact, the more I thought about it, I had an awful craving for Human blood…

NO! a little voice in my head screamed. *Don't you know how much you'd upset Amaury if you did such a thing?* Sighing, I continued to search for a rabbit, or something of the sort.

I began to move deeper into the forest. The trees became so thick that they blocked out the last of the remaining daylight, creating a seemingly artificial darkness. It was so spooky here, in fact, that I nearly jumped out of my skin every time I stepped on a branch. There was a haunting tone to this part of the forest, and I felt as though I was being watched. Though, it was highly unlikely, considering I'd be able to hear the thoughts of anybody near me. Except, of course, the Werewolf James, and, of course, all the other Vampires.

I gulped. What if it was Benjamin? Or even Magdelene? Maybe, even, it was James, planning a sneak attack on me. I tried as hard as I could to block out my paranoid thoughts, and focused instead on finding a rabbit. However, the obscurity lingered around me, a burden I was unable to shake off.

Also, there was an obfuscated silence that surrounded me. Everything was quiet. The birds, the bugs, everything. I knew why of course; they were in the presence of a predator. But was I the only one? Then, out of the blue, I got my answer as a sharp, foul scent hit my nose. Werewolves.

"Fuck it all," I whispered. I was in Chiroux. While this town was closer to Maufanges over Les Bains, it was the Werewolves' territory (considering none of the wolves knew that Amaury was the true ruler of these lands). If a Vampire was found anywhere on Glace Pack's land, even one disbanded from the Coven, they'd be put to death. No exceptions.

I realized too late that my words, while quiet, were very audible. A familiar sniffing noise began to fill the air, and I just barely saw a black pelt sweep around a tree. I hid behind one, chastising myself for having a white shirt. There were only two wolves in the Pack that had black fur, and I began to pray that the one who saw me was James. Thankfully, luck was on my side today.

"Radder?" that familiar voice said. I glanced around the tree to see him standing there, his head cocked to the side in curiosity.

"Yeah James," I said. "It's me."

"What are you doing around here? Don't you know that this is the Pack's territory?"

"I realized that when I remembered what town I was in."

"Where's your girl?" he asked. I could see a smile on his lips, despite the fact that he was in wolf form.

I lied to him, of course. "She went back to our house. I was trying to find something to bring back to her."

"How nice of you lover boy," he said. "What's on the menu? Human?"

"I try to drink as little Human blood as possible," I said. *At least I do now.*

"That's what they all say," he said. "Look, I know I'm supposed to protect the Humans from your kind and all, but really, I don't care what you do. It's how you live. I mean, you can't help it. It's just the way you are."

"So, what are you, a rebel Werewolf?"

"I guess so. Angel is probably plotting my death this very moment for back talking her."

"Well let's hope not."

"Seriously. Anyways, how'd you get kicked out of the Coven? I'm not trying to get into your personal business or anything, but I am rather curious."

"We weren't kicked out," I said. "We left."

"I see. Was it because she got teased for smelling like as wolf?"

"Hey, you listen here-" I said, my voice stopping the second I heard a female voice.

"James?" it said. It was Angel. "James, where are you?"

I whipped back around the tree just as she padded up to him.

"Jeez," she said. "You've been over here forever. I thought something had happened."

"Nope, I'm fine," he said.

"Well, have you found anything?"

"Nothing out of the ordinary, no."

"Well, then come with me. I want you to check around by the lake."

I waited to come out until I was sure they were gone. It was a long, long time before I dared to move from behind the tree, but I eventually mustered up the courage to expose myself. I was afraid of seeing a black or white pelt (or any other color) amongst the trees, but a quick overview of my surroundings told me that I was in fact alone. So, I continued my search for a small animal.

Again, I was struck with luck. A well camouflaged rabbit was hopping around near the tree, unaware of my presence until it was too late. It didn't take long to catch it and take its life away from it, but I was so thirsty it felt like it had taken forever. My fangs had drawn out as I killed the helpless bunny, so I was able to take its blood fairly quickly. When I'd drained its blood, I felt awful for the poor thing. It didn't feel right to just leave it on the forest floor to rot, so I decided to have a show of heart and bury it.

It only took a minute to dig a good-sized hole with my hands, so I buried it in less than three minutes. I was still a little thirsty, but I could feel the redness seeping out of my eyes. I felt better now, knowing that I'd be fine for the rest of the day. And better still, my girl was waiting for me to return to her. The thought made me smile, and I was just turning around to head back, when a voice stopped me in my tracks.

"Well, well, well, if it isn't Radder."

Benjamin.

Slowly, I turned back around to face my brother. He looked, in short, extremely pissed, like he wanted to rip my head off. I thought he was all alone, until a girl came up to him from behind a tree. And I nearly had a heart attack right on the spot. It was Magdelene.

"Surprised to see me?" she said. I couldn't even answer her.

However, words came out of my mouth that I didn't control. "How...? You're alive?"

"I sucked the venom out of her," Benjamin said. "I did just in time too, or she would've died for sure." I figured she must've lost a lot of blood. She was paler than normal, and looked sickly. But, despite it all, she was still alive and breathing.

Then, I noticed something else. Ben had his arm around her waist, and they were standing awfully close. I thought my eyes were playing tricks on me. But, no, it was exactly as it seemed. They were together now. I guess Amaury was right.

Amaury. She was waiting for me. I didn't have time for this.

"Well, it was nice talking to you guys, but I *really* need to get going."

"Oh, you're not going anywhere," Ben said. He stepped away from Magdelene and came closer to me. "And I wouldn't try to run. That'll just make things worse."

"What are you talking about?"

"Revenge, my dear brother, for setting my home on fire and attempting to kill my Coven."

"If I say I'm sorry will you forgive me?"

He chuckled, then became serious. "Not a chance."

Before I could process what was happening, Benjamin lunged for me. I managed to jump backwards though, and I took off. I ran on no particular path, and even climbed to the very top of a tree and jumped from treetop to treetop. I didn't exactly need to get away scot-free, but I had to at least warn Amaury and let her get away, and at least know what had become of me. I owed her that much.

I was nearly to her, still in the trees, when I misjudged a jump and fell flat on my face twenty feet below. It took me a moment to redeem myself and get over the shock, only to find that my nose and left arm had broken in the fall. Plus, I was covered in dirt and had scratches from head to toe; even my shirt was torn so badly it couldn't be called a shirt anymore. I didn't even want to think of how much worse it could've been. My wounds didn't heal fast enough for me to get away, and before my bones had even begun to mend, Benjamin and Magdelene were at my side.

"C'mon Radder," Ben said, "you're just making this worse for yourself."

He picked me up roughly by my right arm, while Magdelene took my broken one. I was hurting too bad to fight back. Plus, it's not like I could've anyways with a broken arm that was being injured further. Together, they practically dragged me all the way to Maufanges. My nose had already healed, but my arm wouldn't be anytime soon.

By the time the castle was visible, so were the stars in the sky. I wish there was someway to tell Amaury what had happened. Otherwise, she'd think I stood her up again. In fact, she might never talk to me again. I felt so awful for abandoning her, that I almost attempted at fighting and running, broken arm or not. But by the time I'd come up with a plan, we'd reached the castle. There was no going back now.

"Welcome back to the castle, Radder," Ben said. "Make yourself at home. You're going to be here for a long while."

The pair then disappeared upstairs, and I was about to

make a break for it when Maryanne and Adam appeared.

"Why are you here?" Adam asked. Back in the day, he'd been one of Ben's supporters in the debate over who should be King. He'd always hated me.

"I'm apparently a prisoner now."

"Good," he said. "Serves you right for trying to burn the place down and kill us all."

"Speaking of which," a voice said. It was Benjamin, coming back downstairs. "I'd show you the damage you did, but I just put Magdelene to bed."

"Wait, did you just say you put her to bed?"

"Well, thanks to that stupid girl of yours, she's been too weak to do much lately. I'm surprised she was even able to help me bring you back here. And, because of your girl, she needs help to do practically everything."

"Hold on," Adam said. "Who's his girl?"

Ben smiled, "Why, she's a-"

"Shut the hell up, Ben," I said.

"If I want to tell the members of my Coven who she is, I will, whether you like it or not." He turned back to Adam. "She's not a Human, nor Vampire, nor Werewolf. She's-"

"Benjamin!" a new voice suddenly called. Suddenly another familiar Vampire appeared, coming from the kitchen.

"What is it Razza?" Benjamin asked, his annoyance showing on his face.

"I was just wondering why that traitor is here, is all." she said. She looked at me and blinked, though of course no real anger showed on her face.

"He's our prisoner," he explained. "In fact, he should be heading for the dungeon in just a few minutes."

I felt my eyes widen. "*What?!?*"

"You didn't think you'd be staying in the actual house, did you? Please Radder, when has the Coven ever kept a prisoner that didn't stay in the dungeon?"

"Never," I whispered. I'd have to think of a way to escape faster than I'd thought. I glanced at Razza, who gave me a sympathetic gaze.

"Exactly," he said. "For now, you can walk around a bit. Maybe reminisce about the old days. But, remember, you'll always be under supervision, and you've got about five minutes before I'm sending you to the dungeon. So, I'd make the most of it if I were you."

Then, he was gone.

I walked a little bit forward, only to get a warning glance from Adam. "You're lucky you even get a single minute to wander around, yet alone five."

"It's just a trick. Don't you see? He's just trying to torture me with this."

"With what, exactly?"

"The fact that I'm in this house again. Don't you remember what happened here all those years ago?"

Adam went quiet then, though his eyes still held a glare.

"Razza," he said. "I want you to watch him. I need to speak with Mary."

Maryanne gave him a rather puzzled look, and I could hear panic in her mind. What did she have to worry about? I tried to see, delve into her mind, but they left in a flash. So, I was left all alone with Razza.

"Hey," she said.

"Hi," I said.

She came a little closer to me, giving me a quick hug. "How's my niece?" she asked.

"She should be OK, as long as Ben doesn't go looking for her."

"I told you to keep her existence a secret, Radder."

"I know," he said. "And believe me, I've tried as hard as I could. But, Magdelene told Ben. I couldn't have stopped her if I tried."

"I wish Annabel had never taken her in. If I had, you wouldn't even know her."

"Well, then I'm glad you didn't get to care for her."

"Ha ha, you're real funny. Stop playing games with her, Radder."

"What are you talking about?"

"You don't really care about her. I can tell."

I felt my anger rise up. "How could you ever think-?"

"Well, Radder, I hope you didn't waste your entire time chatting." Benjamin was making his way towards me from the parlor.

"There's no way it's been five minutes," I said.

"Well, it has. But, I guess you can have a few more to wander around, if you please. Except, Razza, I want you to come with me."

She began to head into the kitchen, right behind Ben. However, she turned to look at me and thought, *I'm sorry.*

Soon enough, I was all alone in this castle that had haunted me my entire life. I found myself wandering into the parlor. It still looked the same as it did hundreds of years ago. Nothing had changed.

There was a doorway in the back of the parlor that led to

Benjamin's room, as well as some vacant others. From where I stood, I could see the doors to the rooms. A shiver went down my spine. One of those rooms used to be Brock's. I left the parlor then, sick of the memories flooding in, and made my way upstairs. I headed toward Magdelene's room, which was giving off a stale scent of smoke. Of course, her room was vacant, she was sleeping somewhere else.

It was just shocking to see the damage. The carpet was completely scorched, as was everything else. Her closet doors had even burned completely off, as did most of her bed and curtains. I walked into her closet, seeing that some of her outfits had been destroyed too. That's when I noticed something. Behind her clothes, there was a wider space in the closet.

Moving aside the tattered shirts and such, I made my way in. There was a small table, holding an unburned box of matches and a bowl that was still full of water, plus a candle. I took a match out of the box, struck it, and lit the candle. I was so stunned at what I saw, that I was barely able to drop the match in the dish of water. There was a wooden crate on the back wall of the room. And on that crate, the bejeweled box that had once held the Fusion Night Necklace.

"You son of a bitch," I whispered. "I knew it was you."

Then, I snuffed out the candle and left Magdelene's room.

As I began to make my way back downstairs, a small voice called to me.

"Radder?"

I turned around to see Maryanne standing in the doorway of Adam's room.

"What?" I snapped. I was sick of being here. I needed to escape, and this was holding me back.

"Can I speak with you? It'll only take a minute, I promise."

I ran a hand through my hair, frustrated. "Fine," I said, making my way to where she stood, annoyance clearly pinned on my face. "What is it?"

"Come in here," she said. She stepped out off my way, motioning me inside.

Cautiously, I stepped into the room. Maryanne leaned out the doorway, checked that no one was around, and shut the door and locked it. Then she turned to face me and Adam, who was sitting on his bed.

"Radder," Mary said. "I've got a question for you."

"What about?" her thoughts were blocked, so I could only guess what was on her mind.

"Do you, um, happen to know a girl? That is, uh- how do I say this? Not a Human, but not a Vampire or Werewolf either? Like, a mix of the two."

I felt my eyes grow wide, my heart skipping a beat. *Amaury.*

Everything in me told me to deny it. But, why lie? She already knew the truth. So, I sucked in a breath and said, "Yes. Yes I do."

She glanced over at Adam, who closed his eyes and let out a deep breath.

"I told you Mary," Adam said in a harsh tone. "I told you they existed."

She just looked down at the ground, like she'd cry.

I couldn't believe I'd betrayed Amaury like that. So, sadly, I asked, "Why'd you want to know? And how'd you find out about her?"

"I think you need to leave," Adam said. I just noticed that Mary had begun to cry. Hesitantly, I nodded, and made my way back into the hallway, shutting the door softly behind me. I needed to get out of here. It was dark now. I knew Amaury would be waiting for me. I knew that right now, she was crying, waiting for me to return.

Once I left, I had to go and find her. I needed to hug her and kiss her and dry her tears and tell her that it's all OK, that I'm OK. But, escaping is my only problem. Until, a thought comes to mind. Magdelene and Benjamin got out of the castle during the fire by jumping out a window. Was it possible that I'd overlooked a broken window in Magdelene's room, and it was my ticket to freedom?

First off, I made sure nobody was around. Then, I crept towards the blackened room. Sure enough, the smaller window near Magdelene's bed was wide open, shards of glass still attached to the sill. I cleared bits of it away with my hand, then, I jumped through, glad my arm had healed in time for my escape. I landed near an old oak tree after falling a whole story, only to be met by Amaury's stale scent. She'd been here? When? And why?

I didn't even have time to think before I heard a noise coming from inside the castle. I snapped straight up from where I'd been crouching and flattened myself against the castle wall, keeping my thoughts to a minimum. Slowly and soundlessly, I crept through the grass and around the castle until I was at its front. Then, I bolted for the fence.

I made it there in no time at all, sliding through the thick iron bars to get into the forest. The second I was out of the Coven's prison of a home, I ran as fast as I could through the forest. *I'm coming Amaury*, I thought, though I knew she couldn't hear me. *Stay where you are. I'll find you. I promise.*

Never had I run so fast in my life. This time, I didn't pause to jump from tree to tree, or do anything else. I just full out ran. It didn't take long for me to reach the forest in Chiroux where, only an hour or so before, I was as happy as could be. Then, before I knew it, I'd reached the lake. It still sparkled, only now by the moonlight. As I searched around, I was hoping to see Amaury sitting, waiting for me. But she was gone.

She'd probably gone home long ago. And, even if she was still here, she probably wouldn't be too happy to see me. But I didn't care. I needed to see her. I began to head towards the spot where we'd been sitting, when I got a growing dread that I was being watched. I tried to ignore it the best I could, just following Amaury's scent, but soon it overwhelmed me.

"Who's there?" I called into the darkness. "Show yourself!"

"I'm here," a voice growled.

I literally felt my heart stop beating. "Who's here?" I asked the voice.

Suddenly, out of the darkness, a black wolf appeared. For a split second, I thought it was James. That is, until I looked into his eyes, which were a deep maroon red over brown.

"My name is Cajun," he growled. "And you are?"

I gulped. "Radder."

"Thor?"

I nodded, silently praying someone would help me.

"What are you doing here Radder?" he asked. "Just because you were banished from Maufanges doesn't mean you can settle in Chiroux. We own this town, not you."

Wrong Cajun. "I'm not settling here, I promise. Just passing through."

"Really?" he asked. "Well, now I know you're lying."

"What do you mean?"

"We found your castle. And not only your scent, but a girl's too."

Oh shit.

"And," he continued, "since we have proof that you live here, and proof that you are in fact alive, and not thirsty by the looks of it, then I can honestly say that you've been hunting on Glace pack's territory. And I'm assuming you do know the punishment for that, correct Radder? And the same punishment goes for your girl too."

"No," I said. "She's Human. Please, leave her be." The lie rolled right off my tongue.

"Human? Interesting that a once high-ranking Vampire would result to being with a Human girl. How pathetic."

"I thought you Werewolves loved Humans, considering you devote your lives to protect them."

"With all do respect," he said, "we devote our lives to killing your kind, not just protecting the Humans from you. And it seems as though we should turn your girl so that you don't kill her."

"Like I said, leave her be. I was never going to hurt her. Ever. I swear on the life of… of my father."

"Brock?" he said. "Aren't you a child to be proud of? Such a disgrace."

"At least I wasn't born a Werewolf."

"No, but you were born a Human. And I'm going to take it that you are so immersed in your long ago past that you've fallen in love with a Human. And, you can't really swear on Brock's life, since he wasn't your real father."

"But he did raise me as his own. I never even knew my real father."

"Well now, whose fault is that?"

I glared angrily at him, not believing those words had just come out of his mouth.

"Not mine," I whispered angrily. "Anyone's but mine."

Cajun growled angrily at me. "Come with me," he said. "You're a prisoner of Glace Pack now."

"I'll go with you when I'm dead."

"Well, you will be soon enough."

He sat down, not once taking his eyes from me, and sent a loud, piercing howl through the night sky. I sighed, not knowing how to get out of this one when the whole pack was coming for me. One bite from one wolf and I'd be dead, at the one time I'd ever wanted to be alive. It didn't take long for the other five wolves to appear. I couldn't believe how many of the Werewolves, and Vampires, were beginning to disappear. The Coven and the Pack had a maximum of six members each. It wouldn't take long for the war to wipe them all out.

Thinking of this, I nearly went into panic as the wolves began to surround me. I saw Angel for the second time today, two brown wolves, Avril and Avery, another named Charles, and, of course, James. James gave me a sorrowful look, knowing what was about to happen to me. Then, that sick realization came to mind. I was going to die.

The wolves crept closer to me, ears fattened, teeth bared. With each paw step, a wave of dread went through me. It didn't really scare me that I was about to die. The only real thing that scared me was knowing that I'd never see Amaury ever again.

What happened next was a complete blur. One minute, I'm fearing for my life. The next, Benjamin is standing in front of me.

"If I were you," he said to the wolves, "I'd back off right now."

"Why should we?" Angel said. "He's been hunting on our lands. According to our laws, we have the right to end his life."

"You're going to hold him prisoner, correct?"

"Yes, of course."

"Well, that's too bad. He's the Coven's prisoner."

"How?"

"We caught him… living in Maufanges after he was banished."

"Impossible," Cajun said. "We found a castle that had the scent of him and another swarming all over it."

"That castle's been vacant for years," Benjamin lied. "For all you know, he could've just been exploring it."

"Again, that's impossible. He admitted to living there."

Benjamin swung his head back and gave me the most vicious glare. *Nice going, dumbass*, he thought.

What are you doing here, Ben? I thought back. *You're going to get us both killed.*

He didn't answer though. Just turned away from me, knowing I was right.

"With whom, then?"

"Excuse me?"

"You said there was another scent there, so he had to be living with someone else. Who was it?"

"He said it was a Human girl."

"Oh, you mean Audrey? Nice girl." He was just trying to kill me.

"Sure..." Cajun said.

"I want her found," Angel said. "Charles, you go and search that castle again."

The golden-furred wolf nodded quickly, then padded off towards Amaury's castle.

Oh God, I thought. *She's going to be there.*

"Angel," Benjamin said. "I promise you that we are going to take care of him. You will never see him on your land again."

"Why should I trust a Vampire?" she snarled.

"If you've forgotten, he's an enemy to the Coven. That's why he was banished in the first place."

Angel paused for a long moment. "For now, Benjamin," she finally said. "But mark my words, this isn't over. Especially when we find that girl."

"I understand."

"Now, if you don't mind, leave our land. Now."

"Of course Angel," Ben said. Then he turned to me. "Let's go Radder."

Slowly, I trailed a little behind him as he began to head towards the castle. I could feel the heavy gazes of the wolves watching us go. Even as we got deeper into the forest, I couldn't help but feel like they were still watching my every move.

Benjamin and I walked in silence until I hissed, "What were you thinking?"

"I was thinking how I wanted to be the one to torture you, not them."

"Why didn't you just let them kill me, Ben?"

"Because, again, I wanted to do that. Anyways, if I'd let them, you never would've seen your precious Fusion girl ever again."

"She has a name you know."

"Yes, I know, but since she's lesser than us-"

I ran up to him and grabbed his shirt collar. "Don't you *ever* say that again."

"Whatever," he said. "Just let go of my shirt."

Reluctantly, I released my grip, matching pace with him as he began to walk again. A short ways in the distance, I could barely see a light. The source: Amaury's castle. I longed to be by her side again. Not only that, but I wanted to make sure she was OK and safe from the Werewolves. I'd take her to the ends of the Earth to protect her if I had to.

"So lover boy," Benjamin said. "You want to see your girl?"

"Of course I do."

"Then I wouldn't try escaping again. The more you try to and the more you do it, the longer stay you'll have in the dungeon."

"Why won't you just let me go?"

"Why should I?"

"Because you know how I feel."

"What are you talking about?"

"I saw you and Magdelene earlier."

His mind went blank. "That was nothing," he said.

"Didn't look like nothing. Amaury called it right. You love her."

"I don't love anyone or anything," he snapped.

"Now that is such a load of bullshit."

"OK," he said. "Then why don't you name everything that I supposedly love."

"Well, the Coven for starters. You'd die to protect everyone that lives in that castle. You loved, and still love, your dad, despite the fact that he was nothing but a cold-hearted bastard. You loved Dina, considering she was like our grandmother. And you love Magdelene. I just know it."

"How are you so sure I love her?"

"Because I read your mind, Ben. I know for a fact that you kissed her. It was all you could think about."

The look on his face when I said that was priceless.

"So, you caught me," he said. "Happy now?"

"Yes, very," I said.

He just sighed.

"You know," I said. "Loving someone is nothing to be ashamed of."

"Love is a sign of weakness."

"Does your whole life have to be centered around power? And anyways, how is it a weakness in any way?"

"It takes up all of your time. Then, loving someone consumes you. After that, it's impossible to want to do anything but spend every second of every day with that person."

"What's so awful about that?" I asked. "Sounds perfect to me."

"That's because you're a softy. You take the time to care for people, while I don't. That's why I'm better than you."

"In status and power, yes. In life, no."

I had him there. We just continued to walk, not another

word passing between us. When I turned around, I could still see the light from Amaury's castle in the distance. God, I missed her.

Not long now sweetheart, I thought to myself. *I'll see you soon.*

Right then is when I made my move. While Benjamin was in his own little world, I ran as fast as had when escaping the castle. Only this time, I jumped a few trees. I was attempting to get home, so when he got there and searched the rooms, I'd sneak back the way I'd come and return to her castle. It seemed simple. And I almost got away with it.

I got down from the trees and began to run again. While it took the same amount of time to jump the trees as it did to run, being airborne made the trip seem longer. About three seconds after I hit the ground though, I was knocked over, falling flat on my face. I tried to stand up, but before I knew it someone had grabbed my hands and chained them together.

"What did I tell you about running away?" Benjamin's voice asked in an angry tone.

He placed his knee on my back, making it impossible for me to stand. "Get off of me you asshole," I said through gritted teeth. He was just trying to piss me off.

He did as I asked, but still kept his hand gripped tightly around the chains. I stood up on my own, shaking a bit of dirt out of my hair. My shirt was in pieces, and the scraps fell away as I stood, one by one. Benjamin kept both hands on the chains and began to lead me through the trees. We were much closer to the Fanges Castle than I thought, considering that within a matter of minutes it came into sight.

We approached the gates, and Ben pulled a key out of his

pocket to unlock them. They swung open on their own once released from the lock, and so Ben led me through them, pausing only to shut and relock them.

"You shouldn't have run away," he said. "Now we're going to give you a more severe punishment."

"What are you going to do other than throw me in the dungeon?"

"Well, you're not going to be the only one getting hurt."

"What do you mean?"

"Let's just say that your girl better watch her back."

"You wouldn't dare lay a finger on her."

"What are you going to do? Yell at me 'til my ears bleed? Please, you're too much of a wuss to do anything to me if I harm her."

"You wanna bet?"

"Either way, you won't be able to, considering you're going to be kept in the castle or a *very* long time."

"That's OK. I'll get out eventually. And when I do, I'll just go and find her and explain what happened."

"How are you so sure that she'll believe you? Or take you back? You never know Radder, she might move on by the time I let you go."

"I doubt it. It took her three-hundred years to get over Rafe."

"But he meant more to her than you do."

"How do you know?"

"Because he understood what it was like to be different, to be forced to live in solitude for your whole life. And, he was the only other of her kind that has ever existed."

"None of that matters."

"It matters more to her than you realize." It struck me

then that he was right. I'd caught her thinking of him more than once, after all.

We approached the doors then, and Benjamin quickly led me back inside the castle's walls. Adam was just coming downstairs, with Maryanne behind him, as we walked in. They both stared at me, appalled by me being shirtless and covered head to toe in mud. Unfortunately, I didn't see Razza anywhere.

"What happened to you?" Maryanne asked. I just looked at her.

"Well, Radder," Ben said then. "Get one last glimpse of the light. Because you aren't going to be seeing it again for a *long* time."

Then, without another word, he led me to a door by the staircase, opened it, and led me inside. I was instantly swallowed by the darkness, and I could just barely see in front of me. As my eyes adjusted to the darkness, though, I was able to see the whole dungeon, including the window Amaury and I had broken to get into the castle. The window hadn't yet been fixed, and it only reminded me that our castle break-in had only been yesterday. But right now, it seemed like a hundred years ago. Ben suddenly swerved to the left, leading me into one of the chambers. For the second time today, I felt my heart skip a beat.

"What?" he asked. "A little too familiar for you?"

I swallowed hard. This was the chamber that Brock had bit me in.

Ben tried to shove me in, but my feet wouldn't budge. I wouldn't allow myself to be forced in here. Not again.

"Scared?" Ben asked.

I didn't even have time to answer before everything went black.

Chapter 8
Lies

Magdelene:

I woke up not knowing where I was. Then, everything came flooding back. I was sleeping in the previously vacant bedroom next to my old one. After I remembered that, a memory of me being in the woods with Benjamin surfaced. It didn't take long for me to recall that I'd been there to help him drag Radder here to be held as a prisoner. I smiled at that thought, wishing I could've seen his face when he was taken back into the room where his life was ruined.

I tried to sit up, but couldn't thanks to my weariness. I didn't understand how I was still so tired. I'd been standing for ten minutes last night and felt like I was about to drop over dead. I still felt like I would, in fact, when I'd been asleep for who knows how long. So, out of exhaustion, I lay back down and tried to remember my last memories from last night. Benjamin had tucked me in, so to speak, and made sure I was asleep before he left the room. He kissed me, and told me he loved me, and I'd never been happier my whole life.

I wished he was here now.

"I am."

I jumped up from where I lay, searching around the room. Ben was sitting in a chair near the door, staring at nothing.

"What are you doing here?" I asked.

"I came to check on you."

"How long ago?"

"About five minutes ago."

"And you've just been sitting there?"

"I was waiting for you to wake up," he said.

"Why?"

"Because I need your help."

"With what?"

"I told Radder we were going to hurt Amaury. So, we need a plan on what we're going to do."

"That's gonna be a little difficult, don't you think?"

"Maybe," he said. "Unless you can think of a plan. 'Cause I'm all out of ideas."

I thought for a long while. Ben came over and lay beside me after a few minutes, and for some reason that made the thoughts come easier. It didn't take very long for me to come up with a master plan after that.

"It's simple," I said. "We hold her prisoner too, and then tell Radder she's dead. All we'll have to do is come up with something to use as "proof" that she's dead. Then, when we let him go, he'll find that her castle is empty, and he'll believe our story. Then, he'll disappear forever and we'll never have to see him again. And we won't let her go until he's long gone so that they can't find each other. It'll take a while and a lot of careful moves, but it'll work."

Benjamin looked at me, his eyes shinning. "That is the absolute *greatest* plan I have ever heard!" he exclaimed.

He pulled me to him then, and kissed me softy. "No wonder I love you so much," he said.

"That didn't make sense."

"Sure it did. It's a great plan, and I love you for coming up with it."

I shrugged. "You could've worded that differently. And I hope that isn't the only reason you love me."

"Of course not," he said. "Just one of many."

"Well, that's good. I guess."

"So, do you think you're OK to get up?"

"Of course," I said. "I'm better than ever."

"Good," he said. "I'll be right outside. If you need anything at all just call for me."

"I will." He got up off my bed then and exited my room, shutting the door softly behind him.

Slowly, I stood, trying to find my bearings in the pitch-black darkness. I was still so unused to this room, and it took me a few moments to find my desk, where a candle, matches, and a dish of water lay. I withdrew a match from the box, struck it, lit the candle wick, and discarded the match into the water within a matter of seconds. Instantly, the room was filled with light.

Finally able to see, I made way to my curtains and opened them. A flood of daylight swept into the room, the glory of the sun's rays shaming the small flicker of light coming from the candle. It was pointless to keep it lit with all the light coming in, so I blew out the candle, watching the ghost-like smoke rise from where the flame had just been. Afterwards,

I began to rummage through the drawers and closet, trying to find something to wear. I settled for a black skirt, the hem laced with frills, and a matching shirt (minus the frills).

Once I was dressed, I quickly ran a brush through my awfully mangled hair. Then, when I seemed ready, I stepped out of my room to greet the world. Benjamin was waiting just outside, as he said he would be.

"Hello," he said. "Nice seeing you again."

"Ditto."

Ben strode over to me and hugged me tightly. "I missed you," he said.

"You were gone five minutes."

"I know," he said. "But any time away from you at all is pure torture."

I smiled in spite of myself. We stood in the middle of the hallway for a long time, just holding each other, when Razza came upstairs.

"Benjamin," she said.

He didn't release his hold on me. "What?" he asked, turning to answer her.

"Have you decided what we're doing with Radder yet?"

He gave her a suspicious look, a lie forming in his head. "No..." he said. "I'm still thinking about it."

"Well," she said. "Let me know right away when you get a plan going."

"Why?" he asked. His suspicion only grew.

"No particular reason," she said, trying to ignore his accusing gaze. "I just want to know as soon as possible so I can help."

"Alright," Ben said. "Well, I'll be sure to tell you as soon as we've got an idea going."

"OK," she said. "Thanks Ben."

"No problem," he said. She began to descend down the stairs, leaving us alone again.

Ben turned back to face me. "Now, where were we?" he asked.

He leaned in closer, just about to kiss me, when again a voice pierced the silence.

Adam came out of his bedroom, saying, "Hey, Ben, what's the plan?"

Benjamin sighed angrily before turning to look at him. "We're not sure yet," he said. "But we're working on it."

"Looks to me like the only thing you're working on is scoring one with your girl."

"Adam!" Ben said. He didn't look very happy.

Adam's face was red from attempting to hold back a laugh. "Dude, chill. Seriously. It was a joke."

"Whatever," Ben grumbled, anger still showing in his voice.

"Really, though, there's no plan in effect yet?"

"No, there's not. Now, I'd recommend you leave before I'm tempted to rip your head off."

Adam put up his hands in self-defense. "Hey," he said. "It's not my fault you chose to make out in the middle of the hallway. You two should get a room."

Before Ben could reply, Adam was gone.

Anger was still in his eyes, but when he turned back to me it began to ebb. He glanced around a couple times to be sure we were definitely alone, whispered "Finally," and then kissed me.

Of course though, there was another interruption.

"Ben?" Maryanne asked, appearing out of nowhere.

"Oh my God, every time!" he exclaimed.

"What?"

"Never mind," he said. "What do you want?"

"I was just curious if you came up with a plan yet."

"Oh my God, *NO*! We haven't come up with *any* plans yet! Jeez! Can no one understand this?!?"

"OK, wow, calm it down a bit. I'm just gonna go now," she said hurriedly, quickly heading downstairs.

Ben rubbed his temples. "Sometimes I think they all gang up and do that just to get on my nerves."

"I'm sure it's just a random coincidence." I said. "Maybe if you told one of them we had a plan, they'd tell the others and you wouldn't have to go through this again."

"Maybe so," he said.

"Why didn't you tell them, anyways?"

"You didn't read Razza's mind, did you?"

"I'm too weak right now," I reminded him. "Why do you ask?"

"I think she's up to something," he admitted.

"Like what?"

"I'm getting the vibe that she doesn't hate my brother as much as she claims."

"Maybe they have a secret relationship."

"You know as well as I do that he's with your sister. And, while he's a little screwed up in the head, I wouldn't take him as the type to cheat on a girl with her aunt."

"Good point, but still. With Radder, you never know what's in store."

"Exactly. That's also why you should never trust him. Amaury's made a big mistake."

Something was starting to bug me. "What if my plan doesn't work?"

"It'll work. Trust me. I know how to make it look like someone's dead. It's quite simple."

"What do we have to do?"

"The only hard part about it is getting some of her blood. The rest of it is easy enough it doesn't need an explanation or extremely careful planning."

"Well, that's good at least."

"Believe me. It won't fail. And if it does, then we'll just find another way to keep them apart. Simple."

"Right," I said. "'Cause that's just so simple."

"Really, it is. Do I have to explain?"

"If you will."

He sighed. "All we have to do, basically, is injure her somehow and get some of her blood. Then, we place it on… What kills a Fusion?"

"You should know," I said. "You killed one."

"But that was a long time ago. Besides, when you told me about your sister I couldn't believe she was a Fusion, and I thought you were crazy. Remember?"

"Yeah, I do. Unfortunately, I've no idea how you're supposed to kill one."

"Well, there a combination of Vampires and Werewolves, right?"

"Yes…"

"So, what if we drove a silver-tipped stake through her heart?"

"That might work. Even without the silver."

"How would that be logical if it had no silver on it?"

"Based on common knowledge, I'm pretty sure Fusions are a little more Vampire than they are Werewolf."

"What gave you that idea?"

"Well, we are fast, and really strong, can read minds or tell the future, and have fangs. Fusions have all those qualities. And, they can turn into wolves, just like the Werewolves can, only Fusion venom not only kills Vampires, but Werewolves too. So, based on all that, they have more Vampire traits than they do Werewolf."

"You know something?" he said. "You might just be right."

"Of course. I'm always right."

"Oh, I'm sure," he said, chuckling as I lightly hit his arm at the offensive comment.

"Anyways," he said. "We get her blood, dip a stake in it, and give it to him as proof. You may have to get some blood on your hands too, if you know what I mean. It'll make it seem more realistic."

"I know that," I said. "Go on."

"So, once he thinks she's dead, everything goes as you planned. So, it really is simple."

"How are we getting her blood, though?"

"We'll do that when we capture her."

"Right."

"I'll have you know that the wolves almost got Radder last night. They found Amaury's castle."

"So?"

"So, I'm afraid that they might get to her before us."

"Oh no they won't," I said. "And if they do, then we'll just go and take her back."

"They won't allow it."

"What?"

"They told me I could have Radder. But if they found Amaury first, they got to hold her prisoner over us."

"But that's not fair!" I said.

"I know. I tried to persuade them to let us hold her prisoner, but, they're Werewolves. They never listen to reason."

"Well, yeah. They're just so proud of owning Chiroux that they think they can control what happens to everyone who lives there. And anyways, I think Amaury should own that town."

"Well, of course. But, if we tell the wolves about her, they'll get greedy and destroy her before we get the chance."

"Good point. In fact, if we told them about her, they might join our side to kill her."

"I fought by the Werewolves' side once before. I'd rather not do it again."

"They must be good fighters though, considering there's more of them than there are us."

"Not necessarily. Radder still counts, even if he isn't part of the Coven. The number is even."

"Boy do I hate him. Why in Brock's right mind did he make Radder the King over you? In fact, why'd he even take him in in the first place?"

"Well, that was a while ago, and a bit off subject," he pointed out. "But, nobody really knows why he was made the King. I guess he just thought that Radder would do better than me. And I've already told you how and why he took him in."

"Well, I don't remember."

"Me and my parents raided his house and killed his parents after setting it on fire. My mother died in the house with them. My father tried to save her, but couldn't get to her. And when he saw Radder was the last one in the house that was alive, he saved him. That's why these days none of us tortures Humans for a while before killing them. Too many of our kind get hurt."

"I'm sorry about your mother," I said. I couldn't believe I'd forgotten that story.

"It's OK," he said. "I barely even knew her."

"You do realize that that makes it even worse."

"Probably. But you can't really cry and grieve for someone you didn't know."

"I'm sure you were crying."

"At her funeral, yes. But I was three, and that's when I knew her. So, of course I was crying."

"Still, that's horrible."

"If I recall correctly, I'm not the only one with a dead mother."

"Amaury killed her," I hissed. "Why do you think I hate her so much?"

"I thought you hated her because of what she is?"

"Well, that too. Why do you hate Radder so much?"

"Well, first off, he stole my rightful position as King."

"Which you got back."

"Yes. Then, he betrayed the Coven by having a relationship with a Human girl. He killed my father. It was partially his fault that my mother died. And, possibly the biggest of all, is that he was raised by us solely to replace my real little brother."

"You had an actual brother?"

"Yes. But I never got to meet him. He died with my mother in the fire."

"That's awful."

"I know. That's why Brock took Radder in. To replace the son he never knew. If only my mother wouldn't have died, Radder wouldn't be alive right now."

"Wouldn't the world just be so much better without him?"

"Yes, it would. Which is why we're keeping him prisoner. Think, in a week or two, we'll never have to see his face again."

"I can't wait for that day."

"Neither can I."

"Do you think Amaury will go searching for him?"

"I highly doubt it. And, she'll probably have limits as to how far she'll go to look for him. I don't think we have anything to worry about."

"Good," I said. "The last thing we need is her finding him and bringing him home."

"Maybe we should actually kill her then," he said. "Then there'll be no risk at all."

"That's a little harsh though, considering we're already taking her boyfriend. We'll end her life another time."

"Deal. Now, what do you say? Should we head downstairs?"

"Why not? I'm thirsty."

"I figured you would be. C'mon, let's go." He took my hand, and we slowly made our way down the steps and into the kitchen. From there, he headed for the fridge and began to rummage through it.

"Any particular type?" he asked.

"No, anything's fine."

"Alright," he said. He pulled a random container out and set it on the counter, while I leaned against the table. While he got two wineglasses, I tried to read the label on the tub, but couldn't since it was turned away from me. Ben quickly poured the blood into the two glasses, then returned the container to the fridge.

"Here you are," he said, handing me a glass.

I took a sip of it, quickly recognizing Type A blood. "Is this your favorite or something?" I asked him.

He smiled. "You know it," he said, before guzzling it down with one drink. Some ran down the sides of his mouth, which he quickly wiped away.

I just sipped mine, trying to act proper, while I was so thirsty that I wanted to just guzzle it down like he had. But if there's one thing my mother taught me, it was how to act in front of the guy you liked.

Ben placed his glass in the sink, then came towards me. He took my glass and set it on the table behind me. Then, he pulled me to him and kissed me. His breath tasted like blood, and I was still incredibly thirsty. It was hard for me to pull away from him. Somehow though, I managed. As soon as I pulled away, I picked up my drink and finished it off, despite the fact that blood would run down the sides of my mouth. Screw manners. I was thirsty.

When I finished it, I wiped the remaining blood from my face and pried myself from Ben's embrace. I set the glass in the sink, then turned around to meet Ben's gaze.

"What?" I asked.

"Nothing," he said, shaking his head. "I was just spacing out."

"OK..."

"I'm going to the parlor," he announced out of nowhere. "Care to join me?"

"Sure…" I said. He turned and left the room then, so I followed close behind.

When we entered the room, the rest of the Coven was scattered about on the chairs and couches.

"Hello, everyone," Ben said. "Why are you all gathered in here?"

"We're discussing some plans," Adam spoke for the trio. "What've you come up with?"

"Well, we aren't exactly sure what we're keeping him away from, but considered just leaving him there forever until he dies of thirst."

"We're keeping him away from a girl."

"A girl?"

"Some Human girl he's in love with."

"But you said she was…"

"Never mind about that," he said. "I was mistaken."

"Well, we could easily kill her then or something."

"Magdelene came up with a plan somewhat similar. I think it's going to work." Four pairs of eyes focused on me.

"Well," Razza said, "what is it?"

"Basically, we fake her death."

"How?"

"We cut her with… something… and spill blood on the floor and on the "murder" weapon, so it seems like she really is dead. Then, we capture her and keep her in the dungeon too. After she's safely locked away, we show Radder the weapon and prove she's "dead." Then, when we release him, he'll go to her house to find the blood on the floor and actually believe us. That'll make him leave forever, and once he leaves this town we'll let her go and live her life without him.

I know it seems lengthy and a little difficult, but I think it just might work."

They all stared at me in silence, until Maryanne said, "That's genius!"

"Exactly what I thought," Ben said. "So, do you guys think we should go through with it?"

"Of course," Adam said. "It'll work perfectly."

"I think we should get her blood for the weapon before we capture her though," Mary stated.

"Why?" I asked.

"'Cause then we can tell him before we capture her, and that'll crush him even more. Because if we wait, all he's doing is standing in the chamber, which isn't complete torture. But if we tell him, he'll probably only be able to think of her and become so upset that as soon as you release him he'll leave Guéret."

"Good idea," I said. "When will we go and do that?" I asked.

"When it gets to be dark," Ben said. "Unless we do it now. But that would involve knocking her out."

"Which means whacking her head with a hard object. I'm in for it."

"Good," he said. "Although, we'll probably end up doing that no matter what time of day it is."

"Yeah, I know," I said, "but I can't wait."

He chuckled. "Well, then what do you say we head to the Sleet Castle for a little visit?"

"I say that sounds like a great idea," I said laughing. "C'mon, let's go!"

Ben turned to face everybody else. "Any of you care to

join us?" They all shrugged, their minds all saying, *I'm good, no thanks*, in near unison.

So, Ben and I headed towards the door, alone. We walked out into the crisp afternoon air, and began the long journey to Chiroux. Unless we ran, it'd take well over an hour to get there.

Ben slid his hand into mine, and inched closer to me. "Are you gonna be OK?"

"Of course I will," I said. "I managed to help bring Radder here, didn't I?"

"Yes, but, you were so weak afterwards…"

"So? I was poisoned and about three seconds away from dying before you sucked out the venom. Do you know how much blood I lost? I should've died. But, I didn't, and I'm OK now. I promise."

He squeezed my hand, then sighed. "I wish you wouldn't talk about that," he said. "It's not my favorite memory."

"Sorry," I said. "Just trying to make a point."

"I know," he said. "I just don't like thinking about how close I was to losing you."

I didn't really know what to say after that. So Ben spoke for me.

"I love you," he said, "more than you'll ever know."

I felt myself blush at his words, and very quietly I said, "I'd say the same thing if I knew how to word it."

He stopped walking them, taking my other hand and pulling me into an embrace so I could be closer to him.

"Promise me you'll be careful today, OK?" he whispered in my ear. "I couldn't stand it if something happened to you."

"You know I'll be fine," I said. "Now, let's get a move

on. We're not gonna capture her easily if we're just standing here."

"Ah, but remember, we're not capturing her..."

"Yeah, yeah, we're just knocking her out, getting her blood for the weapon, yadda yadda yadda. I know. But it's easier to say capture than all of that, isn't it?"

He didn't speak after that. Instead, he just took my hand in his again and began to walk away. He was practically dragging me until I got the right footing to walk on my own.

You could've been a little nicer about that, I thought harshly.

Sorry, he thought back. He looked pretty angry. Probably because of me.

"No," he said. "Not because of you."

"Then why?"

"Because I'm still really pissed off at your sister."

"I see," I said, nodding my head. "She seems to spend every minute she's alive pissing somebody off."

"Very true. But we won't have to deal with her for much longer. Radder will be out of this town within the week, and your sister will never talk to us again. It's a win-win deal for everyone. Except them."

"But it's fine if they're miserable."

"Exactly. Because, if you ask me, we're the only ones who matter."

"I'll have to agree with you on that."

"Good," he said. "Will you be OK if we speed up?" he asked.

"Of course," I said. "Why wouldn't I be?"

He opened his mouth to say something, but changed his mind and snapped it shut. His mind wasn't sending out waves of what he was going to say, so I was left clueless to his words.

Gradually, we increased our pace to a speed walk. Or, I guess, what we call a speed walk. To a normal Human, it'd be more of a fast jog. The time it took to reach Chiroux absolutely flew by at that speed, and soon I saw Amaury's castle looming over the treetops.

You ready? Ben thought to me.

You know it, I thought. *Let's go.*

Silently, we crept through the woods, trying not to make a sound, just in case Amaury was outside tending to her garden. When we got closer to the castle, we peeked through the trees, trying to see if she was there. It seemed that the coast was clear, so we began to exit the woods. Then, suddenly, Amaury came around from the back of the castle, watering can in hand, and made Benjamin and I dive backwards into the shadows of the trees. She moved extremely slowly, like her feet were made of lead. She also kept sniffing. Was she *crying*? If so, *why*?

The reason came to me in an instant. Images of Radder flooded into my mind, like memories. Only, they belonged to Amaury, not me or Benjamin. In fact, Benjamin must've seen them too, because he shook his head and said, "Pathetic."

While I completely agreed with him, I also felt a bit of sympathy for my sister. She thought Radder had left her. She had no idea what really happened. Bit by bit, Amaury got closer to her castle's door. She stopped a few times on the way to water some flowers, and then, finally, she went inside. I let out a deep breath.

"That was close," Benjamin said. "We'll wait a couple of minutes until we're sure she's in another room."

"How can we be sure?"

"Well, I guess we'll just have to play it by chance then. We'll go around to the left side of the castle and find a way in there, so she doesn't spot us by mistake."

"Sounds good to me."

"I say it's about time we go. I can't wait to see Radder's face when we tell him that she's dead."

"Same here," I said. "You brought the weapon, right?"

"A silver-tipped stake?" he asked. "Right here." He pulled the tip out of his cloak's sleeve, causing the silver on it to gleam in the limited sunlight.

"Good," I said. "Now, what're we waiting for?"

Soundlessly, we began to make our way toward Amaury's castle. We weaved through the trees, trying to remain in shadow, until we came to the woodland on the left side of the house. From there, we darted over to the stone walls of the fortress. We scanned along the walls, trying to find a good place to break in.

"Last time I came in through that window," I said, pointing upwards and a ways over to the left. "It leads to her bedroom."

"Do you think she's in there right now?"

"I highly doubt it."

"Then I say we go in that way. How'd you get up there?"

"I jumped and scaled the wall a ways," I said sarcastically.

"Really?"

"No, you idiot. I obviously climbed the tree that is right by her window." About a yard away from her window was a giant sycamore, inched over just so. When you were in her room, you couldn't see its branches unless you stood at a certain angle. If you just waltzed right into her room, you might not even know the tree was there.

Ben and I made way over to the tree. "Ladies first," he said, gesturing at the tree.

"Mind you, I'm wearing a skirt. This time the gentleman will have to go first."

"Fine," he said. "But if I fall and break my neck because I don't know what I'm doing, it'll be your fault."

"If that happens I will gladly take the blame."

"Good," he said. "Just promise that if it happens you'll finish this plan."

"Will do," I said. "It'd be my pleasure."

Luckily, Benjamin made it up to one of the top branches without falling or breaking his neck. He inched forward on a sturdy branch until he was near the window.

"Now what?" he said.

"Jump and grab the sill. You'll have to balance with your feet on the stones and open the window with one hand. Then, when it's open, you have to swing one of your legs over the sill and go in."

"Because that's not completely impossible at all."

"Hey, if I did it before, you can to. It's really pretty easy, so long as you time your jump right."

"Great, that makes me feel better. What if I misjudge the distance?"

"You're a Vampire; it won't happen. And, if by some random chance it does, then you *will* fall and break your neck. Long story short, *don't mistime the jump*."

"Gotcha," he said. "Well, here I go."

Benjamin jumped the three feet to the window clearly,

grabbing the sill with both hands just in time. He reached out and grabbed the window, yanking it open one-handed. Before he lost grip, he swung his leg over the sill and slid into the castle.

He looked out the window and down at me. "Your turn."

Quickly, I scrambled up the tree and onto the branch he'd jumped from. I settled myself on the branch, the leapt for the sill. Up until that point I thought it was the branch I'd jumped from about a week ago, but once I jumped I soon realized it wasn't. I mistimed the jump by a mile, and I felt as gravity began to pull me down.

Suddenly though, I felt as a strong hand gripped my arm and stopped me from falling. Another hand reached out to me, and I slowly placed my hand in it. I felt myself be pulled upward and in through the window, where I met Ben's warm embrace.

"Are you alright?" he asked.

I nodded shakily. "I'm fine."

"What happened?" he asked.

"I don't know," I said. "I guess I just thought I already knew where to jump, but it wasn't the branch I was used to, so it was mistimed. And then I couldn't reach the sill, and I just got so scared-"

"Shh, it's OK," he said. "You're alright now, and you're going to be just fine."

"I know," I said. "Thank you."

"Anytime love," he said. "Now, let's go and find Amaury."

"Alright," I said.

Slowly he pulled away from me and began to walk towards the door. I took a moment to shut the window, then hurried to follow him. He opened the door without making a sound, and slowly began to walk the floor of the house. I followed his tracks perfectly, trying to make as least noise as possible. Once, though, he stepped on a creaky floorboard. It made an awful groaning sound, and I couldn't see how nobody could've heard that. I was sure we'd be caught, but there wasn't a noise anywhere. I realized then that I wasn't hearing any thoughts.

Where do you think she went? I thought.

I've no idea. We'll just have to keep searching for her.

I nodded, although he couldn't see it, and just continued to follow him.

As we got closer to the stairs, I finally began to hear some words streaming through my head that didn't belong to me. By the sound of them, Amaury was writing in her diary. That meant she had to be sitting at her desk. Benjamin and I ducked low, since we were at the very top of the stairwell. She could see us clearly from where she was, since there was no cover for us, but it was harder for her if we kept low.

Now? I thought.

Now.

Fast as lightning, Benjamin and I bolted down the stairs. Amaury heard us about halfway down though and stood up, ready to defend herself. When we reached the last of the stairs, Ben and I jumped and ran straight at her. She tried to dodge us, but we were a little too quick for her. I grabbed her arms and twisted them together in the blink of an eye, promising she wouldn't get away until we were finished with her.

"Well, well, well." Benjamin said, approaching her. "What've we got here?"

Amaury just glared at him.

"Now now, we're not going to hurt you. At least, not *that* bad."

"Why do I find that hard to believe?" she spat at him. Anger was flaring in her pale blue eyes.

"Probably because I've done something like this a few times before. Really though, all we need is a sample of your blood, if you'd just cooperate."

"Why do you need my blood?" she asked. "Gonna prove my existence and turn me in to the Werewolves? Well, go ahead. See if I give a damn."

"That's not really what we were planning, but that is a rather good idea. We'll have to take this to them after we go through with our original plan."

"And what is your plan exactly?" she asked.

"That's for us to know and for you to find out."

"You do realize that I can only find out if you tell me, right?"

"Right you are. And, since we don't want you to know, then we're not going to tell you. It's as simple as that."

Amaury just rolled her eyes at him. "Do your worst," she said.

Benjamin took one of her arms from my grasp and held it himself. "This'll only hurt a little." Then, he grabbed the stake and plunged it through her arm.

Amaury's eyes closed shut tightly, but she didn't make a sound, or any other movements to show it had hurt. Her blood began to seep onto the stake, down her arm, and began to pool on the floor. Benjamin let it flow until the stake was just about soaked before he removed it from her arm. There was now a nice puddle of her blood all over the floor, and Amaury's arm was soaked in it.

We should stitch that for her, so she doesn't die, I thought quickly to Ben.

Why? Don't we want *to get rid of her?*

Yes, but we're only faking her death, remember? It's unnecessary to kill her.

Fine, he thought. *But you'll regret not finishing the job one day.*

Amaury was gripping her arm, obviously in pain. She was trying to hide it, but the look on her face made her pain extremely obvious.

"Do you have stitches anywhere?" I asked.

She nodded, but couldn't speak. *In the upstairs bathroom. The supplies are in the medicine cabinet*, she thought.

I nodded, and quickly ran upstairs to retrieve the kit. It wasn't hard to find, and when I had it I ran back down the stairs to where Amaury and Benjamin stood. I told her to move her hand, and when she did her wound spurted more blood. I took a string that was in the kit and tied it around her lower arm to stop the blood flow. Afterwards, I cleaned the blood that was around the wound and began to stitch it up so it'd heal properly. Once that was time, I quickly returned the kit to where it belonged, and then rushed back downstairs.

"Now," Benjamin was saying. "That wasn't so bad, was it?"

"Not really. I was expecting *much* worse."

"Well, you're going to get a lot worse. Not now, but in good time."

She gave a sarcastic smile. "Great," she said. "Can't wait."

"I'll bet you can't," he said.

"Are you going to be leaving anytime soon?" she asked. "Because I really don't like either of you being in my house."

"Of course," he said. "In just a moment." *Grab something hard to hit her with*, he thought to me. *And hurry*.

Right, I thought. I glanced around, deciding to choose the first thing I saw. And that thing happened to be a candleholder.

Go, now, he thought.

I ran straight past the both of them, absolutely flying, and snatched up the candleholder. Amaury didn't even have time to think before I bashed it against her head. She fell to the floor just as it slammed into her head, her mind slipping into the darkness of unconsciousness. Benjamin took it from me, and slammed it down on her head once more to keep her in that unconscious state. Then, when we were positive she wouldn't be waking anytime soon, we left the castle and headed back to Maufanges.

It didn't take long to reach our home. We speed walked to get there, and since we were so happy everything had gone as planned, our adrenaline made us go even faster. I son saw the Fanges Castle looming over the treetops, and I smiled in spite of myself. Radder's world was about to come crashing down around him.

Benjamin was so impatient to get inside that he didn't bother to unlock the gates. Instead, we both slid through the bars to get onto our land. We strode quickly over to the doors, and when we walked in, we were met by three pairs of eyes. Adam, Maryanne, and Razza all stood at the foot of the stairs, wondering if the plan had been successful.

"Well," Adam said, "did you get it?"

Benjamin held up the blood-covered stake, making all of their eyes grow wide with shock. He waved it around so that they all took it in, and then asked, "Is Radder awake?"

Adam nodded. "Yeah," he said. "I went to check on him a few minutes ago." The look in his eyes told me he wasn't telling the whole truth.

"Good," Benjamin said. "Now, if you'll excuse us, Magdelene and I have some business to attend to."

Benjamin began to head towards the dungeon doors. I felt the Coven's eyes watching me leave, burning into my skin. I tried to ignore it the best I could, but it seemed as though they were watching my reactions to their thoughts, like they were trying to hide something. Something big. I slowly followed Benjamin down the stairs, hoping to break their gazes as quickly as possible. I was a little exhausted, but I wasn't about to show it when the moment I'd worked all day for was about to happen. Walking into the darkness, I suddenly felt a chill. I felt sorry for Radder, having to stay down here in complete darkness. Plus, to make things worse, he was all alone.

"Do you want to tell him, or would you rather have me?" Ben asked, loud enough for Radder to hear.

"I will," I said. "Better he hears it from me, I say. I mean, I am her sister after all."

Ben nodded, and at that moment we approached the cell. Ben opened the door, and I walked into the pit of darkness. The first thing I saw before my eyes focused was glowing red eyes.

"What do you want?" Radder growled. "Haven't you two tortured me enough for one day?"

"Not quite," I said. "I've got something to tell you. It's not the best of news."

I could see him clearly now. He had no shirt, and he was covered head to toe in mud. Ew. His legs were shackled together, his arms chained upwards and outwards, so his hands were even with the crown of his head.

His thirsty red eyes narrowed. "I smell blood," he said. "And the scent is familiar." Just barely, I could see his hands shaking. He knew exactly whose blood he was scenting, and he didn't like it.

"What did you do to her?" he growled. His voice was as shaky as his hands.

I said, simply, "She's dead Radder."

I saw as his eyes widened in shock, although he'd already known what I was going to say. His mind was full of mixed thoughts. But soon, his eyes narrowed again.

"You liar," he said.

"I'm not lying, Radder. Here, see for yourself." I rolled the blood-covered stake toward him. Only the tiniest hint of silver was visible on its tip.

"Wha-? What is this?" he asked, the look of shock back on his face.

"That's the murder weapon. And, as you can see, it's completely covered in her blood."

"No," he said. "No. I don't believe this. I-" While he tried to deny it, the look on his face showed me he bought every word. He saw the silver on it as easily as I did, and he knew it was the ideal weapon for killing a Fusion. I saw his eyes began to well with tears.

"I'm sorry Radder," I said, walking forward to retrieve the stake. "But we had to do it."

He didn't speak; just closed his eyes and hung his head. He squeezed his eyes, trying to hold back the tears, but I could plainly see them stream down his face.

Ever so slowly, I backed out of the cell and shut the door behind me. Benjamin stood outside of the door, waiting for me. I nodded to him, letting him know that the deed was done. He let a small, wicked smile grow across his face. We began to make our way upstairs, and as soon as the door was closed to the dungeon, and Radder was well out of earshot, he gave me a giant hug.

"Well done my love," he said, and then he kissed me.

Chapter 9
Taken

Amaury:

I swung open the doors to my castle, only to find clutter *everywhere.* Somebody had been in here, searching through my stuff. Suddenly, I began to panic. *My diary!* I thought. If anybody had gotten a hold of that, it'd be the death of me for sure. I ran over to my desk, but the worn, leather-bound book still sat where I'd had it last. It seemed to be untouched.

Relieved that it was safe, I surveyed the damage in my house once more. Practically everything I own was on the floor, strewn all over. I scented the air, trying to discover the identity of the perpetrator, when I realized that there were six different scents. *Glace Pack*, I thought. But what had they wanted here?

I began to make rounds, picking things up here and there. Once the parlor was clean and everything was returned to its place, I searched the rest of my house. The kitchen was clean, so I decided to go upstairs. I searched every room but my bedroom, checking that they were all free of clutter, before I searched the room I slept in. It was fairly obvious that most of the damage would be in there.

When I was sure nothing else had been searched, I wandered into my bedroom. The door had been left ajar by the wolf, or wolves, who had searched it, so I'd already gotten a glimpse of the damage. But I never suspected it was this bad. I couldn't even see the floor. There were mostly papers that were on the ground, but other things too, like the contents of my nightstand drawers. To go along with that, my dresser drawers had been opened and searched, as well as my closet.

Sighing, I began to clean up the mess of papers. I sorted through them, deciding they were all trash. I chose to just make a pile and throw them out later, when I wasn't in such a bad mood. It didn't take as long as I thought it would to pick them all up. I guess it just seemed that there was more than there really was. I took the stack of papers to add to the ones that I'd stacked in the closet a few days ago. It's hard to believe that it was only a few days ago that I was crying for Rafe. It seemed like it had been forever since then.

When the papers had been cleared, I took up the task of throwing random items back into my nightstand drawer. *I should really clean that out*, I thought. Again though, I didn't feel up to it. It only took about five seconds to put everything back in the drawers of my nightstands, and then I shut the drawers on my dresser. When I was finished, I surveyed the room. It looked as though nothing had occurred in here.

I left my room, then, and wandered downstairs. I headed to the kitchen and opened my fridge, only to remember that I'd never gone to Guéret to buy food. I'd be sure to do it tomorrow though, first thing. I was starving. Hopefully, I'd be out of the house before Radder inevitably came to apologize for standing me up. Right now, he was the last person I wanted to see. But he was also the only one I wanted to see.

A sudden knock made me jump. Slowly, I crept into the living room. There was another knock on the door. Thanks to the light from my candles in the parlor, though, I couldn't see who stood at the door. Just a tall shadow.

It's got *to be Radder*, I thought. Slowly I approached the door. But when I opened it, I was surprised at who I saw.

It wasn't Radder. Instead, it was a boy about the same height as him, with shaggy blonde hair and smoldering green eyes. He didn't look familiar at all.

"Hello," he said.

"Hi…and you are?"

"My name is Charles Renaud," he said. That name sounded so familiar.

"OK… Well, I'm-"

"Amaury de Pompadour. I know."

"How do you-? Who are you?"

"I told you. Charles Renaud."

"You know what I mean."

"Well, if you must know," he said, stepping closer to me, his green eyes looking menacing. Only then did I catch his scent. He wasn't Human. Or Vampire. He was a Werewolf.

Right as I thought it, he confirmed it. "I'm a Werewolf."

I tried to look shocked. I wanted to convince him I was Human. "Yeah, right," I said. "There's no such thing. Nice try."

"Really?" he said, stepping even closer to me. "Because you smell a bit like Werewolf. Vampire, too."

"Well, if you "Werewolves" are the ones who raided my house, then yeah, I probably do smell like wolf. And, Vampires? *Really*? Come on, don't make me laugh."

"According to my Pack, your boyfriend is a Vampire. Radder?"

"Radder? A *Vampire*? Please. That's ridiculous."

"Wow, I love how you're lying."

"Lying?"

"Radder's brother told us your name was Audrey. You're all trying to protect something. I've got you figured out."

"Radder has a brother? Oh well. Either way, how do you know he didn't just pronounce my name wrong? Because, I mean, Audrey and Amaury are kind of close in pronunciation."

"Maybe so, but I still you know you're lying."

"No, I'm not. I swear. And, even if I was, how could you tell?"

"Most Humans freak out when we tell them what we are."

"Well, just because you say it doesn't make it true."

"Fine. Then do you want me to prove it?"

"Yes, actually. I do."

"Alright then" he said. "Come with me." Slowly, he turned around and walked out of the house. I cautiously followed him out the door, but left it open in case I had to run inside really quickly, for fear of danger. He walked just into the darkness, and said, "Watch this."

Then, right before my eyes, he transformed into a golden-brown wolf. I gasped (it was fake of course) and covered my mouth with my hands. He didn't know it, but it was to hide my smile from him. Then, I made my hands shake as I drew them away from my mouth, and said, "Wha-? What's wrong with you?"

He gave a wolfish grin. "Nothing at all."

I pretended to be terrified. "Stay away from me!" I yelled, then, I ran towards my open door.

When I turned around though, he was standing in the doorway, in his Human form.

"You must really be a Human," he said. "I don't think I've ever seen anyone more terrified in my whole life."

Wow. How gullible.

"On the second thought though," he said, "I've also never seen a Human run so fast."

Shit.

Busted.

"You'd be surprised at how fast we can go when we're in danger," I said, trying to cover up the truth that had been unveiled.

"Oh, I'm sure Humans can. But not that fast."

"It wasn't really that fast."

"You almost beat me. I think that's fast."

"Well, I… uh-" I was at as loss for words.

"You what?" he prompted, a wicked smile plastered on his face.

"I…" I trailed, not even bothering to finish.

"That's what I thought," he said. "Now, tell me, why would you hide the fact that you're a Vampire?"

"Because I don't want to be one," I said.

"I hope you realize that you'll have to be held prisoner of the Pack, correct?"

"What?" I asked, astonished. "But, why?"

"For hunting on Glace Pack's land."

"Wrong," I said.

"Excuse me?" he replied in a supercilious tone.

"You heard me. You can't hold me or my boyfriend prisoner. We don't hunt in Chiroux. We're not stupid."

"Then where do you hunt?"

"In the cities near here, like La Rue and Guéret."

"La Rue is Pack territory."

"Don't try to trick me. It's unclaimed. Everyone knows that."

"Whatever," he said. "It'll belong to the wolves soon enough."

"I wouldn't be so sure," I hissed.

"Well, it's pretty obvious that I'm speaking the truth, but, OK, don't believe me. We'll see how that works out."

I just rolled my eyes at him. "If you don't mind," I said, "I'd like to go inside my house now."

His smile widened. "As you wish."

Slowly, he stepped out of the way, gesturing with his hands for me to go inside. Cautiously, I stepped forward and into the castle, figuring he'd follow me inside. When he didn't, and just stood there in the doorway instead, I slammed the door in his face and locked every bolt I could. I felt thankful to have been relieved from his clutches, not really caring what he did with the "information" I'd given him. Then, I heard a noise behind me.

Ever so slowly, I turned around to see a white furred wolf standing in my parlor. She emitted a low growl, and looked as though she was going to bite my head off. Her bright blue eyes, which looked similar to Radder's (only less vibrant), held a gaze of pure hatred. Not long after I'd spotted her, more wolves began to appear from nowhere, flanking her sides as protection. She had to be the Pack's leader, Angel.

Fucking sons of bitches, I thought. *They must've snuck in while I was outside with Charles.*

There were five wolves, counting Angel, standing before me. Just a moment later, a golden-brown wolf joined there ranks, one that could only be Charles. I surveyed the group of growling Werewolves, trying to pick out the one I knew. There were two black wolves, but I couldn't tell which one was James. Although, I didn't think he was the one with red eyes. But I couldn't be for sure.

"Amaury de Pompadour," Angel suddenly snarled, drawing me away from my thoughts.

"What do you want?" I asked.

She had a wolfish grin on her face. "What do we want?" she asked. "We want you and Radder Thor dead. That's all there is to it."

I sighed. "Can't it wait?" I ask.

"Well, it can, but that would be a favor to you. So no."

"How rude," I said. "And to think I believed that you Werewolves were rather nice."

"Well," the black wolf with red eyes growled, "you thought wrong."

"Apparently," I said. "Now, what is it you plan to do exactly?"

"Simple," Angel said. "We're going to surround you and kill you. It'll be quick, don't worry. Then, once we get a hold of him again, we'll do the same to your boyfriend. Although we may torture him a bit first."

"Why just him? Why not me?"

"Well, since we hold such a grudge against him, he deserves it. But while you haven't really done too much to make us hate you, we won't make you suffer."

I almost protested, saying I wasn't hunting on their lands. *Almost*. But then I thought better about it. If the entire Pack knew, there was a possibility they'd take it up with the Coven. That could very well expose my secret. So, I shut my mouth and just nodded understandingly.

"Now, we have things to do, so let's make this quick," Angel said. "I'm not going to waste the whole rest of my night chasing Vampires around."

With that, the Pack began to close in on me. I began to back away, reaching for the doorknob behind me. Only then did I remember that I had locked every bolt, and they'd be attacking me before I'd be able to unlock them all. I realized then that that had been Charles's plan from the start. I was trapped.

The black wolf with red eyes was the first to lunge at me. I highly doubted now that this was James. I ran, trying to dodge him, but he pinned me to the ground before I was able to take more than a few steps. I struggled beneath him, trying to release his grip on my shoulders, but he was exceptionally strong for a Werewolf.

"Hold her there, Cajun," Angel said. "I'll finish this."

Slowly, she padded over. I was dreading what might happen to me, what she would do. Call the rest of them to sic me, and rip me to shreds? I shuddered at the thought, and slowly she came up beside me. She bared her fangs, and… she bit my arm. That was it. A bite to the arm.

"There," she said. "Now she'll suffer enough to pay, plus it'll kill her. Seems like a win to me."

"Do you want us to stay until she dies?" Cajun asked his leader.

"Not especially," she said. "It'll kill her anyways. There's no point in wasting our time."

Cajun nodded to his leader, then motioned to the rest of the pack to follow him. He shifted into his Human form and unlocked the door for his fellow wolves, who filed out of my castle, one by one. When they exited, they stood, watching and waiting for the others. When all were through, Cajun took one last look at me, and then shut the door. I remained sprawled on the floor for a while longer, afraid to sit up, expecting a wolf's face to appear in the window.

But, after waiting for around half an hour, I got the courage to sit up. I crawled on the floor to avoid the windows, only standing to snuff out the candle on my desk. Then, I moved to peer out the windows. I saw no shadows lurking near the trees, or any sign of wolves anywhere. It seemed that, for now at least, the coast was clear. But I was still going to be cautious.

Ever so silently, I began to make my way upstairs to my bedroom. My house smelled so strongly of the Werewolves' musky scent, it almost made me sick. I had half a mind to spray perfume over every inch of the castle, but it wouldn't mask the scent for more than a few hours. It would only be a waste of time, and perfume.

Once I'd ascended the stairs, I made way to my bedroom. I hastily changed into a nightgown, and ran a brush through my tangled hair. I wasn't really all that tired, but I didn't really have anything better to do than to go to sleep. But when I lay down and pulled up the covers, I realized that sleep would be impossible. So I tried to think of something to do, when I got a rather great idea.

I sprung from my bed and began to head down the stairs. When I reached the second floor, I walked over to my desk, and reignited the candle I'd blown out a few minutes ago. I slid my leather-bound diary towards me, opened to a fresh page, and began to write.

Mars 22, 1874; La nuit
(March 22, 1874; The Night)

Dear Diary,

Today has officially sucked. I figured it would be amazing, considering I got a surprise visit from Radder. He used up one of his favors (which means he only has one left) and asked me to go swimming with him at Ruisseau de Chiroux. It was amazing! But then, the Werewolves came, and we had to hide. They almost caught us hiding under the dock, but we were able to escape their notice. Well, at least all of them but one. After we thought they'd all scattered, a black wolf approached us. His name was James. He believed I was a Vampire, which sent me in the clear, and even promised not to tell the Pack of our meeting. He didn't believe it was right for them to be hunting us down any more than me or Radder did. Once he left, Radder and I went to his house so I could eat. Afterwards, we returned to the lake to sit by the water's side. Everything was just perfect, until I saw his red eyes. I told him to go and get a drink, knowing it wouldn't take him to long. He even promised it wouldn't. But, unfortunately, he lied to me.

Because, big surprise, he stood me up. Again. I returned home after the sun set, figuring I'd waited long enough. When I returned, I saw that my home had been raided. I had to clean it all up, and when I did, someone knocked on the door. I thought it'd be Radder, but instead it was a Werewolf by the name of Charles Renaud. I tried to convince him I was Human, but in the end he would only believe that I was a Vampire. The Pack ambushed me in my own home, sharing his belief. Angel bit me in the arm, believing it'd kill me, and then left with her Pack members. This all just goes to show, I can never, ever have a perfect day.

-Amaury de Pompadour

It didn't take too long for me to write the entry, but it was long enough to tire me out some. Shutting the book, I decided to go back upstairs and attempt to sleep. I had a feeling that tomorrow was going to be a long day. I pushed back my chair and stood, blowing out the candle while doing so. Then, I made my way upstairs and back into my bedroom.

When I entered the room, I walked slowly towards my bed and slid underneath the covers. When my head hit the pillow, I felt a tear run down the side of my cheek. And that one tear turned into several. I couldn't believe that the Werewolves were hunting me down. Not to mention, the Vampires were after me too. But I think the worst thing was that, now, Radder wasn't here to protect me. It was just like the past four days have been a dream, and I'm just now waking up to again realize how awful the world is.

I missed him. Like, *really* missed him. More than I miss Rafe, even. And that's saying something. I need him right now. I can't believe that he stood me up for the second time since I met him. And I've known him for four days. I know the type of person he is. But considering I've had nobody, other than the backstabbing Magdelene, for over three-hundred years, he's all I have left. And I can't even have him.

I awoke the next morning to find the sun shining brightly through my window, brightening my bedroom. I sat up and ran a hand through my hair, gathering all my jumbled thoughts into my head. Then, one realization hit me hard. Radder had never come back. I mean, last time I had to find him, and he had an explanation for why he ditched me. It was a little odd that he hadn't come to apologize, and I thought that maybe, just maybe, something had happened to him when he went out into the woods. But, the thought quickly paced. He was a Vampire. He could take care of himself.

I decided that today, I was going to Guéret to do a little shopping. I badly needed food. I contemplated dropping by Radder's, just to see if he was home, but thought better of it. If he wanted me to forgive him, he'd have to come to me. I wasn't going to forgive him so easily this time. It'd only make him do it again, knowing he'd be able to get away with it.

Unhurriedly, I got out of bed and picked out an outfit. Nothing special; just a skirt and blouse. It was just what I've been in the mood to wear lately. Although, there's not much else to choose from. Once I was dressed, I was going to water my garden. But, judging by the sky, it was around noon. I'd have to get to Guéret before it got too late and the shops closed. The flowers could wait.

Quickly, I ran a brush through my mangled hair. I decided a little jewelry might go along with my outfit, so I checked my necklace rack to see what I had. There were probably hundreds on it, but only one caught my eye, sitting alone on its own hook. The little blue belle necklace.

I swallowed hard when I saw it, and decided to just close my eyes and pick one at random to avoid accidentally seeing it again. It brought back memories of Radder that I didn't want to think about right now. So, I just grabbed a necklace, and peeked to see which one I'd chosen. Ironically, it was the black onyx one, another item given to me by Radder.

Taking a deep breath, I reached to place it back on the rack. That is, until a little voice in my head told me that wasn't the best idea; that I should wear it. I wasn't really sure why, but I chose to listen to it. I didn't even have the slightest clue as to why my conscious was advising me to wear it, but I figured I might as well. I had nothing to lose in doing so.

So, I slipped the necklace's chain around my neck and clasped it. I checked my appearance in my dresser mirror before I left. The necklace was stunningly beautiful, and went perfectly with what I wore. I let a small smile slide across my face, but it quickly vanished. I wished Radder was here to see me wear it for the first time.

Again, I took a deep breath. *Get over it*, I thought, making my way towards my bedroom door. Once I'd left my room, I went down the stairs and searched around my parlor for a basket I could take to the market. Once I'd found a suitable one to take, I left the house, not bothering to lock the door behind me.

Once I'd left the castle, I began to head for the woods. I had to trek through the dense foliage of the forest, but it didn't take me long to find the dirt path that would lead me to Guéret. I wondered if I'd run into Radder here again. Although, the likeliness of that occurring was very slim.

I made my way along the dirt path at a rather slow pace. Still, the hour it took me to get there flew by. Before I knew it, the gates of the city loomed before me. People filed in and out of its gates; the town was as busy as ever. I hadn't seen so many Humans since the bazaar a few days ago. It was incredibly ridiculous that there were so many of them. Humans had it so easy. They have no threat of extinction, or threat of being hunted down like an animal. They also posses no knowledge of Vampires or Werewolves or Fusions or other mythical beings that are more than likely to exist. I envy them for that.

Thinking this, I head straight for the gates. I blend right in with the crowd; nobody suspects a thing about me. The wave of the crowd unwillingly pushes me forward. I'm stuck right in the center of the mass of people, and for the first time since I met Radder, I feel somewhat safe, and away from all danger. But I see that as soon as I enter the square, those thoughts are a lie.

I drift from the crowd once I reach the water fountain, searching among various wooden booths. Usually at the market there is only food, and the trinkets are saved for the bazaars. But today, many people are selling odds and ends things. Probably leftovers from a few days ago.

I go from booth to booth, inspecting what each has. Finally, I find a booth that actually holds food instead of curios. It is full of fruit, in which I take a lot of and place in my basket. I fill it to the top, and once it's full I wait to pay. And when the man in front of me walks away, and I face the owner of the booth, I feel my heart skip a beat.

That's because Anthony Smith, the old man from the bazaar, stood before me.

The only Human who knows what I am.

His gaze instantly goes into a glare the minute he sees me. Warily, I place my basket on the booth's counter.

"What do you want?" he asked in an agitated tone.

"Just the food in here," I said. "I promise."

"And why should I sell any of this to you?" he asked. "You stupid Fusion, you don't even deserve to live!"

"I know that you hate me," I said. "But I am buying this from you, giving you money. That's to your benefit at least."

"But it also benefits you by allowing you to live," he said. "And I don't want that for you or that stupid Vampire Ratter, or whatever the hell his name is."

"*Radder*," I corrected. "And I really don't care if you want us dead or not. I just want the food, and I'll be on my way."

"Well that's too bad," he said, "because I refuse to sell you anything."

Suddenly I felt a tap on my shoulder. I turned around to see a Human behind me.

"Excuse me," she said impatiently, "but could you hurry it up please?"

"I'm sorry ma'am," Anthony said. "How can I help you?"

I didn't hide my annoyance. "Asshole," I hissed, not bothering to move.

A new voice joined in just then. "Excuse me," it said, "but is there a problem here?"

A girl, about twenty or so, walked towards the booth. She came around the back and stood next to Anthony. The girl had some qualities that resembled him, and I figured she must be a relative of his.

"This thing is a Fusion," Anthony whispered to her. To the other Human he said, "I'll be right with you, ma'am."

Luckily she rolled her eyes and just walked away, abandoning her basket.

"Grandpa," the other girl said, "We talked about this. There's no such thing."

"Yes there is!" he shouted, loud enough for a few passers-by to stare at him for a moment. "The proof is right in front of you!"

"Grandpa, keep your voice down!" she hissed.

"No, Abigail," he snapped back. "The world deserves to know that these things are out there."

"Stop, will you?" she asked. Then she turned to me. "I'm so sorry. It's just, he gets this way sometimes."

"Don't talk about me like I'm not here!" he said, causing her to roll her eyes.

"His parents told him all this crap about Vampires and Werewolves when he was little to scare him so he'd stay out of trouble. He accuses everybody of being one it seems."

"She's a Fusion," he grumbled, "not a Vampire."

"Whatever," she said, turning back to me again. "Really, I'm sorry."

"Oh, it's fine," I said, bringing a fake smile to my face.

"Now, I'll take care of your food for you."

I pulled some money out from the basket where I'd stored it and handed it to her.

"Thank you," she said, as I grabbed my basket and began to walk away.

"Wait," a voice said.

I turned around. Anthony was motioning for me to come back to the booth. Cautiously, I stepped forward and back to the booth. "What?" I asked him.

"I just wanted to say how sorry I am…" before he finished what he was saying, he chucked a knife at me.

I didn't have any time to dodge it before it sliced open my arm.

"…that you're alive!" he yelled, finishing his sentence.

Abigail looked at him, then at me. "Grandpa!" she said. "What have you done?"

"Just look at her arm," he said, a wicked smile on his face.

Reluctantly, she looked at the gash, and then gasped in astonishment. Which, of course, I'd been expecting. The wound was already starting to heal itself. Within a minute, there wasn't even a scar to show it'd been there.

Abigail was speechless. But her grandfather sure wasn't.

"I told you," he said. "I told you they were real."

"I- I don't believe this," she stuttered. "You- you're a?"

"I'm a Fusion," I said. "Your grandpa was right about that."

"Then- then…" she couldn't even finish her sentence.

"Abigail, I need you to focus," Anthony said. "I'll need your help for this."

"For what?" she asked in a shaky voice.

"We're going to have to capture her," he said.

"She isn't an animal," she said.

"Yes, she is," he said. "Now, come on!"

I chose that moment to run.

I didn't run too fast though. If I'd gone my fastest, people would definitely know something was wrong with me. So, I kept the pace equivalent to a very fast Human's. I ran about half the length of the square before I stopped to look behind me. I searched through the crowd, but I had completely lost them. So, I turned around, only to see another familiar face before me.

Raven Navre.

She wore the same brown peasant's cloak I'd seen her in before. Her gaze was sharp, and her brown eyes were held with anger.

"Ava," she said, calling me by my fake name.

"Raven," I said back. "Nice to see you again."

"You too," she said. We were both silent for a moment before she said,

"I need to talk to you."

I nodded at her, and she grabbed my arm and led me through the crowd. I took us a moment to weave our way through, but eventually we ended up on a practically empty street. I felt a lump rise in my throat when I realized that this was the street where Radder had first kissed me. Raven kept dragging me until we reached a dark alleyway, which just so happened to be the one where Radder had spoken with the mystery person. Cautiously, we walked into the darkness.

When we were sure we were alone, Raven turned to face me.

"What is it?" I asked.

"Do you know who I am?"

I was shocked at her question. "No," I said. "Of course not."

She nodded. "Good," she said.

A question then exited my mouth without any thought at all. "Do you know what happened to Radder?"

She gave me a very, very serious look. "No," she said.

I fought back tears, making a lump rise in my throat. It burned when I spoke. "I'm so worried about him."

"You'd be better off not being involved with him," she said. "Believe me Ava, he is nothing but bad news."

"I know," I said. "But it's not like I can help it."

"He is pretty irresistible, isn't he? Believe me, you're definitely not the first girl to swoon over him."

"Are you talking about Audrey?"

She shook her head. My eyes grew wide. "What, do you love him too?"

Again, she shook her head; her eyes widened too. "God no," she said. "I know him better than anyone. And, trust me, he's not worth it. All he's going to do is break your heart."

"You think I don't already know that?" I snapped.

"I know you know. But you choose to ignore it. I'm only trying to help you Ava."

"I don't care," I said. "I'm just sick of being alone."

"I'm not saying you should be alone," she said. "I'm just saying that you shouldn't be with *him*."

I felt a streak of water run down my cheek. "I don't think I would be," I said, "except that there's no one else to turn to."

Raven stared at me, her expression blank. "Are you sure about that?"

I nodded, wiping the tear away with my hand. "Well, considering he's the only guy I know."

"What about Benjamin?"

"Please," I said. "I hate him as much as my sister." *At least,* now *I do,* I thought. I swallowed hard before continuing. "And, even if I didn't, he's in love with Magdelene. So either way, it makes no difference."

"Well, I'm sure you could meet someone else."

"Like who?"

"Like, maybe a Human."

"Yeah, right," I said. "What Human would love some immortal freak of nature that was never meant to exist?"

"Well, they will if you don't tell them."

"How could I not tell them? Besides, they'd figure it out sooner or later, considering they would age without me."

"Just let them die without you, and then move on. It's simple."

"That's *horrible*! I couldn't just move on, either; once I fall in love with someone, it lasts forever, no matter what."

"And I'm assuming you think you love Radder?"

"I'm not assuming," I said. "I know that I do."

"You've known him for… what? Five days? And, let's see, he's stood you up twice and lied countless times. Plus, he was a jerk to you the first time you met. And you think you *love* him???"

"Love works in strange ways," I said.

"Not *that* strange!" she exclaimed.

"I guess I'm not really sure why I love him," I said. "Because, I mean, everything you said is true. But, I don't know, it's just like there's this magnetic pull between us. It's like I've known him for my entire life, and I'm just now realizing it. In fact, it's almost like… we were made for each other."

"That's a lot to say about someone you've known for five days."

"I know you say you know him," I said, "But you really don't. You don't know how sweet he can be."

"He's just tricking you, Ava." she snapped. "Everything he says, thinks, and does, is a *lie*."

I glared at her. "You don't know that." And then, I turned and began to walk away.

I expected her to follow me; I really did. But as I continued down the cobblestone road and back into the sea of people, I noticed that she was nowhere in sight. In fact, none of the limited people I knew were in sight, and the crowd had begun to die down. I followed a crowd of people that was heading toward the gates, so that I wouldn't be swept off in the wrong direction. But as I began to head towards them, I felt a strong hand grab my shoulder.

I thought for a hopeful moment that it might be Radder. But then I realized that the grip was much too harsh to be his. I spun around, just in time to see the angered face of Anthony Smith. And just behind him stood Abigail. There was another man there too, who looked just like the two, and aged somewhere between theirs. I assumed he was Abigail's father.

"Just where do you think you're going?" Anthony hissed at me through gritted teeth. He was trying to be intimidating, but we both knew that all three of them put together couldn't stop me if I tried to hurt them.

"Actually," I said. "I was just leaving."

"I don't think so." The other man, who I assumed to be Abigail's father, stepped in. "You're not going anywhere. We know what you are, and we're not going to let you get away."

"How sure are you of that?" I questioned. "You all know as well as I do that I can outrun you, and tear you all limb from limb in a split second if it's necessary. So, I ask, why try?"

"Because you're not going to play us for fools," Anthony said. "We know what your kind does. They kill random Humans just to live."

"That's Vampires," I said. "I'm the only Fusion, and I never drink blood. And if I do happen to, it's from an animal. Like a bunny or something."

"It wasn't a Vampire that killed my sister!" Abigail screamed. A few people around us gave us questioning looks.

"Look," I said, lowering my voice. "The Vampires drink blood. Not me."

"Well, then how do you explain why there were not only bite marks, made by Vampire fangs, in her neck, but also why there was evidence of wolves all around?"

"How do you explain that you're not lying?" I asked.

"Why would I lie?" she asked. "I lost my sister! What's there to lie about?"

"How she died. Not but ten minutes ago you were telling your grandfather that there was no such thing as Vampires or Werewolves or Fusions. Explain that."

Abigail was at loss for words.

"That's just what I thought," I said, taking that moment to turn the other way.

I moved at a quick pace, trying to shake them off. I knew they were behind me, somewhere, trying to spot me in the crowd. Luck wouldn't be on their side today, though. As soon as I was out of sight from the villagers, I was making a mad dash for home.

When I reached the gate and was readying to leave, a guard stepped in my way.

"Sorry," he said. "But I'm not allowed to let you leave."

My heart skipped a beat. "What? Why?"

"Because," he said. "I have witnesses saying that a few days ago at the bazaar you and a man reeked havoc on one of the vendors' stands, causing severe damage. Then, they claimed to have seen you both jump on top of a building and jump among the rooftops to escape. Although, I myself don't find the last part believable."

"And you shouldn't," I said. "But either way, we paid for the damage done."

"Still, you caused panic amongst the townspeople. I have an order to keep you here in the city until we find out more. I'll also need to know the identity of your accomplice-"

"Over my dead body," I hissed through gritted teeth.

"That can be arranged," he retorted.

"It can," I said sharply, "but it won't." And with that, I shoved the guard aside and began to run. I ran at an average Human pace, but went fast enough to escape the guard and his colleagues who had been standing nearby.

I kept running, not stopping, until I was deep into the forest. I stuck to the side of the dirt path to avoid making footprints. I figured that the guards would soon be looking for me, so it was smart to stay as hidden as possible. When I was sure that I was at a safe distance from the town, and that I wasn't leaving any evidence behind telling I'd been here, I noticed that the cloth had blown off my basket. And, to my disgust, a few of its contents had spilled out.

I continued down the side of the road until I could see my castle through the trees. I was glad to see its familiarity, and I hurried toward it. I quickly ran inside, where I went to the kitchen and set my basket on the kitchen counter. It was good to be home. I began to unpack things from the basket and take them to the refrigerator, placing them in in random places.

Once I was done with that, I remembered that I had a garden to attend to. So, I made my way to my mudroom to grab my watering can. I made my way outside and went to the well to fill it with water, which only took a minute. Then, I began to make my way around the house, watering the always thirsty flowers.

I made it just over halfway around the castle before the tears started to come. I wasn't really sure why, but thoughts of Radder flooded my mind. The thought of him just made me so upset, I guess, that it had brought me to tears. All I wanted to do was go inside and write in my diary or something; anything but stay outside. But I had business to attend to before I could do that. I rushed through watering my flowers, but not too fast. I still made sure every plant got water.

It didn't take me too long to complete watering the flowers. I slowly inched toward the door, and ran out of water just as I finished up. Then, finally, I was able to go inside, where the only memories of Radder were minor ones. Ones that didn't break my heart.

Once my watering can was replaced to its rightful place in the mudroom, I went towards my desk and sat down. I grabbed my diary, opened to a fresh page, and began to write.

Mars 23, 1874; L 'apres midi
(March 23, 1874; The Afternoon)

Dear Diary,

Again, another suckey day for me. I went shopping for food in Guéret today, and, what do you know, I run into Anthony Smith (the Human who knows what I am). He was running the booth, and refused to sell me the food. Although, his granddaughter, a girl named Abigail, accepted my money. Anthony tried to convince her I was a Fusion, but she called him crazy. Then, Anthony proved it by cutting my arm with a knife when I wasn't watching him. They both watched my arm heal itself, and I ran from them, trying to escape. When I ran, I ran into Raven Navre for the second time. We talked, and she warned me about loving Radder. But I hadn't wanted to hear anything. So, I left. As I headed towards the gates though, I was stopped by Anthony, Abigail, and a man I assumed to be Abigail's father. They accused me of murdering Abigail's sister, which I had nothing to do with. Those people are just psycho I guess. So, again, I ran from them. On my way out of the city however, I was stopped by a guard. He was trying to arrest me for what happened at the bazaar the other day, and have me reveal Radder's identity. After a rather rude conversation, I ended up just pushing past him and running. When I got home, I began to water the garden, which, for some reason, reminded me of Radder. And I realized something. I miss him. A lot more than I probably should.

-Amaury de Pompadour

I had just shut my diary, when I suddenly heard a loud noise. I swung my head around to see none other than

Benjamin and Magdelene running down my staircase. I stood, ready to defend myself. They were down in my parlor in an instant, and were charging me. I tried to dodge their inevitable blow, but before I could even blink they had me by the arms. Magdelene twisted them together, ridding any possible chances I had of escape. I knew I had no way out until I gave them what they wanted.

"Well, well, well." Benjamin said lividly, stepping forward, just about right in my face. "What've we got here?"

I just glared at him, letting my eyes pierce him.

"Now now," he said in a promising tone, "we're not going to hurt you. At least, not *that* bad."

"Why do I find that hard to believe?" I spat at him. I felt the anger rise up inside me. I hated him so much.

"Probably because I've done something like this a few times before. Really though, all we need is a sample of your blood, if you'd just cooperate."

"Why do you need my blood?" I asked suspiciously. "Gonna prove my existence and turn me in to the Werewolves? Well, go ahead. See if I give a damn."

"That's not really what we were planning, but that is a rather good idea. We'll have to take this to them after we go through with our original plan."

"And what is your plan exactly?" I asked.

"That's for us to know and for you to find out."

"You do realize that I can only find out if you tell me, right?"

"Right you are. And, since we don't want you to know, then we're not going to tell you. It's as simple as that."

I rolled my eyes at his ridiculousness. "Do your worst," I snapped at him.

Benjamin snatched one of my arms from Magdelene's hold, and gripped it so tightly my skin turned white.

"This'll only hurt a little." He promised. Then, suddenly, a stake emerged from nowhere in his hand. A stake that he plunged straight through my arm.

It hurt. I mean, I've felt a lot of pain in my entire existence, but that fucking *hurt.* I tried not to reveal my pain, so to block it out, I squeezed my eyes as tight as they would go, and gritted my teeth to the point that they almost broke. I could feel blood, *my blood*, flowing down my arm. A bit dropped onto my shoes; I could hear it when the drops hit the tip. It went on for about two minutes before Ben finally dislodged the stake from my arm.

My arm hurt so bad, and was still bleeding horribly, that I had to grab my wound in order to somewhat cease the pain and slightly stop the blood flow. I chose then to open my eyes. And the first thing I noticed was the huge puddle of blood was on my floor. Secondly, I noticed Ben and Magdelene staring at each other, deep in conversation. But, no actual words were being spoken. I'd just lived long enough to be able to tell when Vampires are talking through mind reading.

"Do you have stitches anywhere?" Magdelene asked suddenly.

I nodded, trying to speak, but couldn't. The pain had robbed my voice. *In the upstairs powder room,* I thought. *The supplies are in the medicine cabinet.*

She nodded, then disappeared upstairs. And to my dismay, left me alone with Benjamin. He looked rather impatient, as though he had somewhere to be. Before I knew it, my "sister" was coming back down the stairs, the kit in hand.

"Move your hand," she ordered. I did what she said, only to see more blood shoot out of my arm as I removed my hand. She opened the kit, withdrawing a string from its contents, and tied it on my upper arm to slow the blood flow.

Once that was done, she began to clean up the blood that had surged down my arm. Then, she began to stitch the wound. It didn't take her very long, and once she completed, she returned the kit to its rightful place in the powder room cabinet, returning back downstairs soon after.

"Now," Benjamin said. "That wasn't so bad, was it?"

"Not really," I admitted. "I was expecting *much* worse."

"Well, you're going to get a lot worse. Not now, but in good time."

I gave him a sarcastic smile. "Great," I said. "Can't wait."

"I'll bet you can't," he said.

"Are you going to be leaving anytime soon?" I asked impatiently. "Because I really don't like either of you being in my house."

"Of course," he said. "In just a moment."

I pinned a glare at him, my hatred so focused on him that I just barely noticed Magdelene slip behind me. Before I knew what was going on, I felt something hard slam against my head, making my world go black.

When I next awoke, I was lying on my parlor floor. I was lying in a pool of my own dry blood, and my head was throbbing. Benjamin and Magdelene were nowhere in sight.

The sky outside was a dark blue, the moon the only light in the room. One of the candles on my desk had smoke rising from the wick. It had either snuffed itself out, or, perhaps, someone had come inside and done it...

A hand clasped over my mouth. I tried to scream, while I struggled out of their grasp.

"Be quiet and stop struggling," a familiar voice snapped, "and it'll all be over with soon enough. Besides, no one can hear your screams but Magdelene. It's a waste of breath."

Benjamin.

The ungrateful *bastard.*

"I'm going to remove my hand now," he said. "Cooperate?"

I nodded, gasping as he moved his hand off my mouth. "What the hell are you doing back here? And why did you guys knock me out?" I asked.

I couldn't see him, but I knew a wicked smile was on his face.

"Simple," he said. "To do this."

And then my world blackened once more.

This time when I awoke, I was sitting in a chair. My hands were bound tightly together behind the chair. My entire torso was tied to the back of the chair with a rope, and my mouth was taped shut. I tried to break the rope by pushing against it with my arms, but for some reason, it wouldn't break. This was no ordinary rope. I began to struggle against it, trying to escape, but it was impossible. Even the chair itself was nailed to the floor, making it impossible to find something sharp in this place capable of cutting the bindings that held me in place.

Realizing it was useless, I stopped struggling. Instead, I took the time to survey my surroundings. I was surrounded by stone walls. Water dripped rapidly, coming from an unknown source, and I could hear rats shuffling along the floor…

That's when I realized it was just how Radder had described the Coven's dungeons.

That's where I am, I thought. *It has to be.*

Then, as though to confirm my thoughts, the wooden door to the cellar creaked open, revealing Benjamin's evil, smiling face.

Why have you brought me here? I thought quickly to him.

But he didn't answer my question. Instead he said, simply, "Welcome to hell."

Chapter 10
The Escape

Radder:

Darkness. All I saw was darkness. It was all around, consuming me. It was within me, clawing at my insides, begging for blood. The Thirst, that undeniable Thirst, it was going to kill me.

That was what I always felt when I woke up in the dungeon. It had been days, maybe weeks, I didn't know, since I'd been brought here. And, surprising as it may be, it was comforting. Because, when the thought passed, Amaury came into the picture. She was always on my mind, though, no matter what.

I longed for her. All I wanted was to kiss and hold her at least one more time before the Thirst killed me. I had begun to plot an escape, although I had no idea of how I would get out of the chains. But I'd find away. I'd cross an ocean on foot to see my girl, and would just as well break indestructible chains to see her as well. She was the sole reason I wanted to escape, my only motivation. Until, that was taken away from me.

I had been doing nothing, just thinking about Amaury and plotting an escape, when my cell door creaked open. I was expecting Benjamin, but instead saw Magdelene. I smelled a strong scent of stale blood that was just barely familiar.

"What do you want?" I growled at her. "Haven't you two tortured me enough for one day?"

"Not quite," she responded. "I've got something to tell you. It's not the best of news."

I could only think of Amaury as I glared at her. "I smell blood," I snarled. "And the scent is familiar." I felt as my hand began to shake. I knew whose blood was on that stake. *Benjamin,* I thought to myself, *If you hurt my girl, I swear to God I'll tear you limb from limb...*

"What did you do to her?" I growled. I heard my voice shake as I spoke.

She said, simply, "She's dead Radder."

I felt my eyes widen. But I narrowed them again just after. I couldn't believe it. I wouldn't believe it.

"You liar," I accused.

"I'm not lying, Radder. Here, see for yourself." She rolled a blood-covered stake toward me. I could just barely see a glint of silver on its tip.

"Wha-? What is this?" I asked, shocked.

"That's the murder weapon. And, as you can see, it's completely covered in her blood."

"No," I whispered. "No. I don't believe this. I-" But I could plainly see that she was in fact telling the truth. It was the only weapon capable of killing a Fusion. What's more, it was soaked through with her blood. I felt my eyes swell with tears.

"I'm sorry Radder," she said, walking forward to retrieve the stake. "But we had to do it."

I didn't dare say a word, and I couldn't have even if I'd tried. I just closed my eyes and hung my head. I tried to hold back the tears, at least until she was gone, but my emotions overwhelmed me. I felt the water trickle down my cheeks.

Magdelene slowly backed out of the cell, shutting the door softly behind her. A minute later, I heard the door that led out of the dungeon open, and then shut once more. I was alone now. I let the tears come then, not even trying to stifle my sobs. She couldn't be gone. She just couldn't be.

I'd never even got to tell her that I loved her.

Sure, I'd had plenty of chances. Five, to be precise. The first time I almost told her was that night I told her my past, as I was begging her to stay with me. But, I thought it had been to soon then. The second was after our attempt at killing Benjamin and Magdelene, right before I'd left. I'd just given her a kiss, my forehead was resting on hers, and I'd begun to whisper it. I'd just wanted to hear myself say it, confirm to myself that it was true, when Amaury heard me. I'd only said 'I', so I hadn't finished. I'd chosen that moment to leave.

And then, there was that note I'd left her by the flower, the one where there was a blotch of ink above my name. I was going to write it there. But I'd chickened out. Then, there was twice that day we'd been at Ruisseau de Chiroux. The first there was when she was thinking about how much she loved me. At that moment, I'd wanted to scoop her in my arms and say it over and over again: 'Amaury de Pompadour, I love you!' But I didn't. Because, again, I'd chickened out.

And the last, the last chance I'd had to tell her, was when we were discussing all the secrets I was keeping from her.

"If you love me, you'll tell me," she had said.

"I promise I will," I'd said. "Just not today."

She thought I'd meant I promised to tell her my secrets. Which, I had. But really, what I'd meant was, 'Someday I will tell you I love you. Just not today.'

But I would never get another chance. Not now, not ever. And that was probably one of the hardest things to come to concepts with. That, and knowing that I would never be able to kiss her again, or hold her. That I'd never again see that sweet smile that had made my day, or hear that beautiful voice that had wrapped me in a spell of lovesickness.

No. Never again. And it was all thanks to my carelessness. I'd let them take me, hold me prisoner. I'd left her saddened by my disappearance, making her vulnerable. I'd allowed them to harm her. To kill her. That girl, the only reason I'd had to wake up each day for the past three-hundred years, was dead. And it was all my fault.

And so, after Magdelene had released the information about my love's death, I fell into a deep depression. I went in so deep, even, that I didn't think I'd ever be able to come back out. Which, that was perfectly fine with me. Because, in my depression, all I basically did while I was awake was thirst for blood and cry over Amaury. After a few hours of being awake, I'd be so tired of sulking that I'd fall asleep, sometimes for hours on end.

I came to love sleep. I longed for it. Because, when I slept, the Thirst was no longer there. And when I dreamt, it was of my sweet Amaury. Only, I was never sad. Because the dreams were always of us, just being happy together. It was the simplest things, even. Just holding her hand was enough to give us both butterflies. And, always in my dreams, I was able to tell her that I loved her, even though I knew I'd awaken and that nothing had actually happened or been said. But it was nice to think that it had. At least, for a little while.

Gradually though, I felt my mind slipping away from me. I needed blood so badly that it hurt. The Thirst clung to my insides, making me want to puke (although I had nothing in me to throw up). The vastness of its power over me was sickening. It stole away my thoughts, causing me to begin to become mad. I wanted blood. Absolutely needed it. The Thirst told my mind that it was the only thing I needed. But my heart countered with it, refusing for my mind to give in. Because, in my heart, I knew that Amaury was the only thing I needed. As long as I could have her, I'd never need anything else.

Despite the trueness of these words, I kept reminding myself that they were spoken by a crazy man.

While in Benjamin's dungeon, I had become completely insane. In my madness, the ancient memories of Brock turning me, in this very room, began to flood my mind as the Thirst took over me. I begged my mind for them to leave me, but they wouldn't go away. At least I wasn't focused completely on Amaury. Although, she was still in the corners of my mind, as she always was.

It seemed as though I was living it all over again. Sometimes, I swear my cell door opened, and I saw his shadow moving towards me, like it had all those years ago the day he turned me. It would get closer and closer, almost revealing his face, and then it'd be gone. I figured I was either hallucinating, or it was his spirit coming back to haunt me. I figured that, in my condition, it could be either of those.

One day, as I was sleeping, the conscious part of my brain heard the cell door creak open. I blinked open my eyes, just barely making out a shadow in the dim light of the doorway. But as I focused my eyes, I saw that there was not one, but *three* shadows. I'd figured, when the door opened, that it was another Brock hallucination. But it was apparent now that that was not the case.

The shadows began to move closer, and I felt the need to panic. I couldn't make out any scents, which worried me. There were also no thoughts to be heard. I figured that they had to be spirits, angels possibly, coming to take me away. That is, until I thought of crazy that sounded. However, it did seem rather likely, considering I was dying of thirst. And with that thought, I felt a sharp scent hit my nose.

Blood.

These shadows, whatever and whoever they were, had blood with them.

I instantly felt myself pull against the chains (though it was entirely against my will, and instead a work of the Thirst), my arms and legs straining to break them and get the blood that was getting nearer to me. My fangs drew out instinctively at the thought of blood. I must've looked crazy to whoever these shadows were. So I figured I looked just as I felt.

The shadows kept getting closer and closer. I felt as though my mind was playing a trick on me, knowing I needed blood so badly that it was making me manifest its scent in the air. But I didn't think I was capable of doing such a good job at it. No, this blood had to be real. But I still thought then when the shadows came to the spot were I'd last see Brock whenever he came, they would disappear too. Finally though, the shadows were close enough for me to make out their faces. And unlike Brock, they didn't disappear. But I didn't believe who stood before me.

It was Razza, Maryanne, and Adam.

"What do you want?" I growled at them, though my voice cracked. I wanted the blood that I smelled.

"We came to help you out a bit," Razza said.

"By doing what exactly?" I asked.

"Well, first of all, we brought you this," Adam said. He stepped forward, holding two wineglasses that were filled to the brim with blood. Again, I felt myself strain against the chains.

"Calm it down Radder," he warned.

He stepped forward, holding, to my surprise, a key, which he used to unlock my left arm's shackle. Then, he placed one of the glasses in my hand. I took it, my hand shaking so much I thought some of it would spill. Slowly, I brought the glass to my lips, taking small sips. I didn't want to take a huge drink and cause most of it to run down my mouth. Or, worse, drip onto the floor. I wanted every last drop of it.

Everything about the blood was perfect. Now, as strange as it is, it was even just the right temperature. It slid down my throat smoothly, and it tasted so good that I thought it was too good to be true. I finished the first glass quickly, and downed the second even faster. I felt much, much better. Self-consciously, I wiped my mouth when I'd finished to avoid the trio's gaze. I knew they understood how I felt, considering the Thirst was inside them as well, but it was still awkward and embarrassing to go on a blood-craze right in front of other Vampires.

Adam took the glasses from me, and I finally lifted up my eyes to look at them all. Their stares were burning into me. Suddenly, a thought came to my mind, one that would hopefully put their minds off of my blood-craze.

"How did you guys manage to sneak down here without Benjamin and Magdelene seeing? And how did you hide your scents? And block your thoughts so well?"

"One question at a time," Maryanne said.

"Fine," I said. "Then start with the first."

"Benjamin and Magdelene left to have some "alone time,"" Adam said. He shuddered in distaste.

"That's disgusting," I commented.

I had no idea what had to be going through Magdelene's mind for her to fall in love with my heartless bastard of a brother. They all nodded rapidly in agreement with me. I could hear their thoughts now, and saw they had the same thing on all of their minds as I did mine.

"Next question," I said.

"Every Vampire knows how to block their thoughts," Adam answered.

"That wasn't the next question."

"I was getting to that one," he said. "We all know how to hide our scents as well as you do. It's that soap you wash your clothes in."

My eyes narrowed. "How do you know that?" I asked.

"Ben sent us to search your house for anything useful,"

Razza explained. "And we found it by your wash bucket for your clothes. We argued over what it was, and since I thought it was just soap, I smelled it. But it didn't have any scent. So, we took some with us when we left, but didn't give any to Benjamin or Magdelene. And we didn't think about it or anything either, so don't worry."

"OK," I said. "So you caught me having scent-covering laundry soap in my house and then you used some. What's the big deal about that?"

"Well, we want to know where you got it," Adam said.

"I can't tell you that," I said. "I made an oath, a *blood oath*, to the person I got it from that I would never reveal who they were or where they sold that stuff."

"Then how did *you* find them?" he questioned.

"I had a friend who introduced me to them, because I'd mentioned to him that I needed something to disguise myself."

"I see," he said. "But why do you need it?"

"I use it sometimes," I said, "when I have to do something, and I don't want anyone to know I was there."

"Well, we have the clothes covered, but what about the rest of you?"

"I have scent-covering bath soap and shampoo too."

"Very clever indeed," he said. "I'll tell you what, if you can get your hands on some more to give to us, then we'll get you out of here right now."

"I can't do that."

"Why not?"

"Because I'm never going back to get any more. And I told them that. I no longer have any use for it."

He glared at me. "But if you get us some, *we'll get you out of here*."

"The answer is no." I said. "What do you even need it for?"

"None of your concern," he growled. Maryanne hung her head, looking ashamed. I grew suspicious of the two of them.

"Then I definitely won't give you any of the stuff."

"Do I have to say it again? We'll let you out of here! What more could you want?"

"What more could I want?" I snarled. "I'll tell you what I want. I want my girl to still be alive. *That's* what I want."

Instantly, in unison, they placed walls around their thoughts. Then Adam spoke up.

"Your girl?" he said. "You mean the Human? Radder, she's-"

"Dead," Razza quickly put in before he finished. "Remember Adam? Benjamin and Magdelene went and killed her, like, two weeks ago."

"Right," he said, nodding. "I forgot."

"What is today?" I asked Razza.

"Um- I believe it's the 6th."

"The 6th of what month?"

"April."

It had been exactly two weeks today since Amaury was killed.

"I'm proud of you Radder," Razza said. "You went two whole weeks without a single drop of blood. That's impressive. It would've killed me."

"I can go a month without a drink. The only thing putting me on the verge of death was knowing that Am-, my girl, is dead." I thought Razza would kill me right then and there for almost revealing Amaury's name. Instead, she just looked at me, an understanding sorrow in her eyes.

"I'm done in here," Adam said. Before he left though, he relocked my shackle. "C'mon guys," he said as he turned to leave.

When he'd gone, I hung my head. "I miss her," I whispered.

"I know you do," Razza said. "But maybe it's just better this way." With that, she left for the cell door.

"I'll catch up with you in a minute, Razza," Maryanne called after her. Razza didn't even nod; just walked out.

"What do you want Mary?" I asked. She was about the last person I wanted to talk to.

"I need to talk to you about something."

"And what would that be?"

She bit her lip. "I want to know about Fusions."

I felt my eyes grow wide. "Wha- what do you want to know?"

"As much as you do."

"So, everything?"

"Not quite. I didn't know you knew everything about them."

"Here, why don't I just say it? I've got nothing to lose." *Except the last little bit of my sanity.* "They're extinct. There is not another Fusion alive on this planet."

"Oh," she said. Then, realization shone in her eyes. "Ben was telling Adam that night we captured you that your girl was neither Human, nor Werewolf, nor Vampire. But then later on, he came up with a cover-up story telling how she was Human. So, is she a-"

"Fusion?" I said. "Yes. Yes, she *was*."

"They killed her then?"

I shut my eyes tightly. "Yes," I said, so quietly that even Maryanne barely heard me.

"I'm sorry," she said. We were both silent a minute before she asked, "What was her name?"

"Why do you care?"

"I really don't all that much," she confessed. "I'm just curious."

"If you must know," I said, sighing deeply. "Her name was Amaury."

"That's a pretty name," she said.

"I know. And it suited her perfectly for that matter."

"Why? Was she pretty?"

"The most beautiful girl in the world."

"In your opinion."

"I bet I could find a lot of people who would agree with me if they saw her."

She shrugged. "I'm sorry, you know, that she died and all."

"It's OK," I said. "I'll just take out my rage on Benjamin once I find a way out of here."

"Why him?" she asked. "How do you know Magdelene wasn't the one who killed her?"

"I *don't* know," I said. "I guess I'll just have to take out my revenge on both of them."

She shrugged. "Whatever. Well, anyways, what can you tell me about Fusions? Other than the fact that they're extinct?"

"Well, Fusions are pretty unique. They can run ten times

faster than you or I, or any other Vampire alive. Same goes for the Werewolves. Their senses are sixteen times sharper. If they bite a Vampire or a Werewolf, the bitten will die, unless the venom is quickly removed. They can also read minds or predict the future, one or the other, just like us, and can also shift into wolves when they turn eighteen.

They get their fangs when they're three years old. And, for example, if the Fusion's father was a Werewolf and they were to bite a Human, the Human would become a Werewolf with incredible speed. If the Fusion's father was a Vampire, however, the Human would become a Vampire that can read minds *and* predict the future."

"Wow," she said. "That's very interesting. Is that all?"

No, if you count the fact that Amaury was the only Fusion ever worth my time. "Yes," I replied.

She nodded, "I see." Again, we stood in an awkward silence.

"I think I need to leave. You know, before Ben and Magdelene get back. I don't want them to tear my head off."

"I understand," I said. "It was nice talking to you."

"You too," she said. Then she turned around and headed for the door. "Oh, and Radder?" she said, stopping just before she left the cell.

"Yes?"

"Thank you," she said. And then she disappeared, shutting the cell door softly behind her. Once again, I was left alone and in the dark. At least some of my thirst had ebbed.

I thought about how, right at this very moment, Ben and Magdelene were enjoying themselves. And, what's worse, they were together. They were each having the time of their lives with the person they loved. And me? I was stuck all alone in a dark cell. And the girl I love? Dead. Gone. Never again to take another breath on this Earth.

Thinking of Amaury, I vaguely began to remember the silent promises I'd made to her the night I was captured. The night before the day she died.

I'm coming Amaury. Stay where you are. I'll find you. I promise.

And:

Not long now sweetheart. I'll see you soon.

It's funny now to think of how I was so stupid that night, thinking that I would ever get to see her alive again after messing with Ben. If there was one thing in this world I knew better than anything else, it was what my brother did when you pissed him off. And it was never pretty. It didn't matter who you were or what you meant to him, if you made him mad for any reason, he would destroy you.

And that is exactly what he did to me.

I had given him plenty to hate me for. First off, I'd replaced his unborn baby brother. Then, I'd stolen his rightful place as King. During the time that I ruled the Coven, I had fallen in love with a Human girl. And then, after she had died, a Fusion girl. He had every reason to hate me, and he'd had three-hundred years to tear me down. But he'd waited until now, when I was finally starting to enjoy my miserable life.

I hate Benjamin. I hate him for taking away every ounce of respect anybody had for me. I hate him for killing Amaury. I hate him for taking away my life, and every reason I had for existing. I *will* make him pay. I swear it on my parents' graves.

I don't exactly know how, but someday, somehow, I will make him regret everything he's ever done to me. All I know is that I'll start by killing Magdelene, and make him feel how I do now. Lost, alone, and missing the one person who meant the world to you.

And I cannot wait until that day comes.

I have to find a way to escape this cell. I *need* to. If I don't get out of here, I will never be able to get my revenge. They're not going to let me go. If I don't get out now, I'll die in here.

But that's the thing. I can't get out. The chains that are on me are made of some material that I can't break. I have a hunch that the person who sells me the scent-covering soaps and shampoo knows Benjamin. And, since I know they make chains like these, I'm for certain that they were the one who sold these to my brother. And that really pisses me off.

I started to look around my cell, hoping to spot something that could help me in any way to get out of here. Then, something caught my eye. Jammed at an awkward angle in the wall, there was a nail. I hadn't noticed it until now, but that didn't surprise me. All I'd done the entire time I've been in this cell was cry over Amaury.

I had to strain against the chains to their maximum to reach the head of the nail. When I was able to grab it, I pulled as hard as I could. To my advantage, it was extremely long. That meant that, if I was able to make it thin enough, I could use it to pick the locks on my shackles.

It took quite a while for me to press down on the metal. Finally though, it became thin enough to fit through a keyhole. I angled my hand awkwardly, rubbing my wrists raw against the metal, and stuck it in the keyhole. I tried my hardest to angle it just right, and then to my satisfaction, I heard a small *click*. And with that, the shackle came off.

But when my wrist fell away, the chain the shackle was attached began to swing around. And to my horror, the nail slipped from the keyhole and fell to the floor. What's worse; the dungeon door opened right at that exact moment.

"No," I whispered. "No, no, no, no, no!!!!"

I reached down as far as the other shackle would allow me to, which allowed my fingertips to brush the floor. It was enough for me to be able to grab it, except that it was two centimeters farther than I needed it to be. Then, I heard footsteps coming down the stairs. I figured I could attempt to get it later, and make the shackle look like it was secured on my wrist. But if it was Ben or Magdelene coming down the stairs, which I knew it would be, they would check to make sure the shackles were secure. When they found that the one on my right arm had come off, they would relock it, and I'd never be able to escape.

That's when I realized something. If I strained my right foot enough, I would be able to pull the nail towards my hand. It wouldn't be much, but it would be enough for me to reach it. So, I did as planned, fighting back the urge to yell in pain when I felt one of my anklebones crack. After all the effort I put forth, I was finally able to reach the key. Except now, I had a broken ankle. Oh well. It was well worth it.

As quickly as I could, I unlocked the shackle on my left wrist. I then bent down and picked the locks around my ankles, satisfied as they fell off me. The footsteps then began to grow closer. Thankfully, my ankle had healed just in time. As silently as I could, I hid, pressed up against the wall by the door. Then, when the person opened the door and came in, I could run out, and, hopefully, lock them inside.

I held my breath as the footsteps grew closer still. *Just a little more, and-* The footsteps didn't stop at my door. Instead, they kept on walking. Confused, I stood in front of the door, pressing my ear against it. I heard another cell door creak open, and then shut again. I guess there was another prisoner. Either way, whether they were coming in here or not, I was going to choose this moment to escape.

Ever so silently, I slid open the door to my cell. Thankfully, Mary hadn't locked it when she left. I opened it just enough to squeeze through, and walked as quietly as possible down the cobblestone aisle. A familiar scent began to overwhelm me. It was stale, but I knew who it belonged to. It was Amaury's. Was it possible that, maybe, she wasn't dead? And instead, she was *here*?

Get a hold of yourself, I thought. *This scent is from a few days ago, when we broke in through the window. You saw the stake, Radder. She's dead.*

I took a deep, yet silent breath. *The window.* That thought ran through my mind again. It was possible that, if I could get through it on the inside, I could escape. It was a better chance then risking being seen by going through the castle's foyer.

So, I continued down the aisle of the dungeon. I smelled the strong, fresh scent of Benjamin in front of a doorway, and knew he must be in that particular cell. With whom, I had no idea. But, I decided to pass it quickly so curiosity wouldn't get a hold of me. After all, curiosity killed the cat. Or, I guess that in my case, it'd be Vampire.

I made it to the back of the dungeon, where the window was. Luckily, it was still open from a few weeks ago. Apparently, nobody had bothered to shut it. Just as I put my foot on the first crevice in the stone, I heard a cell door creak open.

Fuck. My. Life.

I scrambled up the wall, trying to make as little noise as possible. I heard Ben exit the other cell. Momentarily, I could hear the prisoner yelling, their screams muffled by a cloth or something. It sounded feminine, which only raised my curiosity as to who was behind the walls of that cell. Unfortunately, Benjamin's thoughts gave me no hint as to who it might be.

His footsteps continued down the long hallway. I was silently praying that he would continue walking, and that he wouldn't check in on my cell. He paused in front of my door, though, and I could hear him contemplating over whether to go in or not. I held my breath, but my prayers went unanswered. He opened the door to my cell, and the last thing I heard from him was:

"What the *fuck*?!?"

That's when I made my move. I scaled the stone wall and hopped out of the window so fast that I still can't believe I did it so soundlessly. When I was out in the open, I silently shut the window. If I did, he may not suspect it was how I got out, although, he could always follow my scent. As soon as the window was shut, I ran, not once stopping and not once looking back.

I ran at full speed until I reached the area just outside of Guéret. I moved along the dirt pathway until I saw a small white house in the distance, which I ran towards. Finally, I was home. As soon as I reached my house, I went inside, and got to work.

I went into my small laundry room, where I had some fresh clothes that had been washed in the scent-covering soap. I picked them up and carried them to my powder room, where I was planning on taking a quick bath, just to wash off all the dirt that had caked on me the night I was captured. I didn't know how bad I looked, but I figured it had to be awful. And boy was I right.

The sight of myself almost made me sick. My reflection in the mirror showed me, but, it wasn't me. I didn't look the same at all. My hair was nearly brown with mud, and all clumped together. In some places, you could even see the skin on my head. Aside from all of this, I no longer had a shirt, since it had been torn to pieces. The jeans I wore were completely ruined.

My entire body was, like my hair, completely covered in dirt. Plus, my wrists and ankles hadn't healed yet. Therefore, the skin was raw and pink, and the very sight of it made me want to throw up. Plus, my eyes were a sharp, menacing red, the only proof that I was still thirsty. Although, for once, the Thirst wasn't consuming me with its need for blood. The only thing that I was focused on at this moment was getting myself cleaned up and finding something to drink from.

It didn't take me too long to take a bath. I was sure to use the scent-covering shampoo and soap. That way, if Ben were to track me, it would be a lot harder for him to find me. When I had finished, I put on the clothes that I had washed in the scent-covering soap. I didn't think Ben could find me now, no matter how hard he tried or for how long he searched.

I was almost ready to leave my house, but I had to comb my hair first (Yes, I am a guy. And, yes, I comb my hair. But, considering its length, I kind of have to). Then, I remembered something. I had left my signature coat here the last time I'd gone to get Amaury. I smiled, knowing that it hadn't been ruined. But on the inside, I was frowning at the thought of Amaury.

I shook my head to clear my thoughts as I left the powder room. There was no use in getting all worked up in remembering her. All I wanted to focus on at this moment was grabbing my coat and getting some blood. I had to search for a little while before I remembered I had left it in my room. As soon as I walked in, all I saw was the clutter. I promised Amaury that I would clean this up. And I would keep that promise, despite that fact that she would never get to see that I'd kept one of the last promises I made her.

I blinked back the tears, refusing to let my mind go there. I just walked to my bed, grabbed my coat, and left my bedroom in the darkness. I scented my coat, to see if it needed washing, but it had no scent. Thankfully, the soap hadn't yet worn off, even though it had been two weeks since I'd been able to rewash it.

Putting my coat on, I began to walk out of the house. I decided that the first thing I would do was get some blood, although, I'd already established this. And, afterwards, I would go to Amaury's castle. I would search the crime scene myself. There was a chance that they had only faked her death.

Hell, it might not even have been her blood on the stake.

It might have been someone else's, and my paranoid mind was only playing tricks on me. And if it was all a lie, then she would be there. And if she was, I would finally tell her how much I loved her, and how much I'd missed her. I wouldn't care what she did or said when I told her, because, no matter what, I would love her forever. And, hopefully, she would say the exact same thing to me.

I crossed the field that surrounded my house and went back into the woods. I went deep inside them, straying far off of the dirt pathway. If I did, there was less of a chance that someone looking for me would be able to find me. Plus, there was more of a chance of finding bigger game this far in.

The first thing I spotted, as always, was a rabbit. I caught it and killed it swiftly, sucking it completely dry. I had to kill three more rabbits before my Thirst was satisfied. The death toll would've been higher, had Adam not given me the two cups of blood earlier today.

I wished I could have more Human blood, like the kind Adam had served me, but I didn't feel like risking myself being seen. But, lately, I'd drunk too much animal blood. I needed more from Humans if I wanted to survive. Though, without Amaury, I wasn't sure if I wanted to.

Once I was full, I went back towards the dirt pathway. I didn't walk on it, though. Instead, I stayed on the tree line beside it, under the cover of the foliage. I walked at a brisk pace, but dared not to run. If I did, I risked being heard by someone. And being spotted was never a good thing.

Even at the speed I was walking, I still made it to Chiroux rather fast. I figured that my longing to see an alive Amaury was the thing driving me forward. Soon enough, I saw her castle looming in the distance. Screw walking. I needed to run. I needed to make sure that it was all a lie; that my girl was OK. And if she wasn't, well, I wasn't sure what I'd do. I guess I'd just have to find out.

Finally, I'd reached her castle. My hand instinctively reached for the doorknob, but I stopped myself. This was the moment of truth. Here was where I found out if Amaury was really OK. If she was still even alive. Taking an extremely deep breath, I opened the door.

The first scent to hit my nostrils was blood. Sure, it had been a long time. But the smell of blood sticks around, as strong as ever, for the longest time. And the blood I smelled was emanating from a large puddle near the staircase. And it was hers. There was no denying that it was hers. But I would not, under any circumstances, believe that it was true.

I began running through the rooms of her castle. "Amaury!" I called. I must've said it a thousand times. But, there was never an answer.

The last room I checked was her bedroom. Perhaps she was only sleeping. Maybe she just hadn't heard me calling her. Although, when I opened the door, she wasn't there. Plus, her bed wasn't made. She was always tidy, and always had everything look nice. So, with all logic and reason on my side, it shouldn't be so untidy if there was someone there to fix it up. This was the third sign to me that Benjamin and Magdelene had been telling the truth all along.

Tears had begun to swell in my eyes. I left the bedroom, shutting the door softly behind me. I turned around, surveying the hallway. The powder room door was open, so she obviously wasn't in there. And she never went in the other rooms. I knew that for a fact. Unless, of course, she was in Rafe's old room. But every time she went in there, she cried. So, since it was only two rooms away from hers, wouldn't I be able to hear her sobs from here? I guess that all I could do was face the simple fact. Benjamin and Magdelene had been telling the truth. Amaury was gone. And she was never, *ever* coming back.

I felt the tears come on then. I sunk back against the wall next to her bedroom door, my head buried in my hands. I didn't want to be strong about this anymore. I loved her. I missed her. And if I was gonna be sad about it, then dammit, I was gonna cry.

I remembered then some words Dina had told me when I was little. *"Only the strong cry."*

And how true that was.

When I finally ran out of tears, I wiped my eyes with the back of my hand. The stains the tears had made on my cheeks were too noticeable, and a heavy burden to carry. I quickly went in the powder room and splashed my face with water. As much as I tried though, I could still feel the stains burning into my skin, a constant reminder of what I'd lost.

I decided that I couldn't stand it in that castle any longer. I left the powder room, making my way down the stairs at a vigorous pace. I was about out of the house, just a few feet from the door, when I spotted something on Amaury's desk.

It was her diary.

My hand slowly began to reach for it against my own will, and it was soon in my possession. I wanted to read it. I wanted to know every secret she kept from me. But, mostly, I wanted to see if she'd ever mentioned my name. I was about to open it and start reading, when a voice in the back of my head warned me not to.

Is it fair to read about her secrets, when you're still hiding the biggest secret of all?

I sighed, shutting the book. I couldn't do that to her. I placed the leather-bound diary back where it belonged, and I silently walked out the door.

It didn't take me very long to reach the city of Guéret. When I got there, I quickly hopped into a large crowd, trying my hardest to remain hidden. I didn't even know why I was here. I guess it was just because there were so many people that it would be difficult for anyone to find me. Or, perhaps, it was a good place to escape from your memories, even though the memories were flooding around me.

I was going to turn on the street that led to my secret alleyway, when I felt a hand grab my shoulder. I turned around to see none other than Anthony Smith. I was shocked, and a little frightened, but at least it wasn't Benjamin or anyone else from the Coven. Anthony's gaze was filled with rage, and he looked like he wanted to kill me. And I thought he might.

A young girl came up beside him then. They had a lot of the same features, and I figured they were somehow related. I learned by one glance in her mind that her name was Abigail, and that she was Anthony's granddaughter. She was glaring at me as well, perhaps even more harshly.

"Anthony, Abigail, nice to see you," I said with a smile on my face.

Their glares only narrowed at my words.

"What?" I asked. "Do you both have a cold shoulder or something?"

"Shut up and come with us," Anthony said sharply. "We need to speak with you."

Hastily, he began to walk away, Abigail at his side. Reluctantly, I followed them, pushing against the crowd of people. While we seemed to be in a sea of bodies, it didn't take us long to move through the mass of people. We came out near a booth that had nothing on its shelves but fruits and vegetables. Anthony moved behind it, as did Abigail, so I followed them. We came to a stop in there, and that's when I asked:

"What do you want to talk to me about?"

"A lot of things," Anthony replied.

"Like?"

"First thing on the list…murder."

I felt a lump rise in my throat. "Murder?"

"The murder of Agatha Smith." His eyes saddened, as did Abigail's. "In other words, my other granddaughter. Abigail's older sister. We found her, dead, with two bite marks, *fang marks*, on her neck. But there were paw prints all around her too, like there'd been wolves there. But, the fang marks were from a Vampire, not a wolf."

"What are you implying?"

"We think your Fusion girl is the one who killed Agatha."

I felt my eyes burn with rage. "You're crazy!" I hollered. "Amaury would never hurt anybody or anything!"

"Then explain to me how my granddaughter died!"

"I don't know!" I said. "But whatever or whoever it was, it was *not* Amaury. Get that in your heads."

"Fine," Anthony said. "Then what's your theory? Because if you don't come up with a good explanation, we're blaming your girl. And if we're for sure that she did it, *we will kill her*."

"It's too late for that," I whispered, my heart aching as I said the words. "She's already gone."

"Well, good riddance to her," he said. "Now, start talking."

I felt like ripping his throat out for what he'd just said. But, I restrained myself.

"My theory," I said, "is that one of the Coven's members was hunting her. They'd probably just snatched her away and had begun to drink her blood, when the Werewolves came. And, of course, since it's their job to protect the Humans, attacked the Vampire. That would explain the bite marks on her neck, and the evidence of wolves being there. I'm guessing that, if that were the case, the Vampire had already killed her by the time the wolves got there, and somehow escaped them."

"That sounds reasonable,' Abigail said quietly.

"Good," I said. "Then I'm going to leave."

"Not…yet," Anthony said. "I'm not done with you yet."

"What else could you possibly want?"

"I'm curious as to your past."

"What parts?"

"Like what you killed Brock for. And which of you kids was the one who killed Rafe."

"I killed Brock because I was sick of how he treated me, and just as angry for everything that he'd done to me. And the issue with Rafe is absolutely none of your business."

"Why not?"

"Because nobody but me needs to know the truth of what really happened the day he died. It's a secret I'll take to my grave."

"Why is it so dire that it remains a secret?"

"Because no one can know! I couldn't live with myself if anyone found out about it."

"Is it to protect your little Amaury?"

"I told you," I snapped. "She's gone."

"Gone can mean a lot of things."

"She's gone. Dead. Late. Lifeless. However you want to put it."

"I just thought you meant-"

"Well you thought wrong."

"How did she die?"

"Benjamin and his girlfriend murdered her."

"I'm sorry," he said. "But if she's gone, then who exactly are you protecting the secret from?

"Myself," I said quietly. I never wanted what had happened to ever be put into words, especially coming out of my own mouth. It was too big a burden to tell anyone about, even me.

"I see," he said.

"I'm sorry," I said. "It's…complicated."

"We understand," Abigail said. "You don't have to tell us about Rafe if you aren't comfortable with it. We were just hoping for a brief history lesson. But you've already told us everything we need to know."

"I'm glad at least some of us are happy," I mumbled,

just loud enough for them to hear. They both opened their mouths to say something, but a familiar voice pierced through the silence before they had the chance.

"Excuse me?" the voice said. We all turned to see Ruby Chauvin standing on the other side of the booth, a wide smile on her face. A smile that vanished the very instant she saw me.

"Radder?" she asked. "Wha- what are you doing here?"

"Having a quick little chat," I said. I was *not* happy to see her.

"Hi there," Anthony said, interrupting us. "How can I help you?"

Ruby turned to him. "Um- I just need whatever is in this basket." She slid it towards him so he could count the produce and total up the amount she needed to pay.

"Alrighty then," he said, taking the basket and beginning to count.

Ruby turned back to me. "A chat about what?"

"A chat about the Coven. Why do you ask?"

"I was only curious."

"Well, it doesn't concern you. So don't butt in."

"I'll try not to." She looked uneasy at my company, and I could tell that she didn't care about her produce at all. All she wanted to do was get the hell away from me.

Abigail smiled politely at Ruby. "You two know each other?" she asked the both of us.

"We've seen each other around," Ruby said slowly. I knew she was referring to the night at the Fanges Castle, where Amaury and I had attacked Ben and Magdelene.

"Oh," Abigail said. She looked like she wanted to say more.

"She knows what I am, Abigail," I said. "In fact, she came close to killing me before. Lucky me, she missed my heart with the stake she drove through my chest."

"Serves you right," she said. "I'm guessing you didn't see what happened after that, since it'd knocked you out cold."

"What happened after you stabbed me?

"That stupid girl you were with-"

"Amaury," I said. "Was not stupid."

"Whatever," she noted. "Either way, once you were out, she came at me. She picked up the candle that was still on the ground and trapped me in a ring of fire by igniting the carpet. If that tiny window wouldn't have been there, and open at that, I never would've got out. But I hurt myself pretty bad when I jumped all that way down onto the ground. Apparently, falling a whole story really hurts your feet."

"Thank you for enlightening us on that," I said. "Except, I don't believe that Amaury would do that to anyone."

"Well, she did," Ruby said. "I'd prove it to you if I could."

"Try."

"Well, she was just so overcome with rage. She just, like, went mad when I did that to you. I mean, I don't blame her. I would've done the same if anyone had done that to Sam."

"Ironically, I'd have done the same thing if anyone had done that to her. In fact, I'd have done it to anyone for even thinking about harming her." Too bad I couldn't have done that to Benjamin and Magdelene.

"I figured that," she said. Her voice was starting to grow shaky.

"Here you are," Anthony said. "That'll be-"

Ruby threw some money at him, suddenly panicked.

"Keep the change," she said, grabbing her basket. She was glad to be able to run away from me. And that's exactly what she did.

Oh no, I thought, *you're not getting away this time.* And then I bolted through the streets of Guéret after her.

Chapter 11
The New Vampire

Radder:

I ran. Not too fast, but fast enough to keep up with Ruby. There was absolutely no way that I would be able to take out revenge on Benjamin and Magdelene. It was impossible, considering how well guarded they were by the Coven members. Not to mention, they knew very well how to defend themselves against people like me, ones only driven by rage with no battle plan whatsoever. So, I was going to take out my revenge on the one thing that was easy to get. And at the moment, that thing was Ruby.

She ran through nearly all of Guéret, never once stopping or slowing down her pace. She knew I was after her, though she wasn't sure why. But at least she was smart enough to know that my intentions weren't good. She ran down darkened alleyways, high-populated areas, everywhere, trying to shake me off her trail. Unluckily for her, I knew every corner of this city. If anyone were to get lost, it'd be her.

Gradually, Ruby's pace began to slow. We ended up on a

narrow street that was seemingly vacant before she stopped all together. I thought that this was where I'd get her. However, she seemed to know this street fairly well, and quickly put the rest of her energy into running inside a nearby house.

She was in such a hurry to escape me that she didn't even bother to shut the door. Fortunately for me, she had chosen the absolute worst house to hide in. Nobody else was around to help her, and the house only had six rooms. Figuring this had to be her house, I searched for the bedroom that held the majority of her scent. Obviously, it only took about three seconds to locate. I burst in the door, where I saw her sitting on her bed. She appeared to be crying.

"OK, so you caught me," she said. "Do your worst."

"It won't be so bad what I do to you," I said. "Just what happens to you afterwards."

"What on Earth are you talking about? Are you going to drink my blood or something? Because I figured that there was no after effect."

"No, I'm not going to drink your blood," I said. "Trust me, it'll be much worse."

"What could be worse than you killing me?"

"Doing the exact opposite."

She didn't say anything, just looked at me with confused eyes.

Slowly, I stepped forward toward her. She placed her hands up to block her face, although I wasn't aiming to hurt her like that. Instead of throwing a punch or something, like she was expecting, I grabbed her left wrist and drew out my fangs.

"Say hello to a life without death," I said.

"Wait, no!" she screamed. "Please, anything but this! I don't care what you do; just don't turn me into a fucking Vampire!"

"Too fucking late," I growled. And, with that, I sank my teeth deep into her flesh.

I didn't let go of her wrist, though. If I did, she could suck the venom out before it had time to take effect. I couldn't release her until she screamed in agony. That would be the signal that the venom was doing its job.

She just looked at me like I was stupid. She was thinking about how the venom wasn't doing anything, and that, perhaps, she was immune to its powers. At least, until she started hurting. She was trying to hide the fact that it was hurting her, but it soon became too much for her to bear. She finally let out a scream, and I let go of her wrist.

"What did you do to me?" she shrieked.

"I bit you," I said.

"But…why? What did- I-" she stuttered, unable to finish.

"If you can't talk, just think the words to me," I said. She responded with another scream of pain.

It took her a moment to get her mind back to me. *What did I ever do to you?* she thought angrily. *Because whatever I did, I sure as hell didn't deserve this.*

I didn't have the words to respond to her question. The truth is, Ruby had never done anything to me, other than stab me in the chest with a stake. But it wasn't something that should get me mad enough that I turn her. It was just out of rage and loss that I did what I did to her. And if you put all that together, it made me no better than Brock when he changed me.

But, it was too late now. The venom was pretty much tearing at her insides, making all of her organs shut down. Except, of course, the heart, which still retains an extremely slow beat, even after we've completely turned into a Vampire. It does nothing whatsoever, but, despite its meaningless existence, it still beats.

Anyways, the venom tears away at the insides of the bitten, practically burning them away from the inside out. Along with the heart, the stomach remains. It's practically just a bottomless pit though. The remaining venom totally ends up in the stomach. This venom is what causes the Thirst. And when we Vampires drink, the blood goes straight to our stomachs and is vaporized in the toxins the venom holds. This is why we are always thirsty, no matter what.

Since this is what is beginning to happen to Ruby at this very moment, it can't be undone. The venom has already started eating up her insides. If someone were to remove the venom now, she would have nothing to keep her functioning. So, in a short sense, it would kill her. Once you've been bitten, there's no going back.

"Um- hello? Radder?" Ruby said. She sounded panicked.

"What?"

"How long is this going to go on for?"

"Approximately three hours."

She groaned in anguish. "Just kill me now," she said.

"I'm fine," I noted. Again, she screamed in pain, and fell back on her bed, laying down over sitting. She curled up into a ball and whispered, "Please make it go away."

"That's impossible."

"Then make it more bearable at least," she begged. "*Please.*"

"I'll try," I said. I sat beside her on the bed.

"Well?" she said. "Help!"

"OK, um-" I tried to think of something that would somewhat get her mind off the pain. "Just think of how powerful you'll be once this is all over."

"How much so?"

"You'll be able to lift up three castles with your pinky."

"That's pretty awesome."

"Yeah," I said. "Yeah it is."

"What else?"

"Well, you'll be able to kick anybody's ass."

"Even yours?"

"Yes."

She smiled. "Good, I can't wait." Her teeth gritted in pain. "I would love it," she said, "if you could find Sam and bring him here. Or Hazel. Hugo. Jared. Anyone."

"Unfortunately, I can't do that."

"Why not?"

"Because, they'd probably kill me."

"I wouldn't mind."

"You know what? Neither would I."

"Then why don't you get one of them?"

I sighed. "Because I bit you. In the Vampire society, that pretty much makes me responsible for you in every way. I need you make sure you survive the change, first of all."

"There's a chance that this could kill me?"

"Yeah. But you're tough, so your chances of dying are slim. Now, if you were sickly or something, you'd have less of a chance. The weak ones rarely ever live through the change."

"Good to know," she said. "'Cause I'm not done living yet."

"Well, you've got plenty of time to live now."

"I hate you."

"I figured you would. And I may warn you, the first hour and a half is nothing compared to the last half."

She wrenched in pain. "How could it be worse than this?"

"Trust me, it is. You won't even be able to open your eyes."

"Well, isn't that just great?"

"Not especially, but if you want to put it that way, sure." I elusively remembered Amaury saying that on our first trip to Guéret together, right after our argument. That had been the day that I'd first kissed her.

"Oh, shut up," she said. "This isn't funny."

"I know it's not. Being turned into a Vampire sure as hell ain't no picnic."

"How would you know?"

"How did you think I came to be a Vampire?"

"But, aren't you and Benjamin brothers? Because I know he was born a Vampire, so wouldn't the same go for you?"

"We aren't biological brothers," I admitted. "I was adopted by Brock as a baby after he killed my real parents. I was Human until he turned me on my eighteenth birthday."

"Must've been a pretty shitty birthday."

"It sure was. I didn't get a present or anything."

"Speaking of presents, what's my gift going to be?"

"Your gift?"

"Yeah. Vampires can either read minds or predict the future. I want to know what I'll be able to do."

"Well, since I read minds and I bit you, mind reading will most likely be your ability."

She gave a tiny smile. "Sweet," she said.

"Yeah, it's pretty fun searching through everyone's thoughts. If you want to know anything at all about someone, it takes about two seconds of snooping. It's great."

"So, will I be able to pick through your mind after this?"

"No."

"But, you just said-"

"All Vampires know how to put up shields to keep mind-reading Vampires out of our heads. I'll teach you how to use them," I added. That was a promise I intended to keep. But, at the thought of promises, I could feel tears coming on. I'd promised Amaury so many things; that she could trust me, that I'd pick up my mess of a room, that I'd tell her my secrets, the silent promises I'd made the night I was captured, even. But most of all, the promise that, one day, I'd finally tell her I loved her. But that would never happen now. I tried to stop the tears, but one managed to escape from my eye and roll down my cheek, which I quickly swiped away.

"That's pretty awesome," she said, her voice snapping me away from my thoughts.

"Not only that, but it's also very convenient," I said. I hoped she hadn't heard the crack in my voice.

"Well, I'd hope so."

"It is."

"So, am I gonna have to like, kill people to survive?"

"Unfortunately, yes."

She gulped. "Will I have any control? Or am I just going to be an absolute killing-machine?" The panic in her voice was evident. She doesn't want to become a monster, but she has no idea what I've gotten her into.

"You'll mostly have control. But I'll warn you now, the Thirst *can* take over you if you allow it too. It's not easy to resist it, but it's possible. I'll teach you how to do that, too. If you allow it to control you, though, you will become a blood-thirsty killing-machine. It's inevitable."

She gulped once more. "What will happen to me if I let it take over?"

"It controls your mind, so essentially you become brain-dead, and can't think or reason. That's why you go on a killing-spree. If it's not too far along though, you can be saved, but it takes special Vampires to do that."

"But what happens if I can't be saved?"

"You'll be destroyed."

"I don't want that to happen," she said.

"It probably won't. The only real way it happens is if you give your mind over to the Thirst. The only Vampires who were ever stupid enough to do that just wanted to escape an immortal life."

"Why?"

"In most cases, it was caused by grief. Especially if someone they loved died, and nobody would kill them, even if they begged them to. So, they did the only thing that they thought would make sense. And that was to give their mind to the Thirst."

"Why not suicide?"

"Do you really want to watch yourself drive a stake through your own heart?"

"No, I guess not."

"Exactly."

"I do have one more question about this, though."

"What's that?"

She let out a small whimper of pain and a small sigh before she spoke. "How do you know so much about what it's like when the Thirst takes over you?" she asked.

I took a long pause before I answered her. "Because it nearly happened to me twice."

"Twice? How? Why? Details, details."

I sighed. "Before Amaury, there was another girl I thought I was in love with. I killed her, though I'm not telling you why or how, and I was grieving over her for a long time. So, I starved myself-"

"Wait," she interrupted. "You have to *starve* yourself for the Thirst to take over you?"

"Yeah."

"But, that doesn't make sense. It should be the other way around."

"Except that when you gorge on blood you're satisfying the Thirst. You have to make it angry and thirsty so that it controls you. After all, it tells your brain that all you need is blood, and when you don't get it, then it takes over your brain until it gets what it wants. And all it wants is blood, blood, and even more blood."

"Oh," she thought for a moment. "Well, I guess that makes sense. Anyways, continue with your story."

"Anyways," I said, "I wouldn't drink for the longest time. Everyone in the Coven tried to get me to, but I refused. I wanted my life to end. In fact, for a time, the Thirst *did* take me over. I don't remember anything that happened; only that one morning I woke up in a tent with some ancient Vampire sitting over me. He'd calmed the thirst down before it took over me. I learned from then on to be more careful."

"Then how come it happened a second time?"

"It was an accident. Me and Amaury," I took a breath. It pained me to even say her name. "We had been at the lake, and I got thirsty, and so I left. I planned to only be a few minutes before I returned to her. But, Benjamin and Magdelene found me in the woods and captured me. They kept me in the dungeon, I just escaped today in fact, and they-" I had begun to choke over my words; tears were pouring down my face.

"Radder?" Ruby said. "What did they do?"

"They killed her," I said. I could feel the rage bubbling up inside me once more. "They killed Amaury."

Her eyes opened as wide as they could. "I'm so sorry."

"You should be. It's that reason and that reason only that I chose to ruin your life by making you an immortal, blood-sucking monster."

She sighed in dismay. "Don't remind me." On that note she winced in pain.

We were both silent for a moment before she said. "So, if you just escaped today, then how did the Thirst almost take you over?"

"When I was in the dungeon, Ben was starving me. Hadn't some members of the Coven come and given me blood today it would've taken over me for sure. Although, I'm sure that that was Ben's plan all along."

"You would think so."

"Exact-"

Ruby interrupted my words with a loud, painful scream. She curled into a ball, wrapping her arms tightly around her chest. She began to cough, and continued to whimper and shriek every now and then. Her mind went blank.

Finally, she managed to choke some words out. "Oh my God," she said. "Why the fuck does this hurt so badly?"

"Because the venom is eating up your insides."

"It's doing *WHAT*?!?" she yelled.

"You heard me."

"Oh my God," she repeated.

"Oh, trust me, it's only going to get worse from here."

"I *really* hate you."

"I'm sure you do. And after this is over, if you want to take out your revenge on me, go ahead. You can even end my life if you want to. I really don't care to be honest with you."

"I'm not gonna do that," she said.

"Why not?"

"Because I want you to suffer. And if I killed you, then you wouldn't be suffering anymore."

I sighed. "Haven't I suffered enough? My whole life has been nothing but me being taken advantage of. And every single good thing that's happened to me has been ripped out from under me. It's not fair."

"Yeah, well, life isn't fair. It's not like I asked to be turned into a fucking Vampire."

"I'm sorry," I said. "I'm just starting to realize how stupid it was of me to bite you."

"Well, gee, thanks. I'm sure glad that thought struck you *after* you changed me."

"I said I was sorry!"

She glared at me. "You're an asshole."

"Believe me, I know."

Again, she let out a loud scream of pain. When she stopped, a thought dawned on me.

"Where are your parents?" I didn't want them to barge in on us. I mean, what would you do if you walked into your child's room and saw them being transformed into a Vampire as one sat beside them?

"They're dead," she said. Oh jeez. I'd completely forgotten that she'd mentioned that the day we all invaded the Fanges Castle.

"Right, sorry, I forgot," I told her quickly.

"It's fine," she said. "It doesn't matter anyways."

"You know, if it makes you feel better, my parents are dead, too. Both my real *and* foster parents."

"Well, I guess that makes your rude outburst a *little* better…"

"Good," I said, giving a weak smile. "I'm glad. So, Sam isn't gonna come bursting in here, is he? Or one of your other friends?"

"They shouldn't, no. Anyways, I hope not. You won't hurt them or turn them, will you?"

"Not at all," I said. "I have a limit to how many people I make Vampires each day."

"Oh, you're *real* funny," she said.

"Aren't I?"

"No, not really," she said. "You need to take a lesson in understanding sarcasm."

"Actually, I'm quite good at it," I said with a smirk. "I mean, I have had over three-hundred-thirty years of practice."

She sneered. "Good to know. You'll be using that skill a lot around me."

"I assumed that."

She just sneered at me, then whimpered in pain.

"Please," she whispered. "Just bring me Sam. Honestly you're not helping me all that much."

"Well, I'm sorry," I said, "there isn't much I can do other than try and get your mind off of the change."

"Well, can you at least try harder?"

"I'm doing my best."

"Your best isn't good enough."

"Well, you know what? When I got changed, I was trapped in a dungeon, and the only comfort I had was the dripping noises and the scurrying of the rats in my cell. At least you have someone to talk to. I had nothing."

"Well, that was like, three-hundred years ago. Times have changed."

"Believe me, I know."

"Then stop comparing my change to yours. They're completely different in every way."

"Not quite," I said, "I went through the same thing you're going through right now."

"That's not what I meant. I mean, yeah it's the same, but it isn't. I actually have a life."

"*Excuse me?*"

"You said you were raised by the Vampires. To everyone in the real world, you and your family were dead. But I have friends, neighbors, a boyfriend, a little brother… People are going to know if I disappear. I can't just up and leave."

"We could always fake your death."

"Uh- no thanks. Besides, how would we even do that?"

"You jump off a building when the change is over, you won't be hurt, I promise. Then, I'll dress as an officer and get Razza to help me carry you off so that it all looks official and what not."

"OK, the first thing wrong with that is that everyone who knows me knows that I have great expectations for myself, and that I'd *never* jump off a building and end my life. And secondly, everyone at the station would eventually find out that something was wrong when no records of my death showed up in their files, and when they see that none of the officers know who you are."

"Hmm. True, true. But it's either that, or you just up and leave..."

"Or, let's just think of a better plan."

"Like?"

"We could do a fake-" Again, she interrupted herself with a loud, shrill scream. I realized then that it'd been nearly an hour and a half since I'd bitten her, so it would soon be turning to hell for her. I could hear her thoughts; she wanted to finish what she'd been about to say.

"Think it to me," I told her.

I think, she said, *we should do a fake kidnapping. You know, trash the house and what not, and leave a ransom note. I'm sure that would work. The police wouldn't find anything, even if you leave evidence behind. Nobody knows who you are.*

"That may work," I said. "Except for one thing."

What's that?

"There are a few people who know me."

You mean those people from the booth earlier?

"Yes. And that old man would stop at nothing to kill me."

Hmm, she thought. *Then I guess we will just have to up and leave.*

Suddenly, she cried out again, a bloodcurdling scream this time. It was so loud, I had to plug my ears. Her mind went completely blank, and she then slipped into unconsciousness. My heart skipped a beat. It wasn't normal to slip into unconsciousness when you were changing into a Vampire. Of course, there were some who had that survived the transformation, but usually if you blacked out, it meant that you were weak. And if you were weak and suffered through the change, more than ninety-five percent of the time, you died.

"Shit," I cursed. I didn't know what I was supposed to do. I could probably fish out a magician somewhere in this town, but they would probably be a fraud. It'd just be a waste of precious time. I would have to try and wake her up somehow, but…

Sam. Of course! If I could only find Ruby's boyfriend, or even her best friend, they may be able to awake her from her coma-like state. The problem was, I had no idea where to start. I figured I could track them down, but I'd need a scent. Perhaps, though, something in Ruby's room had the scent of at least *one* of them. And, if that were the case, then I should know who it belongs to. I mean, it's not like I've never met either of them before.

I began to search the room frantically, trying to pick up a trace of any familiar scent. The only one I could find, though, belonged to Ruby. In frustration, I picked up one of her pillows and threw it violently across the room. Just then, I realized something. When I threw the pillow, the slight breeze it made carried a new scent.

I quickly scrambled over to the spot where it landed and picked it up, pressing it to my nose and deeply inhaling the scent. It belonged to Hazel. Once I had it, I was able to sense a scent trail leading out into the streets of Guéret. I stole a quick glance at Ruby, I was certain she'd be OK without me for a few minutes, and then made my way out the door.

I shut the door quietly, glancing up and down the street to be sure that nobody saw me. When I saw no one around, I began to follow the scent trail that lead to Hazel. It began going left from Ruby's house, so I began to head that way. As I progressed, Ruby's street turned into a bad neighborhood. The cobblestone underneath my feet had begun to crack and wither away, and the houses became drab and run-down. The appearance of this place seemed to obscure the sky, even.

I ducked my head low into my collar. It was growing darker with each passing second. The people that lived here always looked and acted trashy. I guess that's why I had a hard time believing that Hazel, always so perfect-acting and rather pretty in appearance, would live in one of these slum houses. But alas, her scent trail weaved among these houses. She had to be here somewhere.

Her trail took a sudden turn off of the streets, and into a dark alley. I could see perfectly fine, but I had no clue as to why Hazel would be traveling amongst these streets. So much trouble occurred in places like these, and it was hard to fathom Hazel wandering around them. She may be nothing but a mere Human, but she's not stupid.

A sudden, unexpected ambush took me by surprise. Five men, all dressed from head to toe in black, hopped off the rooftops in front of me. I'd been so distracted by following Hazel that I hadn't heard their thoughts on their attack. But they were all Human. I'd pass through this easily.

"Why hello there," one of the men said. He stepped out in front of the others. I assumed he was their leader.

"Hi," I said. "How are you?" I smiled gleefully at him, which made him angry.

"What are you smiling about pretty-boy?" he asked nastily.

"Pretty-boy? Why, thank you." I beamed at him, trying my hardest to stifle my laughter.

He grabbed me by the shirt collar and lifted me off the ground. He removed his face mask to reveal a malicious-looking young man, probably about twenty or so, with grimy red hair and dark yellow eyes. He gritted his teeth, which were stained yellow, and got right into my face.

"You're a damn smartass," he growled. "You come waltzing in my alley with your rich-boy clothes and what not, thinking you own the place."

"Um, I beg to differ, but I never claimed to own anything."

His breath was hot in my face, and smelled as rancid as he looked. "I'm going to enjoy kicking your ass."

"And why is my ass going to be kicked?"

"We don't like your kind around here in these streets. We're gonna teach you to stay on your home turf."

"I wouldn't try kicking my ass if I were you."

"And why not?"

I drew my fangs out and felt my eyes go red. "Because I can kick your ass ten times worse."

His eyes grew wide, and he dropped me, placing his hands up in defense. "Hey man," he said. "I don't want any trouble."

"Really? 'Cause just a few seconds ago your view was quite the opposite of that."

He began to get farther away from me, and the other

four around him looked confused and alarmed. He was their leader, and wasn't supposed to show fear in front of their victims. They had no idea what was happening. I began to step closer, and they all turned to the red-headed man.

"What are we supposed to do?" one of them asked.

Red-head's gaze darkened. Then an evil smile drew on his face. "Grab your stakes and let's kill this bitch."

Again, it was my turn to be surprised. *Stakes? But, they're afraid of me, aren't they? And where'd they get the stakes so quickly?*

Each one of them drew a stake from nowhere, but they probably came from the back of their shirts. That's when my mind began to fit the pieces together. I hadn't heard their ambush. I realized then that it was not because I was focused on the trail, but because they had blocked their minds from me. The fear they'd shown had been a charade from the beginning. Also, I knew why Hazel had been safe to cross through here. She was a Human, and I wasn't.

These men were Vampire Hunters.

I began to back up from them. "What's your name?" I asked Red-head.

He smiled at me spitefully. "Jackson, Professional Vampire Hunter. And you are?"

I smile in spite of myself. This kid has no idea who I am or what I'm capable of. I look at him, a wicked look in my eyes, and say, "Pleased to meet you Jackson. I'm Radder Thor."

One of the men dropped his stake. "Jackson," he said. "We need to get out of here."

Jackson looked confused. "Why?" he asked. "It's just another Vampire."

"But-"

"Enough! We're standing our ground, just like we do for every other Vampire. If you don't want to fight this one for whatever reason, then get the fuck out of my sight."

The man shuffled backwards, ashamed, but held his ground. At least he had some sense. I'd spare him.

"You should've listened to your friend," I hissed. "He's smart enough to know when it's time to run."

"What do you mean?" he asked, turning around. The man had chosen to leave after all, abandoning his leader. Wise choice.

Jackson turned back to me, fire in his eyes. "You're gonna pay you little fuck."

Suddenly, he was charging at me. I jumped over him, landed directly behind him, and grabbed his neck in a choke-hold. Two of his followers charged at me. The other ran away like the previous one. He knew this was a fight that they couldn't, and wouldn't, win.

Jackson tried to claw my arm away with his hands. He'd dropped the stake already in his struggle, too. His face was beginning to turn a deep shade of purple; he was nearly dead. His followers were trying to form a plan of attack, but they didn't know what to do. Eventually, as Jackson was in his death throes, one charged straight for me, driving the stake at my arm. Unfortunately for him, I shifted at the last second, and the stake went straight through Jackson's right arm.

He attempted to cry in agony, but wasn't able to by the way I was holding him. Blood began to soak through his shirt, and the sharp scent of it hit my nose. Only then did I realize how thirsty I was. I released my grip on Jackson, and as the color began to drain back into his face, I bit his throat and began to drink.

His followers came at me again, both this time, one on either side. I'd already drained Jackson of blood, so I dropped his corpse and picked up the stake he'd dropped. As they got closer, I swung in a full circle and cut both of their throats open. They died almost instantly, falling to the ground beside their leader. I contemplated drinking their blood too, but decided I was pretty full.

With that ordeal finally over, I began to pick up on Hazel's scent trail once more. I continued to make my way down the alleyway, when I heard something that sounded like a muffled cry. I stopped in my tracks, turning towards the place the sound emanated from. There was a pile of crates sitting in the alleyway, and between the two piles was one of Jackson's followers. His mask was off, and he was stifling his cries into the fabric of it.

I assumed this was the man who'd known who I was; otherwise he may not be crying. He knew I was there, because he was staring straight at me. As I drew nearer, he put his hands up to block his face.

"Please," he begged. "Don't hurt me!"

"I won't," I said. "But only if you promise me something."

"What's that?"

"Don't drive a stake through my heart."

He gave a weak smile. "Alright," he said.

"Good," I said, sticking out my hand. "I'm Radder."

Reluctantly, he took my hand to shake it. "I know," he said. "I'm Devin."

"It's nice to meet you."

"You're not gonna kill me, are you?" His deep brown eyes looked pleading. I'm sure the last thing he wanted to do today was be viciously murdered by a Vampire.

"I wasn't planning on it. You were smart enough to know not to attack me back there. As long as you leave me alone, I'll do the same for you."

"OK," he said, sighing in relief. "I didn't want to be Vampire lunch."

"I figured. But either way, that's what Jackson became."

Devin gulped, his face growing a shade paler. "I didn't want to serve him, I swear," he said quietly. "Jackson took us all away from home and trained us for this. I never wanted to hurt anybody. I told him this'd happen one day. I'm sorry- I didn't mean to harm any of your kind."

I studied the boy. I saw then that he was fairly young, about fifteen or sixteen. "When did he take you?"

"When I was eight. Same for all the others."

"Was it kidnapping? Or did your parents give consent?"

"Kidnapping, I guess. I don't have parents. I was taken from the orphanage. So was Curtis." He must've been referring to one of the others, though I wasn't sure which one. I still couldn't access his thoughts. That raised another question to my lips.

"You said Jackson trained you for this. But where'd he learn to block his thoughts?"

"He never said. All he did was teach us and told us never to open up our minds, especially when we were out hunting."

"That's weird," I said.

"He told us to never ask about his past, or why he knew things and such. We never could figure out why. But we always assumed that he used to be in league with the Vampires, but they did something to piss them off, so he quit working for them and chose to hunt them instead."

"I'm not so sure," I said. "I probably would've heard his name come up somewhere."

"True," he said. He appeared to be deep in thought.

"How do you know who I am?"

"Jackson had us study Vampire history. Your name was mentioned often. But I guess I was the only one who remembered."

"No, you're not. Somebody else ran off too, a little after you did."

His eyes lit up. "Was it Curtis?"

"I don't know," I said. "He still had his mask on."

"Oh," he said, the light dying from his eyes. I had a feeling that he and Curtis were really close friends, considering they'd both grown up in an orphanage. They had probably been through a lot together.

"You know," I said. "I'm an orphan too."

He gave another weak smile. "I'm sure you didn't grow up in an orphanage though? Or with a crazy Vampire Hunter?"

"No," I chuckled. "But I was a Human raised by a whole Coven of psycho Vampires."

"Well, that sounds like it sucked."

"Believe me, you have no idea."

His smile grew slightly. Then, out of nowhere, he asked, "Brock Thor was your father, wasn't he?"

"Adoptive. Not biological. But, yes, I guess you could say that."

He nodded. "I've heard a lot about your turmoil with him. He was an asshole, I presume?"

"The biggest."

"Figures. No offense, but most Vampires are."

"Agreed," I said. "Are you going to go back to Vampire hunting after this? I'm just curious. The Minuit Coven is nearly wiped out."

"I know. And no, I probably won't."

I smiled. "That's good to know, Devin."

"Yeah," he said. He stood as he said it, brushing dirt off of his suit. He was as tall as I was, but rather gangly in appearance, and in the light I could see his features clearly. He had shaggy dirty-blond hair, and scars lined his face. Not the type of guy you'd want to mess with.

"Where are you heading?" he asked. "You obviously came down this alley for a reason."

"I'm looking for a girl named Hazel Deschamps. You know her?"

"Hazel?" he smiled. "Yeah, I know her."

"Great! Do you happen to know where she lives?"

"Of course," he said. "I can take you there, but first, I'd really appreciate it if we could go back to where Jackson is. You said only one of the others fled?"

"Yeah, just one."

He nodded. "I'd like to see which of my comrades have fallen."

I nodded in agreement. I was in a rush, but Ruby still had another forty-five minutes or so to go. She could wait for just a few more. Slowly, we made our way down the alleyway to where Jackson and his two dead followers lay. Blood was pooled all around them. Devin stepped to where the two un-masked bodies lay. He drew the mask off the closest, and nodded in silent respect. When he drew off the other man's mask though, the look of shock on his face surprised me.

"Curtis," he whispered to the dead man's face.

"I'm sorry," I said. Guilt made my chest throb. He bent his head low, but I could still see tears stream down his cheeks. But suddenly, he stood, making his way toward me.

"Let's go," he said. I hinted the anger in his voice.

"OK," I said, trailing behind him.

We wove through the streets of Guéret, until we left the slums. The sky got brighter as we walked back into a good neighborhood, and I smiled in spite of myself. Eventually, Devin stopped walking.

"Go straight from here, then take the first left. Her house is the fourth one on the right."

"Thanks, Devin. I'm still really sorry about-"

Without warning, Devin screamed with rage, flinging a stake at me at full speed. I just barely caught it before it pierced through my heart.

"*What the hell?*" I asked him.

"You killed my brother," he snarled. "So I'm going to kill you."

He and Curtis were *brothers*? Well, of course it made sense. After all, he'd cried for him where he hadn't for his other dead companion.

I gripped the stake tightly. "I don't think so," I growled. Before Devin could even blink, I had slit his throat open with the stake. He was dead before he hit the ground. Once he was out of the picture, I made my way down the street to Hazel's house.

When I knocked on the door, I was relieved to see Hazel

answer, and not some other Human. She looked shocked to see me.

"Radder?" she said. "What are you doing here?"

I hung my head. "I bit Ruby, and she's unconscious. If she stays that way for long, the change will kill her. I need someone she knows really well to wake her up, because I can't."

Hazel nodded quickly. "Let's go."

We made our way through the streets silently, but quickly. I was worried she'd take the alley and witness the bloodshed I'd caused, but she took a different route instead.

"This way's quicker," she said, noting my confusion.

Before I knew it, we were back at Ruby's house. We strode in, and Hazel made her way to Ruby's room, with me right behind her. When we opened the door though, we were both taken by surprise.

Sam was sitting on the edge of her bed. He looked up as we walked in, his eyes filled with pure hatred and rage. His eyes fell on me.

"Radder Thor," he said. "You're dead."

Chapter 12
Leaving

Radder:

Sam stood from where he was, striding over to me. "What the hell is this?" he screamed at me.

I backed up. "I didn't mean to-"

"But *why*? What possessed you to make my girlfriend a blood-sucking *demon*? I ought to kill you where you stand. And I just might."

I felt hot tears run down my face. "You really think I meant to do this? It was out of nothing but pure rage. My brother killed my girlfriend, and I needed something to take it out on. Ruby just happened to be in the wrong place at the wrong time."

His gaze softened. "Can you fix it?"

I shook my head. "The change is too far along. If we were to suck the venom out of her, she'd die for sure."

He let out a long sigh. "Will she have to leave Guéret?"

"I'm afraid so. She'll probably have to go and live with the Coven."

His eyes held a look of sadness. "So, this is the end of us, isn't it?"

It took me a moment to understand that he meant his relationship with Ruby. "Yeah," I said, "unless she makes you a Vampire too."

"I doubt that'll happen."

"Exactly."

"Why is she out cold?" Sam asked, running a little off topic. "I thought you were supposed to be awake when you changed."

"You are," I said. "That's why I brought Hazel here."

"So you expect us to wake her up then?" Sam asked.

"Yes," I confirmed. "Because if you don't, then she'll die."

"How do we wake her?"

"She's in a coma-like state, so I'd recommend talking to her. If she hears two familiar voices it, may be enough to wake her up. Oh, and also, when she does awaken, she'll probably be screaming at the top of her lungs."

"Thanks for the warning," he said.

"Seriously, you'll need to keep your ears plugged."

"Well I figured that one out."

"I'm glad," I said, a slight smirk on my face.

Sam and Hazel made their way over to the bed and sat beside Ruby. Hazel started to tell some story about when they were younger, and Sam just stroked her hand. When Hazel's story ended, Sam began to tell one. They went back and forth, never ceasing to talk, until I could hear her mind waking up.

"Keep going as you are," I said. "Her thoughts are resurfacing."

They both began to talk faster due to their excitement. They couldn't wait for her to wake up. Finally, her eyes immediately began to flutter open. But she just as quickly squeezed them shut, releasing a scream so loud I was surprised it didn't shatter a window. Sam and Ruby covered their ears at the last second, just avoiding becoming deaf. When her screaming ceased, Ruby began to cry. Sam took her in his arms, trying his hardest to comfort her.

She was in far too much pain to talk, but I could hear her thoughts clearly. Pain had numbed her mind, however, so her thoughts were just random, unimportant little phrases. I highly doubted that she was even aware of her surroundings, or the fact that Sam and Hazel were sitting right beside her.

Over the course of time, her screams began to lessen, and eventually ceased. She began to shake though, and the tears still flowed down her cheeks. Soon enough, even those things stopped, and Ruby finally opened her eyes. Her gaze roamed her room, eyes drinking in the sight of the new world she'd been forced into. By the sound of her thoughts, she was overwhelmed by how much the world had changed in her line of vision.

"Oh my God," she whispered. "Everything looks so… different! It's all so clear- I can see everything! And," she turned to look at her two friends, "I can hear everything that you two are thinking." Then she turned to me. "But not you," she said.

"I've established shields on my mind. I'll show you how to put them up in good time."

She nodded. "Will I be able to block other people's thoughts?"

"Yes," I confirmed. "I'll teach you that too."

Again, she nodded. Her hands were clutched into fists, and she was biting down hard on her lower lip. Her eyes, which had once been as blue as mine, were slowing turning a bright, blood-colored red. She was trying to control herself in front of Sam and Hazel, but I knew enough that I could tell how much she was struggling with being in their presence.

I turned to Hazel and Sam. "I think," I said, "that you two better leave, unless you want to become Vampire lunch."

Hazel's eyes grew wide, and she quickly stood from where she'd been sitting. "Goodbye Ruby," she said in a melancholy voice. "Remember, best friends forever."

Ruby didn't even flinch as Hazel made her way out the door. Sam turned to her once Hazel had left, about to say something meaningful. I turned away, but I could still here what they were saying.

"Ruby," he said, taking her hands in his. "I want you to know that I will always love you no matter what, but, we just can't do this anymore. I mean, have you ever heard of a Human and Vampire relationship ever working out?"

I smiled in spite of myself, my mind drifting back to Audrey. To be honest with Sam, I'd never heard of such a thing either. But it didn't matter now, because even though she's gone, Amaury and I would've been much happier than I ever would have been with Audrey. Vampires and Humans just don't mix in the relationship field.

I noticed then that Ruby had begun to cry. Sam was holding her tightly to him, as though he didn't want to let her go. "I'm sorry," he whispered. "If I could do anything about this, you know I would. I don't want to lose you. But this is the best thing for both of us." I saw then that Sam was crying too.

Ruby wanted to plead with him, but she didn't know what she could say to make him stay. She contemplated biting him right at that moment, but decided it was unfair. She didn't want to force him into his fate like I had done to her. So, she chose to let him go, despite the hardships it would bring. Sam bent down to kiss her one last time, then he stood to leave.

Right before he walked out of her bedroom door though, he turned to me. His eyes were red thanks to the tears spilling down his face. "Take good care of my girl, you hear?" he said to me. He slapped me once on the back, and then made his way out of the house.

Ruby was sitting with her arms resting on her knees, and her head on her arms. She was crying softly to herself, mourning her broken relationship with Sam. I made my way over to her bed and sat down beside her.

"Ruby, I'm so sorry," I said.

I expected her to blow up in my face, tell me she hates me, try to kill me, anything like that. But instead, she just turns her head away from me and whispers, "I forgive you."

I am, in a few words, shocked beyond mere belief. "What did you say?" I asked. I mean, I'd heard her, but I felt she needed to say it once more to confirm what she'd said.

"I forgive you," she said. "Obviously this happened for a reason. Of course I'm mad, I mean, I always thought that Sam and I were going to be together forever, and it's not going to happen now. But it's not your fault that your brother killed your girlfriend, which fueled your rage and caused you to change me. I bet you thought you were going to be with her forever, didn't you? And I mean, like, a *real* forever. Not just one Human lifetime."

"Well, I hoped it would eventually come to that," I admitted.

"Exactly. And Benjamin denied you that future, just like he denied me mine. If he hadn't captured you or killed her, you wouldn't be here right now. If anyone's to blame for me becoming a Vampire, it's him."

"Well, yeah, I guess. I still regret it though," I said.

"I understand why," she said. "But hey, maybe someday you'll thank yourself for changing me. I may become of use to you one day."

"It's possible," I said. "Who knows, maybe one day, you'll help me kick Benjamin's petty little ass."

"In good time, my friend, in good time," she said. A smile had finally grown on her face. "I feel like I'm going to puke," she said then, clutching her stomach.

"You won't."

"How are you so sure?"

"Because you can't."

"Oh," she said. "Well, there's one pro to being a Vampire."

"It's about the only one," I said. "The rest are pretty much cons."

"Great," she said. "So, then why do I feel like this?"

"That, my friend, would be the Thirst. It's reminding you that it needs blood."

"Fuck the Thirst," she said. "It doesn't need to hurt so bad."

"I know, right? But, no matter. It's not like we can change how it makes us feel."

"Very true," she said. "So, how do I draw out my fangs?"

"Very carefully. You have to kind of will it to happen."

"How do I do that?"

"Think about how thirsty you are, and focus on that. It should-"

She screamed in agony, holding her hand over her mouth.

"-work," I finished.

"Ow! What the hell?"

"Here, let me see," I said. Reluctantly, she opened her mouth so I could inspect the damage. Her fangs glinted at me.

"Well, you're not bleeding, and they're out all the way." I smiled at her. "Nice work."

"It feels like they're bleeding," she grumbled.

"I'm sure," I said. "But at least they aren't. It hurts ten times worse when they are bleeding."

"How would you know?"

"That's what happened the first time I drew mine out. It took a half hour for them to stop bleeding. And it *hurt*."

"I'd imagine so," she said. "So, now that I got them out, can we go hunting? *Please*?"

"I want you to draw them in and out at least twice more before we go," I instructed. She struggled getting them back in, but she finally became able. It didn't take long for her to get the hang of it, and so we made our way outside of her house and into the city.

"Whoa," she said as we stepped out the door. "This is amazing!"

I looked around with her, taking in the city. I hadn't seen it through Human eyes in over three-hundred years. It looked the same as always to me.

I let her take it in for a few more minutes before I said, "Well, we're going to have to find you a victim."

She turned to look at me. "A victim?"

I nodded. "Someone for you to drink from."

Her face went a shade paler. "I don't want to kill anybody."

"Well it's either you kill them and live or don't kill them and die. And I do believe you said you weren't done living yet."

"I'm not," she said. "But I don't want to kill people so that I can survive."

"Believe me, I know. I wish people didn't have to die for our sakes. But it's their fault for having the most nourishing blood."

She scrunched up her nose. "That's disgusting."

"This life is disgusting. Being a Vampire is anything but magnificent."

"Well, there's no changing it now," she said with a sigh. "So, what's the best way to get someone?"

"By going down a dark alley and finding someone who's cast off from everyone else," I said. She just stared at me.

"What?" I asked. "I'm serious!"

"I know you are," she said. "It's just really sad, picking people off like that. Who knows, they may have a family, kids, friends, a lot of people who care about them. It doesn't seem right for us to murder them for our sake."

I shrugged. "It's just the way things go. We're at the top of the food chain, they're at the bottom. It's life. Besides, these people go for a reason. And either way, if we don't kill them, something else will."

"I see that," she said. "But it's just so vile and wrong."

"It is," I agreed. "But like you said, there's no changing it now. It's just the way things are."

We made our way through the streets of Guéret, seeking an alleyway that would hold the perfect first victim for Ruby. We found one not far from her home, where a middle-aged man was walking past the various buildings, enveloped in darkness. His back was turned to us, and he was seemingly unaware of out presence.

"I want you to sneak up behind him," I said, "and grab him. Hold your hand over his mouth, though, so he doesn't cry out. Then bite his jugular vein and start drinking."

"Is that it?" she asked.

"That's it," I said. "Good luck."

She silently walked down the alleyway, blending in with the shadows, moving gracefully amongst the obstacles the alley held before her. I stepped into the darkness of the alley as well, to avoid being seen by any passers-by. I watched Ruby as she snuck up behind the man, as silent as a mouse, and grabbed him from behind. Her hand slammed over his mouth, and her fangs slid out, about to sink into his throat. But right as her fangs were about to pierce his flesh, she drew her head away.

I quickly strode over to her. "What's wrong?" I asked.

"I can't do it, Radder," she said. "I just can't bring myself to kill someone." The man was struggling in her arms, and I could tell she was contemplating on whether or not to let him go.

"Ruby, listen to me. If you don't do it this time, you won't be able to any other time. You won't survive."

"But... I'll be a murderer. Nothing but a cold-blooded murderer."

"Ruby, come on. Human rules don't apply to you anymore. It's not like you'll go to prison or anything."

"That's not what I'm worried about Radder," she said, her eyes blazing with anger. The man in her arms continued to struggle, so I bent down and hit the pressure point behind his ear. He instantly slumped over, unconscious. Ruby let him fall to the ground.

"Then what do you mean?" I asked her.

"I mean, do you know what it'll do to me when I kill him? It'll just make me want more and more and more, and before I know it I'll have killed a thousand people! And after the thousandth, it'll be the hundred-thousandth, then millionth, then-"

"Enough!" I said. "I get the picture."

"A million souls Radder," she whispered. "A million people dead at my hands."

"Think of it this way," I said. "It's like a Human killing a cow or pig to eat from. They have souls too, and yet people murder them. You know why? Because they're at the bottom of the food chain. It's eat or be eaten, or I guess in our case, drink or be drank from. But, since nobody needs us to survive, but we need people to survive, it's nothing. It's just who we are. We need people to survive, just as people need cows and pigs and such. Understand?"

She nodded. "Yes, but, I'll still be guilty about it."

"The guilt goes away in time."

"Are you sure? Has it gone away for you yet?"

"Not for me, no," I said. I felt my gut swell with shame.

"Well, then it probably won't for me. I mean, I have a soft-heart. You, on the other hand, are extremely cold-hearted."

"I have a soft-heart," I said. "I just don't show it very often." *Unless Amaury was here*, I thought. Then the fact that it wasn't cold would be as obvious as the fact that the sun will rise tomorrow.

"I can tell," she said.

"You know," I said, "I find it funny that you gripe about murdering people to sustain yourself, when you used to be a Vampire Hunter. That's murder if I ever saw it. In fact, you tried to kill me once before."

"That was different."

"How so? Vampires are living, breathing creatures with as much right to live as people. So how come you killed them without thought, and yet refuse to kill a Human for your own survival purposes?"

"Well, if you've forgotten, I was just a Human about three hours ago. Vampires kill Humans to survive. You've made that very clear. But if a Human being preyed upon by Vampires wants to survive, they have to kill the Vampire hunting them. And in doing so, that Human also protects everyone they love around them. At least, until another Vampire jumps into the picture. So, Vampire Hunting is a "survival purpose" as you put it. Oh, and for the record, I tried to kill you because you were about to kill me."

"I was not!" I said. "I just needed information, that's all!"

"Well I'd given it to you, yet you still wanted more, even after I'd told you everything!"

"Except that you hadn't. You *refused* to tell me what I needed to know."

"I didn't know what you needed to know, wasn't that clear enough?"

"Apparently not," I said.

"You are just so persistent with everything you do, Radder. You think everyone is against you and that you have to torture them to make them tell you what you want to know. Except that you usually don't listen to them, because you only hear what you want to."

"That isn't true and you know it!"

"Oh, but it is Radder," she hissed.

"No, it's not. Stop being such a goddamn bitch about this!"

Ruby smacked her hand hard across my face. I grabbed her wrist after it happened, drawing out my fangs to intimidate her. "I wouldn't normally result to hitting a girl," I growled. "But provoke me anymore and I'll kill you where you stand."

"I'm sure you'd love to, wouldn't you?" she hissed back.

"Very much so at the moment," I said.

We stood in the alleyway, staring at each other, ready to rip one another to pieces, when I heard a noise behind me. I let go of Ruby's wrist and saw the man beginning to stir.

"Last chance," I said. "When he wakes up he's going to run, and you'll loose your first meal. And you are in dire need of blood."

She glared angrily at me, I'm sure she wanted to kill me right then and there, but the Thirst almost forced her to go towards the man. She grabbed him right as his eyes shot open. He quickly opened his mouth to scream, but Ruby again slammed her hand over his mouth to shut him up. Then she sank her teeth into his neck and tasted Human blood for the very first time. It didn't take long for her to drain every last drop of blood from his body. When she finished, she dropped his corpse on the ground, wiping the leftover blood from her face.

"I'm still thirsty," she complained.

I nodded. "OK," I said. "Then we'll go find another Human for you to drink from."

"Sounds good to me." A smile grew on her face. Her temper had certainly gone down after she'd drunk the blood.

"I want you to track this next one," I said. "Think you can handle it?"

"Of course," she said. "It'll be easy."

She headed out of the alleyway, and began walking around the neighborhood. It took about five minutes, but we finally found another alleyway. Again, only one person inhabited it. This time, it was a woman, about twenty or so. Ruby snuck up behind her, as quietly as she had for the man, and grabbed her from behind. She covered her mouth before the woman could scream, and then sucked her dry.

When Ruby had finished, she walked back over to me. "Are you satisfied?" I asked her.

"Yup," she said. "So, what now?"

"We have to take these corpses and bury them."

Her eyes grew wide. "You're not serious."

"Oh, but I am." I remembered Jackson and his three followers that I'd killed earlier today. I contemplated going and getting their bodies to bury as well, but I figured that their bodies had already been found. It had been over a few hours since then, after all.

We walked down the alleyway and picked up the woman's body. "Why do we have to bury them? Shouldn't we just leave them? Then, when they're found, their families can bury them properly."

"We're going to bury them properly," I said. "We aren't just dumping their bodies in the woods."

"I know, but, it's more proper when they're surrounded by the people who love them, and not their murderers."

"*Murderer*, you mean."

"Yeah, murderer," she said, giving a very weak smile. "But also her accomplice."

I smiled. "Alright, I'll take that title any day."

"I feel really bad about this. Their families won't ever know what happened to them. It's pretty sad, really."

"I know," I said. "I wish it didn't have to be this way. But like I've said before, it's just the way it is."

She only nodded as we made our way through the back alleyways, trying to find the man's corpse. I hoped nobody would spot us. Eventually though, we came to the alleyway where he lay. Ruby picked up his body. Her face went a shade paler; she looked as though she was about to get sick. I also caught a tear run down her face.

"I killed this man, Radder," she whispered.

I placed my hand on her shoulder. "I know it's hard for you to comprehend that, but it'll all be OK in time. I promise."

She nodded. "How are we going to bury them, exactly?"

"What do you mean?"

"I mean, how are we going to get outside the city with them so we can bury them?"

"We have to put them on our backs and scale the wall," I said.

"Please tell me you're joking."

"I'm not."

"Oh my God," she said. Her face grew even paler.

"You'll be fine," I said. "It only takes about five seconds. But you *have* to be quick. We can't risk letting anyone see you."

"OK," she said. "Let's just get it over with."

Together, we both swung the corpses over our backs. I had done this a thousand times before, but it still made even me feel sick. Ruby and I walked through the alley until we got to the wall. We grabbed onto the cracks in between the stones and climbed up the wall as fast as we could. When we reached the top of the wall, we jumped down into the grass and ran towards the trees. When we were deep under the cover of the forest, we slowed our pace. Ruby stayed behind me as I led her through the forest. Finally, we came to a rather large clearing.

"What is this place?" Ruby asked, amazed. Hundreds of thousands of small wooden crosses dotted the landscape, marking an unknown number of graves.

"This," I said. "Is the Vampire Victim Cemetery. No Humans ever come around this area; it's a wasteland, so the Coven decided to bury their victims here. Only Vampires know about it. And even if you're banished, like me, you're still welcome to use it. It's universal, almost."

"This is sick and twisted in every single way imaginable,"

she said. She looked horrified. "All of these poor people."

"Well, at least it's better then just dumping them here. This could just be a giant pile of bodies for all the Coven cares. But at least we Vampires have enough humanity left in us to properly bury the dead."

"That's a good point."

"And at least we mark the graves. I mean, yeah, they're nothing but makeshift crosses made out of sticks and tied with string. But it's a helluva lot better than nothing. If I were one of these people, I'd be pretty grateful that my killer cared enough to bury me and mark my grave. Then again, that may just be me. But still, at least we aren't all that cold-hearted."

"Yeah, I guess," she said.

We stood silently for a moment, gazing across the vast amount of graves. Finally though, Ruby broke the silence between us. "Let's hurry up and bury these two," she said. "This place gives me the creeps."

"Me too," I said. "Let's get to work."

I found two spots in the cemetery where no graves were. I told Ruby to wait beside them so that I could get a few shovels. I walked across the clearing to a hollowed out tree. There were ten shovels hidden inside of it, of which I grabbed two. Shovels in hand, I headed back to where Ruby stood, waiting.

I handed her a shovel. "Bury the man here," I said pointing to a certain spot in the field. "I'll bury the girl."

She nodded, then plunged her shovel into the soft earth. I did the same, and I soon had a six foot deep hole. Ruby was a little behind me, but close enough. I placed the woman neatly into the hole, then shoveled the dirt back on her. It didn't take long to recover the grave. By the time I'd finished, Ruby was still at work.

"I'll be right back," I said.

I made my way back over to the hollow tree, placing my shovel back in it neatly. Along the side of the tree, there was also a wooden box full of string. I sought it out quickly, and removed two pieces of string. After I had them, I searched for small twigs amongst the trees. I found four of a considerable size, and made my way back to Ruby. She was just finishing up.

"When you're done," I said, "return that to the hollow tree over there." I pointed so she'd know where to go.

"Alright," she said quietly.

As she threw the last of the dirt on the grave, I got to work on the crosses. I placed one of the sticks across the other, tying it carefully with the strings. I did the same with the other two sticks, and I soon had two crosses. Ruby finished covering the man's grave, and then returned the shovel to the hollowed out tree. When she came back to the graves, I handed her the crosses.

"They were your kills," I said. "You owe them some respect."

Ruby took the crosses from me with a cold expression on her face. She drove them into the ground at the head of the graves, positioning them so they weren't crooked.

"There," she said. "Can we leave now? Please?"

"Of course," I said.

"Lead the way, then," she said.

"With pleasure," I said, smiling.

I lead the way by weaving through the graves. They were

scattered randomly about; I wished the other Vampires had cared enough to dig the graves in an orderly fashion, so that they lined up symmetrically. It would sure make this horrible place seem much more inviting. Not that it would be inviting under any circumstances, but still. A little order never hurt anyone.

We were still making our way through the cemetery when Ruby asked, "So, can I go home now?"

"Home? You're kidding, right?"

"No, I'm not. I'm sick of this. I want to go to my house, fall asleep, and wake up to find out that this was all just a bad dream." She began to fall behind me after she'd said it.

"Well, I hate to tell you, but this isn't a dream. I wish I could go home, too, and crawl in bed, and wake up to find that these past few weeks were all a bad dream. Then, Amaury would still be alive. But, unfortunately, she isn't, and I'll never see her again. Plus, I have a Vampire King and his whole Coven after me. Those are things you just can't sleep off."

"I realize that it's not a dream," she said, sighing. "But I wish so, so badly that it was."

"Well, no matter how much you wish, it won't come true. You'll just have to accept that you're not a Human anymore."

She nodded. A moment later, she spoke up again. "Who are they?"

I whipped around to face her. "Who is who?" She had her back turned toward me, pointing across the cemetery. Two figures stood, holding the body of another, shovels in hand.

"How long have you known they were there?"

"I just noticed, honest."

"How'd you see them in the first place?"

"I heard one of their thoughts. It was almost like a whisper. They're trying hard to block them."

I hadn't heard anything, but I understood how she had. She'd just been bitten today, so her senses would be stronger than mine for a while. I tried to focus on their thoughts, but they were heavily blocked. Then, suddenly, they turned towards us.

"Ruby," I said. "How do you feel about testing your amazing speed for the first time?"

"Sounds like a whole lot of fun," she said with a smirk.

"When I say to, run for your life. Got it?"

"Got it."

The two figures turned back to face one another. They appeared to be talking, though I couldn't tell from the distance between us. One of them continued to dig. But the other turned toward us, and in an instant, was running full speed to where we stood.

"Ruby, run!" I shouted.

We tore off through the woods. Ruby flew past me; like I said, she'd be a lot tougher than me for a while. I struggled to keep pace with her through the trees. It felt like we were going a hundred miles an hour, and I could almost feel the other Vampire's breath running down my neck. I figured it was just a figment of my imagination, but it sure as hell made me run faster.

Ruby kept the same pace the whole while we ran, never running out of breath. I however, was actually starting to get winded. A Vampire can only run so fast for so long, and I was going ten times my usual speed. I hadn't run this fast since the night I'd been captured. And I definitely hadn't gone for this long of a distance.

We were already to Maufanges by this point, and that was nearly two hours away from Guéret in walking distance. I began to think we were far enough away from our chaser. Ruby must've too, because her speed gradually decreased. It took a few minutes, but we finally stopped. We were both gasping for air, but we were alive and safe.

"Wow," Ruby said once she'd finally caught her breath.

"Tell me about it," I said. "So, how was that?"

She took a second to search for the right word. "Exhilarating," she said.

"That's a nice way to put it," I said.

"Well, it's true," she said. "Totally beats my Human speed."

"I wouldn't doubt it. But did you run fast enough? Jeez."

"Hey, *you're* the one who told me to run for my life."

"Fine, you win. Sorry," I added.

"Don't be," she said. She smiled widely. "That was so much fun! I'm so glad we got away from that person."

"Yeah, me t-" I stopped talking when I heard a twig snap behind me. I snapped my head around, only to see a man behind me. And I could not believe my eyes.

The man was rather lanky, and his brown eyes had been replaced by a bright, menacing red. Scars lined his face, only partially hidden by his unkempt dirty-blond hair. His black outfit was torn all over, and he had a pair of fangs that glinted in the sunlight. They were tinged with red. There was also a scar that covered the whole length of his throat.

"Devin?" I asked.

"That's right, Radder," he said.

"But- you're dead! I killed you in back in Guéret!"

"Correction: you *thought* you killed me. But no, I was perfectly alive. I'd just blocked my thoughts to the maximum so you'd believe I was dead and move on. Of course, I would've died, had a Vampire not crossed my path."

"Which Vampire?" I inquired.

He smiled ominously. "I cannot say the name of the one who changed me. They forbade it."

"C'mon, you can tell me. Benjamin? Magdelene? Adam? Maryanne? Razza?"

"None of them," he said.

"Then who else?" I asked. "That's the entire Minuit Coven."

"I never said it was anyone from the Minuit Coven."

"But you never said it wasn't. Besides, there aren't any other Vampires around here."

He smiled. "As far as you know."

I just glared at him. He spoke once more. "Anyways, my changer bit me almost right after you slit my throat. I only just survived the change. In fact, it was only about ten minutes ago that I finished the transformation. I just made my first kill, and my changer brought me here to bury them. I never dreamed I'd ever see you again. And you're going to be sorry that we had the privilege to meet once more."

"And why do you say that?"

He gave me the most wicked smile I'd ever seen. "Because I'm still thirsty."

He lunged for me, fangs bared, prepared to rip me to shreds. He was quick, but I was faster than he ever dared imagine. I grabbed him by the throat, his fangs only inches from my own neck. He struggled in my grasp, attempting to claw my hand away from his neck. His eyes grew redder by the second.

"You psycho little fuck," I said. "You can't drink the blood of your own kind. It'll kill you!"

"That's not what my changer said," he hissed back.

"Well then they, whoever they are, lied to you, Devin."

His eyes glowed with anger. "He would *never* lie to me!"

"How do you know?"

"Because," he said, "I'm part of his family."

"Wha-" I cut myself off when I realized what he said. "Is Curtis the one who changed you?"

"Very good, Radder," he said. "I'm pleased you were able to figure that one out."

"But, he was Human. And he died back in the alleyway with Jackson and that other guy!"

"No, he was a Vampire the whole time. We led you into a trap."

"Explain. NOW."

"Jackson, Alec, and Raoul were all Humans, as was I. Curtis was too, in the past. A long while ago though, we were hunting Vampires, when one got the better of us. It bit Curtis. Jackson sucked all the venom out, or at least, he *thought* he did. That night though, Jackson and the others were out, and Curtis and I were alone in our house. Curtis changed into a Vampire.

Meanwhile, Jackson had struck a deal with the leader of the Minuit Coven. He wanted you dead, and was going to give us a large sum of money. He later backed out of the deal, however, because he wanted to rid of you himself. Then, to-day, he called us up, saying that if we tracked you down and killed you he'd give us even more than he'd previously promised. He just wanted you dead.

We'd kept the secret of Curtis's change to all the others until today. We told only Raoul of this secret though. We ordered that if you came down that alleyway, which we figured you would, then he was to run away soon after I did. When that happened, I killed him, and as you left the scene where the other three lay, I ran around the alleyway with his body.

Curtis, of course, was alive when I arrived. He had already healed from the slit you put in his throat. I placed Raoul's dead body next to Alec's and Jackson's, then quickly ran ahead to the crates where you found me. Then, you know the rest. And after you "killed" me, Curtis came and bit me to ensure my survival. It was rather simple, really."

"Simple? Sounds pretty complicated if you ask me."

"That's because you're not the sharpest person around."

"So, Ben's behind this all?" I asked, mostly to myself.

Devin answered me anyways. "Yup."

"Well, how'd you know I'd be crossing through that particular alleyway?"

"When Ben noticed you escaped from his dungeon, he knew you'd be taking your rage out on something, most likely in Guéret, so we ended up there. Not long after we arrived, we saw you chasing Ruby, and we knew you'd turn her. We hoped something would go wrong that would require Hazel's assistance, and we knew she passed through that alleyway often. It wasn't surprising that her scent trail would lead there.

And, I guess luck was on our side, because you came striding through, just as we'd thought."

"So, essentially, you were stalking him? And my best friend?" Ruby asked.

"In a sense, yes," he answered.

She sneered at him. "That's extremely creepy," she said.

"Only a little," he said.

"No, actually, quite a lot," Ruby said.

I cut off their argument. "Where's Curtis?" I asked Devin.

"I told you, he's burying the man I killed," he said.

"Is he coming here afterwards?"

"Of course," he said. I hadn't noticed until now, but his scars had all already healed.

"Ruby," I said, "get ready for your first fight."

"OK," she said. She got in a stance for battle. "I'm ready," she said with a smirk.

"He could be here any second now," Devin said. "He was just starting to cover the grave when I left."

Almost at that exact moment, something black flashed past me. I threw Devin a few feet away, to stall him for a few seconds. I whipped around to see a man standing beside Ruby, clutching both of her arms. He had a twisted-looking smile on his face, and his eyes blazed with a look of pure evil. He looked a lot like Devin, except he had black hair, and a more muscular figure.

"Curtis," I hissed his name.

"Hello Radder," he said. "What a pleasure it is to meet you."

"Oh, I'm sure it's quite a privilege," I said.

"You know," he said. "I really wish we had time to chat,

but, duty calls. So, I'm sorry, but I'm going to have to rid of you."

"I'd like to see you try," I said.

"Really?" he asked. "Well, that can be arranged."

Curtis let Ruby go, but pushed her against a tree so she couldn't help me. He pulled a stake from nowhere, just like he had earlier, and plunged it at me. It missed its target by a mile, but managed to graze my leg. Curtis swore under his breath, then charged at me again. He bit my shoulder, but I managed to punch him square in the jaw. He was thrown back so far that I couldn't even believe I'd been the one to hit him.

I considered going to grab the stake, but before I could make up my mind, Devin snuck up behind me and grabbed me in a chokehold. It wouldn't suffocate me, but it would sure as hell slow me down. I strained against him with all of my might, and managed to harshly bite his hand. He yelped in pain, but refused to let me go. So, I did the only other thing I could. And that happened to be to kick him as hard as I could in the shin.

That made him release his grip on me. I turned to check on Ruby. Curtis had again set his sights on her for attack. She was holding up pretty well, but I could plainly see that she was struggling. Therefore, I made my way for the stake that Curtis had thrown. Once I'd grabbed it, I lunged at Devin.

He didn't even see me coming. I stabbed the stake through his heart before he could even think twice about what was happening. He fell to the ground in an instant, dead for real this time. I pulled the stake from his corpse and made my way to where Curtis was fighting with Ruby. He had her in a hold that she couldn't escape from.

"Let me go you insane freak!" she shrieked.

Instead of letting her go, he hit the pressure point behind her ear, causing her to pass out. Then he dropped her, and turned to me. He pulled out another stake from absolutely nowhere and gave me an evil smile.

"I bet you planned to play hero today, huh?" he asked. "Well, unfortunately, that's not going to happen. You're going to die, your girl is going to die-"

"*My girl*?" I questioned.

He pointed at Ruby with the stake. "Aren't you two together?"

"No," I said. "My girl is dead. I just bit her, and I'm teaching her the ropes of being a Vampire. Once she knows enough I'm taking her to live with the Coven."

"Well, I'm afraid you're not going to be able to make that trip."

"You're all talk and no action," I said with a sneer. "If you're seriously going to kill me, go ahead and give it a try already."

"My pleasure," he said with a hiss.

Again, he lunged at me, stake in hand, but this time I was prepared. I threw my stake at his to block his attack, using it as a sort of sword. Every move he made from then on, I was able to block with my stake. At one point he aimed for my heart, but I grabbed his stake with my left hand, and thrust my stake through his chest. By the look on his face I knew I'd plunged it straight through his heart. Before he'd even hit the ground, he was as dead as his brother.

I kneeled down beside Ruby where she lay. It didn't look like she'd be waking up on her own anytime soon. I wanted to wake her, but I wasn't quite sure how. I figured splashing water on her face would help, but I didn't know of any water sources near here, other than at the Fanges Castle. *Unless*, I thought, *I go to the Enfer Castle.*

The Enfer Castle was the now abandoned meeting place of the Minuit Coven. Despite that it was well hidden in the woods, it was only about a five minute walk from here, considering we were about ten minutes from the Fanges Castle. I thought it would be a pretty good idea, so I picked Ruby up and carried her to the neglected castle of the Vampires.

It didn't take long for us to arrive at the Enfer Castle. The Gothic castle wasn't nearly as big or magnificent as the Fanges Castle, but it was still a beautiful building. I remember coming here once I month when I lived with the Coven. We would hold a meeting discussing how to rid of the Werewolves and things like that. Afterwards, we'd have a ball.

Nobody was left out of the dancing, and everyone had a blast. Those nights had always been fun, and something to look forward to. After I'd left, it was one of the few things about the Coven I missed. But they ended the meetings here when most of the Coven died off. Now they hold meetings in the parlor of the Fanges Castle. Such a waste of such a wonderful place.

I opened the doors to the castle, brushing away the cobwebs that blocked my entry. I made my way inside once they'd been demolished. I was surprised to see this place. It had been destroyed. Cobwebs covered nearly every inch of its interior. Tables had been knocked over, the tile floor was cracked, and all the priceless lamps had been shattered.

I would've turned around and left right then and gone elsewhere, had Ruby not begun to stir.

I carried her into the parlor, where there were at least sixteen couches. Most of them had been ripped to pieces. I managed to find one that was undamaged, however, and set Ruby down there. I, meanwhile, walked around the room. I couldn't believe what a mess this place had become. Plus, where it had always had always been bright, even in the darkness, it was now darker than a moonless night. I searched around for a candle and matches, but I couldn't find any anywhere.

Finally, Ruby awoke. She shot up when she noticed the darkness, and how she was no longer outside. "Radder?" she called out frantically.

"I'm right here," I said. I was only standing a few feet away from her.

"Where are we? And why is it so dark?"

"We're at the Enfer Castle."

"*Where*?"

"The Enfer Castle. It used to be the Minuit Coven's meeting place, but it's been long since abandoned."

"Hell Castle," she said. "Perfect name for something belonging to Vampires."

I chuckled. "Isn't it though?"

"Well, why are we here? And again, why is it so dark?"

"It's dark 'cause there's not a damn candle in this place. And we're here because Curtis knocked you out, and I didn't really know where else to take you. Plus, I wanted to try to wake you up by pouring water on your face, and this was the only place I knew of that may have water."

"Hmm," she said. "What about Devin and Curtis?"

"They're dead."

She nodded. "Well, can we leave now then, since I've woken up, and we're out of danger?"

"Of course," I said. "Follow me." I left the parlor and made my way towards the front doors. Ruby stayed close behind me.

"This place is creepy," she said.

"It didn't used to be," I said, stepping back outside into the brightness of the day.

We made our way out of the forest before Ruby asked, "So, what's going to happen to me now?"

"I'm going to take you to live with the Coven."

"Oh," she said. "Is that the only option?"

"I'm afraid so," I said.

"But, you still haven't taught me how to block my thoughts, or-"

"The Coven members will teach you that," I said.

She stayed silent the rest of the way. When we reached the gates of the Minuit Castle, we had to slide through the bars. Together, we walked down the cobblestone pathway to the giant oak doors. I knocked loudly on the door, dreading the fact that Benjamin might be the one to open the door. Unfortunately, my suspicions were correct. My brother swung open the door, a look of anger on his face. That anger deepened the moment he saw me.

"Radder?" he said. "What the hell are you doing here?"

I partially ignored the question. "This is Ruby," I said, motioning to her. She gave a small wave at Benjamin, and I wondered if he remembered her as being one of the Humans that had raided his home only weeks before. "I changed her," I explained, "and she wishes to join the Coven." She opened her mouth to protest, but a quick glance from me shut her up.

"Ruby?" Ben asked. "Ruby Chauvin? The same who raided my house not long ago?"

OK, so he remembered. Ruby gave a small nod. Ben smiled at her. "You fought pretty toughly for a Human," he recalled. "I'm sure you're even better now that you're a Vampire?"

"Yeah," she said weakly.

He smiled. "Then I'll welcome you to my Coven with open arms." He turned to me. "And as for *you*-"

"Benjamin," I said. "You won't have to hold me prisoner anymore. I'm leaving Guéret for good, and I'm not coming back. You won't have to worry about me ever again."

He nodded. "Very well. I will be sending out some of my Warriors to make sure you're gone though, understand?"

I nodded. "I do. Goodbye Benjamin," I said.

"Farewell, Radder," he said. He motioned for Ruby to go inside, gave me a wave, and then shut the doors.

Sighing, I made way back down the pathway and through the fence. I walked silently to Guéret, wishing so badly that I didn't have to do what I was about to. When I finally reached my home, I went inside and went straight to my bedroom. I pulled a large bag out of my closet and began to throw things in it. Clothes, a comb, my scent-covering shampoos and soaps, money, the blue suede bag on my nightstand that Amaury had been so keen to open, and a few more odds and ends things. When I was packed, I made my way out the door, and began to walk away from the town and home I knew so well.

I walked for nearly an hour and a half until I reached a new town. By then, it was already night. I laughed quietly to myself; I couldn't believe the intensity of the day I'd had. When I walked into the city, I went up to one of the townspeople and asked him where I was.

"Why my boy," he said. "You're in Fremont."

"Fremont," I said. And then I asked him, "Where can I find a house for sale?"

Chapter 13
Released

Amaury:

I didn't know how long it had been since Benjamin and Magdelene had taken me as their prisoner. All I knew was that it had been a very, very long time. I wanted out of the bindings that denied me my freedom. And I wanted to see Radder. I had the feeling that he was very close to me, as though he were right beside me, although, I was alone in this cell. That much I knew.

I wondered what had become of him. I hadn't heard anything about him or from him since the night he stood me up for the second time. The more I thought about, I just couldn't shake the belief that Ben and Magdelene had to do with his disappearance that night. But, why? I mean, I know how much they hate the both of us, but is that reason enough to try and separate us forever? If they get to be happy together, then shouldn't Radder and I be able to too?

Regardless of what I thought, though, whenever Benjamin came into the cell to see me, he ignored my pleas to be set free. Instead, he only inflicted pain on me, both physically and emotionally. However, it wasn't as bad as he'd planned to make it for me. Occasionally he'd draw a knife on me, cutting open my arms and legs. He'd meant for it to cause incredible pain, but it wasn't too bad. I healed fast, and even though the cuts were deep, they vanished almost instantly. The worst part about it was that for some odd reason, the scent of fresh blood caused the rats to swarm around me. And I do not like rats.

The other physical pain was the food and water. I was so hungry and thirsty that I wasn't. I was for the longest while, but eventually my Vampire side took over, begging for blood instead of food. I'm sure the Thirst would've taken me over, but the Werewolf in me wouldn't allow it. It was like my own personal Yin and Yang. So, in short, sometimes I was starving, and other times I only craved blood. It was never balanced; the scale always tipped one specific way.

I guess that was another reason Ben cut me with the knife. He must've hoped that it would eventually trigger my Thirst to an extreme, letting it conquer my hunger. If that happened, I'd loose my mind for sure. That had to be what he wanted. It'd certainly guarantee that I'd be out of his and Magdelene's hair for good. And then with Radder out of the picture, they could finally live in their sick little fairy tale world that they forced upon everybody else around them. I mean, what would they tell their kids? That they killed their adopted aunt and uncle to make life better for themselves? Now that was a demented thought.

Despite all the physical pain he caused me though, it was nothing compared to the emotions I was being forced to feel.

The guilt that whatever happened to Radder was my fault, the sadness that he wasn't here beside me, the worry of what had become of him. It was unbearable. I didn't care if I never got out of this cell. I didn't care if the Thirst took over me. I only cared about him, and I wanted my questions answered. But Benjamin and Magdelene wouldn't say a single word about him, and I didn't know enough to piece it all together myself. I was, literally, being kept in the dark.

Despite my knowing that I couldn't piece what little information I had together, I had nothing better to do than to try. I started with the notes that Ben and Raven had given me. I could recite the words perfectly in my head. There was Raven's note of course, which read: '*You can run Fusion, but you can't hide, find who you're looking for, and they'll serve as your guide.*' And then there was Ben's: '*You can run Fusion, but you can't hide, learn to trust no one, because everyone lies.*'

These, unfortunately, weren't of much help. The only person I was searching for was Radder, and I couldn't search for him while I was being held prisoner. And I already had lost trust in everyone I know, and so far doing so has done nothing for me, other than confirm that I was truly alone. If only I could find out who Raven really was, maybe that would give me the information I need. I mean, whoever she was, she has to be in league with Benjamin somehow. Their notes had been so similar in structure that it was hard not to think that.

Then again, Raven had been trying to protect me from Radder. She'd told me he'd only hurt me, but I hadn't believed her. And look where I am now. I'm hurt and alone, tied up against my will in a Vampire's dungeon, all because I hadn't taken heed to her warning. Or perhaps that had been the plan all along. I had no idea. Nothing fit together at all.

I didn't realize how lost in thought I'd been until I heard the creak of a door opening. Footsteps echoed throughout the dungeon, sending a chill down my spine. Suddenly though, the footsteps ceased, and I heard no more. *That's odd*, I thought. *I know I heard someone*. Minutes continued to drag on though, and there was still no sound to be heard. I had just begun to relax, thinking I'd imagined it after all, when they started up again.

I felt my muscles tense as the steps grew closer and closer. Finally, my cell door creaked itself open. In the doorway stood a very masculine figure, one that could only be Benjamin. His voice confirmed my suspicion.

"Hello Amaury," he said maniacally. "And how are you this evening?"

I'm fine, thank you, I thought sarcastically.

"Good to hear," he said, stepping closer, little by little, in an intimidating manner. He reached into the pocket of his jeans and pulled out a sharp knife that was covered in blood. *My* blood. He stopped a few feet in front of me and then asked, "Do you know what this is?"

Duh, it's the knife you cut me with, I thought crossly.

"True, it is, but the answer I was looking for was simply just a knife. Now, other than slicing through skin, what else can this be used for?"

Cutting practically anything, I thought.

"Right you are again. But, what if I told you that this is a special knife used for a specific purpose?"

I'd say, "OK, I don't care," I thought. He was beginning to bore me.

"You don't care?" He faked astonishment. "Well, then what if I was to say that its specific purpose is to cut the ropes that are keeping you in that chair?"

My eyes flew open, then narrowed. *I don't believe you*, I thought. *It's nothing but an ordinary knife.*

"That's what you think," he said with a smirk. He suddenly drew another knife from his other pocket, about the same size and texture as the other one, pointed it at me, and said, "Observe."

He covered the last few feet it took to be right in front of me in one swift movement. He picked up a segment of the rope and tried to cut it with the new knife he'd just removed from his pocket. He began to saw at the rope, but not even a fringe of it came loose. Then, he took the other knife and began to cut on a different part of the rope. A partial amount of the rope broke almost instantly when it came into contact with the knife.

"Each coil of rope comes with a single knife like this," he explained. "Each knife is made specifically for that coil of rope, and that single knife is the only thing that can break it."

How is that possible? I thought.

"Don't ask me," he said. "Ask the guy I got it from. Anyways, if this is destroyed, I can almost guarantee that you'll never leave this cell."

And how exactly are you going to destroy it? I thought.

"That's the funny thing about these knives," he said. "The ropes they cut through are as tough as steel, and are unable to be cut with a normal knife. But where as a normal knife is extremely hard and nearly unbreakable, these knives are so fragile that it isn't even funny."

What do you mean? I thought. I couldn't believe what I was hearing.

"I mean that it's so fragile, that I can do this." He gripped the blade of the knife in one hand, the handle in the other, and snapped it in half as I watched him in horror.

"Oh, and one more thing," he hissed. "The broken pieces can still be used to cut the rope. But only if they haven't come into contact with blood." A wicked smile grew on his face. "Have a fun lifetime in here," he said. "Or at least, have a nice one up until you die."

You're a sick, twisted–

He raised his hand up to stop my thoughts in their tracks. "Now now, we'll have none of that," he said. Slowly, he made his way toward the door, only stopping for a moment to turn and say, "Au revoir." Then, he had vanished, and I was alone once more.

I felt hot tears burning into my skin. I couldn't believe that he'd just taken my last chance at freedom. But that was so like him, to build you up and then tear you down. As long as he benefited from it, he didn't care what happened to anyone else. But even so, that crossed the line. I'd never get out of here now, unless he was lying about the knife fragments being unable to break the rope once blood touched them. But there was only one way to find out.

He'd left the pieces on the floor of the cell, right in front of me. It was possible that if I could reach far enough with my foot, I could grab a hold of the knife fragment. I slid myself down as far as I could go, and was able to just barely take hold of the broken knife. Luckily, I'd grabbed the sharp segment of it, so if it could still cut it wouldn't take so long.

I brought the piece closer and closer to me, until I was able to sit normally and still have it within reach. I used both of my feet to take hold of its sides, flipping it so that the sharp end of the knife pointed towards the ceiling. It took a few tries, but I finally managed to get it right. After that was done, I inched the knife closer to rope, until they came into contact.

It was awkward trying to cut the rope. I had to move my feet up and down in unison, but it came to no avail. I kept trying for a long while, but the rope refused to break. I guess what Ben had said was true. I'd never be getting out of here now.

I could instantly feel my hope dying inside of me. I didn't know what else there was for me to do. Then, all of a sudden, an idea sparked in my mind. What if I tried to force a vision? I mean, they were only supposed to come to you every once in awhile. But I'd bent the rules once before, and I was almost certain that I could easily do it again. It'd take a lot of time and effort, but I sure had plenty of both to spare. It's not like there's much else to do. So, I decided to try this insanely genius idea of mine.

I wasn't exactly sure what to do, because I don't think anything like this has ever been attempted before. But I decided to start by pressuring my mind to let something through; anything. Unfortunately, that did nothing except for give me a headache. So, I decided to try something else. I let my mind go completely blank, and let nothing surpass through my train of thought. All I could see was blackness, and I thought of nothing. Not a word, not an image, nor a memory; I allowed myself to see nothing besides the darkness in my mind. And then the vision came.

It came on suddenly, very much like a bolt of thunder after the lightning paints the sky. I still couldn't see anything, but I heard sounds. The whisper of the wind as it raced through the trees, the sound of rain as it pounded into the earth, and ironically, the roll of thunder across the valleys. Lightning forked across the black night sky, illuminating the few remaining stars that had not yet been hidden by the dark gray clouds up above.

Amongst the trees, there was a muddy path. A girl was walking fast-paced along it, half running, half sliding in the mud under her feet. I couldn't make out her details; only that she was wearing a long black cloak that had a hood. Or, maybe she wasn't. It was much too dark to tell.

She took a moment's pause in the middle of the path, then turned to her left and headed into the forest. My mind followed her, but as much as I searched, I couldn't find her in the darkness of the forest. In time though, I saw her figure crumpled in a heap on the ground. She was clutching something tightly to her chest, and she was sobbing loudly. I could see no more than that fact, and then, the vision came to a close.

I felt my eyes open wide, and I noticed that I was breathing heavily. Who was that girl? Raven perhaps? The vision had only raised even more questions than I'd had before. I tried to keep my anger in control, but it had finally got the best of me. Nobody, not even my own mind, would give me any hints as to where I was or what was going on. I just couldn't take it anymore. I wanted to scream so badly, but I couldn't manage anymore than a muffled cry through the tape that covered my mouth. I couldn't wait until I could find a way out of here; I was going to rip Benjamin's head off, and he'll regret the day he messed with me and Radder.

I began to struggle against the ropes that kept me in the chair. No matter what though, nothing would damage the rope. I tried rubbing the part of it that held my hands together against an edge of the chair, but even that did absolutely nothing to help my cause. Deciding I was wasting my time, I started to try something that might actually benefit me, and that was attempting to remove the duct tape that covered my mouth and denied me my voice.

I contemplated the best way to remove it, and figured the best way was to wet my lips where the tape closed around them. So, I started this, and was rather shocked when, eventually, the tape unstuck from around my mouth. I kept at it, trying to at least loosen an edge of the tape. That way, I could rub it up against my shoulder and, hopefully, peel it off.

With each passing minute, the tape began to come looser and looser. It eventually stripped away from the whole area around my mouth, and so I began to rub it against my shoulder. It didn't take long for the edge to begin to cur away from my skin. Then, finally, after many long minutes of working on it, it came free, but only from one side of where it'd been stuck. It still hung loosely on the right side of my mouth, so I had to use my right shoulder to get the remnants of the tape off. I watched it flutter to the floor in a curled up mess, and then shrieked with joy.

I took in a long, dramatic breath through my mouth. The air wasn't exactly fresh though, and I could taste it with the breath I took, but I didn't care. It had been so long since I'd opened my mouth that even the foul taste and rancid scent of the air couldn't bring me down. In fact, nothing could, except for the remembrance of why I'd been trying to get the tape off in the first place.

I felt my anger boil up inside me again, and it flared once more. Something I wasn't controlling, probably the ever-angry Thirst, caused me to shout in pure anguish.

"So Ben?" I hissed to nothing, minus the walls and the rats. "This was your plan huh? Trying to keep me away from my voice, trying to drive me insane? Well guess what, it didn't work! I'm tired of your sick little games, and look at how easily I can get out of them! It'll just take a little time, and effort, but I'll get out of here soon enough! You'll see, you'll all see!"

After this little rampage, I was winded. I'd lost control of my head for awhile there, but when I just thought I'd got it back, the rage took over again. I managed to realize why this time, though, before my head left me. It was because I'd heard all my words echo back at me. They hadn't traveled anywhere farther than this cell. Whoever built this dungeon had made it so that the prisoner could hear what was going on around them, but everyone else couldn't hear a single thing that escaped their mouths. It was a sick way to drive someone completely insane.

Again though, I shouted at the walls. "What, aren't you going to answer me?" I screamed. And even though I already knew the answer, I added, "Won't anyone answer me?" When nobody did, I cried out, "Somebody tell me something! *Anything*!"

Of course, no answer came. When my echoes faded, the silence began to emanate around me, reminding me of how alone I truly was. I had nothing here but the walls and the rats. That's when I began to cry. The tears came on strong, refusing to cease, no matter how hard I tried to make them stop.

I wanted out of here. I wanted to go home. I wanted Radder to be beside me, and hopefully find out that this was all a dream, and that none of this hellish nightmare had been real. But I couldn't go on thinking like that. I had to face reality for what it was. I was stuck here, I wouldn't be going home anytime soon, Radder was gone, and this was anything but a dream.

But maybe I could make part of it a dream. I closed my eyes tightly. They felt heavy after I'd cried so much; I was *still* crying, in fact. I just tried to escape from where I was, and willed myself to see blackness once more. Only, this wasn't completely thoughtless like it had been before. Instead, images of Radder began to run through my head, and before I knew it, I'd fallen into a deep, dark sleep.

When I awoke, I was lying in a field. All around me were flowers of every different type of shape, size, and color. My skirt and blouse had been replaced by a thin, but not see-through, white dress, that ran to abut the length of my knees and had very thin straps. I stood then, brushing pieces of grass and flower petals off my dress, and began to walk. Before me, there was a castle, three times the size of the Minuit Castle and bigger than any I'd ever seen before. The bricks were made of an odd peach-like color, and on the top was a giant clock tower.

Although I was very far away from the castle's doors, it took me almost no time at all to reach the vicinity of the castle. As I walked toward it, I stirred up about a hundred butterflies, which began to dance in my path. Each one had its own unique color and design, and each was as beautiful as the last. I didn't get to admire them for long, however, because I finally approached the oversized doors of the castle. I raised up my hand to knock on the wood, but they swung open before I had the chance.

Cautiously, I entered the castle. In front of me was a long and very tall stairwell, which was covered by an elegant red carpet that stretched all the way to the entrance. The floors and stairs were made of a luminescent white linoleum, and there were large, curtain-less windows everywhere. With the light of the sun against the linoleum, the whole inside of the castle appeared to be glowing. I began to walk along the red carpet, but about halfway to the stairs, I came to a stop. I'd heard a noise somewhere in the castle. The echo of it didn't help much though; the castle was so big and roomy I couldn't pinpoint the direction. Quickly though, I found out.

At the top of the stairwell were two doors. They swung open, and a figure dressed in a black shirt and a pair of jeans began to make his way down the stairs. I had a suspicion of who it was, but his head has ducked low. I wouldn't be able to see until he lifted his head. And when he did, I nearly shouted with joy. I had been correct. It was Radder.

"Radder!" I shouted excitedly. He hadn't noticed me until

that point, and after his moment of surprise passed, a smile quickly grew on his face.

"Hello Amaury," he said.

Unable to contain my excitement, I began to run toward him. For some reason though, I couldn't go very fast. Catching the gist of my idea though, he began to quickly make his way towards me as well. I finally managed to reach the bottom of the stairwell at my snail-like pace, as did he, but before he could take me in his arms and hug me, we froze. I began to get scared. I had no idea what was going on.

Before I knew it though, for some strange, unknown reason, Radder burst into flames. He fell to the ground, nothing but a pile of ashes. I tried to hide my utter shock and horror, but I was unable to. It took me a moment afterwards to realize that the castle had become darker. The sun had stopped shining in the windows, the carpet had turned a deep black, and the linoleum a vermilion red. While I was taking all of this in, I noticed something. The ashes had been picked up by a wind that had suddenly begun to blow, and were swirling around rapidly. Then, they turned into something that made my heart skip a beat.

They had turned into Benjamin.

I looked at him with a look of utter horror. He returned my expression with a wicked smile and said, "Hello Amaury. Did you miss me?"

When I said nothing, his smile only grew. His fangs were drawn out, and he clearly displayed them in his smile. They were soaked through with blood. "I certainly missed you," he said.

"Why do you say that?" I said.

"I awfully missed your company once you left the dungeon."

"But I'm still there-"

"Not quite," he said.

"What are you talking about?"

"I mean you're not exactly "there." You've made yourself drift into this dream world as an escape, but I won't allow it. You're supposed to be in agony at this moment, and just a moment ago you saw Radder. Or rather, an image of him. If I'm to keep you my prisoner, I can't allow you to have any enjoyment."

"You're psychotic."

"Maybe," he said. "But at least I'm not alone, and resorting to my dreams to be happy." Now that stung. "He's never coming back you know," he said. "Radder I mean."

"Yes, he will," I protested. "I know he wouldn't abandon me."

"Are you sure?" he questioned. "He did once before."

"That was different. He had a reason."

"Well he has a reason now, too."

"And what would that be?" I asked.

"He's tired of you," Benjamin said. "He doesn't want you around anymore; you don't mean anything to him."

"You're a damn liar," I hissed.

"Maybe so, but not this time," he said. "If you think he's going to be Prince Charming and come to rescue you, you're sadly mistaken."

I didn't say anything in response to him. I couldn't usually feel any emotions in my dreams, but this time I felt like I wanted to cry. I didn't, of course. But it would've made me feel a whole lot better. Also, I wanted Ben to be gone, and to have my dream in peace. He could torture me when I awoke back into hell.

Ben spoke up then. "I'm sick of the small talk," he said. "Now, how about the real reason I'm here?"

"And what would that reason be?" I asked skeptically.

His smile grew even more devious, and his eyes shone with a demented new light. "That reason," he said, "is to make sure you never wake up."

My eyes grew wide. "*What?* But why? "

He shrugged. "It's what Magdelene wants. She says she's sick of having you around." He paused for a moment. "Not only that," he added then, "but she wants you to die in the most terrifying way that I can muster. So, what better way than to have you perish inside of your own nightmare?"

He didn't give me time to answer before he lunged at me. I noticed then that he was holding a knife. He kept attempting to stab me with it, but I dodged every blow. The evilness in his eyes was directed at nothing but me, and had the look of insaneness inside them. I knew then that Benjamin would not give up until I was dead. Unless I could do something to make him stop.

"Why use a knife as your weapon of choice?" I asked him, still continuing to dodge the knife with each attempt he made.

"Because," he hissed. "I'm going to make you bleed to death."

"Is that even possible?" I asked. "I thought Fusions could only be killed with a silver-tipped stake."

"Yes, it's possible," he said. "If the wounds are deep enough and inflicted in the right places at the right moments, it's possible for any immortal creature to bleed to death. We're no better than those worthless mortals."

"You used to seem to think that," I growled.

"True," he said. "But I no longer think so shallowly."

"Yeah," I said. "Like I'm going to believe that."

He said no more, and he also stopped trying to stab at me as much by this point. Instead, he started to grab for me so he could keep me still. But I refused to let him take me like that. Unfortunately, I had backed up all the way to the doors. I tried to make a run for them, but they slammed shut in front of me. When I tried the handle, it wouldn't budge. I was locked in, and I was trapped.

Ben continued to move forward, graceful and lithely, like a cat on the prowl. He clutched the knife so tightly that his knuckles were as white as the floor had been when I'd first entered the castle. And then, there was his eyes again. Every trace of evil I could think of was hidden in their depths. Ben had completely lost his mind.

He was getting closer and closer by the second, even though he was taking his own sweet time. I told myself not to panic; I had to find a way out of here, after all. If I let my mind focus on the fact that I was about to be murdered senselessly, I'd never be able to escape. And that's when I got a great idea.

I took a deep breath, then looked him square in the eye and said, "OK, Ben, you win. I'm not going to fight a war I know I can't win."

"What are you up to Amaury?" he asked. The smile remained on his face, and he seemed almost delighted as he said those words.

"Nothing Ben," I said. "I surrender. There isn't anyway I can get out of this. You got me."

"That's what I like to hear," he said. "Just for being so cooperative, I'll try to make your death as painless and quick as possible."

"Thanks for being so considerate," I said with a smile.

"You're so very welcome," he said. "Now, without further ado." He covered the last few feet it took to be in front of me in an instant, and snatched my right arm. "We'll start here, now-"

He had started to explain the process, but I didn't even give him one chance to finish. Instead, in the blink of an eye, I transformed into a wolf. The force of me ripping my arm away was enough to knock him back. It wasn't much, but it was all the time I needed to make a fast getaway. In my wolfen state, I was much stronger than in my "Human" one. So, I rammed into the giant oak door behind me. A hole was immediately punctured into it, which I slipped through. Once I was out of the castle, I began to run as fast as I could.

The outside had changed as much as the inside of the castle had. The grass was a dark, sickly green. The sky was now a deep red, and black clouds covered its vast expanse. Even the butterflies had changed. Their wings were now a pitch black, and scarlet blood ran down there wings, dripping off every time their wings fluttered. The blood spattered in the grass, beginning to turn it into a field of blood. I continued to run, but changed out of my wolf form. It took only a split second to do so, but somehow Benjamin managed to end up in front of me. If I hadn't skidded to a halt in the nick of time, he'd have had me for sure.

"Going somewhere?" he asked in a taunting manner.

"How'd you get in front of me?" I questioned. "I'm faster than you, plus I had a head start. It's impossible."

"In this place, I can bend the rules however I wish. In fact, I can even do this." He didn't move a muscle, didn't even flinch, but suddenly I was caught in his grasp. I struggled, trying to break free from him, but I couldn't escape.

"Now, now," he said. "There's nothing to worry about. It'll all be over soon."

Then, he drew his knife along my arm.

After the first cuts he'd inflicted, I woke up. I was back in the dungeon, and my head felt groggy. I could feel the three cuts he'd made burn into my skin, and felt the blood trickle down my arm in a rather disturbing way. I thought the cuts would heal, but after a long while the bleeding continued and refused to cease. I was starting to get light-headed, and I figured that this would be the death of me.

Then, a miracle happened. Or, at least, what *I* would call a miracle. My cell door opened wide, revealing a figure. I panicked at first, thinking it was Benjamin, until I realized that the shadowy form before me was much too feminine. Plus, it was much too thin to be Magdelene; this person before me was as thin as a twig. They began to come closer and closer, until they came into view. And their identity nearly took my breath away.

It was Raven.

I tried to speak, but she put her finger to her lips, ordering me to remain silent. For once she wasn't wearing her cloak, and I could see that her hair was a wavy mass of blonde. I felt like I'd seen her before, but not in Guéret, where I'd seen her all those other times before. There was something even more familiar about her that I just couldn't place. And it wasn't until she looked at my arms, and clearly displayed the defined expression of horror combined with disgust that I remembered so well. The only time I'd ever seen it, though, was on the face of Vampire outside this castle the day Benjamin broke into my home. This Vampire was not, as I'd always suspected, Raven Navre.

She was Razza Lacoste.

My only living relative.

"You have to be very quiet," she whispered to me, nearly soundlessly. "I'm going to stitch up your arm and stop the bleeding as much as I can. OK?"

"Razza," I choked out her name. "Why are you helping me?"

She didn't seem surprised that I'd figured out who she was. She answered me then. "Because," she said. "You're my sister's daughter. I promised her I'd protect you."

"But you're supposed to be loyal to the Coven."

"Fuck the Coven," she said. "Benjamin and Magdelene are just thirsty for power. They're running through a corrupt system. They'll fall eventually, and the Wolves will take over us. We don't stand a chance. I'm just playing along for now, but I'm working against them. That way, when the Werewolves kill them all, at least I'll be around to make sure the Vampire race survives."

"How thoughtful of you," I said. I was beginning to get drowsy.

"Just hang in there Amaury," she said. "You better not die on me."

"I'll try not to," I whispered. She began stitching up my arm then, and was finished in no time at all. I then felt something cold touch my arm, and I flinched away from her.

"Relax," she said. "It's just a wet rag. I'm trying to clean up the blood on your arm."

I nodded silently, allowing her to rid of the blood. It took her only a few short minutes to finish up. When she had, she took my face in her hands, forcing my eyes to open, although I hadn't been aware that they were closed. She looked directly into my eyes, and said, "Amaury, don't let them take your head away from you. Keep yourself sane and they'll let you go soon enough. I promise. Do you understand?"

I nodded solemnly.

"Good," she said. "Good luck."

"Thanks," I said.

By that point, she had let go of me, and was making her way to the door. She was about to open it when she said. "Oh, and one more thing."

I lifted my head as much as I could to see her before she departed, but all I could see was her shadow. "What is it?" I whispered.

"You'll find who you're looking for," she said. And with that, she was gone.

After Razza was gone, my head began to pound. I was in so much pain, though I didn't really know why. Thanks to the stitches, my wounds were already starting to heal. I had no idea what was going on. All I knew was that the pain was unbearable. That was my last thought, and then, before I knew it, my world went black.

When I next awoke, all I could hear was noise. It stirred me from my dreamless slumber, and I must say, it also scared the living crap out of me. When I woke though, I found that my head was no longer gone from me, and I was able to think clearly. Therefore, I realized that the noises I was hearing were footsteps, coming from above my head. It sounded like a bunch of people running around, most likely frantically, or in a hurry.

I had only been awake for a few moments when I heard the cell door open. Someone made their way quickly down the stairs, and were then on the pathway to my cell. It didn't take long for them to approach my door, which swung open suddenly. In the doorway stood Benjamin. His hair was in a mess, and he looked angry and disheveled.

"Amaury," he said with a snarl.

"Yes Benjamin?" I asked.

"You haven't seen anything...suspicious recently, have you?"

"No," I said. "I've been asleep for... I don't even know how long. But it's been a long while. Why do you ask?"

His expression lightened. "No particular reason," he said. "It's just that we've had an... incident."

"What incident?"

"That doesn't concern you," he said.

"Then why would you mention it to me?"

"I had to make sure you didn't see anything you weren't supposed to."

"Well, I'm sure I didn't," I said. "I just woke up a few minutes ago, in fact."

He breathed a sigh of relief. "Good," he said. "That's exactly what I wanted to hear."

"That's great news," I said sarcastically. "Now, will you please leave me alone?"

He smiled. "Maybe I will," he said. "Or-"

More footsteps sounded down the stairs. They were at a full blown running pace, and reached the cell in seconds. The Vampire approached Benjamin, and I felt my rage grow. It was Magdelene. She took no notice of me; instead, she went right beside him and began to whisper into his ear.

She hid her mouth with her hand so that I couldn't read her lips. I did, however, manage to catch the last few words she said. And they were, "…at the door." When she finished talking, Benjamin's eyes widened in frustration and surprise.

"*What?!?*" he said suddenly.

"What happened?" I asked.

Magdelene finally glanced my way, giving me a dirty look. "None of your concern," she hissed. Then she turned back to Ben, softening her gaze. "We need to go," she said, grabbing his sleeve.

He nodded, then turned to me. "I'll be back later," he promised. Then, he slammed my cell door shut, and together they quickly made their way up the stairs. The cell door shut behind them, and I was left alone once more.

It was a long while before I heard the cell door open again. I'd managed to fall asleep again, but I was only for an hour or two, or so I assume. The rest of the time I sat in waiting for whatever it was Benjamin would bring when he returned. But now, I was about to find out. The footsteps were nearly silent, and extremely slow, seeming to drag on forever. Still though, whoever it was approached my door in just about no time at all. When my cell door came open, I prepared myself for the worst. But Benjamin disregarded my fear, and instead strode over to me casually. I gave him a confused look, and he just shrugged.

"So," I said. "What's your plan this time? Gonna sweep me into another dream and try to kill me? Or knock me out and finish the job? Or even-"

"Shut up Amaury," he said, placing his hand on his forehead. "You're lucky I'm not going to put more tape over your mouth."

"Why?" I asked. "Because you know I'll get it off?"

"No," he said. "Because I'm letting you go."

I opened my mouth to say something, until his words sank in and I realized what he'd just said. "*What?*" I asked, completely bewildered. I had *not* seen that one coming.

"You heard me," he said. "I've decided that you've been here long enough, so I'm letting you go scot-free."

"Are you bullshitting me?"

"No."

"Then there's a catch? There's gotta be."

"The only catch is that after I let you go you have to promise to stay out of my hair from now on. If you don't, I'll kill you."

I was still suspicious of him, but Ben didn't appear to be joking. He approached me then and began to untie the rope around me. He did my feet first, then my torso, and then my hands. I was really free from his clutches. I stood up as soon as he untied my hands, preparing to make a run for it if it was necessary.

"I'm not going to recapture you after I just let you go," Ben said.

"Whatever," I said. "Now, I have two questions for you."

He shrugged. "Ask away," he said.

"First of all, what day is today?"

"April 7th."

I nodded. "Secondly, where is Radder?"

"Radder," he said. A wicked smile replaced his bored look. "My brother is long gone by now."

"What do you mean?"

"I mean he up and left. Didn't even take the time to search for you."

"How do you know he's gone?"

"I sent the Coven members out to check out every square inch around his house and Guéret, plus all the woodland. There's no trace of him anywhere."

My eyes narrowed. "I don't believe you," I said.

"Go ahead and check it out for yourself then," he said. "He's not around anymore. He's probably in a different country, even. Who knows?"

"I know he wouldn't leave," I said. "Not without searching for me. And he'd never stop looking for me. I know that."

He shrugged. "Go see for yourself," he said. "Just don't be mad when you find out that you're wrong."

"I will," I said. "And I'll be sure to rub it in your face when I find him."

And with that, I turned and walked out of the dungeon. I headed up the stairs and out the cell door, entering the castle's foyer. Nobody was around to try and stop me, so I headed straight out the door. From there, I began the nearly two-hour-long trek all the way to Guéret. I waited until I reached the dirt path, and then I changed into my wolf form, and began to run. My muscles felt extremely sore, but it felt so good to run and breathe in fresh air after being in that musty dungeon for so long.

I knew it hadn't taken long for me to reach Guéret, but the trip had seemed to take forever and a day. I decided to go to the town first before I checked out Radder's house. I wasn't sure why, but something in my gut told me that if I'd gone there first, it would be evident that he'd really departed. *No*, I thought, *I can't think that. He wouldn't have left me by myself.*

I ended up in the field before the town of Guéret. There, I changed out of my wolf form, and inspected my looks. Thankfully, Razza had cleaned up the blood that was on both of my arms, and legs. Probably my face, too. I didn't remember her doing so, but who else would've? My skirt had a few stains, but you couldn't tell it was blood. So, figuring I looked as nice as I would, I made my way towards the over-populated city.

I walked through the gates of Guéret, searching for a scent of Radder. But, I couldn't find one. I walked down every alley-way, searched every street, but I only found two traces of him. They were extremely stale, and it was obvious that he hadn't been here for a long while. So, coming to no avail, I left the city and headed to its outskirts, to where Radder's house lay.

It didn't take very long for me to find his little white house. I approached the door, taking a deep breath. Then, I turned the knob, and stepped inside. The house looked like it always did, but all the scents of Radder were stale. So unless he was in his room and had been there for a long while, there was no way he was in this house.

I didn't loose my hope yet though. I began to weave my way through the living room and to where his bedroom door lay slightly ajar. No candles were lit inside, that much I could tell. So, unless he was sleeping, he wouldn't be in there. I opened the door quietly, in case he was asleep. But as soon as I opened the door and saw his empty bed, I knew that he really was gone for good. I just didn't want to make myself believe it.

In the darkness though, I could see that some items were missing. A few of the outfits that had been strewn on the floor, his comb, and the blue suede bag that he never let me open. Also, one of his bags was gone. It was obvious that he'd taken these possessions with him wherever he went. I thought that maybe he'd left me a note somewhere in case I came across his room with the missing items, but a quick search told me that no such thing existed. He really had left me. And he hadn't even taken the time to try and find me. Or tell me goodbye.

I felt tears burning my eyes. I crossed my arms over my chest and made my way out of Radder's house. From there, I began to walk home. And that's when the tears began to roll down my cheeks. I began to realize then how stupid I had been for thinking that Radder loved me back. I should've listened to Razza when she told me that'd he'd break my heart. But at the time, I hadn't believed that it was possible.

I didn't realize it for quite a while, but I had accidentally taken the long way home, and I was walking along the dirt pathway. Also, while I'd been deep in my thoughts, thick black storm clouds had covered the sky. They were swelled, and I could tell that it would be raining any second. Right as I thought it, in fact, the first rain droplets of the storm had begun to fall. I began to quicken my pace, but it didn't help any. It was pouring within seconds. The wind began to pick up too, and it was so dark that I almost couldn't see. *Almost.* Unfortunately, I was able to make out a familiar part of the trail.

I veered left into the forest then. I wasn't sure how I would find it, but I knew I would eventually. Surprisingly though, it didn't take me long to reach the rotten log buried amongst the trees. This was the place where I'd almost kissed Radder for the first time; the place where he'd given me that precious little wood violet. I wasn't sure why, but I was drawn over to the log. Memories of that day began to flood through my mind, making my tears stronger. Although, the rain was falling so hard, that it would be impossible for anyone to tell that I was crying.

Suddenly then, I remembered something. I fell to the ground in front of the log and began to dig frantically. I wasn't sure if it was still there or not, but it was worth a shot. Thankfully though, I was able to locate it in the dark. I pulled it out of the dirt, and watched as the rain washed the mud off of that little heart-shaped gray stone with the black flecks. I clearly remembered when Radder had placed it back in the ground that day, and the words he'd said.

"Let somebody else have it."

I gave a weak smile for a brief moment, but it was gone just as quickly as it came. I clutched the little rock to my chest, feeling the tears come on even stronger than before. Lightning illuminated the sky right then, and a deep roll of thunder rolled across the sky. I figured by then that it was time for me to head home. I stood, tears still rolling down my cheeks, and began to half-run, half-walk, home.

However, the rain had turned the dirt pathway into nothing but mud and puddles. I kept slipping and falling, which only made me angry. And the angrier I got, the more I cried over what I'd lost. I was so mad and depressed by the time I saw my castle, I almost didn't want to go inside; I was afraid of destroying something that was dear to me. But it was cold and wet, and I was tired, so I went in anyway.

As soon as I was inside, I shut the door behind me and locked it. A puddle of rainwater had formed where I was standing, but I didn't care. I just walked around my living room, lighting candles. I didn't want to be in the dark for a minute longer. So, from there, I went to the kitchen, providing more illumination. Once I could see in there though, something caught my eye. And that's when my rage went over the boiling point.

I saw the little wood violet in its big wineglass vase, still alive after all this time. I got so mad over Radder leaving me, that I took the little gray rock and threw it as hard as I could at the wineglass, shattering it into a million tiny pieces. The little flower fell on the countertop, unscathed, despite all the destruction around it.

I made my way over to where the flower was. My rage still wasn't satisfied, so I picked up the delicate little flower. From there, I ripped off its four petals, one by one, watching them flutter to the floor. I was crying nonstop the whole time, and it took me a moment to realize what it was I'd just destroyed.

I fell to my knees on the floor, picking up each individual petal and placing them in the palm of my hand, along with the stem. Even more tears swelled in my eyes, and I crumpled up the demolished flower pieces as I clenched my hand into a fist. I opened my hand then, watching the petals fall to the floor once again. And then, I placed my head in my hands and cried even more.

Chapter 14
The Return

Radder, three years later:

I was roaming the streets of Fremont, weaving through the crowds, when I saw it. It was an ordinary day in my town, and so far I had been fitting in here really well. I was pretending to be a Human, and the townspeople loved me; I was well-known amongst them. Therefore, I couldn't bring myself to hunt in this town, so I only did in the ones somewhat nearby. That way, nobody in Fremont would grow suspicious of me. I had lived here for such a long time that I got caught up in my own charade. I had thought of trying to maybe find another girl and move on. But I knew that would never be able to do that, nor could I. I couldn't forget the girl that I still loved, and I could not wait until the day I saw her again.

Despite this though, I tried to block her from my mind. But today, her memory appeared vivid and clear in my head. The reason was because I saw a couple that acted so much like her and I had. They were clearly deeply in love, walking hand in hand through the streets. By the sound of the girl's thoughts, she had only known him for a week, and like Amaury had been, she wasn't sure of how she'd fallen in love so fast, or if it was even true love. But the boy didn't doubt it for a second; he knew that what they had between them was real, and he never wanted to leave her side.

I had been going the opposite direction as them, but I quickly changed my course and began to follow them, but I never got too close. After a few minutes, they stopped at the entrance to an alleyway. The boy took the girl in his arms and kissed her, then told her to wait there until he came back. He began heading straight again, and once he was out of her sight, I approached him.

"Hi," I said.

"Hello?" he said. "And you are-?"

"Radder," I said.

"Oh, well, hi there," he said. "I'm Jordan. Um, I don't mean to sound rude, but do you need something, or what?"

"Not in particular, no," I said. "But I saw you with your girlfriend. And I just wanted to give you some advice."

"OK," he said with a shrug.

I nodded. "Don't break her heart," I told him. "She loves you. You love her. And you need to remind her everyday. Because you never know when it'll be too late, and you won't realize what you had until it's gone. Remember that." My throat went tight as I spoke those last two sentences, and I had to fight back my tears.

He studied me for a moment, but nodded in agreement. Then he gave a weak smile. "I don't think I'll ever forget," he said. "You must be in the same situation, huh, to be able to read us so well? People say we're stupid, we've only known each other for a week, but I know something's there. It's too evident to look past."

"I was in the same situation," I said. "And you're not stupid," I added. "I can see it in both of your eyes. You two were meant to be together. And please, for her sake, don't let her go."

"I won't," he promised. "Now, if you'll excuse me, I need to go."

"Of course," I said.

He began to walk away, as did I, but a moment later he called my name. I turned to look at him, and the last thing he said was, "Thank you," and then he went on his way.

Again, my throat felt tight, and only grew more so as I began to walk away. I made my way through the streets at a rather fast pace, heading the opposite direction as everyone else. It didn't take long for me to find my house; it was a tiny little cottage near the gates of the city. I had bought it within three days of coming to Fremont, and was probably the smartest purchase I'd ever made. However, in a few years, I would have to sell it. The citizens of Fremont believed me to be twenty-one, so I'd have to be leaving this town within the next five years. If I stayed much longer, somebody would soon figure out that I wasn't aging at all.

I approached the door to my cottage then, and went inside. It was a nice, cozy little place, absolutely perfect in every way. The only problem with it was that every time I entered it, Amaury popped into my mind. This was the exact kind of place that she would've loved to live in. Not to mention, the interior looked so much like the inside of her castle that it wasn't even funny. I'd attempted many times to remodel it after I bought it, but I couldn't bring myself to do it. I had already erased enough of my life before I'd come to Fremont, and I was afraid I'd only forget more if I changed the inside of my new house. So, everything stayed as it was.

Still, the memories that swelled into my mind were always painful. My mind would go back to that day at the lake, that day that my whole world changed forever. I could clearly recall the sound of her laugh, the words she had spoken, everything. And every time I reminisced about that day, no matter where I was or what had triggered it, tears would always fall from my eyes. Just like they were right now.

I made my way to the kitchen after I'd shut the door behind me. I approached my countertop once I was in there, and then I picked up a small green vase that had been sitting on it. In the vase was a small little wood violet, just like the one I'd given to Amaury all those years ago. It had sprung up in my yard a few days after I'd bought the house, all by itself. Three years later, it was still living. How, I wasn't sure. It made me wonder if, all the way back in Chiroux, if that little violet was still somewhere in Amaury's castle. Who knows, maybe it was still alive, even after all this time.

Next to where I'd set the vase was another relic from my past. I had found it in my coat pocket after I'd moved in, and I didn't want to loose it, so, I kept it on the counter. It was that shiny, white, heart-shaped rock that I had found in Maufanges, when Amaury and I had been sitting on that log in the middle of the forest. I had stuck it in my pocket that day, and thought that I had lost it a long time ago. But one day I just pulled it out of my coat pocket, and so, I kept it. And when I found the little flower in my yard, I decided to keep them both beside each other on my countertop, where Amaury had kept her flower. It was my own personal little tribute to Amaury, and I reminder to me that no matter how far I went to escape my past, it would always be with me.

The tears continued to roll down my face as I held the vase and rock in my hands. I missed Amaury. I wished so badly that I hadn't left her that day at the lake. If I could take it all back and not have left her that night, I would in a heartbeat. I'd have done anything to ensure that she would be by my side forever. But, you can't change history. And there's no point in wasting your hope on things that you can't change.

By the time that my tears had finally ceased, my eyelids felt heavy. I decided to go to bed; it was late anyway. I had spent hours crying over Amaury, so many that the sky was now pitch black. The last I'd checked though, the day was still bright and sunny. Plus, I had to work my shift tomorrow at one of the produce stands set up around town.

I didn't really need the money, but the townspeople would've grown suspicious if I'd been living perfectly fine without having any source of income. I usually gave my extra money to the poorer people of the town, though, because I knew they needed it more than I did. I also figured that tomorrow I needed to hunt, I hadn't for a few days, which meant I had to be up even earlier. So, I made my way to my bedroom, and lay on my bed. And I was asleep before my head even hit the pillow.

The next morning I forced myself to awaken bright and early so that I could hurry and get to one of the surrounding towns. I chose to go to Teix, since it was the closest town, only a ten minute walk from Fremont. I got out of bed in a dazed state, and went through my usual routine of combing my hair, and then changing my outfit. I decided last minute though to change once I returned form Teix, as to not get my uniform dirty. At my produce stand, we were required to wear black pants, a green shirt, and, to my disgust, aprons. I figured I may look a little suspicious if I went to work with blood on my shirt, so I went to Teix in the clothes I'd worn yesterday.

I slipped quietly out of my house, trying not to disturb any of my neighbors that would still be asleep. It was four in the morning, after all. And, if I didn't slip out unnoticed, then someone in town might know that I had killed someone. Word of the murders or disappearances in other towns always got back to Fremont, and I couldn't risk anybody knowing that I had been the cause of them. That would mean that I would have to expose the secret that I had been trying so hard to keep.

I had begun to walk silently down the cobblestone street, and quietly slipped out of the entrance. Unlike in Guéret, Fremont didn't close its gates at night; they were always open. Also, there were no guards, so ensured escape each time I went out to hunt was guaranteed. Once I had walked out of the city, I walked alongside the road that led to Teix, as to not leave any traces that I'd been there in the dirt road. It was the only dirt road for a few miles, the rest were cobblestone, so I always had to be careful when I went to Teix.

It didn't take me long at all to reach Teix. I slipped through the entrance of the city unobserved, and searched out my victim. I went through every alleyway, and walked every street. Finally, I found a man walking by himself. I followed him, but he never noticed that I was there. Finally, he went down a dark alleyway, the perfect place for me to kill him. I was about to strike, in fact, when I saw another figure in the darkness The man approached the figure, and they started talking in very low voices. I slunk closer, sticking to the shadows, until I could hear what they were saying.

"Who do you think it is?" the mystery figure said. I could tell it was a man, but his thoughts were blocked, although I had no idea how.

"I'm not sure," the other man said. "But we need to find him. He's been killing someone nearly every two weeks for the past three years. In fact, he's killed so many people, the police don't even search for the missing people anymore. They know that they're dead."

"I know that," the mystery man said. "Whoever this person is, they're sick minded and don't deserve to be alive."

"Exactly. So, why exactly did you call me here?"

"Because I want you to help me find this man," the mystery man said. "I have a feeling that this is no ordinary person."

"What do you mean?" the other man asked.

I held my breath as the mystery man spoke once more. "I mean," he said. "The person killing all these people… is a *Vampire*."

"*What?*" the other man said, trying to stifle a laugh. "You're crazy."

"I'm serious."

"Yeah, whatever," the other man said, turning to walk away. "Forget it. I'm not going to help you if you can't be reasonable. A *Vampire*! What a ridiculous thought!"

He shook his head the whole time he spoke, and when he finished talking he waked out of the alleyway. Thankfully, he didn't see me. In a few moments, he was gone, and I was left alone with the mystery man, who was probably a Vampire Hunter. The man was obviously stunned, and hadn't turned to walk away, so I made my move. I slunk around behind him, grabbing him suddenly by the neck. I covered his mouth so that he couldn't scream, which he tried to. Once he'd calmed down though, I removed my hand.

"Wha- what do you want?" he asked in a panicky voice.

"Tell me everything you know about Vampires," I hissed.

"There's not much that I know," he said, his voice still shaky. "All I know is that one has been killing people."

"How'd you find that out?"

"I found the body of one of the missing people. There were bite marks on their neck, and they were drained of blood. That's how I know. There's nothing else. I swear."

"Then how do you know how to block your thoughts?"

He was clawing at my arms by this point; I was sure he knew that I was the Vampire he'd been searching for. "Well?" I asked. "Tell me!"

"I found a man," he said. "Who knew about Vampires. He came here two years ago and sold produce, and he told me about them, and how he'd moved here to escape the ones in his old town. I told him what I'd found, and he taught me how to block my thoughts, trying to keep me safe."

"Where is he?"

"He died last year," he said. By the sound of his voice, I knew he was telling me the truth.

"What was his name?" I asked.

"Anthony Smith," the man said.

I nearly lost my grip on him when I'd said that. I couldn't believe that after all these years, Anthony had been so close to me. I thought I'd left him behind along with everything else in Guéret. It just goes to show, you really can't run away from your past.

"You said he's dead, right?" I said.

"Yeah," he said.

"Well," I said. "Prepare to join him." And then I bit his throat.

About a half hour later, I was making my way back to Fremont. It was a little past five by now, and I needed to get home before anybody saw what a bloody mess I was. I approached the gates quickly, and glanced around to make sure nobody was out and about. Then, I ran all the way to my cottage, shutting the door and locking it behind me. From there, I took a bath, and got ready for work.

I put on my shirt and pants, and quickly ran a comb through my hair. I made sure that my teeth had no blood on them, too. They had none, but my fangs were soaked in it. That was OK though. It wasn't like my fangs would be drawn out at all.

It was five 'til six by the time I was done getting ready. I grabbed my apron and swung it over my shoulder, then walked out the door. I locked the door, sticking my key in my pants pocket, and began to head for the produce stand. I got there right at six, and my boss, Mr. Taylor, was just beginning to get everything ready.

"Ah, Radder," he said. "Good to see you this morning."

"And you, Mr. Taylor," I said, sliding my apron over my head and tying it in the back.

He handed me a bushel of apples, just like he did every morning I worked for him. He didn't even need to give me directions; I knew exactly what to do. I carried the large basket around to the front of the stand and began to place the apples in the little wooden boxes that were on top of the stand. I had to inspect each apple to make sure none of them were rotten. Once that was done, I would lay out the grapes, then the lettuce, broccoli, cauliflower, tomatoes, oranges, bananas, carrots, potatoes, and anything else we had in stock. It usually took around two hours, which was about the time people started their days. I would work until six PM, and then Mr. Taylor's grandson, Harry, would come to help us clean up. It was the same thing each day.

I was done stocking the produce before I knew it, and soon enough it was nine o'clock. We'd had three customers already, and today seemed as though it would be very productive. By eleven, I'd lost track of how many people had come to the stand. The sun was climbing higher into the sky, and it had become extremely hot. We didn't have any customers at the moment, so Mr. Taylor had begun to count the money. A long while passed, and there was still no one around. Having finished his counting, Mr. Taylor pushed his glasses up higher on his nose and said, "Go ahead and take an apple or something, boy. You look thirsty."

I tried hard not to laugh. "I'm alright, Mr. Taylor," I said.

"No, really, have one," he said, tossing one to me. I caught it just before it flew past me.

"Really Mr. Taylor, I'm fine."

"Now I may be nothing but an old man," he said. "But I can tell when people need food or water. That fruit is both. Plus, it'll do you good. You're so damn scrawny, and I 'tain't never seen you eat a bite of anything. You need it." I was about to say something back at him when I heard a loud shout. I looked out across the stand and saw a large crowd gathering around something.

"Uh-oh," Mr. Taylor said. By the sound of everyone's thoughts around the stand, a fight had just broken out. I set the apple down on the stand.

"I'm gonna go break it up," I said, beginning to head towards the crowd.

"Good luck," he said.

I made my way over to the crowd and pushed my way through the people. I saw two men fighting. One of them, a rather small guy, was getting his ass kicked. There was also a girl in the crowd trying to reach him, but was being held back by some friends. I realized then with a sudden stroke of shock that the girl was the one I'd seen Jordan with yesterday. Which meant that, since I had no idea who the other guy was, Jordan was the one being beat up so badly. I had to stop this.

I went to the center of the circle of people and yanked the other guy away from Jordan. Jordan crawled as far away from the man as he could once I pulled him off him. The man was very muscular and had blue eyes. One was a deep blue, but the other looked like the sky. It had a scar over it, and I could tell that he was blind in that eye. But for being half-blind, he sure could throw a punch.

Once I'd pulled him away from Jordan, his expression turned to a sneer. "You scraggy little bastard," he said.

He drew his arm back, and then swung it full force at my face. However, I surprised him when I caught his hand mid-air and pushed it backwards. Then, I swung my fist at him. His nose made a loud cracking sound when my fist came into contact with it, and he fell to the ground, hands over his face. Blood had begun to seep through the cracks between his fingers, but I couldn't care less. I was more concerned about Jordan. I walked over to him, where he lay in a heap on the ground.

"Need a hand?" I asked, extending my arm out towards him.

He looked up at me and blinked. His face was swollen, bruised, and bloody, and I'm sure he had a hard time making out who I was. But he finally came to and grabbed my upper arm. From there, I helped him get back on his feet. He smiled at me.

"Thanks Radder."

"No problem," I said.

He began to scan the crowd. "Have you seen Lee?" he asked.

By his thoughts, I could tell that Lee was his girlfriend. I scanned the crowd and found her in seconds. She was biting her fingernails nervously. I motioned her over, and she sprinted over to Jordan. That seemed to break the trance over the crowd; many either walked away or went to help the other guy. Some police officers had arrived as well, and were asking people questions. When Lee reached us, she fell right into Jordan's arms. She appeared to be extremely upset at first, but once he was holding her all the worry on her face had disappeared. Then, she turned to look at me.

"Thank you," she said.

I shrugged. "Who was that guy, anyways?" I asked her.

"My brother," she said. "He hates Jordan to death, and kept picking fights with him. Finally he just snapped and punched him."

"Well that's not good," I said.

"Believe me, I know," she said, rolling her eyes. "I can't believe you broke his nose. Stark is the toughest guy I know. Plus, you don't look like the tough-guy type."

Again, I shrugged. "People say that all the time. But I can kick ass if I absolutely have to."

"Apparently," she said. "Anyways, thanks again. I hate to go, but I think I need to take Jordan to a doctor." I agreed completely with her. He looked like death warmed over.

Jordan did manage to look at me once more before they left, though. "I owe you one, Radder," he said.

I turned around to head back to the produce stand, only to see Mr. Taylor standing right behind me. His arms were crossed, and he was tapping his foot impatiently. The fake-angered look on his face almost made me crack up laughing at him. And with his cheesy-looking mustache and white hair pulled back in a ponytail, it only added to the humor of it.

"Boy," he said. "I didn't think it was possible for a youngster like yourself , let alone one who works at a produce stand, to throw a punch like that."

I just smiled. "It was nothing, really." I said. "Now, let's get back to the stand."

We continued working from there on. Nothing else eventful happened, so things went back to normal. Around two o'clock, though, we'd sold all of our apples. Mr. Taylor gave me another bushel to put in the boxes. In the midst of doing this, someone tapped my shoulder.

"Just a second," I told whoever it was. "I'm almost finished."

"I don't think you'll want to wait a second," a familiar voice said.

The bushel fell from my hands, and I whipped around to face them. "*Adam?!?*" I said. I was taken completely by surprise. Adam Carpentier, a face from the past, was now standing right before me.

"That's right," he said. "I'm surprised you still remember me."

"How did you find me?" I hissed.

"It wasn't easy," he admitted. "I had to ask around. Thankfully, I met someone heading to Guéret for this year's bazaar, and they claimed to know you. They said you were in Fremont. So, here I am," he said with a shrug.

"What do you want, then?" I asked. "Did Benjamin send you here?"

"No, he didn't," he said. "But I came to tell you something kind of important."

"And what would that be?"

His silver eyes saddened. "Razza is dead."

The news took me aback. "*What?*" I said. "How? Why?"

"Benjamin found out that she was doing some work against the Coven," he explained. "So, he sentenced her to death. They killed her yesterday, and I came to search for you and tell you the news. I knew you and her were pretty good friends, so I felt obligated to tell you."

"Oh," I said. "Well, thanks."

"Thanks? That's all I get?" he said. "I hope you realize that I could be put to death now for coming to find you."

"How? Ben will never know."

"Yes, he will," he said.

"What do you mean?"

"I mean, I'm asking you to come back to Guéret with me. She told me before Ben killed her that she wanted you to come to her grave."

"But, why?" I said. "It's not like she can tell me anything. And anyways, I swore to myself that I would never go back to that place for as long as I live. I can't."

"Please," he said. "If you won't do it for me, then do it for her."

I hung my head. "You just don't understand," I said. "I-"

"What's the trouble here?" Mr. Taylor had approached us then. He looked back and forth between the both of us, then asked, "Do you two know each other?"

I stared at Adam. "Yeah," I said. "We go way back."

He looked at Mr. Taylor. "Are you his boss?" he asked. Mr. Taylor nodded. "Well," Adam said, "do you think Radder could come back to Guéret with me? A… family member of his just passed away, and he wants to attend her funeral."

My eyes widened. "Actually Mr. Taylor-" I said.

"Oh, of course you can go," he said. "Don't even let me try and stop you."

"But-"

"Come on, Radder," Adam said, grabbing my arm. "Where's your house? Go pack up your things. We're leaving."

I tried to fight him, but he'd gotten a lot stronger since I last saw him. Either that, or I'd become a lot weaker.

Once we were out of earshot of people, Adam spoke. "Pathetic," he said with a growl. "The strongest Vampire in the world, reduced to selling produce and pretending to be a Human. I can't believe you Radder. What are you hiding from?"

I thought about that for a moment. Of course, Amaury was the first thing that came to mind. But I wasn't about to tell him that. So, instead I said, "Honestly, I don't know anymore."

"Well, then man up," he said. "You can't escape Benjamin forever, you know. He'll catch up with you eventually. He may've told you that you could leave, but he still wants to punish you for what you did. And I guarantee, he won't give up searching for you."

"I really just don't want to go back to Guéret, or Maufanges-"

"I don't care," he said. "Face your fears. There's nothing for you to be scared of. You're a Vampire for Christ's sake, not a damn Human. So stop acting like one. Now, where is your house?"

Of course, we just so happened to be right in front of my cottage right as he asked. I sighed. "Right here," I said.

"Well, go in there and pack up. And hurry," he said. "I need to get back before Ben starts getting suspicious."

I made my way to the door of my house and unlocked it. I stepped inside, about to shut the door, when I realized Adam was behind me. "Sorry," I said. He just glared at me.

The first thing I did was go to my bedroom and change

into my normal outfit. I thought about leaving my jacket off, it was pretty hot, but chose to wear it anyways. Once I'd changed, I grabbed a bag from my closet and started to place things in it. I almost forgot the blue suede bag, but grabbed it at the last second. I don't know what I would've done if I'd forgotten it. Once I had everything in my bag, I left my room and went into the bathroom to grab my comb. Then, I was ready, so I went to the living room, where Adam stood, waiting.

"You ready?" he asked.

I nodded, and so we were about to leave, when I remembered something. "Wait!" I said "I forgot something!" I dropped my bag and ran into the kitchen. I grabbed the rock from the counter, and stuck it in my pocket. I turned around to head back out to the living room, only to see Adam was behind me.

"You came in here to get a rock? OK, whatever floats your boat. Now come on, let's go." I followed him back out to the living room and grabbed my bag. From there, we left my cottage and Fremont for good.

The moment I laid eyes on Guéret, I wanted to turn tail and run. It had been three years since I'd been here, and my memories came flooding back in a rush. We walked alongside the walls of the city, heading to the Vampire Cemetery. It felt weird to be walking next to the city. It was all so familiar, and yet foreign to me. It almost seemed like I was dreaming. But I knew I wasn't. The hurt feeling in my chest was too great to be from a dream.

We walked at a brisk pace, and I soon saw the tree line leading to the cemetery. Adam and I quickened our already rather fast pace until we were under the cover of the trees. From there, we weaved our way through them, until we came to the cemetery. Thousands of graves dotted the wasteland that we were in, and at least ten of them were fresh. We had no trouble finding Razza's grave though. We Vampires buried our dead with the ones that we have killed. The only way you could tell a Vampire's grave from a Human's was that, instead of tying the crosses with string, the two sticks were held together with a blood red silk ribbon.

Adam walked right up to the only fresh grave that was marked with a red ribbon. I didn't go straight there, though. I walked back to the tree line and picked a few wildflowers to place on her grave. I also realized then that I was still carrying my bag, so I placed it next to the remaining flowers. Then, I walked back to where Adam stood. His head was bent in respect to her. They had never been too good of friends, but it was always hard to lose someone you were used to being around. After all, with the exception of Ruby, everyone in the Coven had grown up together. They were almost like a big family; they may hate each other, but they all miss their fellow Vampires when they're gone for good.

Adam stood aside when I came up next to him. I kneeled on the ground in front of her grave, placing the flowers right in front of the cross. I bowed my head and closed my eyes, as did Adam. A slight breeze whipped across the land as I did this, toying with my hair. I thought that with the breeze, a strange noise had come as well. But it ended as abruptly as the breeze did, so I didn't think much of it. Well, that is, until I opened my eyes. I stood and jumped backwards, away from the grave.

Adam opened his eyes and gave me a confused look. "What?" he asked.

"Look," I said. "On her cross." I pointed at what I was talking about. His eyes widened.

"What the-?"

The breeze had started up again, as did the noise I'd heard before. I realized then that the noise was emanating from the small piece of paper that had been nailed to the cross. The small piece of paper that had not been there when we arrived. It was flapping around manically, as though someone was telling me to read its words. Cautiously, I stepped forward, and leaned across the grave to rip it from the nail. The words on it sent a thousand chills down my spine:

You can run Radder,
But you can't hide.
Your flower hath not wilted,
Your flower hath not died.

The note was clearly written in Razza's scrawl; that much I couldn't deny. I felt as though I was going to get sick. Adam took the note from me to read, and his face went three shades paler.

"That's impossible," he said. "This isn't forged, either."

"I know," I choked out. For a split moment, I suspected that maybe Adam had placed it there. But, that was untrue for two reasons. First of all, his thoughts weren't blocked, and the thought would've crossed his mind at some point. And secondly, I would've sensed him moving to place the note on the cross, which I hadn't. The note had, literally, come from nowhere.

"Well," Adam said with a gulp. "She did say she wanted you to come to her grave. I just didn't think anything would actually happen."

"Neither did I," I said.

"What does this even mean? 'Your flower hath not wilted, your flower hath not died.' What flower?"

"I'm not sure," I said. *Could she be talking about Amaury's wood violet?* I thought. That was the only thing that would make sense. But even if that was what Razza's note had been talking about, then why did it matter so much? It was just a flower, after all.

"Well, I am officially creeped out. I think I'm going to leave now," Adam said, handing the note back to me. I stuffed it in my coat pocket.

"Me too," I said. I didn't want to stay here for a moment longer.

"Where are you going to stay?" Adam asked.

"At my old house," I said.

"What if some Humans found it and moved in?"

"They wouldn't have moved into that rundown excuse for a house. And if some were stupid enough to, well, then I guess I'll be getting a free lunch, huh?"

"I guess so," he said.

"Good luck with Benjamin," I added. "I hope he's not too angry with you."

"He shouldn't be," he said. "Unless he scents you on my clothes."

"Well," I said. "I hope that won't be the case. I don't want to visit anymore graves for a long while."

He gave a weak smile. "Don't worry about me," he said. "I'll be fine."

"I know," I said. "You can weasel your way out of anything."

He just nodded, and then he turned to leave. I headed back to the patch of wildflowers to retrieve my bag. I picked it up and was about to head into the forest when Adam said my name. I turned to where he stood about fifteen feet away, waiting for him to speak.

"Thanks for coming with me," he said. "And trust me, you won't regret it." And with that, he disappeared into the forest.

I had no idea what he had meant by that. So, I just shrugged it off, and also went into the forest. It didn't take long to navigate through the trees, and I soon saw the walls of Guéret looming before me. Once I reached them, I began to walk beside them until I could see the field. I cut through it and began to head to my little white house. The first hour of dusk had begun, and I hoped to make it home before nightfall.

I reached the little white house just before the sun disappeared. The moon was clearly visible now, as were many of the stars. It was very much like the night that I had first met Amaury in this very yard. That had been a great day, if not for her, then for me. I just wish that she had left me alone after I'd been so rude to her. I was trying to prevent anything from happening to her, since everybody that I ever loved died. But, she was so persistent to have my company that I just couldn't refuse. And look at where it had gotten me.

I walked up the steps and onto my tiny porch. It took me a moment to get the door to budge open, but in time it did. The inside of the house was musty, and cobwebs had appeared in just about every spot imaginable. I couldn't believe that this was the house that I had lived in for over three-hundred years. I hadn't been here for a mere three years, and already it was unfit to live in. But I didn't plan to stay here for very long anyways; just one night, and then I'd be heading back to Fremont.

I walked across the kitchen into my living room. Where it had once been warm and inviting, it was now very cold and dismal. It deflated my spirits to a maximum. Finally though, I reached my bedroom, and no longer had to stare into my opaque living room. I found a match on my dresser the moment I walked into my room, and lit the candle that was beside it. The room was illuminated instantly. I blew out the match and surveyed my room, setting my bag down beside the door as I did so. There were less cobwebs here than anywhere else, which was a good thing. A few dead bugs were on my bed sheet, though, which I had to shake off. Thankfully, though, nothing was lurking under the covers. So, with that, I crawled under the covers. And soon enough, I was fast asleep.

I awoke the next morning not because of the midday sunlight coming in through the window above my bed, but because I felt something crawling on me. I sat up to see a huge ass spider crawling up and down my leg. I thrashed my leg out, flinging the spider across the room. It scuttled into my open closet and didn't emerge again. I figured that that was my cue to leave. I checked my hair in the mirror, making sure I looked at least a little presentable. I was about to pick up my bag and head back home, but I stopped myself. There were a few things I wanted to do before I headed home.

I abandoned the bag, deciding to come back for it later. But before I walked out the door, I removed the blue suede bag from my suitcase and stuck it in my pocket. Its content was too valuable to leave alone in this place. So, once I had it in my possession, I made my way out the door.

The first place I decided to stop by was Guéret. It didn't take me long to reach it from my house, and I instantly noticed that the city was different the moment I walked inside its walls. I mean, everything looked the same. But where all those years ago it was always swarming with people, it was now nearly empty. I saw a man sweeping in front of his produce stand, and I went up to him.

"Where is everybody?" I asked.

"Oh," he said. "Everybody left after the bazaar yesterday."

"OK," I said. "But even after the bazaar, this town always used to be filled with people. What gives?"

"A bunch of people moved out a few years ago because a bunch of murders began to happen. Why? Are you looking for anyone in particular?"

"Not especially, no," I said. "I was just curious." He just shrugged at me, so I began to walk away from him and down the street. Nothing really caught my interest, and I was contemplating leaving when I saw three familiar faces walking my way.

It was Hugo, Sam, and Hazel.

The boys didn't even see me, but Hazel noticed me right after I saw them. "Guys!" she said. "Look!"

They both turned and looked in my direction. Hugo looked confused, but Sam's eyes had widened drastically. "Wait here," I heard Sam say to Hugo. Then, Sam and Hazel began to walk as fast as they could over to me.

"Radder!" Hazel said, running up and giving me a giant hug. "Long time no see, huh?"

"Yeah," I said as she pulled away from me. "Three whole years."

"Where have you been all this time, anyways?" Sam asked.

"I moved to Fremont," I explained.

"Fremont?" Hazel said. "Jeez, that's far!"

"Not for a Vampire," Sam said with a smirk. "They can get anywhere in about five minutes."

"True," Hazel said. "So," she added, "if you live in Fremont now, what brought you back to Guéret?"

"My friend Razza died."

"Oh, I'm so sorry," she said. "How'd she die?"

"Benjamin killed her for betraying the Coven. I knew she'd get caught one day, but she didn't believe me."

"Sounds like she should have."

"Yeah," I said. It hit me then that Razza had been Amaury's only living relative. It was almost as if she'd never existed now.

"Well," Sam said, "we'd love to stay and chat for a while longer, but we really need to get going."

"I understand," I said. "I won't keep you then."

"It was nice seeing you," Hazel said. "I hope you'll have a nice life in Fremont."

"Me too," I said.

"Bye, Radder," they said in unison. By this point, Hugo had walked up next to them, and the trio headed on their way. They turned on the next left from where I was, and soon disappeared from sight.

I began to head back out of the city, when I felt a sharp pang in the pit of my stomach. I knew the feeling though, so I wasn't too worried. It was only the Thirst, telling me it was about time for some blood. So, once I had left the city, I made my way to the woods to find some kind of animal to drink from. It had been awhile since I'd had animal blood, and I would make me feel better knowing that I hadn't killed a person.

Once I was amongst the trees, I saw a rabbit right away. It was hopping along the dirt pathway, unaware of my presence. Within seconds, I had it in my clutches, dead and completely drained of blood. My Thirst was satisfied after just the one rabbit, so I killed no more. From there, I went to the side of the pathway and dug a small grave for the poor bunny. I buried him quickly and then stood. I hesitated on deciding which way to go. I wasn't sure if I should I head back to Fremont or stop by Amaury's castle to reminisce one last time. Ultimately though, I decided to head to Chiroux.

I was nearly to Maufanges when I noticed something odd about where I was walking. The trees here were extremely familiar, although I wasn't sure why. But suddenly I remembered; the old rotten log was buried amongst these trees. I went into the forest and sought it out. It took me only a moment to find. I sat down on its surface, not believing that it didn't fall in on itself with my added weight. I sat there for quite a while, taking in the forest around me, when I remembered something.

I bent down over my feet and begin to dig in the ground. I didn't know if the rock would still be here or not, but it was worth a shot. After a long time of searching though, I came to no avail. I guess that after three years it had to be completely buried by now. So, I wiped my dirt-covered hands on my jeans, stood, and began to head back to the dirt pathway. When I found it, I was back on my way to Amaury's castle.

I walked rather slowly through the forest, trying to enjoy the beauty around me. But, I had realized with a miserable feeling that Amaury had died about three years and a month ago. It was nearing the end of April after all, so it may even be longer. I couldn't fathom how I had gone on for so long without her. But I didn't think I'd be able to for much longer. I missed her more than I ever imagined I would.

Even at my snail-slow pace, her castle had begun to appear in the distance. I instinctively sped up when I saw it, though I told myself to slow down. She wouldn't be there, I knew, so there was no point in getting excited over nothing. Still, the thought that she would greet me with open arms as soon as I entered the castle stayed in my mind, unceasing.

The castle grew closer and closer with each step I took. I began to become nervous; I had no idea what I'd find here, although I was sure it wouldn't be pretty. In fact, after three years, the inside of her castle might even look like my house had. Before I knew it, I had reached the edge of the forest. I came out of the trees and began to head towards the castle's doors. When I reached them, I took a deep breath. It was also a big déjà vu moment, since I'd done the same thing the last time I was here. So, after I'd taken a breath, I opened the door and stepped inside. And I could not believe what I saw.

The first thing I noticed was that the inside of the castle was completely clean. There were no cobwebs anywhere that I could see. Also, there wasn't any dust on anything. But there was one thing that caught my eye the most. The giant puddle of blood that had been by the stairwell three years ago was gone. And there was no trace of it to tell me that it had ever been there at all. I had no idea what was going on. Benjamin and Magdelene had proved to me that Amaury was dead a long time ago. It was impossible for the inside of this castle to be utterly spotless.

Unless, I thought, *Ben and Magdelene came in to clean it up. Who knows? Maybe they're selling it or something, As long as it benefits them, they don't care what happens to anyone else. Maybe that was the case here.*

I took a deep breath, choosing to believe that thought. Nothing else made sense, nor could explain anything. Strangely enough though, the words on Razza's note had begun to swim through my head. *Your flower hath not wilted, your flower hath not died.* I took a shuddery breath at the thought, when I remembered something. If Amaury's flower were still here, then maybe, just maybe, it would give me the answer to Razza's riddle. So, I made my way to the kitchen. Unfortunately, when I walked in, I could plainly see that her counter was bare. Both the wineglass with the violet and the vase with the rose in it were gone. I sighed in anger.

"Razza," I whispered. "What is it you wanted me to find?"

I walked back into the foyer then, since I had no more business in the kitchen. I began to wander around the room, surveying everything, taking it all in. My recollections of being in this room with Amaury began to flood my mind. I felt a smile grow on my face, but it just as quickly went away. Every memory I had of her was filled not only with happiness, but with the pain and sorrow of losing her. I decided that I couldn't stay here for much longer. If I did, the memories would kill me for sure.

I had just turned to leave, when I heard a noise behind me. It was a loud creak, and I felt the hairs on the back of my neck stand up. I realized with a growing dread that I wasn't the only one inside the castle. Another creak sounded, and another. I figured it had to be Ben, or Magdelene. But I didn't have enough time to get away though if it was one of them. I was trapped. Taking a deep breath, I turned, expecting to see either one of them. But the person on the staircase behind me wasn't Benjamin, or Magdelene.

It was Amaury.

Chapter 15
The Necklace

Amaury:

I had been sitting in my room, reading a book, when I heard a creaking noise. But it was no ordinary creak; it was clearly the sound of my front door opening. I froze the second I heard it. *What the hell?* I thought. *Nobody is supposed to be here*. I thought it might be Ben or Magdelene, but they had promised a long while ago to leave me alone from now on, as long as I returned the favor. I'd stuck to my promise so far, so they should've as well. But who else would it be?

Slowly and silently, I slipped off my bed and set my book down. I began to creep along the floor, hoping not to make any noise. Without making a sound, I opened my bedroom door and began to head for the stairwell. I kept my mind blank (I'd been practicing how to do it lately, and had gotten pretty good at it) just in case the intruder was a mind-reading Vampire.

After a few moments, I heard more floorboards squeak. Then they ceased, and I heard footsteps on tile instead. In the meantime, I crept closer and closer to the stairs. The steps suddenly switched back to the floorboards; the intruder was back in the parlor. My heart was pounding in my chest. I was scared at who might be in my parlor. So scared, in fact, that I stepped on the wrong board, creating a long, droning creak. *Shit.* I thought. Whoever it was froze. I decided to just continue from here on out, not caring if I made anymore noise or not. They knew I was here, whoever it was.

Finally, I reached the stairs, and began to descend them. I could see the back of the person clearly now; they had been making a beeline to the door when they heard me. There was something oddly familiar about the figure standing in my parlor. It was obviously a man, and I could tell even in the darkness that his hair was pitch-black. Also, he was wearing a light yellow, nearly white in color jacket, and a pair of jeans. One particular name came to my mind just then.

No, I thought, *it can't be.*

But it was.

The split second Radder turned around, my heart skipped a beat. Or four. I felt my eyes widen as I drank in the sight of him, standing right before me. His eyes widened as well when he saw me. And then, a smile bigger than any I'd ever seen before grew on his face.

"Amaury?" he said, so quietly that I barely heard him.

Suddenly, I couldn't contain my excitement any longer. "Radder!" I cried back at him.

I ran down to the bottom of the stairs, were he already stood, waiting for me. I jumped into his arms the very moment I came off the last step. He held me as tightly to him as he could, slowly rocking us back and forth.

"Oh my God," I heard myself whisper. "I can't believe you're here." I looked up to see him staring down at me. His smile was gone.

"What's wrong?" I questioned. He squeezed his eyes shut after I asked, and before I knew it, tears were streaming down his cheeks.

"Radder?"

"Amaury," he said. "I can't believe I'm here either. I swore I'd never come back, and now look at where I am."

I was shocked by his words. "What do you mean 'you swore you'd never come back'?"

Even more tears streamed down his face. "Because," he said. "I thought you were dead."

His words hit me hard. "You thought I was dead? *Why?*"

"Ben and Magdelene brought me a silver-tipped stake with your blood on it."

"When?"

"That's not important right now," he said. "I'll explain everything later." He held me even tighter. "Don't you know how much I've missed you?" He opened his eyes then, and stared deeply into mine.

"Amaury," he said, very seriously, "I love you."

I didn't even have time to think about what he'd just said before he kissed me. His hand was suddenly tangled in my hair, and my arms had snaked around his neck. He didn't pull away from me for the longest time. Instead, he pulled me as close to him as possible, so that not even an inch of air was between us. I'm not sure how long we stood there with our lips locked together, but it must've been a long time. Eventually though, I pulled away from him, because I had to catch my breath. He was smiling at me, but I wasn't at him.

"You don't love me," I said. "Don't lie."

He looked taken aback. "Why would you say that?" he asked.

"You disappeared for *three years*, Radder. And then, one day, you randomly decide to show up, tell me you missed me and that you love me, and then kiss me so I can't say a damn word back to you."

"It's not like that," he protested.

"Really? Then what is it like? *Where the hell have you been?*"

"Amaury, calm down," he said in a low voice. He looked hurt.

"Fine, I'm calm," I said, taking a deep breath. "I just don't understand why you left." I began to feel tears in my eyes then; one managed to make its way down my cheek. Radder quickly swept it away, and kissed me lightly.

"Come on," he said. "Let's go sit down. It's a long story."

I nodded, following him to the couch. I felt like I was dreaming all of this. Nothing seemed real here at all. The only thing I had to convince me that I really was awake, and that Radder really was back, was that first kiss he'd given me. You can't dream something like that.

Radder sat down on my couch, hands folded on his knees, his head bent down. I sat right beside him and leaned against him. Yeah, I was mad that he had just now come back, but that didn't mean that I hadn't missed him. Plus, I didn't really have much to be mad at him over. He'd already explained that all this time he'd thought I was dead.

"I'm sorry," I told him.

"For what?"

"Getting mad at you."

"That's alright," he said. "I don't blame you. I'd have said the same things to myself if I'd been in your shoes."

I just nodded. Then he asked, "So, what do you want explained first?"

"Where you went that night at the lake."

He nodded. "Well, you know I went hunting, right?"

I nodded again. "Yeah, because your eyes were red, so I told you to go."

"And do you remember me saying that I didn't want to leave? Well, if you hadn't made me go, nothing would've happened that night."

"What do you mean?"

"I ran into some trouble in the woods. Before I found anything to drink from, I ran into James again. We were talking for a little bit, though I can't remember what about, when Angel came up to talk with him. I just barely evaded her, and then they left. So, from there, I searched for something to hunt again, and I found a rabbit. I drank from it, of course, and then buried it, because it felt wrong to just leave its body there. Right when I finished that though, and I was heading back to the lake, Benjamin and Magdelene appeared out of nowhere.

I ran, of course, trying to get as far away from them as possible. I wasn't going fast enough though, and they were right on my heels, so I decided to jump trees instead. I had almost reached the lake, but I mistimed a jump and fell. I would've gotten up and kept going, but when I fell, I broke my arm and my nose. I was trying to get up and ignore the pain, but Ben and Magdelene came right then, and dragged me back to their castle. Ben had my right arm, and Magdelene my broken one, so I couldn't fight them off. When we reached the castle, I got left alone to wander. I remember telling Mary something about Fusions, because she figured out that you existed-"

"Wait," I said. "What did you tell her?"

"Babe, I don't remember," he said. "It was such a long time ago."

"Well, why tell her anything in the first place?"

"I don't know why I did," he admitted. "Now, can I continue?"

I nodded, though he'd kind of ticked me off there. He must've realized that, because he slid his arm around me and pulled me closer to him. Then, he began to speak again.

"Well, after I told them whatever I did, I went into Magdelene's room. I remembered that day we attacked them, her small window had been smashed, and I was sure they hadn't repaired it yet. And, they hadn't. My arm and nose had healed by then too, and so I jumped down to the ground and began to run." He paused for a moment. "Come to think of it," he said. "I'm almost certain I caught your scent there."

"Were you next to a tree?"

"Yeah."

"Well, I used to deliver letters to Magdelene, before she totally betrayed me. I slid them through that window."

He nodded. "Well, that explains that," he said. "Anyways, I ran, and I finally made it to the lake. But, you had already left, so I figured you'd gone home. So, I headed to your castle, but I heard a voice in the trees. Cajun, one of the Werewolves, was there. He was ready to attack me, and the rest of the pack came. I thought I was going to die for sure, but, get this, *Benjamin* came and rescued me. He talked with Angel as to why I was his prisoner, not hers, and we started to head back to Maufanges. I managed to get away one more time though, very near your castle, but he caught me again. Then, when we returned to Maufanges, he stuck me in a cell. And, of course, it just so happened to be the same cell that Brock had changed me in. I would've escaped after I woke up, but the chains that were holding me were indestructible. But, I tried Amaury," he whispered those last words. "I tried."

"So, that's why you didn't come back," I said. "But where'd you get the idea that I was dead?"

"When I was in the cell, Magdelene brought me a silver-tipped stake soaked with your blood. She told me you were dead, and I believed her, since I know that's the only weapon that can kill a Fusion. Plus, when I finally did get free from those chains, I came here. And the first thing I saw when I walked in was a giant puddle of blood. I panicked and ran around the house, calling your name, searching every room for you, but you weren't here." Tears had begun to stream down his face. "I was entirely convinced that they had killed you. I mean, there wasn't any proof that you were still alive, only that you weren't. What else was I supposed to think?"

"Oh my God," I said. I was stunned. But then I thought of something that didn't make sense. "How'd you know what my blood smelled like though?"

"Don't you remember that day in the woods where Ben and Magdelene ambushed you and made you bleed after you left my house? And then I came here extremely scared for you? Well, I remembered the scent of it from that day. I'm not sure why, but the second its scent hit my nose I knew it was yours."

I nodded. "I guess that makes sense."

Then he asked me something. "So, Amaury, if I may ask, where were you?"

"The day after the night you left," I said. "I went to Guéret and ran into Anthony. He proved to his granddaughter that I was a Fusion, and they were chasing me. And then I ran into Raven-"

"Who's Raven?"

"Well, I didn't know it at the time, but I found out later that she was Razza." He looked shocked by my words. "Do you remember the bazaar?" I asked him. "When I left you at the fountain? Well, I ran into her then, too, and she gave me a note. But this time, she warned me to stay away from you, because you'd do nothing but break my heart. And she was right."

He kissed me on the cheek. "I'm sorry," he said, choking on the words. "I didn't mean to hurt you like I did."

"Well, I know that now," I said. "But at the time I didn't."

He nodded. "What did your note from Razza say?" he asked out of nowhere.

"Um-" I thought for a moment, but the words soon came into my head. 'You can run Fusion, but you can't hide. Find who you're looking for, they'll serve as your guide.' Do you understand?" After three years, the words still didn't make any sense to me.

"No," he said. "I don't. Um, by the way, did you know that Razza is dead?"

I was shocked. "No- no, I didn't. How'd she die?"

"Benjamin killed her for betraying the Coven. He found out everything she did against them." I nodded. It made sense after all; I distinctly remember her telling me she was working against them in the dungeon all those years ago.

"In fact, to visit her grave was the reason I came back. Adam came to my new city and brought me here, because Razza told him before she died that she wanted me to come to her grave. When we were there yesterday, a note appeared on her little cross out of nowhere. It said: 'You can run Radder, but you can't hide. Your flower hath not wilted, your flower hath not died.' It was clearly written in her handwriting, too. I've no idea what it means."

"Seriously?" I asked. "That's easy to decipher."

"Well then tell me what it means."

"She said, 'You can run Radder, but you can't hide.' You ran off to a new city, but she brought you back here so that you couldn't hide from my "death" three years ago. And then, 'Your flower hath not wilted, your flower hath not died.' She was telling you that I wasn't dead."

A deep realization grew into his eyes. "So you were what she wanted me to find," he whispered. "But she told me that you were dead, too. She was helping him keep us apart."

"I guess she changed her mind after she died."

"Well, I'm glad," he said. "So, do I get to hear the rest of the story about where you were?"

"Oh, right," I said. "Well, after I left Guéret, I came here and wrote in my diary. And right when I finished my entry and shut it, Ben and Magdelene came running down my staircase. I didn't know how or when they'd gotten in my house, but they forced me to let them stab me in the arm with a silver-tipped stake. I bled all over it and the floor, and would've died of blood loss, had Magdelene not stitched up my arm afterwards. But right as they were about to leave, they hit me in the head with something and knocked me out. I remember waking up here, but they knocked me out again.

The second time I woke up though, I was in a dungeon cell, tied to a chair with unbreakable rope, and my mouth was taped shut. Ben would cut my arms too while I was there, I was in the Fanges Castle dungeons, trying to trigger my Thirst and make me go crazy. But, it didn't work. Then, one day, he randomly just let me go. He told me not to look for you though, because you were already long gone, and that you hadn't even searched for me or anything. But I didn't believe him. So, I searched Guéret and your house, but I couldn't even find a trace of you. And that's when I knew that you really had left me for good. I just never thought you'd come back. But, here you are."

"Wait," he said. "What day did they let you go?"

"April 7th."

"You're kidding," he said, his eyes growing wide. "The day before that was when I escaped. Are you telling me that they waited until I'd left Guéret to let you out of that dungeon?"

I nodded. "I guess so."

A tear was running down his cheek. "Those assholes," he said through gritted teeth. "I can't believe they'd do that to us."

"Me neither," I said. "I don't see why they worked so hard to keep us away from each other."

"They're jealous of us," he said. "And they hate us."

"Why are they jealous, though?" I asked.

"Because they know they'll never be as close as we are," he said. "It took them more than three-hundred years to even like each other; you fell in love with me after five days."

"Whoa whoa whoa," I said quickly. "What makes you think that I love you?"

He leaned closer to me. "I heard your thoughts that day we went to the lake."

I felt my face flush. I'd completely forgotten about that. "That was a long time ago."

He shrugged. "It still happened."

"Yeah, but that's not the case anymore." I knew I'd lied to him the second the words left my mouth. The truth was, I never had stopped loving him. But he already knew that.

"Amaury," he said. "Nobody's going to shun you for telling the truth."

"But that's the thing," I said. "I'm telling the truth, and you aren't."

"What do you mean?"

"I told you; you don't love me. You're just saying that you do."

"Amaury, yes I do," he said. His eyes held hurt in their depths. "I don't know why you don't believe me."

"Because if you loved me, you would've told me when you heard me think about how much I love you."

"I was going to," he admitted. "But I chickened out, just like all the other times before that when I could've, and should've, told you."

"Well, why'd you chicken out?"

"Because I wasn't sure you'd accept it at first. And after

you thought that, I was afraid you'd stop loving me after I told you."

"I could never stop loving you, Radder," I said.

He leaned even farther forward at that moment, pressing his lips to mine. When he pulled away, he spoke. "You don't know how many times in that dungeon," he said, "that I had wished I had told you. And when Magdelene said you were dead, I was begging to just have five more minutes with you, so that I could tell you. And now, I have the rest of forever to tell you every day. It's a- a-"

"Miracle?" I finished for him.

"Yes," he said with a smile. "It's a miracle. And it's one that I won't *ever* take for granted."

I smiled at him. "I have one more question for you," I told him.

"Ask away."

"What town have you been living in since you left Guéret?"

"Fremont," he said.

"That's pretty far away," I said. "I never would've guessed you'd go that far from home."

"Everywhere around here that I went to reminded me of you," he explained. "If I didn't leave, it would've killed me. It was easy living there though, because nothing brought back those painful memories." He hesitated for a moment, his eyes clouding over. "Well, maybe a few things," he said.

"I see," I said. I felt a little hurt that he'd been trying to forget me. But I couldn't judge; I'd been trying to do the same thing for the past three years.

"Which reminds me," Radder said. "You still owe me a favor."

I had completely forgotten that too. I smiled. "And what would you like this time?" I asked him.

He pulled me into a tight embrace. "I want you to run away with me," he said. "We can live in Fremont together," he added, "and we'll never have to deal with Benjamin and Magdelene ever again."

I couldn't believe what I'd just heard. "Radder," I said. "You can't ask me to do that. In case you've forgotten, I still have a war to stop here. And everyday I put off the peace-making, the more blood is shed. I can't just wait until the Vampires and Werewolves all kill each other."

"Right," he said.

"Are you going to go back there anyways?" I asked him.

"Are you kidding?" he asked. "If you don't want to go, that's fine. I'll just stay here with you." He smiled at me. "Although, we will have to go back sometime, just so I can get the rest of my things. Oh, and quit my job"

"That's fine with me," I said. "So, what would you like me to do for that last favor instead?"

He thought for a long moment. "First of all, I want you to kiss me," he said with a smile. "Second of all, I actually want you to tell me that you love me, and mean it."

"I did tell you," I claimed.

"Not directly," he said.

"Whatever," I said. "I so did. But that's OK, I'll just tell you again." I leaned forward, staring deep into his eyes. "Radder Andrew Thor," I said with a smile. "I love you."

"Amaury Roslyn de Pompadour," he said, smiling back.

"I love you too." I leaned in to kiss him then, but after a few seconds he pulled away. He looked hurt. And not only that, but guilty as well.

"What's wrong?" I asked, confused.

He let out a long, deep sigh, and let me out of his grasp. He put his head in his hands and whispered, "Babe, there's something I need to tell you that I should've a long time ago."

"What?" I asked. I had no idea what he was getting at.

He lifted his head, not so much as glancing at me. Guilt was written all over his face. He swallowed hard before he spoke. "This- this is something that happened three-hundred-three years ago."

With a growing dread, I realized that he was referring to the year Rafe died. "Radder?" I said. I hoped with all my heart that he wasn't going to say what I thought he was indicating.

"You know I was raised by the Vampires, don't you?" he asked. I nodded. "Well," he said, "you obviously also know that the Vampires and Werewolves are in an everlasting blood feud, since you're trying to stop their war. Vampire young, even if they are, or were, Human like myself, are raised to believe that Werewolves are the scum of the Earth. Well, not long after I'd become the King of the Minuit Coven, I lost Audrey. But you already knew that, too. So, needless to say, I had become very angry over my loss.

Then, Baron, one of our Coven's members, reported to me that he'd discovered an abominable creature who was half-Vampire, half-Werewolf. He showed me two books, though I don't remember the titles of them, and proved to me that he wasn't lying. And of course, he was referring to

Rafe. We informed the Werewolves of this and killed his parents. Then Brock, Benjamin, and I had taken the leadership roles in going after him.

Of course, we tracked him all the way back here. I was so mad over Audrey dying, and out of my hatred for the Werewolves that I- I attacked him first. I didn't even give Ben or Brock a chance at him. I wounded him so badly that he bled to death, right before my eyes." Radder began to shake then, and tears spilled out of his eyes.

"Amaury," he said. "I killed Rafe."

"Radder," I said, my voice shaky. "Don't say that. It's not true."

"But it is, Amaury," he said, turning to look at me. His eyes were full of so many emotions: anger, guilt, sorrow, even a hint of jealousy. "Don't try and convince me otherwise. You weren't even there; you can't possibly defend me. I killed him by myself, with no help from anyone else. *It's all my fault.*"

"But Radder," I said, tears spilling out of my eyes. "I know you'd never do anything like that to me-"

"You're right, I wouldn't have," he said. "If I had known at the time that you were alive, I would've spared him. Nothing else in the world would've made me happier than to see you being happy with him. I've never wanted anything more than for you to be happy, and he was the only thing that caused it. If I could go back in time, I would make sure no harm ever came to either of you."

"Well, you can't go back in time. And either way, you didn't know that I existed until three years ago."

"That's not true."

"What do you mean?"

He took another deep breath. "I've known about you since the day Rafe died."

His words shocked me beyond mere belief. "*What?!?* How?!?"

"After I killed Rafe, I ordered the Warriors and Guards to search every room in this house, to make sure that no other Fusions were hiding out. Nobody thought that anymore existed, but I wanted to be sure. I ordered them to search downstairs, and I made my way upstairs. I was searching around the rooms, and I found a certain one that to me seemed oddly suspicious. It was that closet of yours at the end of the hallway. Most wouldn't have thought to look there for anyone, but I did. And when I opened the door, I saw you." His face had turned a bright red. "And when I saw you, I thought that you were the most beautiful girl I'd ever seen. And I fell in love with you right from the start."

"You said the same thing about Audrey," I noted.

"I thought I loved her," he said. "But I know I really didn't. What I felt when I first saw her was no match for what I felt when I first saw you." His face was now completely red in embarrassment. "You were sound asleep, and-"

"Wait," I said. "Now I know you're lying. I never fell asleep in there. I was too terrified."

"Terror can exhaust you," he said. "Believe me, I know."

"Anyways," I said. "I would've heard that door open. It creaks."

"It might now," he said. "But it didn't three-hundred-three years ago."

I opened my mouth to protest, but no words came. I realized just then that he was right. And, come to think of it, I didn't remember every part of hiding in the closet that day.

"I could've killed you," he said. "I could've dragged you out of that closet and drove a silver-tipped stake through your heart, or made you bleed to death, or anything else. But I spared you. And when Benjamin and Brock came upstairs, I told them I'd already checked every room, and made sure they stayed away from that door. Then, as we were leaving, I realized that you and Rafe had to have been together, and that you had meant a lot to him for him to hide you from us. I'd never felt so guilty about anything else in my entire life."

"Well, if you knew about me, then how come you waited three-hundred years to talk to me?"

"Because I was scared," he said. "All my life I'd despised Werewolves. The thought of Rafe existing, being a mix of a Vampire and Werewolf, it made me sick. And then there was you, a girl just like him, who I was falling in love with. I didn't know what to believe anymore. Benjamin saw my confused state, and that's when he challenged me to fight for kingship. And, I'll admit, I lied to you," he said. "I didn't loose that fight because I couldn't stop thinking about Audrey. It was because I couldn't get my mind off *you*."

"You lost that all because of *me*?"

"Yes," he said. "But it was worth it. I didn't care that I had been banished. If I had given the fight my all, I would've let my thoughts loose, and all the mind reading Vampires would've found out about you. They would've killed you, and probably me too, for keeping your existence a secret. Either way, there was a plus side to being banished. I could keep an eye on you and keep you safe without getting in trouble with the Coven."

"What do you mean you 'kept an eye on me'?" I asked.

His face was still glowing red. "I was, sorta, watching you that whole time."

"So, essentially, you stalked me for three-hundred years?"

"Yes, I mean, no. It's hard to explain." He placed his head back in his hands, shaking his head. "God, this is so embarrassing."

"I'll bet," I said.

"I didn't stalk you," he said. "I just dropped by about twice a month to make sure you were OK. And more than once, I caught people trying to harm you. If it weren't for me, you'd have died over fifty times already."

"Who was trying to harm me?"

"Random Vampire Hunters, Werewolves, and Vampires who somehow discovered you existed. I made sure they never came close to hurting you."

"Wow," I said. "How long were you planning to do that for?"

"As long as it took. The whole while, too, I was coming up with a plan to meet you. Coincidentally, the night you came to my house was the night I was going to set that plan in action."

"What were you going to do?" I asked.

"I was going to fake that I had been in a fight and have really bad injuries, and I was going to ask for your help."

"Wait, if it was fake, how would you have gotten the injuries?"

"How do you think?"

I felt my eyes grow wide. "You would've hurt yourself just to talk to me?"

He nodded. "Honestly, I would've done anything."

"Oh," I said. A sick feeling had begun to grow in the pit of my stomach.

"In fact," he said. "I was just on my way to your house when you came into my yard. I was scared, because I didn't know what to say to you."

"Is that why you were being so rude to me?"

"Yeah," he said. "I wasn't really sure how to be anything but rude."

"But why were you trying to push me away?"

"Because I suddenly realized that eventually, I'd have to tell you I killed Rafe. I was hoping it'd never come to that. But I had to tell you sometime. I wouldn't have been able to live with myself if I ended up with you and I hadn't told you yet. So, I changed my mind right then, and tried to keep you away. But then I ran into you the next day, and I realized that I loved you too much to stay away."

"I guess that explains a lot," I said. I really felt sick now.

"Are you OK?" Radder asked me.

"I don't know," I admitted. "This is a lot for me to take in." I didn't want to believe any of it, especially that he'd killed Rafe. But his story fit together too well. I couldn't deny the facts.

"I'm so sorry," he said. "I wish I hadn't done what I did. But you're right, I can't go back in time. But if I could, Amaury, you know I would've kept him alive. I didn't know I was going to hurt you."

"I know, Radder," I said. I felt a tear streak down my face. "I just don't want to believe it. And I'm not going to unless you can prove it."

He leaned forward, as though to wipe away that one tear, but then thought better of it. His eyes held a look of pain. "I don't want to hurt you anymore than I already have. And proving it to you will just make this worse. Please, just believe me."

"I can't," I said. "I don't want to believe that you're a killer. And if you want me to believe it, then you'll have to prove it."

He sighed. Radder was deep in thought for a moment, but suddenly his eyes lit up in realization. He began to dig through his many pockets until he found what he was looking for. He withdrew a small piece of paper, stained yellow with age.

"Here," he said, showing me the writing on it. My eyes grew wide as a read the note from so many years ago:

Rafe,

Just so you know, we've alerted the Werewolves of your existence. We're all plotting on when we're going to come for you.

If you have anything to hide, we suggest you do it NOW.

We're coming for you, Rafe. There's no escaping us.

"Where did you get this?" I asked.

"It was blowing around your yard outside the day I came here to take you to the lake. I picked it up before I came here and put it in my pocket. I found it again shortly after I moved to Fremont. Somehow, it hadn't gotten damaged by the water, and it made its way into my coat pocket. I'm not sure how it got there undamaged, but it did. Besides, stranger things have happened."

"I'll say," I said, taking the note from him. "I was going to burn this."

"I figured that," he said.

"What exactly does this prove?" I asked.

"The first scrawl is Brock's, the second Benjamin's, and the third is mine."

"How do I know that for a fact?" I asked.

He sighed again. "Do you have a pen?" he asked.

"Yeah," I said, standing up. I went to my desk and picked up my feather pen, dipping it in ink. I returned to the couch, holding my hand under the pen to stop the ink from dripping. I sat down next to Radder again, giving him the pen.

"Thanks," he said, taking it from me.

He turned the paper over and began to write. Within seconds he finished, set the pen down, and handed the paper to me. On the back, he'd rewritten the last two sentences from the front of the paper. I turned it over countless times. The scrawls were completely identical in every which way. After I had confirmed this, I crumpled up the piece of paper in my hand and began to cry.

"Amaury, don't cry," Radder said. He moved toward me, put I pushed him away.

"How could you?" I said.

"I didn't mean to," he said. "Amaury, please-"

"Don't," I said. "Just leave me alone."

"Please," he begged. "Don't say that."

"Radder," I said. "Please. Just, go."

The look in his eyes when I said that brought even more tears to mine. "Amaury," he said. "I'm sorry. You know I am. But I can't change it now, even though I wish I could. Anyways, he's been gone for so long. He wouldn't want you to still be mourning him. I'm sure he'd want you to find someone else and be happy."

"Of course he would," I said. "But answer me this: Do you really think that he'd want me to date his killer?"

"No, I guess not," he admitted. "But if mine and his roles were switched, I would only want you to be happy, and it wouldn't matter to me who you were with, as long as he treated you right and loved you with all his heart."

I didn't know what to say to him. After a moment of silence, he spoke again. "Honestly Amaury," he said. "Have I ever intentionally hurt you?"

"No," I said, drawing out the word.

"Exactly," he said. "And you know I never would and never will. And you must know how much I love you." His eyes clouded over. "Don't you?"

"I don't know anymore," I said.

He nodded. "I understand." He took me by surprise then by standing. "I'll be leaving for Fremont at dawn tomorrow, since it seems you don't want me around anymore. But if you happen to change your mind, you know where to find me," he said. He bent down and kissed me lightly on the cheek. "Oh, and one more thing," he said.

I looked up at him. "What's that?"

He gave me a tiny smile. "I really do love you," he said. "I always have and I always will."

Then, he kissed me on the lips. Radder took my hand as he kissed me, placing something in my palm. The kiss itself didn't last long, and before I knew it, Radder drew away from me and made his way out the door. Once he'd shut the door behind him, I looked at what he'd placed in my hand. I was stunned to see the blue suede bag that I'd been so keen to open so long ago. Nervously, I undrew the strings that held the bag closed, and dumped its contents into my open palm. And when I saw what lay in my hand, I felt my heart skip a beat.

It was the Fusion Night necklace.

I heard myself gasp. I could not believe that he'd just returned the gift from Rafe to me. I dropped the blue suede bag and the crumpled up note, then stood and rushed outside. Radder was just to the tree line; he was walking extremely slowly. I cupped my hands around my mouth and shouted his name. He stopped, turning around to look at me. He looked confused.

"Radder!" I called again, making my way toward him as fast as I could walk. I was standing right before him in seconds.

"What?" he asked in a cracked voice. This close to him, I noticed that he had tear stains running down the length of his cheeks.

"Where did you get this?" I asked.

"I knew it'd been stolen," he said. "So I tracked down the path of who took it. I spoke to Razza when it went missing, and she found it in Magdelene's room. She took it to the bazaar with her and gave it to me. She was the person I spoke with in the alleyway."

"That was Razza?" I asked.

"Yes," he said.

"Wait, how'd you know that it was stolen that night though?"

"I was checking up on you that night, and I saw Magdelene sneak into your castle. I saw her leave with the necklace, so after she left, I followed her back to Maufanges. I snuck into the castle and woke up Razza, telling her to get it for me. I had to lend her some scent-covering stuff that I had, so that she could get it for me without getting caught. After I had it, I was waiting for the right moment to give it to you. And now seemed like the best time."

"Oh," I said, feeling ashamed for being angry at him. "Well, thanks for getting it back for me. It means a lot."

"I know," he said. "And it was no trouble. I was happy to do it."

I looked down at the necklace in my hands. It was just past dusk by this point, so the necklace would be shining in the moonlight soon enough. For some odd reason, that thought brought tears to my eyes.

"Did you give it back to me now," I said, "because you didn't think I would go to your house in the morning?"

"Yes," he said. "Honestly, I thought that was the last time I'd ever see you."

I felt a tear run down my face. "You shouldn't have thought that," I said. "I was going to come."

A look of shock grew on his face. "You were?"

"Of course," I said. "Radder, I will always be mad at you for killing him. But I can't blame you, even though I want to, because I know it isn't your fault. And-" I took a deep breath before I spoke the last few words. "I forgive you," I whispered.

"What did you just say?" he said.

I looked up at him. "I said that I forgive you." I said. My voice shook as I repeated the words.

He looked at me with a new light shining in his eyes. "Do you really mean that?" he asked. A small smile grew on his lips.

"Of course I do," I said. "I love you, and I don't want to

loose you. And I know I will if I can't get over Rafe. Besides, it's like you said. He's been dead a long time, and he'd want me to be happy. And if you're what makes me happy, then he'd understand."

"But do I make you happy?" he asked.

"The happiest," I said. He took me in his arms then, holding me in a tight embrace. Then I asked him, "Are you still going to go back to Fremont?"

"Fuck no," he said.

"Good," I said. "I don't want you to leave."

"Well, that's a good thing, because I don't know what I would've done without you."

"My guess would be exactly what you did before."

"All I did in Fremont was try and keep you out of my head. But I couldn't even think of trying to do that ever again. You have a permanent residence inside my mind."

I laughed at that. Radder smiled at me, and then leaned down to kiss me. But before he could, he stopped himself. The necklace was still in my hand, and had suddenly begun to glow brilliantly in the moonlight that now shone throughout the sky. I smiled up at Radder.

"It's beautiful, isn't it?" I asked him.

"Just like you," he said. I felt my smile widen, and watched as his did too. Then he cupped my face in his hand and kissed me deeply. Everything about this night was so perfect, even though for a while it seemed just the opposite. But I decided that right then and there, while under the watch of the moon and the stars and locked inside Radder's arms, that I had never, ever been happier.

Epilogue

Amaury, two months later:

Mai 23, 1877; Midi
(May 23, 1877; Noon)

Dear Diary,

It's been two months since Radder came back to Chiroux. I can't believe I haven't written in here since the night he came back, but I've been so busy spending time with him. Well, I guess I should explain everything that has happened since that night. Two days after that night, we went on a trip to Fremont. Radder had to get the rest of his things that he'd left behind at first, and went to quit his job. His boss was a really kind man by the way. He seemed rather disappointed that Radder was quitting, but when Radder told him that it was because of me, he didn't even try to argue. He said, and I quote, "Love is more important than anything, so don't let anything stand in its way." I love that saying. Anyways, after Radder got everything he needed and such, we left Fremont and came back to Chiroux. I didn't exactly ask him, nor did he me, but for some reason he decided that it was OK for him to move in with me. Which, I have no problem with. But it would've been polite if he'd asked first. Oh well. Anyways, I better wrap this up, because he's reading over my shoulder as we speak and it's bugging me. So for now I'll say farewell. And, don't worry; I'll come back later to write more when Radder falls asleep so that he won't be able to read this.

-Amaury de Pompadour

Radder laughed at the last few sentences. He really had been reading over my shoulder the entire time I was writing, but it didn't make any difference to me. But I pretended it did. I elbowed him lightly in the gut, with a mischievous grin on my face. "You're a jerk," I said.

"I'm quite aware of that," he said with a smirk. "But you still love me regardless."

"True," I said. I turned to look at him. His head was hovering right over my shoulder, and he was smiling widely. "What?" I asked him.

"Nothing," he said. "I'm just happy to see you."

"You've seen me all day."

"Precisely," he said. He leaned forward to kiss me. "Am I not allowed to be happy about that?" he asked after he drew away.

"Of course not," I said. "If being with me for every hour of every day from now until the rest of forever makes you happy, then feel free to smile about it. Just, no creepy smiles, if you will."

He lessened the intensity of his smile, but it still remained. "Will do," he said. "And, for the record, that does make me happy."

"Well I'm glad," I said.

He decided to change the topic then. "Are you done writing in that?" he said, motioning toward my diary.

"No, Radder. That's why I said 'farewell' to the page and signed my name at the bottom of it. That always means I'm going to continue writing."

He glowered in a joking way. "Smartass," he said.

I smiled. "I get it from you. After all, you taught me by being one 24/7."

The smile returned to his face. "You'll have to pay for those lessons, you do realize."

"Really?" I asked. "And the price?"

"A kiss," he said. "And-"

We both jumped when a knock sounded at the door. "What the hell?" Radder asked, mostly to himself.

Since he was already standing, he made his way to the door. I quickly stood from my chair though and followed him. By the time I got to him, he'd already opened the door. Nobody was there though. In fact, the only things that were there were a trace of the person's scent, and a letter lying in the dirt. Radder bent down and picked up the letter, then shut the door and locked it.

"What's it say?" I asked.

"Your name is written on the outside," he said, handing me the note. "So you tell me."

I took the letter from him and opened the envelope. Inside was a note, and I almost couldn't believe my eyes. It was written in Magdelene's neat scrawl, and the words shocked me:

Dear Amaury,

As you know, Benjamin and I have been together for quite some time now. And I felt the need to inform you that three days ago, he asked me to marry him. Of course, I said yes. I mean, how could I refuse? Our wedding will be sometime in August, though we're not quite sure on the date yet. Oh well. You know, I feel pretty bad for you, having nobody anymore. Oh, wait, silly me! How could I have forgotten that Radder returned, even though we've been trying to keep you two far apart? Well, "sis," this will not go unheeded. I can guarantee that a disaster is about to come your way.

-Magdelene

I was too stunned to speak after I'd read it. Radder took it from me after I refused to speak, and after he was finished he said, "Oh shit."

"How did they find out you're back, Radder?" I asked with a shaky voice. "We've been so quiet about it."

"They must've caught me hunting somewhere," he said. "I'm sorry."

I shook my head. "It's not your fault," I said.

"Yes it is," he protested. "I should've been more careful."

"It's fine," I said. "It doesn't really matter how they found out. Just what they're going to do about it. You know as well as I do that that isn't an empty threat. They'll do something."

He took me in his arms. "It'll be OK," he said. "They can't keep us apart forever. After all, their last attempt at that failed miserably."

"But they did manage to keep us separated for three years, Radder. I don't want to be away from you for that long ever again."

"It won't happen," he said. "I promise. But fretting about it is only going to make it worse. I'm not going to let them get the better of us again like I did last time. Everything will be just fine."

"It better be, Radder Thor," I said. I buried my head in his chest.

He kissed the top of my head. "Seriously though," he said, "don't let that letter scare you. I'll never let anyone come between us ever again."

"You promise?" I asked him.

"I swear," he said. "Because we're going to be together for forever and a day. And nothing, not even Benjamin and Magdelene, is going to change that." He smiled down at me then, looking deeply into my eyes.

"I love you," he whispered.

"I love you too," I said.

And when he kissed me, I knew that every word he'd said was true. After all, love really is more important than anything. And we weren't going to let anything stand in our way.

CPSIA information can be obtained at www.ICGtesting.com
Printed in the USA
LVOW091941021011

248720LV00001B/1/P

9 781432 778521